# The Hungry Heart

David Graham Phillips

# *A LilliBan Classical Edition*

## LilliBan Arts, LLC

U.S.A.

ISBN 978-1-63703-101-8 (Paperback)
ISBN 978-1-63703-100-1 (eBook)

# Chapter 1

Courtship and honeymoon of Richard Vaughan and Courtney Benedict are told accurately enough by a thousand chroniclers of love's fairy tales and dreams. Where such romances end in a rosily vague "And they lived happily ever after," there this history begins. Richard and Courtney have returned from Arcady to reality, to central Indiana and the Vaughan homestead, across the narrow width of Wenona the lake from Wenona the town.

The homecoming was late in a June evening, with a perfumed coolness descending upon the young lovers from the grand old trees, round the Vaughan house like his bodyguard round a king. Next morning toward eight Courtney, still half asleep, reached out hazily. Her hand met only the rumpled linen on Richard's side of the huge fourposter. She started up, brushed back the heavy wave of auburn hair fallen over her brow, gazed down at his pillow. The dent of his head, but not he. Her eyes searched the dimness. The big room contained only a few large pieces of old mahogany; at a glance she saw into every corner. Alone in the room. Her eyes, large and anxious now, regarded the half-open door of the dressing room to the rear.

"Dick!" she called hopefully.

No answer.

"Dick!" she repeated, a note of doubt in her voice.

Silence.

"Dick!" she repeated reproachfully. It was the first morning she had awakened without the sense of his nearness that had become so dear, so necessary. It was the first morning in this house strange to her—in this now life they were to make beautiful and happy together. She gave a forlorn sigh like a disappointed child, drew up her knees, rested her elbows upon them, and her small head upon her hands. Sitting there in the midst of that bed big enough for half a dozen as small as she, she suggested a butterfly poised motionless with folded wings. A moment and she lifted her drooped head. How considerate of him not to wake her when the three days and nights on train had been so wearing!

Swift and light as a butterfly she sprang from the bed, flung open the shutters of the lake-front windows. In poured summer like gay cavalcade through breach in gloomy walls—summer in full panoply of perfume and soft air and sparkling sunshine. She almost laughed aloud for joy at this timely rescue. She gazed away across the lake to the town where she was born and bred! "Home!" she cried. "And so happy—so utterly happy!" Her expression, her whole manner, her quick movements gave the impression of the impulsive self-unconsciousness of a child.

It was a radiant figure, small and perfect like a sun sprite, that issued from the room three quarters of an hour later to flit along the polished oak hall, to descend a stairway glistening like hall above and wider and loftier hall below. With hair piled high on her small head, with tail of matinee over her arm and tall heels clicking merrily on the steps, she whistled as she went. Some people—women—criticised that laughter-loving mouth of hers as too wide for so small a face. It certainly did not suggest a button-hole. But no one could have found fault with the shape of the mouth or with the coloring, whether of the lips or within, or with her teeth, pearl white and seeming the whiter for the rose bronze of her skin—the shade that seems to be of the essence of youth, health, and summer. Her nose was rather large, but slender and well shaped. It was the nose of mobility, of sensitiveness, of intelligence, not at all of repose. And there were her eyes, of a strange soft emerald, with long dark lashes; the brows long also and only slightly curved, and slender yet distinct. These eyes were her greatest beauty—greater even than her skin. It would have been difficult to say whether in them or in her mouth lay her greatest charm, for charm is not always beauty, and beauty often wholly lacks charm.

But woman feels that figure determines the woman—"the woman" meaning, of course, efficiency as a man catcher. It was upon Courtney's flawless figure that the sour glance of old Nanny, the head servant, rested—old Nanny, whose puritanism aggravated for her by suppression all the damned charms of "the flesh." Nanny had reigned supreme in that house ever since Dick Vaughan was left alone; so from the first news of the engagement she had been hating Courtney, whom she regarded as her supplanter. As Courtney entered the dining room, stiff and dim and chilly, like all the rooms in that house, old Nanny was superintending fat, subdued Mazie at work at the breakfast table. It occupied the exact center of the room, formal as for a state banquet.

"Good morning," cried Courtney in her charming manner of bright friendliness. "Good morning, Mazie. Am I late? Where's Richard?" Her voice was deeper than one would have expected, but low and musical.

Mazie smiled a welcome, then cast a frightened glance of apology at Nanny, who did not smile. "Mr. Richard's down to the Smoke House," said she.

The Smoke House was the laboratory Dick's grandfather, Achilles Vaughan, had built for him on the site of the smoke house of the pioneer Vaughan, settler there when Wenona was a trading post in New France. "Of course!" said Courtney. "I might have known. He wanted to go last night, but I wouldn't let him."

Nanny scowled at this innocent, laughing "I wouldn't let him." She turned on Mazie, who was gazing open-mouthed at Courtney's simple, fresh finery. "What'r ye gawkin' here fur, with your mouth hangin' like a chicken with the gaps?" she demanded in a fierce aside. Mazie lumbered through the door into the kitchen. "As I was saying," continued Nanny to her new mistress, "he's put in most nigh all his time down to that there smoke house day and night—ever since his aunt, Miss Eudosia, died. Yes, an' before that, while Colonel 'Kill, his grandfather, was still alive. He's got sleeping rooms and everything in the upstairs. He often don't come here even to meals for weeks. Mazie or Jimmie carry 'em to him."

Courtney nodded. "A regular hermit. It was the merest chance that we happened to meet."

"You was the first young woman he'd laid an eye on in a long time."

Nanny's tone was colorless. Only a very stupid woman puts both barb and poison on a shaft when either is enough. Courtney, who understood and felt remorseful about the old woman's jealous anger, answered with good-humored gentleness: "I guess that *was* why I got him. But he'll not be a hermit any more."

"He's begun already," said Nanny.

"We mustn't allow it," replied Courtney, not quite so good-humoredly. The old woman's steady bearing down was having its effect.

"There's no goin' agin nature. The Vaughan men ain't ever bothered much about women. They don't let foolishness detain 'em long. And this one's his gran'paw over agin. When he gits at his work, he's like a dog after a rabbit."

"It seems a little chilly and damp in here," said Courtney. "Do help me open the windows. I love sun and air."

"Miss Eudosia—" began Nanny, and checked herself with a considerable shortening of the distance between chin and end of nose.

Courtney understood what that beginning meant. But she ignored. "And," she went on, busying herself with curtains and fastenings, "we'll move the table in front of this big window. I like breakfast near the window in summer, near the fire in winter."

Nanny lowered upon the small straight young figure, so bright and graceful. "Miss Eudosia—" she began fiercely. Again she checked herself, but it was to say with bitterness, "But then she's dead—and forgot."

"No, indeed!" protested Courtney. "You'd have thought she'd gone only a few months ago instead of four years if you'd heard Richard talking about her yesterday. And I'm sure she'd have done what I'm suggesting if she'd happened to think of it." Then with a look that might have softened any but a woman resolved to hate another woman: "Do try to humor me in little things, Nanny. I'll be very meek about things that do matter. I've had no experience in keeping house. You'll teach me, won't you?"

Nanny stood inflexible, her wrinkled hands folded tightly at the waist line of her black alpaca. She could not help Courtney displace that table from its ancient site. It was as if this frivolous, whistling, useless chit of an ornamental wife were violating the sacred Eudosia's coffin—the graves of all the Vaughans—for traditions are graves, and Nanny, like all who live by tradition, lived among graves. After a time Courtney, more nervous under those angry eyes than she showed, got the table at the open window. The room was livable now, and after she had rearranged the dishes the table looked invitingly human. But her buoyant young enthusiasm had oozed away. With wistful gaze out over prim lawns and flower beds, stiff and staid as Sunday, she said: "I guess I'll bring Richard to breakfast."

"He et before he went."

"Oh!" Courtney's tone showed that she was hurt. But she instantly brightened. "I'll get him to come and sit with me while I have breakfast."

A covert sneering smile in the depths of Nanny's eyes made her flush angrily. "If I was you I wouldn't interrupt him," said the old woman. "He don't allow it."

"How absurd!" cried Courtney. But straightway she was amazed and shocked at herself—on this her first morning in the new and beautiful life, to be drawn nearer a vulgar squabble than in all her nineteen years—and with an old woman toward whom it would be cowardice not to be forbearing. "I'm cross because I'm hungry," she said contritely. "While breakfast's coming I'll run down for him."

"He's set in his ways," said Nanny.

"He'll not mind me—this once." And she took up her train and went by the long French window to the broad veranda with its big fluted pillars. At the end steps she paused. Yes, it was summer in the Vaughan grounds as elsewhere. But that prodigal wanton had there been caught, had had her tresses sleeked and bound, her luxuriant figure corseted and clad in the most repellant classical severity. Courtney, of the eyes keen for color and form and fitness of things, felt rebuked and subdued once more. She glanced farther round, saw Nanny's parchment face and sinister gaze watching and hating her. There is a limit beyond which youth refuses to be suppressed and compressed, and defiantly expands in more than its natural gay audacity. This climax of Nanny, representative of Vaughans not so rigid in death as they had been in life, was just the necessary little-too-much. With a laugh and a toss of the head, she swung her skirts very high indeed above her pretty ankles and ran like a young antelope across the lawn, and into and along the path leading away toward the eastern part of the grounds. Through a carefully artificial thicket of lilacs, elders, and snowballs she sped, then through a small wood with not a spray of underbrush anywhere. She came out in a clearing at the water's edge. Before her, one of its walls rising sheer from the retaining wall of the lake, stood the laboratory.

She paused astonished. She had expected a temporary sort of structure. Before her rose a fitting temple for the mysteries of the "black art." It was a long two-story building of stone and brick, not visible from the lake proper because it stood upon the bank of a deep, narrow inlet. The weather had stained its walls into the semblance of age wherever they showed through the heavy mantle of bitter-sweet that overspread even the roof. Around the place hung an air of aloofness and seclusion, of mystery, that appealed to her young instinct for the romantic. The brick path divided into two. One went to what was obviously the entrance to the second-story bachelor suite; the other turned to the left, rounded the corner of the house, ended at the massive iron door of the laboratory proper.

This door was wide open. Courtney stood upon the threshold like a bright bird peering from the sunshine into the entrance to a cave. The air that came out was heavy with the odors of chemicals, but not sharp or especially unpleasant. Besides, in high school and college she had done a good deal at chemistry, enough to be seized of its fascination. She stood gazing into a big high-ceilinged room, filled with a bewildering variety of unusual articles—gigantic bottles, cylinders, vials, jars of glass, of stone, of metal; huge retorts with coils of pipe, lead and rubber; lamps and balances and mortars; tiers on tiers of crowded shelves of glass and porcelain and iron; drying ovens, distilling apparatus, condensers and generators, crushers and pulverizers, cupels and cupel trays, calorimeters and crucibles and microscopes; floor all but filled with batteries and engines and machines of gold and platinum, of aluminum and copper, of brass and steel and glass and nickel. A thousand articles, in the orderly confusion that indicates constant use.

She was more and more amazed as she stared and reflected. "He works with all these things!" thought she, depressed for no clear reason. "I had no idea—no idea!"

She ventured a step farther. In a twinkling her expression of wonder and vague pain vanished before a love light that seemed to stream not from her face only, but from her whole body, with those rare eyes of hers as radiating centers. She was seeing Richard—near a window, so standing that his long high-bred face was in profile to her. He was tall, well above six feet; his careless flannels revealed the strong, slender, narrow form of the pioneers and their pure-blooded descendants. His fairish hair was thick and wavy—"Thank Heaven, not curly!" thought Courtney.

She did not interrupt. She preferred to watch him, to let her glance caress him, all unconscious of her presence. In one hand he was balancing a huge bottle; the other held a long test tube. He was slowly dropping the bottle's contents of quiet colorless liquid into the test tube, which was half full of a liquid, also quiet and colorless. Each drop as it touched the surface of the liquid dissolved into black steam. It was this steam that gave off the pungent odor. As she watched, there came a slow tightening at her throat, at her heart.

"I never saw him look like this," thought she. No, it wasn't his serious intentness; one of the things she had first noted about him, and best loved, was the seriousness of his deep-set dark gray eyes—the look of the man who "amounts to something," and would prove it before he got through. No, it was the *kind* of seriousness. She felt she was seeing a Richard Vaughan she did not know at all. "But, then," she reflected, "there's a side of me he doesn't know about either." This, however, did not satisfy her. The man she was now seeing disquietingly suggested that the Richard Vaughan she had been knowing and loving and had been loved by was not the real man at all, but only one of his moods. "I thought he just amused himself with chemistry. Instead— Nanny is about right." A pang shot through her; she would have recognized it as jealousy, had she stopped to think. But at nineteen one does not stop to think. "I do believe he cares almost as much for this as he does for me."

He lowered the bottle to the table. As he straightened up, he caught sight of her. His expression changed; but the change was not nearly enough either in degree or in kind to satisfy her. "Hello!" cried he carelessly. "Good morning."

She got ready to be kissed. But, instead of coming toward her, he half turned away, to hold the test tube up between his eyes and the light. "Um—mm," he grumbled, shaking it again and again, and each time looking disappointedly at the unchanged liquid.

Like all American girls of the classes that shelter their women, she had been brought up to accept as genuine the pretense of superhuman respect and deference the American man—usually in all honesty—affects toward woman—until he marries her, or for whatever reason becomes tired and truthful. She had been confirmed in these ideas of man as woman's incessant courtier, almost servant, by receiving for the last five lively years the admiration, exaggerated and ardent, which physical charm, so long as it is potent, exacts from the male. No more than other women of her age—or than older women—or than the men had she penetrated the deceptive surface of things and discovered beneath "chivalry's" smug meaningless professions the reality, the forbearance of "strength" with "weakness," the graciousness of superior for inferior. Thus, such treatment as this of Dick's would have been humiliating from a casual man, on a casual occasion. From her husband, her lover, the man she had just been garlanding with all the fairest flowers of her ardent young heart—from him, and on this "first" morning, this unconcern, which Nanny's talk enabled her to understand, was worse than stab into feminine vanity; it was stab straight into her inmost self, the seat of her life.

She dared not admit the wound—not to her own secret thought. Bravely she struggled until her voice and manner were under control. "I've come to take you to breakfast," said she. It seemed to her that her tone was gratifying evidence of triumph of strength of character over "silly supersensitiveness—as if Dick could mean to hurt *me*!"

"Breakfast," repeated he. His gaze was discontentedly upon the bottle whose contents had acted disappointingly. "Breakfast— Oh, yes— Don't wait on me. I had coffee before I came down here. I'll be along in a few minutes." He took up the bottle again, resumed the cautious pouring.

The tears sprang to her eyes; her lip quivered. But sweet reasonableness conquered again, and she perched on a high stool near the door. She gazed round, tried to interest herself in the certainly extraordinary exhibits on floor and tables and shelves. She recalled the uses of the instruments she recognized, tried to guess the uses of those that were new to her. But her mind refused to wander from the one object that really interested her in that room. Perhaps ten minutes passed, she watching him, he watching the unchanged liquid in the test tube.

She had been born in her father's and mother's prime. She had been taught to use her brain. Thus, underneath the romantic and idealizing upper strata of her character there was the bedrock of good common sense, to resist and to survive any and all shocks. As she sat watching her engrossed husband her love, her fairness, and her good sense pleaded for him, or, rather, protested against her sensitiveness. What a dear he was! And how natural that he should be absorbed in these experiments, after having been away so long. What right had she to demand that his mood should be the same as hers? What a silly child she had shown herself, expecting him to continue to act as if love making were the whole of life. If he were to be, and to do exactly as she wished, would she not soon grow sick of him, as of the other men, who had thought to win her by inviting her to walk on them? Her eyes were sweet and tender when Dick, happening to glance seeingly in her direction, saw her ensconced, chin on hand, elbow on knee. "Hello," said he half absently. "Good morning."

There was no room for doubt; he had completely forgotten her. As her skin was not white, but of delicate pale yet rosy bronze, it did not readily betray change of emotion. But such a shock had he given her sensitive young heart, in just the mood of love and longing to be most easily bruised, that even his abstraction was penetrated. He set the bottle down. "Didn't I speak to you—" he began, and then remembered. "I beg your pardon," he said, contrite and amused.

Pride always hides a real wound. She smiled. "I'm waiting to take you to breakfast," she said.

He looked uncertainly at the bottle and the tube.

A wave of remorse for her thoughts swept over her. "Also," she went on, and she was radiant again, "I'm waiting to be kissed."

He laughed, gazed lovingly at her. "What a beauty she is, this morning," he cried. "Like the flowers—the roses—the finest rose that every grew—in a dream of roses."

Her eyes at once showed that his negligence was forgotten. Their lips met in a lingering kiss. He drew away, threw back his head, gazed at her. "Was there ever woman so lovely and fresh and pure?" he said. With impulsive daring she overcame her virginal shyness, flung her arms round his neck, and kissed him. "I love you," she murmured, blushing. "When I woke up and found you gone—it was dreadfully lonely." She had dropped into the somewhat babyish manner natural to any affectionate nature in certain moods and circumstances. It seemed especially natural to her, on account of her size and her exuberant gayety; and she had been assuming it with him in all its charming variations from the beginning of their engagement because it was the manner that pleased him best. "Next time, you'll wake me and take me along—won't you?"

He patted her. "Bless the baby! A lot of work I'd do."

"I'm going to help you. I can soon learn."

He shook his head in smiling negative. "You're going to be the dearest, sweetest wife a man ever had," said he. "And always your womanly self."

"But," she persisted with an effort, "I can help. I'm sure I can." There was no trace of the "baby" in her expression now; on the contrary, her face and her voice were those of an extremely intelligent young woman, serious without the dreary, posed solemnity that passes current for seriousness, but is mere humorless asininity. "I really know something about chemistry," she went on. "I liked it, and took the courses both at high school and at college. Last winter I won a prize for original work." His smile made her color. "I don't say that," she hastened to explain, "because I think I'm a wonderful chemist, but just to prove to you that I do know a little something—enough to be able to help in a humble sort of way."

His expression was still that of grown people when laughing at the antics of children, and concealing amusement behind a thin pretense of grave admiration. "Yes, I've no doubt you're clever at it," said he. "But a refined woman oughtn't to try to do the man sort of thing."

"But, dear, I'm not so superfine as you seem to think—and not altogether foolish." She glanced round the laboratory. "You don't know how at home I feel here. What a wonderful, beautiful equipment you have! Everything of the best— and so well taken care of! Dick, I want to be your—wife. As I watched you I realized I've got to fit myself for it. That is—of course, I always knew I'd have to do that—but now I know just what I must do."

"What a serious child it is!" he cried, pinching her cheek. It was delightful, this baby playing at "grown-up."

She laughed because she loved him and loved laughter; but she persisted. "Being wife to a man means a great deal more than looking pretty and making love."

"That's very dear and sweet," said he, in the same petting, patronizing way. "I'm content with you as you are. I don't want anything more." And he set about putting things away and locking up.

Quiet on her high stool, she struggled against a feeling of resentment, of depression. Her instinct was, as always, to hide her hurt; but it seemed to her that if she did, it would not get well, would get worse. "Dick," she began at last.

"Yes?" said he absently. "Come along, dear." And he lifted her down with a kiss.

She went out, waited for him while he locked the door. "Dick," she began again, as they walked along the path, "I don't want to be shut out of any part of your life, least of all out of the realest part. I want to be truly your wife."

No answer. She glanced up at him; obviously his thoughts were far away.

She slipped her arms through his. "Tell me what you're thinking about, dear."

"About that test I was making."

"What was it?"

"Oh, nothing. Is the house satisfactory? How do you like old Nanny?" As she did not answer, he looked down at her. "Why, what's the matter with my little sweetheart? Such a discontented expression!"

"Nothing—nothing at all," replied she, forcing a smile and steadying her quivering lip.

"I'm afraid those two days on the train——"

"Yes," she interrupted eagerly. "And I guess I'm hungry, too. *That's* very upsetting."

With a little forcing she kept up the semblance of good spirits through breakfast and until he was off to the laboratory again. Then she gave way to her mood—for it could be only a mood. With old Nanny as guide, she went through the house, through all its spacious solidly and stiffly furnished rooms. At every step Nanny had something to say of Miss Eudosia—how good Miss Eudosia had been, how Miss Eudosia kept everything as her mother had it before her, how particular Miss Eudosia had been. And when it wasn't Miss Eudosia it was Colonel 'Kill—that splendid-looking, terrible-looking old Achilles Vaughan; as a child she had decided that the awful god the family worshiped must look like Achilles Vaughan. Nanny talked on and on; Courtney's spirits went down and down. In one respect the house should have appealed to her—in its perfect order. For she had inherited from her mother a passion for order—an instinct that would have a neatly kept ribbon box almost as soon as she could talk, and had prompted her, long before she could talk distinctly, to cry if they tried to put on her a dress the least bit mussed or a stocking with a hole in it. But there is the order that is of life, and there is the order that is of death. This Vaughan order seemed to her to be of death. She felt surrounded,

12

hemmed in, menaced by a throng of the Vaughan women of past generations—those women of the old-fashioned kind, thoughtless, mindless, cool, and correct and inane—the kind of women the Vaughan men liked—the kind Richard liked—"No—no. He does *not* like that kind!"

Assisted by Nanny and Mazie, she unpacked the trunks into drawers and closets. When the last box was empty, Jimmie took them down to the cellar. She was established—was at home. She and Dick were to have the same bedroom; he would use the big spare bedroom directly across the hall and its bath for dressing. It was all most convenient, most comfortable. But she could not get interested, could not banish the feeling that she would soon be flitting, that she was stranger, intruder here. And the last sweet days of the honeymoon kept recurring in pictured glimpses of their happiness of various kinds, all centering about love. How tender he had been, how absorbed in their romance—that wonderful romance which began ideally in a chance meeting and love at first sight. And now, just as she was getting over her deep-down shyness with him, was feeling the beginnings of the courage to be wholly her natural self, to show him her inmost thoughts, o release the tenderness, the demonstrativeness that had been pent up in her all her life—just as the climax of happiness was at hand—here was this shadow, this relegating her to the chill isolation and self-suppression and self-concealment of a pedestaled Vaughan wife. "He acts as if a woman were not like a man—as if I had no sense because I'm not tall, and don't go about in a frown and spectacles." And it depressed her still further to recall that his attitude had been the same throughout courtship and honeymoon—treating her as a baby, a pet, something to protect and shield, something of which nothing but lover's small talk was expected. She had liked it then; it seemed to fit in with the holiday spirit. "I gave him a false impression. It's my fault." To pretend to be infantile for purposes of a holiday of love-making is one thing; to have one's pretense taken as an actual and permanent reality—that was vastly different, and wearisome, and humiliating, and not to be permitted. "But," she reflected, "it's altogether my fault. And the thing for me to do is not to talk about it to him, but just quietly to go to work and make myself his wife—fit myself for it." A wonderful man she thought him; and it thrilled her, this high and loving ambition to be worthy of him, and not mere pendant and parasite as so many wives were content to be.

They were to go the scant half mile across the lake in the motor boat at noon and lunch at her old home. She was ready a few minutes before time, and started toward the Smoke House. Halfway she stopped and turned back. No, she could not interrupt him there again. His manner, unconscious, more impressive than any deliberate look or word, made her feel that the Smoke House was set in an enchanted wood which she could not penetrate until She smiled tenderly.

At half past twelve he came on the run. "Why didn't you telephone?" exclaimed he. "We'll be scandalously late. I'm so sorry. When I get to work down there I forget everything. I even forgot I was married."

She busied herself with the buttons of her glove, and the brim of her hat hid her face. And such a few hours ago he and she were all in all to each other!

"Do you forgive me?"

She thought she was forgiving him; the hurt would soon pass. So she gave him a look that passed muster with his unobservant eyes. "Don't worry. We'll soon be there."

They got under way, he at the motor, she watching his back. On impulse she moved nearer. "Dick," she said. "Don't turn round. I want to say something to you that's very hard to say.... I feel I ought to warn you. At college the girls called it one of my worst traits. When anyone I care for hurts me, I don't say anything—I even hide it. And they don't realize—and keep on hurting—until— Oh, I've lost several friends that way. For—the time comes— I don't let on, and it gets to be too late— and I don't care any more."

"You mean about my keeping you waiting?"

"No—not that—not that alone. Not any one thing. Not anything at all yet—but a kind of a shadow. Just—you've made me feel as if I weren't to be part of you—of your life. No, I don't say it right. I've felt as if I were to be part of you, but that you weren't to be part of me."

He began to laugh, believing that the proper way to dispel a mood so unreal. But glancing at her he saw she was shrinking and literally quivering with pain. His face sobered. He reminded himself that women could not be dealt with on a basis of reason and sense, since they had those qualities only in rudimentary form. As his hands were occupied, he was puzzled how to treat this his first experience with feminine sweet unreasonableness in her. All he could do toward pacifying was to say soothingly, as to a sensitive child: "I understand, sweetheart. I must be very— very careful."

"Not at all!" she cried, ready to weep with vexation at her complete failure to make him understand. "I'm not a silly, sensitive thing, always trailing my feelings for some one to step on."

"No, dearest—of course not," said he in the same tone as before. "If there weren't so many sail boats about, I'd show you how penitent I am."

"But I don't want you to be penitent."

"Then what do you want?"

"I want you to—I want us to be comrades."

"What a child it is! You girls are brought up to play all the time. But you can't expect a man to be like that. Of course we'll play together. I'd not have wanted to marry you if I hadn't needed you."

"But what am I to do when you can't play?" she asked. "And I'm afraid you won't play very often. That is, I know you won't—and I'm glad you won't—for I'd not care as I do if you were that kind. I didn't realize until this morning. But I do realize now, and—Dick, you don't think of me as just to play with?"

Facing her earnestness, he would not have dared confess the truth. "No, indeed!" said he. "Your head's full of notions to-day. You're not at all like your sweet loving self."

She felt instantly altogether in the wrong. "It's the strangeness, I guess," she said penitently.

"That's it, exactly. But in a few days you'll be all right—and as happy as a bird on a bough."

As they were about to land she mustered all her courage, and with heightened color said: "You'll let me come down and try to help, won't you? I'll promise not to be in the way—not for a minute. And if I am, I'll never come again. I can at least wash out test tubes and bring you things you need."

"Oh, if you really want to come," began he, with good-humored tolerance.

"Thank you—thank you," she interrupted, eager and radiant.

"Not right away," he hastened to add. "Just at present I'm clearing things up."

"I understand. You'll tell me when the time comes."

"Yes, I'll tell you."

# Chapter 2

In late July, after he had not appeared either at dinner or at supper for four days, she said to him, "You're becoming a stranger."

The idea of reproaching him was not in her mind. She had been most respectful of what she compelled herself to regard as his rights, had been most careful not to intrude or interrupt or in any way annoy. The remark was simply an embarrassed attempt to open conversation—not an easy matter with a man so absorbed and silent as he had become. But he was feeling rather guilty; also, he had not recovered from the failure of an elaborate experiment from which he had expected great things in advancing him toward his ultimate goal—the discovery of a cheap, universal substitute for all known fuels. "You know, my dear," said he, "in the sort of work I'm trying to do a man can't control his hours."

"I know," she hastened to apologize, feeling offense in his tone, and instantly accusing herself of lack of tact. "I'm too anxious for you to succeed to want you ever to think I'm expecting you. I've been busy myself—and a lot of people have been calling."

This, though bravely said, somehow did not lessen his sense of guilt. "You're not lonely, are you?" he asked gently. And he gave her a searching, self-reproachful look.

"No, indeed!" laughed she. "I'm not one of the kind that get hysterical if they're left alone for a few minutes." Her tone and expression were calculated to reassure, and they did reassure.

"Really, you ought to have married a fellow who was fond of society and had time for it. I know how you love dancing and all that." This, with arms about her and an expression which suggested how dreary life would have been if she had married that more suitable other fellow.

"I used to like those things," said she. "But I found they were all simply makeshifts, to pass the time until you came."

"We *are* happy—aren't we?"

"And just think!" she cried. "How happy we'll be when our real life begins."

"Yes," said he vaguely.

He looked confused and puzzled, but she was too intent upon her dream to note it. "When do you think you'll get time to teach me the ropes?" asked she.

After a little groping he understood. He had forgotten all about that fantastic plan of hers to potter at the laboratory. And she had been serious—had been waiting for him to ask her down! A glance at her face warned him that she was far too much in earnest to be laughed at. "Oh, I don't know exactly when," said he. "Probably not for some time. Don't bother about it."

"Of course, I'll not bother you about it," replied she. "But naturally I can't help thinking. It won't be long?"

He detested liars and lies. Yet, looking on her as a sort of child—and it's no harm to humor a child—he said, "I hope not."

He blushed as he said it, though his conscience was assuring him there was absolutely nothing wrong in this kind of playful deception with woman the whimsical, the irrational. "Certainly not," thought he. "She'll soon forget all about it. I don't see how she happened to remember so long as this." Still, it was not pleasant to tell even the whitest of white lies, facing eyes so earnest and so trusting as were hers just then. He changed the subject—inquired who had been calling. She did not return to it. She was content; his long hours and his complete absorption were proof of his eagerness to hasten the day when they should be together. "Of course," thought she, "he likes what he's doing—likes it for itself. But *the* reason is 'us.'" And some day soon he would surprise her—and they would begin to lead the life of true lovers—the life she had dreamed and planned as a girl—the life she had begun to realize during courtship and honeymoon—the life of which, even in these days of aloneness and waiting, she had occasional foretastes when overpowering impulse for a "lighter hour" brought him back to her for a little while.

She had been puzzled when in those hours he sometimes called her "temptress." The word was tenderly spoken, but she felt an accent of what was somehow suggestion of reproach—and of rebuke. Now she thought she understood. He meant she stimulated in him the same deep longings that incessantly possessed her; and when those longings were stimulated, it was hard for him to keep his mind on the work he was hastening with all his energy—the work that must be done before their happiness could begin. "I must be careful not to tempt him," thought she.

From this she went on to feel she understood another matter that had puzzled her, had at times disquieted her. She had noticed that his moods of caressing tenderness, of longing for the outward evidences of love seemed to be satisfied, and to cease just when her own delight in them was swelling to its fullness. Why should what roused her quiet him? This had been the puzzle; now she felt she had solved it: He had greater self-control than she; he would not let his feelings master him, when they would certainly interfere with the work that must be done to clear their way of the last obstacles to perfect happiness; so he withdrew into himself and fought down the longings for more and ever more love that were no doubt as strong in him as in her.

Thus she, in her faith and her inexperience, reasoned it all out to her satisfaction and to his glory. She had not the faintest notion of the abysmal difference between her idea of love and his. With her the caresses had their chief value as symbols—as the only means by which the love within could convey news of its existence. With Dick, the caresses were not symbols at all, not means to an end, but the end in themselves. Of love such as she dreamed and expected he knew nothing; for it he felt no more need than the usual busy, ambitious man. His work, his struggle to wrest from nature close-guarded secrets, filled his mind and his heart.

He soon assumed she had forgotten her fantastic whim, and forgot it himself. She often wished he would talk to her about his work, would not be quite so discouraging when she timidly tried to talk with him about it. And in spite of herself she could not but be uneasy at times over his growing silence, his habitual absentmindedness. But she accepted it all, as loving inexperience will accept anything and everything—until the shock of disillusion comes. So stupefying is habit, there were times when her dream became vague, when she drifted along, leading, as if it were to be permanent, the ordinary life of the modern married woman whose husband is a busy man. She was learning a great deal about that life from her young married friends of the neighborhood and of Wenona. Many of them—in fact, most of them—were husbanded much like herself. But they were restless, unhappy, and for the best of reasons—because they had no aim, no future. She pitied them profoundly, felt more and more grateful for her own happier lot. For she—Dick's wife—had a future, bright and beautiful. Surely it could not be much longer before he would have the way clear for the life in common, the life together!

She fell to talking, in a less light vein than she usually permitted herself with him, about these friends of hers to him one evening as they walked up and down the veranda after supper. She described with some humor, but an underlying seriousness, their lives—their amusing, but also pitiful, efforts to kill time—their steady decline toward inanity. "I don't see what they married for," said she. "They really care nothing about their husbands—or their husbands about them. The men seem to be contented. But the women aren't, though they pretend to be—*pretend* to their *husbands*! Isn't it all sad and horrible?"

"Indeed it is," he replied. He had been only half listening, but had caught the drift of what she was saying. "It's hard to believe decent women can be like that."

"And the men—they're worse," said she; "for they're satisfied."

"Why shouldn't they be?" said Dick. "They don't know what kind of wives they've got."

"I—I don't think you quite understood me."

"Oh, yes; you said the wives were dissatisfied. They've got good homes and contented husbands. What right have they to be dissatisfied? What more do they want?"

"What we've got," said she tenderly. "Love."

"But they've got love. Didn't you say their husbands were contented? When a man's contented it means that he loves his wife. And a good woman always loves her husband."

She laughed. He often amused her with his funny old-style notions about women. "You can't understand people who live and feel as they do, dear," said she. "Of course, you and I seem to be living much like them just now. But you know we'd never be contented if we had to go on and on this way."

With not a recollection of the "whim," he stopped short in astonishment. "What way?" he asked. "Aren't we happy?"

She smiled radiantly up at him in the clear, gentle evening light. "But not so happy as we shall be, when you get things straightened out and take me into partnership."

"Partnership?" he demanded blankly. "What do you mean?"

"I call it partnership. I suppose you'd call it working for you. I suppose I shall be pretty poor at first. But I'll surprise you before I've been down there many weeks. I've been brushing up my chemistry, as well as I could, with only books."

It came to him what she was talking about—and it overwhelmed him with confusion. "Yes—certainly. I—I supposed you'd forgotten."

She gazed at him in dismay. "Forgotten!" Then she brightened. "Oh, you're teasing me."

He began to be irritated. "You mustn't fret me about that," he said.

"I didn't even mean to speak of it," she protested, her supersensitive dread of intrusion alert. "I know you're doing the best you can. But I couldn't help dreaming of the time when I'll have you back again.... Now, don't look so distressed! Meanwhile, we'll have what we can. And that's something—isn't it?"

What queer, irrational creatures women were! To persist in a foolish, fanciful notion such as this! Why couldn't she play at keeping house and enjoy herself as it was intended women should? A woman's trying to do anything serious, a woman's thinking—it was like a parrot's talking—an imitation, and not a good one. But the "whim" and his "harmless deception" became the same sort of irritation in his conscience that a grain of dust is on the eyeball. He was forced to debate whether he should not make a slight concession. After all, where would be the harm in letting her come to the laboratory? She'd soon get enough. Yes, that would be the wise course. Humor a woman or a child in an innocent folly, and you effect a cure. Yes—if she brought the matter up again, and no other way out suggested, he would let her come. It amused him to think of her, delicate as a flower, made for the hothouse, for protection and guidance and the most careful sheltering, trying to adapt herself to serious work calling for thought and concentration. "But she'd be a nuisance after a day or so. A man's sense of humor—even his love—soon wears thin when his work's interfered with." Still, she'd be glad enough to quit, probably after a single morning of the kind of thing he'd give her to discourage her. "Really, all a woman wants is the feeling she's having her own way."

This decision laid the ghost. As she said no more, the whole thing passed to the dark recesses of his memory. One evening in late September, when he was taking a walk alone on the veranda, she came out and joined him. After a few silent turns she said, "Let's sit on the steps." She made him sit a step lower than she, which brought their eyes upon a level. The moon was shining full upon them. The expression of her face, as she looked intently at him, was such that he instinctively said, "What is it, dear?" and reached for her hand.

He had given the subject of children—the possibilities, probabilities—about as little thought as a young married man well could. There are some women who instantly and always suggest to men the idea motherhood; there are others, and Courtney was of them, in connection with whom the idea baby seems remote, even incongruous. But as she continued to look steadily at him, without speaking, his mind began to grope about, and somehow soon laid hold of this idea. His expression must have told her that he understood, for she nodded slowly.

"Do you mean—" he began in an awe-stricken voice, but did not finish.

"Yes. I've suspected for some time. To-day the doctor told me it was so."

Her hand nestled more closely into his, and he held it more tightly. A great awe filled him. It seemed very still and vast, this moonlight night. He gazed out over the lake. He could not speak. She continued to look at him. Presently she began in a low, quiet voice, full of the melody of those soft, deep notes that were so strange and thrilling, coming from such slim, delicate smallness of body and of face: "I can't remember the time when I wasn't longing for a baby. When I was still a baby myself I used to ask the most embarrassing questions—and they couldn't stop me— When could I have a baby? How soon? How many? And when I finally learned that I mustn't talk about it, I only thought the more. I never rested till I found out all about it. I came very near marrying the first man that asked me because——"

He was looking at her with strong disapproval.

She smiled tenderly. "I know you hate for me to be frank and natural," she said with the gentlest raillery. "But, please, let me—just this once. I must tell you exactly what's in my head—my foolish, feminine head, as your grandfather would have said."

"Go on, dear. But you couldn't convince me you weren't always innocent and pure minded."

"You—a chemist—a scientist, talking about knowledge being wicked! But I'll not discuss those things with you. I never have and I never shall." She drew closer to him, put one arm round his neck. "Now do listen, dear," she went on. "Then— you came into my life. It's very queer—I don't understand why—at least not clearly—but from the moment I loved you I never thought of baby again—except to think I didn't want one."

"My dear!" he exclaimed. He drew away to look at her. "Courtney! That's very unnatural. You're quite mistaken."

As she did not know men, it seemed to her a unique and profoundly mysterious case, this of him so broad-minded, scandalously broadminded most Wenona people thought, yet in the one direction a puritan of puritans. With a wisdom deeper than she realized she said smilingly: "Dear—*dear* Dick! I guess the reason you men think women irrational is because you're irrational on the subject of women yourselves. To a crazy person the whole world seems crazy."

He did not respond to her pleasantry. She sighed, drew his arm round her, went on: "Well—anyhow, it's true. And, do you know, I think that whenever a woman really loves a man, cares for just him, she doesn't want a baby."

"You're quite mistaken," he assured her gravely. "It's natural for a woman to want children. *You* want them."

"Do *you*?"

"I? I've never given it much thought."

"I did hope you'd say no," said she, half in jest. "Now honestly, doesn't it seem reasonable that when two people love each other they shouldn't want any—any intruder?"

20

He looked at her with more than a trace of severity in his expression. "Where did you get these unnatural ideas? I don't like you to say such things even in joke. They're most unwomanly."

She felt rebuked and showed it, but persisted, "You must admit it'll interfere."

"Interfere with what?"

"With the life we've been looking forward to—with my helping you."

"Oh—yes—" he stammered. Again that exasperating ghost! What possessed her to persist in such nonsense?

"You know it would interfere—would put off our happiness for a year or two. A year or two! Oh, Dick!"

When she had the child, thought he, the ghost would be laid forever. "Well—we'll do the best we can," he said. His tone and manner of regret were as sincere as ever mother used in assuring her child of the reality of Santa Claus. And Courtney believed and was reconciled.

"I do want the baby," she now admitted. "But I want you—love—more, oh, so much more. I'm glad your life work is something I naturally care about. Still, I suppose, when a woman loves a man, she cares about whatever he is and does, and fits herself to be part of it."

He smiled with patronizing tenderness, as he often did, always evidently quite sure she'd not understand. If we could but realize it, how our mismeasurements of others would enable us to study as in a mirror our own limitations! "Wait till you have the baby," said he.

"Do you think that with me love for a baby could ever take the place of need for love—grown-up love? You're always making me feel as if you didn't know me at all, Dick."

He laughed and kissed her. "You don't know yourself. Wait till you have a baby, and you'll be content to be just a woman."

"But I'm content to be that now."

"Well—let's not argue."

# Chapter 3

Except courtship and honeymoon never had she been so happy as in the last two months before the baby came. "Every-one is spoiling me," she said, dazzled by the revelations of thoughtfulness and affection. Her friends, her acquaintances, showered attentions upon her. Even her mother, austere and cold, unbent. Her father, the shy, the silent, betrayed where she had got her silent, shy, intense longing for love. The two sour old-maid sisters were all tenderness and chaste excitement. As for Dick, he actually neglected his career. Again and again he would stop in the midst of an experiment to dash up to the house and inquire what he could do for her—this when there was a private telephone at his elbow.

She was intelligent about diet and exercise; so she suffered hardly at all. As for the baby, he came into the world positively shrieking with health. Finally, she had none of the petty vanity that leads many a first-time mother into fancying and acting as if maternity were a unique achievement, original with herself. Thus the agitation quickly died away, and life resumed its former course, except that she had a baby to take care of. At first it was great fun. Dick helped her, forgot his chemistry, seemed in the way to become a father of unprecedented devotion. But this did not last long. He loved playthings and played with them; but the call of his career was the strong force in his life, and he went back to the laboratory. She might have given the baby over to a nurse, as all the other women were doing. But it seemed to her that, as she was responsible for the coming of this frisky helplessness, she could not do less than guard him until he was able to look out for himself. "When he can talk and tell me exactly how's he treated when I'm not around," said she, "why, perhaps I'll trust him to a nurse—if he needs one. But until then I'll be nurse myself."

Many and many a time in the next eighteen months she wished she had not committed herself openly and positively. She loved her baby as much as any mother could—and a good-humored lovable baby he was, fat and handsome, and showing signs of being well bred while still a speechless animal. But, except in romances and make-believe life, the deepest love wearies of sacrifices, though it gladly makes them. This baby—Benedict they named him, but he changed it to Winchie as soon as he could—this baby made a slave of her. She understood why so many women retrograde after the birth of the first child. The temptation to go to seed is powerful enough in the most favorable circumstances, once a woman has caught a husband and secured a living for life. A baby, she soon saw, made that temptation tenfold stronger. She wondered what it was in her that compelled her to fight unyieldingly against being demoralized.

Dick was deep in a series of experiments that forbade him a thought for anything else. He did occasionally spend a few moments in mechanical dalliance with his two playthings; but that interrupted his thoughts little if at all. By the slow, unnoted day-to-day action that plays the only really important part in human intimacies of all kinds, she had grown too shy and strange with him to ask his help or even to think of expecting it. She did not judge him—at least, not consciously. She assumed he was doing the best he could, the best anyone could, the best possible. To have complained, even in thought, would have seemed to her as futile as railing against any fundamental of life—against being unable to fly instead of walk. She made occupation for herself, as will presently appear. But, after all, it was Winchie who saved her. But for him she, with no taste for "chasing about," would have withdrawn within herself, would have become silent, cold, ever more and more like her mother, with barren cynicism in place of Mrs. Benedict's equally barren religiosity. Winchie's spirits of overflowing health, his newcomer's delight in life were infectious and stimulating. In keeping him in perfect health—outdoors, winter and summer, and always active, she made her own health so perfect that the cheerful and hopeful side of things was rarely so much as obscured.

One evening after supper Richard, moved by the intermittent impulse to amuse himself, sought her in her sitting room, where she was reading. She always sat there in the evenings because she could hear Winchie if he became restless. He never did, but that fact no more freed her to go off duty than the absence of burglars the policeman. Dick gave her the kind of kiss that was always his signal for a "lighter hour." She merely glanced up, gave him the smile that is a matrimonial convention like "my dear," and went on with her book. Theretofore, whenever he had shown the least desire to take an hour off from that career of his, she had instantly responded. She assumed this readiness meant love; in fact, love had no part in it. She responded for two reasons, both unsuspected by her: because she did not know him well enough to have moods with him and to show them, and because refusal would have been admission of the truth of indifference to him which she had not yet discovered. That evening, for the first time, she did not respond. It was unconscious on her part, unnoted by him; yet it was the most significant event in their married life since the wedding ceremony two years and a half before.

He stood behind her and began gliding his fingers over the soft down at the nape of her neck. It has become second nature to women to repress their active emotions, no matter how strong, and to wait upon the man—an evidence of inferior status that is crudely but sufficiently disguised as "womanly delicacy and reserve." In response to the signal of those caressing fingers Courtney mechanically put up her hand and patted his. Her gesture was genuinely affectionate—but there had been a time when it would not have been mechanical. She did not lift her eyes from the page.

"Is that a good love story?" asked he. "As good as ours?"

A tender little smile of half absent appreciation played round her lips. But—her glance remained upon her reading. "It isn't a novel," replied she. "It's a treatise."

"A treatise?" mocked he. "Gracious me! What a wise fairy it is! Put it away, and let's go on the balcony. There'll not be many more sit-out nights."

He moved to pick her up in his arms. But she smilingly pushed him away. "I want to finish this chapter," said she.

"All right. I'll go out and smoke. Don't be long."

And he sauntered through the window door. After perhaps a quarter of an hour she joined him in the hammock. Matrimony is a curious fabric of set phrases, set thoughts, and set actions. It was their habit, in such circumstances, for her to snuggle up to him and for him to put his arm round her. The habit was on this occasion observed. It was her habit to assume that she was happy—and she now so assumed. He began the conversation. "I've been watching you as I sat here," said he lazily. "What are all those books on the table? They look serious—businesslike."

"Let's not talk about anything serious. You always laugh at me or get absent-minded."

"But you seemed so absorbed. What was it?"

"Oh, I've been doing a little reading and thinking and studying for the past year. You see, when a woman takes care of a baby, she's got to look out or she'll become one herself."

"But you are a baby." And there followed the usual caresses.

"Not a real baby," said she. "We both act like children at times—very little children. But we'd not care for each other as we do if either of us were really infantile. It takes a grown person to play baby attractively."

"Baby," he insisted fondly. He was smiling with the masculinely patronizing tolerance to which she had grown so used that she never noted it. He appreciated that she was clever—with the woman sort of cleverness—bright, witty, sometimes saying remarkably keen things. But, being a man, he knew that man mind and woman mind are entirely different—never so different as when woman mind seems to be like man mind—just as purely instinctive actions of animals seem to display profound reasoning power. "And what was the baby wrinkling its brow over, in there? The care and feeding of infants?"

"Dear me, no," replied she with perfect good humor. "I went into that before Winchie came. You think it's all a joke—my reading and studying. But the real joke is your thinking so. You must remember I can't afford to let myself go, as you do."

He had been chiefly absorbed in caresses and caressing thoughts. At this last remark he laughed. "Now, what does that mean?" he inquired.

"You've given up everything for chemistry. Haven't you noticed that we can hardly talk to each other—that you can hardly talk to anybody?"

"I never did have much talent for small talk."

"But I didn't mean small talk. You care only for chemistry, know only chemistry. You never did know or care much about literature or art or music or any of the worth-while things except just your own specialty. And you can afford to be that way. It's your career, and also you're not a woman and a mother."

He had stopped caressing her. "I confess I don't understand," said he stiffly.

"A man can afford to be narrow—not to know life or the world. But a mother—if she's the right sort—has to try to know everything. She's got to bring up children—and how can she hope to teach and train successfully if she doesn't know?"

"I don't agree with you," said he, a certain curtness in his voice. "A woman must be pure, innocent, womanly—as you are. Nature didn't make her to be learned or wise—to think. She has her instincts to keep her straight, and a father or a husband——"

"Dick—Dick!" she cried, patting him on the cheek. "What an old fogey it is! You talk like—like an ordinary man. How bored you'd be if you had that kind of wife—one who couldn't be comrade and companion, and didn't want to be—one who was merely a mistress."

Vaughan was sitting bolt upright now. "Those books in there— Courtney, you're not reading impure, upsetting books?"

She laughed delightedly.

"What are those books?" he insisted.

"They're—now, Dickey dear, please don't be shocked—they're on landscape gardening and interior decoration." She looked up at him mischievously in the starlight. "Are they womanly enough to suit you?"

"Yes, indeed," said he heartily. "But I might have known you'd not read anything a good woman oughtn't. I love you as you are—and I'd hate to see you changed, my spotless little angel."

She submitted to his caresses. And presently, in that brain which he would have thought it absurd to look into except for the very lightest kind of amusement, there formed the first really disloyal thought she had ever permitted to be born. The thought was: "Dick certainly does take himself terribly seriously. If it weren't Dick, I'd say he was getting to be a prig." She was instantly shocked at herself, as one always is at the first impulse to doubt the idol one has set up for blind worship. She felt there was but one way to prevent the recurrence of such perilous blasphemy. After a brief silence she said in a constrained voice: "Dick, I was not a stupid, incurious fool as a girl, and I went to college, and I'm a wife and a mother. If by innocence you mean ignorance, I'm anything but innocent."

She saw that he was highly amused.

"Women," she went on earnestly, "always tell each other that before men it's wise to pretend to be ignorant and too refined to know life, and to be shocked at everything. They say it pleases men. But I'm sure you're not that sort of man. Anyhow, I can't be a hypocrite."

"That's right, dear," said he, nodding approvingly, the amused smile lingering. "Go on with your interior decoration and landscape gardening. You can't learn too much about them." He was leaning back again, secure, comfortable, happy, enjoying the sensation of caressing her.

She gave it up, as she always did when she found herself being ruffled by that strange antiquated prejudice of his. It would yield in time. Besides, what did it really matter?—since they loved each other, and would be happy once their real life got under way. "I'd have taken up chemistry," she continued, "but one can't go far alone in that, with only books. And you wouldn't help me. I'm afraid you'll find me very rusty when I come down to the laboratory next spring."

His lips were open to inquire what she meant, when he was unpleasantly spared the necessity. Out of a dark recess of memory sprang the ghost—the "whim." He was astounded, irritated, alarmed. He had supposed he had heard the last of that silly notion about helping him; she hadn't spoken of it in nearly two years. Now—here it was again!

"Dick," she was saying, her hand clasping his, "I've appreciated your not speaking of it, or even talking about what you were doing. If you had, the delay'd have been much harder to bear. For, as long as Winchie needs me, I simply can't come."

"I understand, dear," said he, much relieved.

"It's a dreadfully long delay, isn't it?" she went on, dreamily gazing up into the great quiet sky. "The more I see of married people, and the more I think about married life, the clearer I see that two must have a common interest, a common career, or they drift apart, and usually the woman sinks down and down into a gadabout or a fat frump or a professional minder of other people's business—a gossip or a charity worker."

If she had been looking, even in that faint light she could have seen his expression of gathering displeasure.

"Or else," she went on, "she seeks love elsewhere. Isn't it strange, Dick, how in unhappy marriages the so-called good women are the bad ones, and the so-called bad ones good? I mean, when a weak woman finds herself married wrong she accepts it and gently rots, and people say she's a good soul, when she's really degrading herself and rotting everybody round her. While a strong woman—one that's worth while—refuses to be crushed, and people call her bad. But then I've begun to think life's like one of those exhibitions where some cut-up slips round and changes the labels so that everything's named wrong."

She was talking along lightly, talking what seemed to her the plainest common sense, and was all unconscious that she had brought him and herself where both were almost peering into the abyss between them. He was sitting up, was getting ready to deliver himself. Her next remark checked him. "Thank Heaven, Dick, you and I are going to have the interest that makes two lives one—makes it impossible to grow apart. It seems to me I can't wait for Winchie to release me so that I may come and work with you. Aren't you glad I really, naturally, like chemistry, and already know something about it?"

He winced, and instead of speaking, put his cigar between his opened lips.

She leaned her head affectionately against his arm. "I feel close to you to-night—feel that we're in perfect sympathy. Sometimes—I—I don't feel quite that way. Of course I know it's all right, but I get—afraid. It's such a long, long delay—and your work absorbs you—and we almost never talk as we're talking to-night. There have been times when——I've almost—been afraid *we* were drifting apart."

"What nonsense!" he cried sharply. "How could that be? Do you suppose I don't know you're a good woman? You talk foolishly at times—things you've picked up from loose people. But you are a lady and a good woman."

She saw he was for some unknown reason irritated. She swiftly changed the subject. "Anyhow, dearest, we shan't be in danger much longer. We're nearly to the end of the life we've been leading ever since we got back from our wedding trip. Just think—ever since then! How time has gone!"

He stirred uncomfortably, ventured: "We've been happy, and, even if things were to go on just as they are, we'd continue to be happy."

"Of course, you've had your work and I've had Winchie, and once in a while we have each other. But most of the happiness has been in looking forward, hasn't it?"

She assumed that his silence was assent.

"But don't think, dear," she said, "that I've been content just to wait. As soon as I saw it was going to be a long time before I could come to the laboratory——"

He rose abruptly, under the pretense of lighting a fresh cigar.

"——I made another occupation for myself. It'll be next spring at the earliest before I can come to you. And even then I'll be able to spend only part of the day. Winchie'll have to be looked after when he's not at the kindergarten. Now that he's talking and understanding, it's more necessary than ever to watch over him. I've had to watch only his body. Now it's both his body and his mind; for, if any harm came to either, it'd be our fault, wouldn't it?"

"There's no doubt of that," said Dick with strong emphasis, as he seated himself in a chair opposite her. He thought this remark of hers opened the way out of his perplexity. "I don't see how you can come to the laboratory at all."

"Oh, yes. It's not so bad as that. If it were, I don't know what I'd do. It'd be choice between losing you and neglecting him."

"Trash!" exclaimed Dick impatiently. There seemed something essentially immoral in her whole attitude, an odor of immorality exuding from everything she said. It exasperated him that he could not locate it and use it as the text for the lecture he felt she greatly needed. "Your good sense must tell you there's not the slightest danger of your losing me."

She laughed with raillery. "Oh, I know you're far too busy with your chemistry to wander. But that isn't what I meant. You understand." Her eyes shone upon him. "Sometimes—when we're holding each other tight and your lips are on mine—I can scarcely keep from crying. It seems to me we're like two held apart and trying to be one—and trying in vain. It's as if we touched only at the surface, and our bodies were keeping us from each other. But all that will soon end now, and we'll be really one. Closer and closer, day by day——"

She sat on his lap, and he clasped her in his arms. He felt ashamed somehow, and in awe of this emotion that was beyond him. "How wonderful a pure woman is!" he thought.

After a pause she sat up, went back to the hammock, seated herself, leaning toward him. "But I started to tell you my plans."

"What plans?" he asked, in high good humor with her again and overflowing with "lighter-hour" tenderness. "Tell me quick and we'll go in. It's getting late." He moved to seat himself beside her.

"No," she said, laughingly. "Sit where you are. I want you to listen. It isn't often I can get you to listen. As I said, I've got to have something worth while to fill in as I look after Winchie when he's not at kindergarten. I've been getting ready for a year, and it has given me occupation when he was sleeping or playing, for I taught him to amuse himself and not to look to me for everything. That was good for him and saved me. Well, I studied gardening and interior decoration."

"What a fuss you do make," said he, amused. "Why not just settle down and be a plain woman?"

"Shame on you! Tempting me to go to pieces."

"You'll not improve on the good old-fashioned woman, my dear."

"You deserve to be married to one of them."

"I am," declared he. "Your whims don't deceive me. I know you. Let's go in, dear."

She shook her head in smiling reproach. "Then you don't care to hear my plans?"

"Oh, yes. What are they?"

"I've got everything ready to make those changes we discussed on our honeymoon."

"Really!" exclaimed he, seeing that enthusiasm was expected, though he hadn't the remotest idea what she was talking about.

"Of course, I'm going slowly at first, as I want to be sure, and mustn't be extravagant. I've been very careful. I've made drawings and even water colors, for I thought I ought to see how things would look."

He was puzzled and alarmed. "I don't believe I know which scheme you mean," he said. "We discussed so many things on that trip."

"I mean, to change the house and grounds," explained she with bright enthusiasm. "They'll not be ugly and stiff and cold looking much longer."

He started up. "Courtney, what are you talking about?" he demanded.

"Why, Dick! Don't you remember? I told you some of my ideas on gardens and interiors, and you said——"

"I don't know what careless, unthinking remark I may have dropped," interrupted he angrily. "I certainly never intended to let you tear things up and make a mess." He walked up and down. "What possesses you anyhow?" he cried. "Why can't you behave yourself like a woman? I never heard of such nonsense! I want you to stop meddling in things that are beyond you. I want you to do your duty as a wife and a mother. I want you to stop annoying me. I didn't marry a blue-stocking, an unsexed thinking woman. I married a sweet, loving wife."

She sat on the edge of the hammock, perfectly still. It was as if he had struck her unconscious so suddenly that she had not yet fallen over.

"What devil keeps nagging at you?" he demanded, pausing in his angry stride to face her. "It must be some woman's having a bad influence on you. I'll not have it. I'll not have my home upset and my wife spoiled. Who is it, Courtney?"

She was silent.

"Answer me!"

"It's myself," replied she in a quiet, dumb way.

"It's not yourself. *You* are womanly."

"I've got to have something to do—something worth while—or I can't live."

"Attend to your house and your baby, like all true women."

"It isn't enough," replied she in the same monotonous, stupefied way. "It isn't enough for me, any more than it'd be for you."

"Nonsense," said he, with the man's feeling that he had thereby answered her.

She said dazedly: "You didn't mean it. No, you didn't mean it."

"Mean what?"

"All my plans—my year's work—and such a beautiful house and place I'll make." She started up, clasped her hands round his arm. "O Dick—don't be narrow—and so distrustful of me. I know I can do it. Let me show you my plans—my sketches——"

He took her hands, and said with gentle, firm earnestness, for he was ashamed of having lost his temper with a woman: "Courtney, I cannot have it. I will not let you disturb the place my grandfather gave his best thought to."

"But you don't like it, dear," she pleaded.

"I respect my grandfather's memory."

"But on our wedding trip you said——"

"Now, don't argue with me!"

"It's because you think I couldn't do it?"

"I know you couldn't—if you must have the truth."

"Let me show you my sketches and paintings," she pleaded, in a queer kind of quiet hysteria. "Let me explain my plans. I'm sure you'll——"

"Now, Courtney! I've told you my decision. I want to hear no more about it."

She looked up into his face searchingly. He was like the portrait of his unbending grandfather that made the library uncomfortable. Her arms fell to her sides. She went to the balcony rail, gazed out into the black masses of foliage. Taken completely by surprise, she could not at once realize any part, much less all, of what those words of his involved; but she felt in her heart the chill of a great fear—the fear of what she would think, of what she would know, when she did realize.

His voice interrupted. "While you're on the unpleasant subject of these notions of yours," he said, with an attempt at lightness in his embarrassed tone, "we might as well finish it—get it out of the way forever. I want you to stop thinking about the laboratory."

She turned, swift as a swallow.

"I admit I've been at fault—encouraging you to imagine I'd consent. But I thought you'd forget about it. Apparently you haven't."

A long silence.

"I repeat, I'm sorry I misled you. It seemed to me a trifling deception."

She did not speak, did not move.

"When you think it over, you'll see that I'm right—that we're much happier as we are."

After a long silence, which somehow alarmed him, though he told himself such a feeling was absurd, she crossed the balcony to the window. As she paused there, not looking toward him, the profile of those sweet, irregular features of hers stood out clearly. That expression, though it was quiet, increased his absurd alarm. "It's getting late," she said, and her tone was gentle, apologetic. "I think I'll go in."

"Are you angry, Courtney?"

"No," she replied. "I don't think so."

"Why are you silent?"

"I don't know," she said slowly. "I seem to have stopped inside."

He went and put his arms round her. She was passive as a doll. "Why, you're quite cold, child!"

"I must go in. Good night."

"I'll join you in a few minutes."

She shivered. "No," she said. "Good night."

He was somewhat disconcerted. Then he reflected that she could hardly be expected to give up her whims without a little struggling. "It shows how sweet and good she is," thought he, "that she took it so quietly." And he went to bed in the room across the hall—the room he had been occupying most of the time since three months before Winchie came. As he fell asleep he felt that he had laid "the ghost" and had settled all his domestic affairs upon the proper basis. He slept, but she lay awake the whole night, watching, tearless, beside her dead.

# Chapter 4

Next morning, after her usual breakfast alone, she took Winchie and went across in the motor boat to her father's. If she had been led blindfold into that house she would have known, from the instant of the opening of the door, that she was at home. Every home has its individual odor. Hers had a clean, comfortable perfume suggestive of lavender. She inhaled it deeply now as she paused a moment in the front hall—inhaled it with a sudden sense of peace, of sorrow shut out securely. She left the baby in the sitting room with her sister Lal, and sought out her mother in the pleasant old-fashioned back parlor with its outlook on the hollyhocks and sunflowers of the kitchen garden. Mrs. Benedict, a model of judicial sternness, as her husband was of judicial gentleness, sat reading a pious book by the open window. She glanced up as her daughter entered, and prepared her cold-looking cheek for the conventional salute. But Courtney was in no mood for conventions. She seated herself on the roll of the horsehair sofa. "Mother," she said, "I want to talk to you about Richard."

The tone was a forewarning—an ominous forewarning because it was calm. Mrs. Benedict, for all her resolute unworldliness, had been unable to live sixty-seven years without there having been forced upon her an amount of wisdom sufficient to store to bursting the mind of any woman half her age. She closed the heavy-looking book in her lap, leaving her glasses to mark the place. "I don't think I need tell a daughter of mine that she cannot discuss her husband with anyone."

Courtney flushed. "That's just it," replied she. "He is no longer my husband."

She was astonished at her mother's composure. An announcement about the weather could not have been less excitedly received. She did not realize how plainly she was showing, in her changed countenance, in stern eyes and resolute chin, the evidences a mother could hardly fail to read—evidences of a mood a sensible mother would not aggravate by agitation. "I cannot live with him," she went on. "I've brought Winchie and come home."

Her words startled herself. In this imperturbable, severely sensible presence they sounded hysterical, theatrical, though she had thought out the idea they conveyed with what she felt sure was the utmost deliberation. Her mother's gray-green eyes looked at her—simply looked.

"I know you don't believe in divorce, mother. But he and I have never been really married. He's entirely different from the man I loved. And he— What he feels for me isn't love at all. He doesn't know me—and doesn't want to know me."

"Has he sent you away?"

"Oh, no. *He's* satisfied."

Mrs. Benedict folded her ladylike hands upon the pious book, said coldly and calmly: "Then you will go back to him."

"Never. I refuse to live with a man who classes me with the lower animals. I—"

Her mother's stern, calm voice interrupted. "Don't say things you will have to take back. You will return because there is no place else for you."

"Mother! Do you refuse to take me and Winchie? Oh, you don't understand. You—who believe in religion—you couldn't let me——"

"Your father," interrupted her mother in the same cold, placid way, "is not to be made judge again. We shall have to give up this house and retire to the farm. We have nothing but the farm. It will take every cent we can rake and scrape to pay the insurance premiums. The insurance premiums must be paid. The insurance is for your sisters. They have no husbands." And with these few bald statements she stopped, for she knew that under her daughter's youthful idealism there was the solid rock of common sense, that behind her impetuosity there was her father's own instinct for justice.

"The farm," said Courtney, stunned. "The farm." Twenty miles back in the wilderness—a living death—burial alive. "Oh, mother!" And the girl flung herself down beside the old woman and clasped her round the waist. "You shan't go there! I'll go back to Richard and we'll see that you and father and Lal and Ann stay on here."

Her mother was as rigid as the old-fashioned straight-back chair in which she sat. The blood burned brightly in the center of each of her white cheeks, but her voice was distinctly softer as she said: "You will go back. But we accept nothing from anybody."

Courtney hung her head. "Of course not," she said, hurried and confused. "I spoke on impulse."

"You'd better sit in a chair," said Mrs. Benedict. "You are rumpling your dress."

But Courtney was not hurt. She had an instinct why her mother wished her to sit at a distance. "Very well, mother," said she meekly, and obeyed.

After a pause Mrs. Benedict spoke: "I was not surprised when you told me. I suppose there is not one woman in ten thousand who doesn't at least once in the first five years of her married life resolve to leave her husband."

"But it's different with me. I must have something—and I have nothing."

"You have your home and Winchie."

"That house—those prim, dressed-up looking grounds—they've always oppressed me. And I hate them—now that—" She checked herself. How futile to relate and to rail. "As for Winchie, he's not enough."

"There will be others presently."

Courtney gave her mother a horrified look.

"You will do your duty as a wife, and the children will be your reward."

Courtney could not discuss this; discussion would be both useless and painful. "There may be some women who could be content with looking after a house and the wants of children," said she. "But I'm not one of them, and I never saw or heard of a worth-while woman who was. How am I to spend the time? I'm like you—I don't care for running about doing inane things. I can't just read and read, with no purpose, no sympathy. It seems to me I could do almost anything with love—

almost nothing without it.... Brought up and educated like a man, and then condemned to the old-fashioned life for women—a life no man would endure!"

Her mother was looking out through the window, a strange expression about her stern mouth—the expression of one who, old and in a far, cold land, thinks of home and youth when the sun warmed the blood and the heart.

"What shall I do if I go back?" repeated Courtney. "But why ask that? I've simply got to go back. As you say, there's no place else for me." A flush of shame overspread her cheeks. "Oh, it's so degrading!"

"You forget Winchie," said her mother, and her tone was gentle.

"No, I thought of that excuse. But I was ashamed to speak it. It seemed like hypocrisy. Of course, I've got to go back for his sake. But if I hadn't him I'd go back just the same. Mother, you ought to have had me educated more or else less. If I knew less I could be content with the sort of life women used to think was the summit of earthly bliss. If I knew more I could make my own life. I could be independent. I begin to understand why women are restless nowadays. We're neither the one thing nor the other."

Up to a certain point Mrs. Benedict could understand her daughter, could sympathize. She could even have supplemented Courtney's forebodings as to the future with drearier actualities of experience. But beyond that point the two women were hopelessly apart. "You are warring with God," she rebuked. "He has ordained woman's position." And to her mind that settled everything.

"It isn't God," replied Courtney. "It's just ignorance."

"It is God," declared her mother, in the fanatic tone that told Courtney her mind was closed.

The mother and daughter belonged to two different generations—the two that are perhaps further apart than any two in all human history. Courtney saw how far apart she and her mother were, thought she understood why her mother could sympathize with her restlessness in woman's ancient bondage, but could only say "sacrilege" when the younger and better educated woman went on from vague restlessness to open revolt.

"God has seen fit to make the lot of woman hard," said the mother.

"If that is God," cried the daughter, "then the less said about Him the better."

"Courtney, your sinful heart will bring you to grief."

"Is it a sin to think?"

"I sometimes believe it is—for a woman," replied the mother, with the kind of bitter irony into which the most reverent devotee is sometimes goaded by the whimsical cruelties of his deity.

Courtney had long since learned to be unargumentative before her mother's somber and savage religion, so logical yet so inhuman. She had dimly felt that if she ever investigated religion, the misery of the world would compel her to choose between believing in her mother's devil god and believing nothing. So she left religion aside in her scheme of life, like so many of the men and women of her generation.

"I ought to have had more education or less," she repeated. "I ought to have had more, for it wouldn't have been fair to give me less than the rest of the girls have."

She fancied it was her formal education of the college that had made her think and feel as she did. In fact, that had little, perhaps nothing, to do with it; for colleges, except the as yet few scientific schools—stupefy or stunt more minds than they stimulate. She was simply a child of her own generation, and the forces that were stirring her to restlessness were part of its universal atmosphere—the atmosphere all who live in it must breathe, the "spirit of the time" that makes the very yokel with his eyes upon the clod see things in it his yokel father never saw.

She knew her mother would gladly help her, but she realized she might as hopefully appeal to Winchie. All her mother could say would be: "Yes, it is sad. But the only thing to do is to return and pretend to be the old-fashioned wife, and perhaps custom will make the harness cease to gall." Well, perhaps her mother was right; perhaps there was no solution, no self-respecting hopeful solution. Certainly she could not support herself, except in some menial and meager way that would more surely kill all that was aspiring in her than would submission to the lot which universal custom made abject only in theory. She could not support herself—and there was Winchie, too. Winchie had his rights—rights to the advantages his father's position and fortune gave. Dick had made it clear that he did not and would not have the kind of love, the kind of relationship, she believed in. She must go on his terms or not at all.

She ended the long silence, during which her mother sat motionless in an attitude of patient waiting for the inevitable. "I will go," she said. "And I will try to be to him the kind of wife he wants."

Mrs. Benedict looked at her daughter; there were tears of pride in her eyes. "That is right," she said, and they talked of it no more.

But on the way back in the motor boat, and for the rest of that day, and for a good part of many a day and many a night thereafter, Courtney Vaughan's mind was stormily busy. It teemed with the thoughts that in this age of the break-up of the old-fashioned institution of the family force themselves early or late upon every woman endowed with the intelligence to have, or to dream of, self-respect.

Thenceforth Dick Vaughan, if he had thought about it at all, would have congratulated himself on his wise and thorough adjustment of his threatened domestic affairs. But he gave no more thought to it than does the next human being. We do not annoy ourselves with what is going on in the heads of those around us. We look only at results. And usually this plan works well; for, no matter what the average human being may have in mind, the habit of a routine of action ultimately determines his or her real self. Once in a while, however, circumstances interfere, encourage the latent revolt against action's routine apparently so placidly pursued. But this is rare.

The weeks, the months went by; and Courtney seemed, and thought herself, a typical "settled" wife and mother. That is, as "settled" as an intelligent, energetic, and young woman, restless in mind and body, could be. She did not attempt to come to a definite verbal understanding with him. What would be the use? There was nothing to change except herself. There was nothing to explain. She understood him. He did not understand her, did not wish to, could not on account of his prejudices, however carefully she might explain. "No," thought she, "the only thing is for me to accept my position as woman and adapt myself to it, since I haven't the right, or the courage, or the whatever it is I lack, to do as I'd like." The only outward difference in their relations was that she rarely talked with him, and when he was about, fell into his habit of abstraction.

That winter he became extremely irregular about coming to dinner, and as the days lengthened with the spring he often worked on through supper time also. In late May or early June he began to note that when he did come up to the house for supper, his wife was sometimes there and sometimes not. Gradually her absence made an impression on him, and her always answering his inquiry with, "I was over at the club." As that meant the Outing Club, established and supported and frequented by the young people of Wenona and its suburbs, he was entirely satisfied. This, until about midsummer. One evening, when she returned in the dusk from supper at the club, she found him seated on the bench at the landing stage, smoking moodily. He was scantily civil to Shirley Drummond, who had brought her in the club launch. When Shirley was well on the way back to the north shore, Courtney, who had seated herself beside her husband, spoke of the heat and unwound the chiffon scarf about her bare neck and shoulders. Dick glanced round. In some moods he would not have seen at all. In other moods those slender shoulders, that graceful throat, and the small head with its lightly borne masses of auburn hair would have appealed to his pride and joy of possession. But things had gone wrong at "the shop," and he was in the mood that could readily either turn him to her for the consolation of a "lighter hour" or set him off in a rage. He frowned upon the exposed shoulders.

"Where did you get that dress?" he demanded.

She heard simply the question. Her thoughts were on the events of the evening at the club. "Had it made here," said she, unconscious of his mood. "It's something like one I saw in a fashion picture from Paris. Like it?"

To her amazement he replied angrily: "I do not. I've never seen a dress I disapproved of so thoroughly. Don't wear it again, and please be careful how you adopt a fashion you get that way. French fashions are set by a class of women I couldn't speak to you about. Respectable women have to alter them greatly."

"Why, what's the matter with the dress?" exclaimed she. "Everyone admired it at the club."

"It isn't decent," replied he. "I know you are so innocent that you don't think of those things. But it's my duty to protect you. I won't have men commenting on my wife's person."

"But, Dick," protested she, "this isn't a low-cut dress. It's higher than those I usually wear. It has bands across the shoulders and a real back———"

"Then change all your dresses. You must not make yourself conspicuous."

"Conspicuous! The other women wear much lower-cut dresses than I do."

"I know about such things," said he peremptorily. "I don't believe in low-neck dresses anyhow. What business has a good woman flaunting her charms—rousing in other men thoughts she ought to rouse in her husband only?"

"Don't you think it's all a matter of custom?" she said persuasively. She was not convinced, or even shaken. But she admired the shrewdness of his argument. The reason she had never grown to dislike him was that even in his prejudices he was always plausible, and not in his narrowest narrowness was he ever petty. "Now really, Dick, if that were carried out logically, a woman'd have to cover her face and not speak, for often it's a woman's voice that charms a man"—with a little laugh—"and once in a long while what she says."

"I would carry it out logically," replied he promptly, "if I had my way. That reminds me. You're away from home very often these days, I notice. You're over at the club a great deal."

"The weather's been so fine, everybody goes."

"I've no objection to your going occasionally. But after all the place for a good woman is at home."

She thought so too, as a general principle; home undoubtedly was the place for a good woman, or any sort of woman, or for a man; that was to her mind the meaning of home—the most attractive, the most magnetic spot on earth. However, the Vaughan place was not "home." She could not discuss this with him, so she simply answered, "But I get bored—here alone—and with nothing to do. And nobody'll come at this time of year, with something on at the club every day and evening."

"You don't even stay home to meals."

"Neither do you."

"But I haven't Winchie to look after."

"He plays with the other children at the kindergarten. And Miss Brockholst can keep a child amused as I couldn't. When I stay out to supper I see that Nanny or Lizzie brings him home and puts him to bed. And I'm not out to supper often."

"I don't like it," said Dick imperiously.

"You ought to come with me," rejoined she. "But you never will."

"I've no time for foolishness. And I'm sure you haven't either."

"What ought I to do with myself?"

"What other good women do. Our mothers didn't hang about clubs."

"No. But these aren't pioneer times. Things are entirely different nowadays. That was why—" She did not finish. She did not wish to remind him how he had refused to let her either share his life or make a life of her own. She refrained because the subject might be unpleasant to him. It was no longer unpleasant to her; she now had not the least desire to share his life, was in a way content to drift aimlessly along with the rest of the aimless women.

"Yes, many of the women are different nowadays," said he. "The more reason for my wife's conducting herself as a woman should."

She flushed with sudden anger. "Why can't you accept a woman as a human being?" exclaimed she. "Oh, you men—tempting—compelling—us to be hypocrites—and making our natural impulses rot into vices because they have to be hid away in the dark."

"We will not quarrel," said he, in the calm superior tone he always took when their talk touched on the two sexes. "I simply say I will not tolerate my wife's being a club lounger."

To have answered would have been to say what must precipitate a furious and futile quarrel. She kept silent, with less effort than many women would have to make in the circumstances. She had had the conventional feminine training in self-suppression, that so often gives women the seeming of duplicity and only too often imperceptibly leads them into forming the habit of duplicity. She had also had special training in self-concealment through having been brought up austerely. She kept silent, and made up her mind to obey. She had heard much talk among the women at the club about the "rights of a wife"; but it had not convinced her. She could not see that she, or any other of the women married as was she, contributed to the family anything that entitled her to oppose the husband's will as to how it should be conducted. And she would have scorned to get by cajolery what she could not have got honestly. She was thus the good wife, not through fear of him, for she was not a coward and he was not the sort of small tyrant that makes the women and the children tremble; nor was it because she was faithful to her marriage vows, for she never thought of them. Her submissiveness was entirely due to the agreement she had tacitly signed the day she went back to him, after the talk with her mother. In return for shelter and support she would be, so far as she could, the kind of wife he wanted.

She kept away from the club, stayed at home; and soon the telephone bell was ringing, and pleading voices were giving the flattering proof that in her abrupt divorce from the social life of the town the sense of loss was by no means altogether on her side. And presently over came Sarah Carpenter escorted by her big handsome brother, Shirley Drummond, "as a committee of two," so Sarah put it, "to investigate and report on your cruel and inhuman treatment of us." It was dull, frightfully dull, at the club house, she went on to explain. They did nothing but sit round and try to guess why Courtney Vaughan had dropped them. "And have you forgotten the flower show you were planning? and the play you were going to organize? and the Venetian fête?"

"Oh, that was just talk," replied Courtney. "It's far too hot. I'm resting, and looking after my boy. I'll be over some afternoon soon."

Sarah pleaded and coaxed. Shirley took no part, but sat on the veranda rail, his long legs swinging, his eyes on the interior of the straw hat he was turning round and round between his hands. When Sarah realized that there was unalterable resolution under Courtney's light and gay laughing off of her entreaties, she bade Shirley wait there for her and went to call on Molly Donaldson. Courtney looked admiringly after Sarah's long willowy figure and striking costume—sunshade and hat, dress and stockings and ties, all of various cool, harmonious shades of red.

"Your sister always was pretty," said Courtney. "But since she's married it seems to me she gets prettier all the time."

"Marriage does bring out those women that don't go to pieces," said he. "I guess it's because they get the courage to be more like themselves. Girls are such hypocrites—always posing. You were the only one I ever liked. You weren't a hypocrite. Where you didn't dare be yourself you simply kept quiet."

"I like your impudence—attacking women for being what you men compel."

"Maybe so," said he absently. "But I didn't come over here in the hot sun to talk generalities. Look here, Courtney, there's something I've got to say to you." His good-humored commonplace face was even redder than the heat and his bulk—for he wasn't a thin man—warranted. His voice was low and confused, yet suggested a man talking against a mob and determined to be heard. "I've got to tell you that I care for you—and have ever since we used to walk from high school together—whenever some other fellow didn't slip in ahead of me."

Courtney, puzzled, rapidly reviewed her conduct toward Shirley the past two months—since he came home from Harvard Law School. She recalled nothing that could have given him encouragement to this speech. "I should hope you did like me," she said carelessly. "Of course, we're good friends, as always." She rose. "Let's go over to Donaldson's." Her tone and manner contained the subtle warning to desist that reaches through the thickest skin into the dullest brain.

"You know what I mean," said Shirley doggedly. "Now listen to me while I make a proposition. You're a sensible, up-to-date woman, and this is the twentieth century, not the dark ages. I'm not as clever as some, but neither am I as much the muttonhead as maybe you think. Anyhow, I appreciate you."

"Drop it," said Courtney.

"I want you to get a divorce and marry me."

He spoke as tranquilly as if they were at a dance and he were asking her for the next two-step. She stared. "Well, I never did!" she exclaimed.

"I see you're surprised," said he. "I've thought about it so much that I've got used to it."

"This is something new—a woman getting proposals after she's married, just as if she wasn't." She was laughing.

"Why not?" retorted he, unruffled. "Nobody looks on marriage as the finish any more. I don't think you love me—not for a minute. You've got better brains than I have—a lot better, for I'll admit I'm pretty slow. But you've tried brains and you see they don't amount to much when it comes down to solid living. You don't love me now. But, Courtney, if you'll marry me, I'll guarantee to treat you and the youngster so that you'll simply *have* to love me."

She was slowly recovering from her utter amazement, when he spoke those last words in his simple, honest way with his love in his voice, in his eyes—love that makes bright the dullest face, quickens into bloom the barrenest fancy, puts sweet music in the most tedious voice. Her words of rebuke dropped back unsaid, her throat choked up and tears welled into her eyes. While she was still trying to control this sudden treachery of her hungry heart, he went on: "I was away to college when

I heard you were engaged. I cut exams, and everything and rustled out here. But I saw you were dead in love. It nearly knocked me out. Then it occurred to me that marrying's only a trial go and that in a few years I might get you and you'd be all the better for the experience."

What he said did not shock her. But she was shocked that she was not shocked. Still, it isn't easy to meet a wholly new form of attack; and less easy is it to be stiff and stern with a person one has known always and liked always—a person one knows to be through and through sincere and profoundly respectful. "Shirley," said she, "you mean well and you are slow—so, you don't realize that what you've said is perfectly outrageous."

"Why?" demanded he. "Is it an insult to a woman to tell her you love her? Is it a crime to let her know that, if she isn't suited, there's some one waiting to try to help her get suited? Where's the outrage?"

"I don't know just where," admitted she. "But I feel that it is an outrage—that you've taken advantage of our friendship."

"On the contrary, I've shown I *am* your friend; ready to stand by you. I haven't laid a finger on you, and, so help me God, Courtney, I couldn't try. I'm that old fogey, at least. And I haven't tried to wheedle or win you—have I? I just made a plain statement that if you want me, I'm waiting—and eager. I've seen how things are with you——"

"You've seen nothing of the kind!" Her pride and her loyalty were in arms now.

He looked at her with eyes that were as honest as an open sky. "You don't love your husband, nor he you," he said. "If you did, you'd not see as little of each other as you do."

"Shirley, it's cowardly to say those things," she began angrily.

"Oh, I'd say 'em to him, if it wasn't that I'm afraid you'd have to suffer for it. You needn't get mad. I've been so damn miserable this past week, not seeing you, that I don't care what happens to me. I know why you don't come over any more. He's shut you up here. I saw it in his face that night."

"It was about time he stopped me, I see," said she quickly. "Evidently he understood better than I did. But you mustn't go away thinking I'm obeying a jailer. Do you suppose I'd stay here at the request of a man unless I cared for him?"

"Certainly," replied he. "A right sort woman'll put up with most anything to avoid a row. You needn't try to fool me, Courtney. I know—everyone knows—the truth."

"The truth!" cried Courtney. "How dare you sit there insulting me!"

"Now, Courtney!" begged he.

"Go join your sister and take her back without coming here."

She felt she ought to leave him; but her hungry heart would not let her go. She lingered, looking at him angrily, watching the utter love in his countenance—and enjoying it. He slowly dropped from the veranda rail and faced her. His look was that same mingling of gentle and fierce qualities that makes a bulldog's face fascinating. "If I've said anything I shouldn't, I beg your pardon," said he. "But I stick to my proposition. You can take it or leave it—now, or next year—or whenever you like. It's you or nobody for me." He put out his hand.

She clasped her hands behind her. But she had to lower her head that he might not see—"and misunderstand"—her swimming eyes, her trembling lip.

"Please shake hands," he begged.

She shook her head.

"That hurts," said he shakily, and she turned hastily away. "But," he added, "I'm used to hurts."

He lingered, embarrassed. At length, with a huge sigh, he descended from the veranda and plodded across the lawn toward the hedge. She darted upstairs and shut herself in her room and cried, lying on the bed face down. She felt guilty; would not the right sort of woman have been able to meet such talk from a man, even a Shirley Drummond, with effective fiery resentment? But she knew it was not her guilt that she was weeping for. No, her tears were flowing from the wounds in her heart—the wounds she had thought healed. She had not the faintest feeling in the least akin to love for Shirley Drummond. She never could love him. She had always avoided him as far as her instinct against hurting people's feelings permitted. His grotesque proposal, in itself, appealed only to her sense of humor. But at the mere sound of loving words, words of considerate tenderness, how her whole being vibrated! It terrified her, this heart of hers suddenly and fiercely insurgent.

The next evening after supper she interrupted Dick in the library. "Richard," she said gravely, "I want you to come upstairs with me a few minutes."

"Certainly," said he. "Directly." And he worked on—and would have continued to work until bedtime had she not insisted.

"No. Right away, please."

He glanced up. Her eyes prevented him from returning to his calculations. "All right," said he.

Her sitting room was changed into a painting and drawing exhibition. On the walls, on tables, on sofas and chairs, and leaning against the baseboard were pictures and plans of interiors and of gardens, many in colors, more in black and white, most of all in ground-plan drawings.

"What's this?" said he.

"You were right about my going to the club too much," replied she. "I shall stay at home more. But I *must* have something to occupy me. These are my plans for making over the house and grounds. Please don't try to stop me. I am going to explain it all to you, and I ask you to be considerate and polite enough to listen."

Her manner was compelling; the exhibit was interesting. And he looked and listened as she talked, rapidly, intensely, yet clearly and calmly, describing the whole scheme in minutest detail, not forgetting expense which she demonstrated would be small. He asked several questions—enough to show that he was giving his attention. When she finished she was trembling all over. He continued to inspect the water colors that showed how things would look when the changes had been made.

After a while he smiled and nodded at her. "Very clever," he said. "Really, I had no idea you could do anything like this."

Her mouth and throat were dry; her eyes gleamed. She was giving out the force that flows from a soul in desperate earnest—the force that sweeps away any opposition not already aggressive, before it has a chance to gather. "I may try it?" she asked.

"That's another matter," reflected he aloud. "I ought to say no, for I'm sure you'll be disappointed and your mistakes'll have to be covered up." Now that he was reminded of it he was ashamed of the curt ill-humored way he had issued his orders about her going to the club. "But you can only learn by trying. So, I've no objections to your making a start." He laid his hands on her shoulders. "A little at a time—remember!" he cautioned. "A *very* little."

With that unconsciousness of her being intelligent enough to see his thoughts in his expression—an unconsciousness to which she had long since got used, but never hardened—he was showing that he wished to refuse her, but that, being taken by surprise, he in his kindness of heart could not frame a pretext. His manner took from her all desire or ability to thank him. "I'll be careful," said she.

The smile in his eyes was like a parent's at a precocious child. He kissed her, patted her cheek, went back to his work. He had read the anthropologies, all written by men. Anthropology being out of his line, he accepted as exact science the prejudice and baseless assertion and misleading "statistics" there set down as "laws." Nature had made man active, woman passive; thus, action in woman was contrary to nature, was inevitably abortive and whimsical, was never, except by rare accident, valuable. "She's clever," thought he, by way of finis to the subject. "But she'll soon tire of this thing and drop it. Well, I suppose a few more years'll wash away the smatter she got at college, and this restlessness of hers will yield to nature, and she'll be content and happy in her womanhood. A few more children would have an excellent effect. She's suffering from the storing up of the energy that ought to have outlet in childbearing. As grandfather often said, it's a dreadful mistake, educating women beyond their sphere. But it hasn't done the dear child any permanent harm. She's far too womanly."

# Chapter 5

By the time Winchie was four years old—and in looks and health, in truthfulness and self-reliance a credit to her—she had about completed the transformation of house and grounds. The Vaughan place was no longer an example of those distressing attempts to divorce beauty from its supreme quality, use, that are the delight of the unfortunates whose esthetic faculty has been paralyzed by the mediæval monastic education still blighting the modern world. It was, throughout, beauty applied to use, use achieved in beauty. She had no theory in doing this; she followed the leadings of a courageous and unspoiled taste which was thoroughly practical, as practical as that of the artists of the age of Pericles, a taste which abhorred the bizarre and the blatant. The results would not have pleased Colonel Achilles; they would not have stirred the enthusiasm of anyone who has been enslaved by false education to admire only what has been approved by tradition. But charm no one could have denied. Winter and summer the house, livable and restful in every corner, bloomed within—for over no other part of nature is man's dominion so complete as over the plant kingdom. From early spring through the last warm days of autumn the grounds were delightful to behold; it was as if summer were living there freely and at ease, with no restraint upon her except keeping her clear of the restraint of her own profuse and careless litter. In winter the lawns and clumps and hedges were by no means dead or filled only with evergreen's mortuary suggestions; there are many plants that bloom with bright berries and leaves in the midst of snow and ice, and Courtney knew about them. Winter indoors seemed a millennium in which winter and summer lived amicably together. There were snows and icy storms without, huge open fires within; the windows were gay with blossoming plants, and from a conservatory she built and stocked at surprisingly small cost there came cut flowers for vases and bowls as well as plants that replaced those which had done service and needed rest. Courtney was one of those for whom things grow; her own vivid life seemed to radiate throughout her surroundings and infect all things with the passion to live vividly. With the flowers, as with Winchie, she was patient, intelligent, understanding—never expecting too much, always encouraging to the least disposition to develop.

All this wonder of transformation was not wrought in a day, nor by dreaming. It came as the result of tireless and incessant labor of brain and hand. She had dreamed her dream; she was determined that it should be realized. Failure did not daunt her; it taught her. Nor was she halted by her sense, rather than experience, of a latent reluctance in Richard about giving her money he wanted for the laboratory; for, as his work there expanded, its expenses grew rapidly heavier. She did not ask him for the money; she did not let him know she needed it; she got along without it. In such work as she was doing it takes a vast deal of thought, of planning and contriving, to take the place of money. She did that necessary thinking. When she could get a little money, she spent it to amazing advantage; when she could not, she went on without it. Some of her most satisfying results came through the work made necessary by lack of money. Very powerful, too, was the influence of this upon her character—in developing self-reliance and self-respect which come only through successful independent action.

Now, after nearly three years of days of toil that was also play, since she loved it, she saw, but a short distance ahead, a time when she would have little to do beyond taking care that Jimmie and Bill kept the grounds up, and that Nanny and Mazie and Lizzie did their work properly in the house. There would be minor changes, new features; but the task as a task was almost done. And, in spite of Nanny's opposition, she had put the household on a systematic basis, so that with a little daily attention every part of the routine went smoothly, each servant doing his or her share of the work in the same way always and at the same time. She was about to have many hours each day liberated—and this, in a quiet place, where time refuses to take wings, but insists upon being definitely employed every moment of it.

What should she do next? She had grown through her work. She had educated her originality and her instinctive good taste, had educated them so intelligently that originality had not lost its courage nor good taste its breadth. It had not "settled" her to make a home, as it "settles" a human or lower animal that acts largely from instinct and example and that conceives a home to be chiefly a place to eat and sleep. On the contrary, it had unsettled her the more. Her character had not changed. Character never does change; it simply develops, responding to its environment like any other growing thing. Her character had developed.

What next? What should she do to occupy hand and brain, now grown far more skillful? What should she do with heart? It was now grown far bolder in its dreams and longings; and from time to time it was giving ever more imperious notice that not much longer would it be content with solicitude about a child and makeshift interest in interior decoration and landscape gardening, but would demand its right to the fullness of experience. She temporized with these ominous threatenings. She hoped there would be more children—for children would compel her. From Richard, the absorbed, the well pleased with his "settled, womanly wife," she expected nothing—and wished nothing. The routine of matrimony had become as unconscious as breathing or winking. Her sense of moral obligation to him was also automatic; she felt its restraint not definitely as the wife of a certain Richard Vaughan, but generally as a woman of the married estate. She knew little about him beyond what he thought of her, of marriage—and that knowledge killed all further interest in him. He knew nothing whatever about her beyond the surface—her physical charm, enhanced by good taste in dress. The comfort of his home and its order, the surprising success of her "tinkerings" with house and grounds made small impression upon him. The changes had come about gradually; and he was absorbed at the Smoke House. Before the next change was made he had got used to the one preceding, and had come to regard it as something that had always existed. And she was not one of those who see to it that they get full credit by preceding, accompanying, and following every act with blast of trumpets. She did things because she liked to do them, just as she learned because she liked to know. She worked without friction or bluster. Also, having dismissed him from her inner, her real life, as he had dismissed her from his, it never occurred to her to talk to him about herself—and her work was herself.

What next? She often asked the question as she paused to look about her and saw so short a distance ahead the end of her task. But she was not troubled because she could not answer the question. She waited with a certain confident tranquillity until an answer should be imperative. Meanwhile— One look at her was enough to convince that her lot had been better than the lot of the gay, discontented young married women of Wenona society who pitied her because of her solitude. They did not realize that not only were they unhappy, but also were without the capacity to enjoy happiness if it should offer, had lost the capacity as utterly as a deaf man the capacity to enjoy music. One may abuse intellect or heart with impunity no more than body. Transgression and punishment are simply cause and effect. There were times when Courtney wished she could be gayer; but at least she was never bored, never did the things that do not amuse in the doing, and have an aftermath of disgust. She had an intense, ever intenser desire to live life to its uttermost limits of interest and joy; but that did not seem to her to mean changing her clothes many times a day, rushing from house to house, from party to party, gossiping, eating indigestible sauces and desserts, and playing bridge. She knew what she did not want. She did not know what she wanted—did not dare inquire. She feared life was a good deal of a cheat—not altogether a cheat, not by any means—but still a raiser of longings it had no way to satisfy, of expectations it had no way to fulfill.

She fancied herself little changed since her marriage. And she was hardly changed at all physically. But in mind she was a woman full grown—a rarity indeed in our civilization which tends to make odalisques and parasites out of the women it does not crush under toil. She was ready for a strong part in life, should opportunity offer. Meanwhile, she was living her placid routine with the originality and interest with which intelligence can invest the humblest, the most usual acts.

She wrote in her commonplace book this sentence:

"Love is a tune we whistle in the dark of our aloneness to keep up our courage."

In Winchie's fourth year, in the spring, Judge Benedict had an illness so severe that Courtney went to the farm, taking Winchie with her to stay until the crisis passed. It was nearly three weeks before decision for life was rendered and she could return home.

She had been gone during what ought to have been her busiest season. She rather expected to find the place in some confusion. Instead, so far advanced toward completion were her plans, and so thoroughly had she trained Jimmie and his son Bill and the house servants, everything was well under way. All her instructions, both those given before she left and those written to Jimmie from her father's—had been carried out exactly. They had worked as hard as if she had been there, had done it because they loved her—for only love can arouse and inspire the sluggish energies of those who serve. The lawns were trim and freshly green, the walks were covered with new tan-bark; and its red brown harmonized with the colors of lawn and trees as its odor harmonized with the odors from the grass and the foliage, from the brilliant flowers in great beds at either side of the house. All the windows were gay with boxes of blooming plants. Railings of verandas and balconies were draped with mats of budding creepers. The gardens—the beds in the lawns and along the verandas—the edges of walks and drives—the thickets and trellises—all were blossoming and odorous. Lovely contrasts of light and shade, delicious perfumes, birds flashing to and fro, singing in the trees and bushes—the Vaughan place illustrated what Pope meant when he called landscape gardening nature plus a soul. The soul that had given form to nature's color and perfume was Courtney's.

As the carriage drove down the deeply shaded main drive from highway to drive-front porch, she gazed round with a creator's pride and joy and love. She had two children—Winchie and this lovely place. All the servants gathered to welcome her—all except old Nanny, who had never forgiven and who resented the changes as sacrilege. They watched eagerly for signs of approval. Her expression, as she looked at what they had done, then at them, the unsteady voice in which she said "Beautiful—beautiful" went straight to their hearts. Within the house, everywhere open wide to June's enchantment, there was evidence of the same creative impulse—order without stiffness, art without any trace of art's labor.

Winchie would go straightway to look at his rabbits; she went upstairs alone to bathe and change after the dusty journey, telling Lizzie to bring him as soon as he had satisfied himself that his rabbits were all right. The door of the bedroom immediately across the hall from hers stood open, and with the thorough housekeeper's instinct she glanced in. It was the room Dick usually occupied. Instead of Dick's belongings she saw, spread about, toilet articles and clothing strange to her. She entered. On the bureau she instantly noted a pair of tasteful silver and ebony brushes; the monogram was "B.G." She opened a drawer; neckties, more attractive than any she had ever seen, filled two compartments to overflowing with their patterned silks and linens. In the third compartment several dozen line handkerchiefs; the monogram on them was again "B.G."

She opened the nearest closet. On forms hung perhaps a dozen coats; she recognized the cut and materials as foreign. Beneath was a long row of boots, shoes, pumps, slippers, all of the kind a woman of taste at once knows and appreciates. As she was closing the door there swung out from the hook high up a suit of beautiful striped linen pajamas monogramed in gray and faintly perfumed with lavendar. She went on into the adjoining front room—the room Dick had used as a study. Obviously, he no longer used it. The books of fiction and poetry—the big silver cigarette box—the gaudily trimmed silk dressing gown flung carelessly on a chair—none of these belonged to him or suggested his studious and rather Spartan temperament.

In the hall she saw Lizzie just come with Winchie. "Who's in these rooms?" asked she.

"Mr. Gallatin," replied Lizzie. "Mr. Vaughan put him in here and moved down to the suite at the Smoke House."

Lizzie's tone indicated that she was assuming Courtney knew all about Mr. Gallatin. That tone put her on guard. "When did he come?" asked she, feeling her way.

"Two weeks ago yesterday. He's very nice. He's as particular as you about his things, but it's a pleasure to look after them."

Had Richard forgotten to tell her he expected this Mr. Gallatin? Or had she, fallen long since into his absent-minded habit, failed to hear as he told her? Was it a chance visit from some college or scientific acquaintance? The character of the stranger's installation—the quantity of clothing—did not speak for a brief chance visit. The quality of the clothing, the taste, the care, the worldly interest and knowledge it suggested, were all against the idea of "B.G.'s" being a devotee of science. At least, if there were such scientists, this was the first she had known of it. After she had changed for the evening, and had given Winchie his supper and sent him to bed, she went into the stranger's quarters again. These personal belongings of his attracted her; they so clearly revealed taste and refinement, a refinement unusual in a man; they so strongly hinted a personality more in sympathy with her own passionate joy in life than with Richard's intellectual abstractions. In the early days of their married life Richard had been rather particular about himself; but he had got more and more indifferent, no longer shaved every day, was at times distinctly slovenly. "B.G. is a bachelor," thought she. "Married men—except those that are at heart bachelors—soon lose this sort of gloss." Usually she had not the faintest interest in anything concerning Richard. But this man interested her.

She was in the sitting room downstairs, playing and singing in an undertone when Richard came. "Hello," said he. And he kissed the cheek she turned to a reachable angle. His manner was as casual as hers. It was their habitual manner, and long had been. The difference between his habit and hers was that his yielded from time to time to the intermittent gusts of desire, while hers remained always tranquilly cool. "Your father's quite all right again?" was his careless first question.

"I hope so. I think so."

He was not merely looking at her now, he was seeing her. His eyes lighted up and into his voice came the wooing note. "Glad you've not dropped into my sloppy ways," said he. He was admiring her pale-green chiffon dress that left the slender column of her throat bare and her forearms, but almost concealed her shoulders. "Gallatin won't think we're altogether barbarians here. He dresses for supper. He's at it now."

His eyes showed that he was not thinking at all of Gallatin, but of her—thoughts which did not leave her entirely indifferent, but gave her an unwonted sense of vague distaste, after her long absence and complete freedom. As he moved toward her she said: "There's time for you to dress. And you need a shave badly. Is he from the East?"

"From Philadelphia by way of Pittsburg. He's been doing a little chemistry in his amateurish way in the mills there. I'd not have him about if I didn't need his money."

Dick was coming on toward her again. "The bell will ring in ten minutes," she reminded him. Perhaps through perverseness, the impulse to evade was a little stronger.

But he came, put his arms round her, kissed her again, this time with undivided attention. She lost the impulse to evade, submitted, smiled amicably, and, to extricate herself, rose. The lines of her dress brought out the perfection of her small, slim figure; its color harmonized with her deep-sea eyes and with the delicate bronze of her skin. "What a beauty you are!" he exclaimed. "No wonder I'm so proud of you."

Usually she was indifferent, without being conscious of it; this evening of her return from freedom to married life she felt her indifference. She said coldly, "If you're going to dress——"

"A shave'll be enough," protested Dick. "Your finery'll more than make up for my absence of it. Bachelors like Gallatin have to sleek themselves up. They've still got their brides to win."

"You'll be late."

"I want you to be extra civil to Gallatin. He's likely to get bored in this quiet place after a few months. He's rather gay, I imagine. At least he used to be. And I don't want him to pull out."

"After a few months," repeated Courtney, interested. "Why, how long is he to stay?"

"A year or so—perhaps longer."

"Here in the house!"

"I can't put him down at the laboratory, so near my secrets. I'm not going to let him in on everything. That's part of our bargain. We're partners, you understand."

"Here in the house!" exclaimed Courtney again. The very idea of an outsider as spectator at what was going on there made her acutely conscious of it, all in an instant.

"Oh, you'll like him—at least, you must for my sake. He doesn't amount to much, but he's agreeable—well mannered—good family—entertaining in a light way."

"There goes the bell."

Dick rushed away to shave. He had been gone but a few moments when Courtney was roused from her agitated reverie by the sense of some one in the room. Near the threshold stood the newcomer, who was to be a factor in her intimate life, a spectator of it, whether she willed or no, for "a year or so—perhaps longer." He was a blond young man, fair and smooth of skin, his hair almost golden. He certainly was not handsome; only his coloring and a pair of frank gray eyes saved him from downright homeliness. As their eyes met, his heavy, conventional face was suddenly transformed by as charming a smile as she had ever seen. He was of about the medium height, his figure neither powerful nor weak. He wore a dinner suit of dark gray, fashionably draped upon him, pumps, gray socks that matched his gray silk tie, a plaited French shirt, an unusually tall, perfectly fitting collar. If he had not been so well and so tastefully dressed, he would have attracted no attention anywhere—unless he had smiled. That smile meant a frank nature, a kind and generous heart—rarities to make their possessor distinguished in whatever company.

Courtney, with woman's swift grasp of surface details, noted all this and more while she was advancing with extended hand and saying, "Mr. Gallatin, is it not?"

He was obviously confused and embarrassed. Her natural, self-unconscious manner encouraged him candidly to explain. "I feel very shy," said he, speaking with a strong Eastern accent, "and very guilty. Shy because, before I came, I had somehow got the impression Vaughan was not married—and that we were to keep bachelor hall. I was astonished to find he had a wife." His eyes added without impertinence that he was amazed and dazzled now that he saw the wife. "I feel guilty," he went on, "because I seem to be thrusting myself in upon you. But Vaughan assured me I'd not be intruding."

"You needn't trouble yourself about that," said she. She liked his accent; it was pleasant as a novelty, and rather amusing. She liked his manners. They were of the best type of conventional manners, the type affected by fashionable people everywhere, the type that is excelled only by the kind of manners of which it is an artful and insincere imitation—the simple manners of those rare self-unconscious people who have the courage—or, rather, the lack of fear—to be natural and spontaneous. "We'll not wait for Richard," she said, as the supper bell rang. "He's got a great deal to do before he can come."

She had just finished the sentence when he entered, exactly as he was when he went out. "I forgot I'd taken all my razors down to the laboratory," he explained.

During supper he and Gallatin talked chemistry; that is, he talked and Gallatin listened—listened and ate. Courtney noted—with increased liking for him—that he had a vigorous appetite and that he liked the things they had to eat. But her thoughts soon wandered away to her gardening, to retouching her plans for bringing the grounds a little nearer her ideal than they had been the summer before. When the men lighted cigars, she went to the veranda to stroll up and down in the moonlight. She forgot everything unpleasant in the delight of being home again. As she looked about her, her heart was singing the nightingale's song. She was startled—and her heart's song was stopped—by the newcomer's voice. "Vaughan's gone to the library," said Gallatin. "Do you mind if I walk with you?"

She did mind very much indeed. She had somehow lost interest in him as soon as he ceased to be the mystery B.G. She liked him well enough, admired his manners, his really delicate tact in what must have been for him an extremely difficult position. But she had got the impression that Dick was right in estimating him as a "don't-amount-to-much." And just now he was distinctly a kill-joy. However, she acquiesced courteously, though with no unnecessary cordiality. She felt that now was the time to get him in the habit of respecting her privacy; she could establish a barrier now, where an attempt to establish it later on would offend him. At best, the barrier would be a poor enough makeshift; he would be bound to see, to make her feel uncomfortable about things she had been able to keep unconscious of or indifferent to. Still, she was far too generous to blame him.

"Do you have much spare time?" she asked, her manner more cordial than if she had not been wishing him out of the house.

"A great deal. Vaughan realizes I'm only an amateur."

"I'll take you over to the club and introduce you. You'll find some very agreeable people."

"Thank you. It has been rather dull these two weeks—especially of evenings."

"I don't see how you had the courage to come."

"I had to," said he, in the curt way in which a young man gives himself the pleasure of hinting a secret he cannot with good taste give himself the pleasure of telling.

She glanced across the lake at the twinkling lamps of the town. "The women over there will fill every minute you give them," said she. "You see, most of our men are busy all day and tired in the evening. You'll be a lion."

"That sounds attractive. I'm amazed at the West. I had no idea civilization was so advanced."

The implied condescension in this amused her. But she merely said: "Oh, I guess the same sort of people are much alike the world over."

The conversation languished through a to her tiresome discussion of differences of accent, dress, manners, and such trifles until he happened to say: "This place of yours here was a revelation to me. I've been talking to Vaughan about it—admiring it. He tells me his grandfather's responsible for it. He must have been an extraordinary man."

"He was," said Courtney, in a queer voice. She glanced out over her creation and the blood burned in her cheeks.

"He'd certainly be proud of the way you keep it up."

Her sense of humor had come to the rescue; besides, vanity was not a dominating emotion with her who had too much else to think about to have much time for thought of self. "I'm fond of gardening," was her placid noncommittal reply to his compliment.

"Yes, Vaughan's grandfather must have been a wonder," Gallatin went on reflectively. He had paused, was leaning on the rail, looking out over the lawns and gardens. "I don't mind confessing to you—if you'll not tell your husband—that I'm a chemist only by profession, with landscape gardening as my real passion."

Courtney glanced at him with interested eyes.

"I know a little something about it," he continued. "I learned long ago in a general way that a personality is always revealed in any work, and I at once looked for the personality in this place. That old man must have been an artist.... I can't reconcile these grounds with the portrait of him in the library."

Courtney was smiling to herself. A thrill of pride and pleasure was running through her. She began to like Basil Gallatin, to feel that he was by no means commonplace, but a man of breadth and artistic instinct, something at least of the man of the big world, not merely the man of the little world of well-cut manners and clothes.

"That portrait is of a stern, narrow man—strong but conventional," he went on, confirming her more sympathetic judgment of him. "This place—the house as well as the grounds—shows a very different individuality. It's feminine and sensuous and poetical. Yes, it's distinctly feminine—and delightfully disdainful of the conventional—of everything and anything 'cut and dried.' I don't mean the details— the things you're probably responsible for—and they're very charming. But I mean the whole conception—so free, so daring, and so lovely. Yet Vaughan tells me that the old gentleman made the plans himself and superintended their carrying out. It's very curious. Don't you think so?"

"I hadn't thought about it."

"You're not interested?"

"Why do you say so?"

"Your tone. I suppose a man is tedious when he gets on his hobby. I noticed you were bored when we were talking chemistry at supper."

"I wasn't bored. I simply wasn't listening."

"You don't like chemistry?"

"I did. But my enthusiasm cooled as I got interested in other things."

Again the conversation languished. She suspected that his opinion of her was rapidly declining. But some instinct withheld her from making any effort whatever to rehabilitate herself. Finally he said: "Well, I guess I've disturbed you long enough. I'll go to my room and read."

"I'm going up myself after I've had a little talk with Nanny about the house."

As soon as he disappeared, she dismissed him from mind with a few pleasant and friendly thoughts—"he may not have any great amount of brains or force, but he certainly has good taste. He will be a distinct addition." When she ascended to her sitting room, perhaps an hour later, she halted on the threshold, coloring with anger. Dick was seated at her center table reading a newspaper; Gallatin was inspecting the books in one of her cases. Dick saw her and said: "Come in. Don't mind us."

Courtney, struggling against her anger at this climax to the impudent intrusion upon her privacy, remained upon the threshold.

Dick's eyes had dropped to his paper. "Gallatin," he went on, "was complaining that the books in the library were too old and solemn. So I brought him here. I knew you'd laid in a stock of the frivolous kinds that grandfather wouldn't have tolerated. Finding what you want, old man?"

When Dick's speaking warned him that Courtney had come, Gallatin had startled guiltily and had hastily put away the book he was examining. But he didn't turn round until Richard directly addressed him. His face was red and his eyes were down. "I feel sleepy," said he awkwardly. "I'll look again some other time if Mrs. Vaughan will let me."

"Certainly," said Courtney, cold as a flower blooming in the heart of a block of ice.

The case into which Gallatin had been delving was filled with works on landscape gardening and interior decoration—modern works. As he almost stumbled from the room he cast a further glance round at the walls—walls covered with the original plans, sketches, and paintings Courtney had made for her revolution in house and grounds—very modern-looking drawings all, and unmistakably feminine. She knew that the newcomer had her secret—all of it—not merely the secret of her authorship, but also, through it, the secret of this loveless married life in which the husband had not the remotest idea who his wife was or what she had done. In passing her on his way out, Gallatin visibly shrank and grew as white as he had been red. She went to the window to compose herself, for her blood was boiling in the greatest rage of her life.

Richard went to close the door after Gallatin, then turned on her. "My dear," said he in his "grandfather" tone, which sometimes amused and sometimes angered her, "you are so cold by nature that you don't realize it, but you were almost insulting to Gallatin."

"I hope so!" cried she, facing him. "How dared you bring him in here without my permission? There are not many women who would have accepted quietly your bringing him to this house to live without a word to me. I wish you to understand you cannot thrust him upon my privacy. I don't allow anyone in this room without my consent. It must not occur again."

"Now—now—my dear," said Dick soothingly. "All that is very unreasonable. Of course, I have the right to do as I please in my own house, and you're too good and too sensible a wife to dispute it."

"I do dispute it!" she cried, her bosom heaving. "This room is—*me*!"

"What a tempest in a teapot! Child, what has made you take such a sudden dislike to him—and so violent? He isn't worth it—an amiable, well-meaning, commonplace chap. Really, you mustn't act this way. I've told you I need him, and you must be polite to him."

"The impertinent, prying——"

"I brought him here, Courtney," he interrupted, magisterially. "And I repeat, I had the right to do so."

Like most people of sweet and even temperament, she lost all control of herself in this unprecedented rage, where those in the habit of raging learn a sort of etiquette of bad temper. "You had not the right!" she declared, her eyes blazing into his. "And if you ever do such a thing again, I'll make it impossible for him to remain here. Do you understand?"

"I do not quarrel," said Richard with gentle superiority, "especially not with women—with my wife."

"And why not? You call it chivalry. I call it contempt. And I detest it. If you could appreciate how absurd you are, with your antiquated notions of superior and inferior sex, of rights and duties, and all such nonsense!"

Richard was in full armor of masculine patience against feminine folly. "You are beside yourself, my dear. I'll leave you until you are calm and courteous." And he added, as if he were meting out severe but just punishment, "I shall occupy the spare room."

Courtney gave a strange laugh. He turned away, went into her bedroom. Presently he reappeared exclaiming: "Why, where are my pajamas? I told Lizzie to put them in there."

Courtney's smile was of the same quality of strangeness as her laugh of the moment before. "They are in the spare room," said she. "I put them there before I came in here."

He looked puzzled, vaguely discomfited. "Oh—very well." He glanced inquiringly at her, decided against the trivial question he had been about to ask. "Good night." He was again puzzled when what he heard about the location of the pajamas was recalled and made vivid by the sight of them on the turned-down bed in the spare room. But for an instant only. He dismissed the trifle and went to bed and to sleep. Husbands do not bother their heads about the petty feminine eccentricities of wives. The mystery of these transposed pajamas was too petty to detain a masculine mind.

# Chapter 6

She did not go down to breakfast next morning until Richard and his guest would surely be gone. Her anger against the guest had evaporated because it was clearly unjust. Her anger against Richard was subsiding because it was clearly futile—and also because she hadn't it in her to foster harsh feeling. But there remained a dislike and dread of Gallatin because he had her secret. She could not think with composure of facing him, intolerably her partner in a secret she was ashamed of, was hiding from her husband, was trying to hide from herself. She would be unable to look at him, to remember his existence even, without at the same time having it thrust at her that her married life was a sham, a hypocrisy.

Half an hour before dinner Richard came to her in the big greenhouse she had built back of the library. As the day was warm, all its doors and sashes were open. Richard sent Jimmie's son Bill away and said with agitated abruptness: "Courtney, Gallatin seems determined to take rooms over at the hotel."

"I'm glad of that," replied she. "It's much better." She had not paused in her delicate task of extricating plants from their winter bed and arranging them in a basket for taking into the garden.

"But it's the first step toward going away. He'll never put up with the hotel's discomforts." Her indifference, her inattention made him impatient. "My dear, you don't understand. I need him. I've branched out on the strength of the capital he's supplying and has promised to supply. If he leaves, I'll be in a hole. We'll have to cut down in every direction, for I simply can't abandon my new plans."

"I don't like him," said Courtney. She had abruptly stopped work, was leaning against the frame facing him. "I want him out of the house."

Dick took the tone of gentle, forbearing remonstrance. "It's too late to change him to the Smoke House. He feels your dislike—is eager to get away. If there were any ground for dislike, I'd say nothing. As it is, I— I don't like to assert authority, but your frivolous whimsicality makes it necessary. I want you at once to convince him that you wish him to stay."

"But I don't." Her voice showed that those brief words were all she could trust to it.

"You do, since I wish it."

"Why should I consider what you wish? When have you considered what I wish?"

"When have I been inconsiderate of what was for your good?"

She was silent—silenced, he thought. His handsome face and his voice were gentle; but underneath there was sternness in both as he said: "You'll not oppose me in this. It'd be a very severe strain upon my love for you, if I found you so contemptuous of my interests. I'm sure you'll not risk that strain."

She saw into what an impossible position her anger had hurried her. Usually women, through playing upon the husband's passions and weaknesses generally, get enough control over him to be able to maintain—with only an occasional slight lapse—the pleasant fiction that they are of full human rank. They take care to avoid such crises as was this. Courtney, by long keeping away from the bars of her cage, had been lured into believing her pretense that they were not there. She now found herself bleeding and exhausted against them. "Very well," said she, after a moment's silence. It had taken her quick mind only a moment to see the alternatives—submission or a clash in which she could not but be defeated. "I'll try to get him to stay." Her voice was low and broken, but not from anger. Deeper than the sense of Richard's tyranny burned the humiliating sense of her servitude. In fact, her own plight so mortified her that she had no emotional capacity for raging against him as the author of it. She felt, as always in these sex conflicts, that the fault was not his, but fate's; he was simply playing his part as man, she her part as woman.

"That's a good girl," cried her approving husband, kissing her brow. It did not occur to him, the deep-down reason of sordidness that enabled him to compel; but she could think of nothing else. "Be sweet to him," Dick went on, in an amiable, petting tone. "And you may rest assured, dear, I'll get rid of him as soon as I can. I don't like intruders into our happiness any more than you do."

Her cheeks flushed, and she turned again to the frame, to resume her digging. Her whole body to her finger tips was in a tremor.

Through dinner she was silent and cold; Gallatin hardly lifted his gaze from his plate. Whenever Richard could catch her eye, he frowned and glanced significantly at Gallatin. But her eyes met his hints with a vacant look that made him twitch in his chair with nervousness and exasperation. As soon as Gallatin in politeness could, he excused himself and left the family of three alone.

Richard, unmindful of Winchie, burst out, "What's the meaning of this?

"You must let me humble myself in my own way," said Courtney coldly. "Come, Winchie." And the two went out on the lawn.

As Gallatin a few minutes later issued from the front door with Richard, she called: "Oh, Mr. Gallatin, I want to speak to you a moment."

He halted. The color flared into his face. Richard said, "I'll go on. You needn't hurry," and strode along the path into the eastern shrubbery. Gallatin hesitatingly crossed the grass. Winchie, who had on first sight taken an instinctive dislike to him, held a fold of Courtney's walking skirt and glowered like a small but very fierce storm.

"Go to the veranda, Winchie," said his mother.

The boy released his hold and reluctantly obeyed. Gallatin stood before her like a prisoner arraigned for sentence. "Richard tells me you're talking of moving to the hotel over in town," said she.

"Yes, I'm going to-morrow."

"Because you feel I want you out of the house?"

"I think a man in my position couldn't help being an intruder."

"I want you to stay."

His fair skin paled. "I thank you," said he, "but I must go."

"I want you to stay. I ask you to stay."

"That's very kind. I appreciate it. But I really must go."

"I did wish you to go. But now I sincerely wish you to stay."

Their eyes met. She was as pale as her bronze complexion permitted. She went on, her deep, clear voice steady, "If you go, you'll put me in a very painful position."

Gallatin looked at her, flushed, looked hastily away. In a voice of intense embarrassment he said: "I've another reason for wishing to go. It's even stronger than the knowledge that you're—very naturally—displeased at my being forced upon you."

"Oh," said Courtney, baffled. Then, "Please tell Richard what it is."

"I cannot." His gaze was on the ground now.

Somehow Courtney was liking him better. As he glanced up, her eyes met his. "Be frank with me," she urged winningly. "Is it because you dislike it here?"

"No." His gaze was wandering again. "No, indeed."

"I'm glad of that," said she. "Do you believe me when I say I wish you to stay?"

He lowered his eyes, remained silent.

"If I were free to choose, I would wish you to go," she went on, speaking with the utmost deliberation. "I am not free. So, I wish you to stay because it will be most unpleasant for me if you persist in going. I venture to ask you, if it is not too great a sacrifice, to stay on—at least, for the present. But if you still say you must go, I shall not misjudge."

"I'll stay," was his prompt response. "Gladly." And his tone and eyes were sincere.

"Thank you," said she simply.

He looked at her with an appeal that was very engaging. "I know you'll hate me for having created this situation."

"I thought I did a few minutes ago," replied she. "Now, I feel I don't. I feel I'd like to be friends with you—" Her small, sweet face lit up with a faint smile—"since we can't be enemies."

"You mean that?" he asked with an eagerness that sounded only the more eager for his effort to restrain it.

"Indeed, I do," replied she. "Will you help me with the gardening—when you have time?"

"There's nothing I'd like so well."

"Then—it's all settled?"

"Quite."

They smiled gravely; they shook hands; they laughed. "And a little while ago I was thinking I never could forgive you!" exclaimed she gayly. "Now I'm wondering what on earth there was to forgive." And she felt and looked very well acquainted with him. It was part of her upright-downright nature either to like thoroughly or to be so indifferent that she was little short of oblivious.

Before her generous friendliness the laughter died out of his face. "I'll try to be worthy of your friendship and your trust," said he gravely.

"That sounds mysterious—somehow."

"Does it? ... When may I help you?"

"Whenever you can get off. Soon?"

"To-morrow, I think."

"That's good."

"I'll join Vaughan." He hesitated, blushed. "He knows you were to ask me to stay?"

"Yes. But not how," was her calm answer.

"I understand." Their eyes met. He colored; but her expression, sweet and grave, did not change. As he went Winchie, seated morosely afar off on the veranda steps, scowled at his back.

That evening Richard said: "Well, I think he's going to stay. How did you manage it?"

"I've asked him to help me with the gardening. He's fond of it."

"A good idea," approved Richard. "I'll back you up."

She gazed silently out over the unruffled lake, so peaceful, so suggestive of peace unchanging, endless—the lazy, graceful sails—beyond, the town among its trees, lights coming out as the dusk gathered.

But their friendship, thus auspiciously begun, did not prosper. Gallatin almost pointedly avoided her. He helped her only when Richard, disturbed from time to time by his unrelaxed reserve, urged him to take a day or an afternoon off "and amuse yourself with the flowers, since you like that sort of thing." If it had not been that occasionally in talking or working at the gardening he seemed to forget his solemn and formal pose and showed unmistakable enthusiasm, she would have thought his profession of interest a pretense. She had a peculiar horror of gloom—doubtless born of the austerity of her bringing up. There was in her circumstances only too much to discourage her natural brightness, and she had within herself a struggle as incessant as that against weeds and destructive insects in her gardens. She had no desire to make this struggle harder; so she saw as little of him as she in courtesy could—the only course open to her, since she did not know him well enough to try to help him.

"What's the matter with Gallatin?" Richard asked her one day. "He says he likes it here and is going to stay, yet he acts as if he were revolving something different. He used to be full of fun and life. Now he's enough to give anyone the blues."

"He *is* rather heavy," admitted Courtney.

"I wonder if it's the booze," said Richard reflectively.

"The booze?"

"He always drank a lot more than was good for him. And there in Pittsburg he got to lapping it up like the get-rich-quick crowd he traveled in. That was why he wanted to come here—to break off and take a fresh start. I suppose he's gloomy because he's fighting his taste for rum."

"Probably," said Courtney.

Drink was a vice she could not comprehend—and we always are unsympathetic toward the vices we do not comprehend. She associated drinking and stupidity; the Wenona men who drank to excess were the dull ones, like Shirley Drummond. When Richard thus disclosed to her what Gallatin had meant by his mysterious hint as to his reason for coming to Wenona, she lost the interest in him started by his fine frank way of meeting her advances and his appreciation of her work. She recalled his other mysterious hint—about there being a hidden reason for his wishing to go. "No doubt," thought she, "he meant he's finding it hard to keep straight here, where it's so quiet. I wish now that he'd gone—though, when a man can give way to such a dull, dirty habit as drunkenness, he'd find excuse anywhere."

As the mail came in the middle of the morning and the middle of the afternoon, she saw it first. Thus, she noted that about once a week there was for him a foreign letter so heavy that it carried several stamps. These letters were from the same person, the same woman. And as the writing was large, rapid, and affectedly angular, she more than suspected that the woman was young. Somewhat tardily these facts, obvious though their leading was, wove together in her mind, incurious about other people's affairs; she knew that there was traveling abroad a young woman who taking the trouble to write their guest regularly and at great length. But when she happened to recall that he had a young married sister, she assumed the letters were from her.

One day he casually said that his sister had taken a house at Bar Harbor for the summer. The moment he said this, she for some unknown reason, or for no reason at all, jumped to the conclusion that his depressed state was due to the lady of the letters—to her being so far away—perhaps to some difficulty in their love—the objection of her parents to his drinking habit.

All was now clear to her. And thenceforth she looked at him with deep sympathy. He was not handsome; his mouth, for example, was so heavy that it flatly gave the lie to his idealist, poetic eyes. His nose was not good, was too small for a man's face. Somewhere there lurked a suggestion of weakness, and this was not lessened by his attention to dress—though she liked his clothes and his way of wearing them. He was far from her ideal of a man. But the longer one knew him, the better one thought of him, chiefly because the more confidence one had in his essential generosity and kindness. And she felt that he had capacity for tenderness of a very manly sort, and for appreciation of love and of all the beautiful things; just the kind of nature fate seemed to delight in making the sport of its maliciousness.

One night, in the pensive mood to which she sometimes yielded for an hour, she was at the piano softly playing; and singing that saddest of sad love's songs:

> "Alas for lovers! Pair by pair
> The wind has swept them all away—
> The young, the yare; the fresh, the fair—
> Where are the snows of yesterday?"

Through the window she saw him leaning against a pillar of the veranda. His profile was outlined clear against the luminous dusk. Its expression made her voice die altogether in a sob. She forgot her own sense of fleeting wasting youth, of supreme joy forever denied, of love never to be hers. This sorrow before her in those profiled features—they were strong features now—was no vague dream, but a living reality. She longed to go to him and try to console him; and at the same time, no matter how well she had known him, she could not have gone—for in that unsuspected strength of his there was the hopelessness that is beyond consolation. From that time he was the foremost figure in her thoughts; and her fancy put its own color into everything he said and did. If he had begun to drink she would have been only the more sympathetic; for, she could comprehend how unhappy love might drive its victim to any excess—were not her own longings, for three years now latent except for an occasional outburst, once more throbbing and aching day and night?

It was part of her routine to make a careful tour every day to see that everything was up to the mark. One day, in their guest's sitting room, she happened to see half fallen from the stationery rack a letter from his foreign correspondent. It was apparently unopened. The shock of this made her take a second look before she realized how she was intruding upon his sacred privacy. But she had seen; the letter was indeed unopened. And she knew that the last come of these letters had been at least three days in his possession.

Her heart ached for him; she felt she understood. His love affair had been going more and more badly—his increasing silence and sadness made that certain. And this letter must contain some news he dared not read—some words that meant the burial of his dead hope. She went downstairs with a heavy heart, and out into the sunshine—out to the rose garden in the western part of the grounds. She had been dreaming all along that this romance of which she was unsuspected, deeply moved spectator would surely "come out all right." Life did not always mock the story books. Love was not always sad, not always mere deceptive echo of one's own heart call—echo that flitted mockingly on as one pursued. No; this love that meant so much to him would prove real. Such had been her dream. Now— The flowers, their perfume, the gay birds, the sunbeams—all the sights and sounds she loved seemed tricks of a black enchanter. She remembered the day they buried her little brother. There had been just such radiant glory as this. She remembered the day she had seen that her own dream of love was dead. There had been just such sunshine and music and perfume. How could anyone with a human heart even for a moment laugh, jest? To be light was to make oneself party to this cruel levity of bird and flower and sunbeam. Laugh, when loved ones were dying somewhere—and the living were bending over dead faces with cracking hearts? Jest, when the winds of time and change were blowing love and lovers all away?

She caught her breath in a kind of terror when, on her return to the house, Lizzie told her that Mr. Gallatin had dashed in, had packed a bag, and had rushed off to

Chicago. "He has business there," Richard explained at dinner. "And I've asked him to buy some stuff for the laboratory." She was uneasy, at times unhappy, throughout the following week, as she thought of him trying to rid himself of his too heavy burden. Probably he was dissipating—she hoped he was, if it would give him relief. She began to debate whether she ought not to tell Richard what she had accidentally discovered, and suggest that he go to Chicago to help his friend, who might have fallen ill or worse. At dinner and at supper, even at breakfast, where she had seen him only occasionally, she positively missed Gallatin. Until he came, the time spent at table had been the stupidest part of each day—Richard and she in silence or abstraction, or exchanging disconnected commonplaces about the weather, the food, their friends. While Gallatin was far from lively, still he and she had talked— usually about gardening and plants, the difficulties and mysteries of inducing things to grow, the comparative merits of various species for flowering and for hardiness—not exciting conversation, but interesting, a relief to a monotony the dreariness of which she did not appreciate until he came—and went.

On the eighth day, as they were at supper, he appeared unexpectedly on the threshold. There was no forcing in the cordiality of her smile. At first glance, she suspected that he was in much better spirits. And this impression was soon confirmed. Certainly good news—the best—must have reached him in Chicago. Otherwise he could not sit there eating heartily, laughing, making amusing remarks, telling funny incidents of the trip. Courtney tried to continue to feel delighted that he had found surcease from sorrow. But her spirits went steadily down. She felt horribly alone. She had been company for him in his unhappiness—though he did not know it. Now, she quite unreasonably felt as if he had deserted her. She was ashamed of this, so ungenerous, so selfish, but she could not help it.

After supper Richard left them alone; they went out on the veranda—out where the full beauty of that place, now at summer's climax, could be seen in the soft sunset light. She stood watching a belated bird, a tall white sail—listening to the faint sounds of the town that came tinkling across the water. But she was thinking of the man beside her. "You've been enjoying yourself in Chicago," said she.

"No," was his unexpected answer. "I've been impatient to get back." He glanced round at trees and lawns, gardens and shrubbery, with delighted eyes. "I had to go away, to appreciate how well off I was." He went to the edge of the veranda to get a broader sweep. He seemed to be noting, reveling in, every detail. He drew a deep breath, returned to the big lounge chair, and lit a cigarette. "Yes," continued he. "Yes—I didn't dream it, or imagine it. It's all true. It's all here." Without looking at her: "And you happen to be wearing the same dress you had on the evening I came. Now, don't tell me you made it—as you've made those gardens and these rooms."

"I superintend," said Courtney, thinking him a pleasant and agreeable, if deplorably shallow person. "I'm not one of those dreadful original women who get up their own awful costumes, and think they're individual because they're different."

"If you lived in Paris, you'd set the styles," declared he. "And you're equally good at gardening and decorating houses."

"That's laid on with the trowel," laughed she. "But I like it." She returned to the subject that fitted her thoughts. "You're much livelier than when you went away; I'm sure you've had good news."

"No—nothing. I simply took myself in hand." He reflected in silence, then lifted his head and looked at her with a boyish simplicity and candor. "You see," he proceeded to explain, "I've had something on my mind ever since I came—that is, almost ever since—something that was my own affair entirely. And I let it prey on me—made myself a nuisance and a bore, I've no doubt."

There was a gleam of mischievous humor in her eyes as she nodded assent and said: "You were solemner than I thought a human being could be."

"Precisely. Well, that's over. As I said before, I didn't realize how well off I was, how much I had to be thankful for, as the pious people say. I do realize it. And I'm going to behave myself."

Courtney felt she ought to be scandalized by this vanishing of the last solemn tatters of the tragic romance she had woven about him; for it was clear as the lake that he had gotten over his bereavement in that one brief week, had gotten over it entirely. But somehow she was not scandalized; was, on the contrary, taking quite cheerfully this confirmation of his fickleness, of his incapacity for deep emotion. After all, wasn't that the best way to be? Wasn't he perhaps philosopher rather than shallow changeling? Wasn't he simply exemplifying the truth that fire burns out, that the dead are forgotten, that life leans always at the bow of the ship, never at the stern? She, eager to escape from her own shadows and thorns, slipped easily into his mood. "I should say you did have a lot to be thankful for!" answered she. "And you'll soon forget her." She colored at her slip. "I assume it was a love affair," she hastened to add. "We women always do."

"Yes, it was."

"You'll get over it."

"I do not wish to get over it." He was not smiling back at her. She felt his thoughts traveling over land and sea, into Europe, whence came those letters—there were two of them waiting on his desk upstairs. "I do not wish to get over it," he repeated. "I've learned—" His voice, full of earnest young seriousness, sounded as if he were thinking aloud rather than talking to her—"I've learned there's a love deeper than the love that demands—a love that appreciates where it dares not aspire—a love that asks nothing but just silently to love."

There was a long silence, broken by the snapping of the match, as he lit a cigarette. She startled, rose, and leaned against a pillar. With eyes half veiled by her long lashes she watched the gardens wane dreamily in the evening light. She inhaled the odors of rose, of lilac, of jasmine, of honeysuckle—perfumes so sweet that they were sad. How cruelly she had misjudged him! She felt a kind of reverence for him now, him with this nobility of soul so unconscious, so lofty. Here was a man worth a woman's while. "Why couldn't I have had such a love as he is giving?" she thought. "Oh, if she had learned what I've learned!"

"Come into the sitting room, Gallatin," called Richard from that direction.

Gallatin went, and for a few minutes Courtney heard, in intervals between her thoughts, snatches of the talk between the two men about the shopping Gallatin had done for the laboratory—talk about a new crusher, about a promising bomb calorimeter. After a while came in Vaughan's voice, "Courtney, what do you think of that?"

She stood in the window with an inquiring glance.

"I've been telling Gallatin you're going to introduce him round among the Wenona girls. And he says he has no use for women."

"I!" exclaimed Basil. "On the contrary, I think women—a woman—the most important element in a man's life."

Richard laughed. "Why, the man's in love!" cried he.

Courtney saw Gallatin wince as his wound was struck by this careless, jovial hand.

"Only a lover," proceeded Dick, "would exaggerate woman in that frenzied fashion. To live isn't to love. It's to do—to achieve."

"I don't agree with you," said Gallatin. "Love's the center—the mainspring—the purpose—the meaning."

"You ought to have been a woman."

"Why not?" retorted Gallatin. Courtney saw that Dick had irritated him. "In one respect I envy women. A woman *knows* whether or not a man loves her. A man can only hope and believe." And he glanced swiftly at her.

He looked confused, frightened, as her expression showed that she, the married woman, the lovelessly married woman, understood. She turned away abruptly, two bright red spots burning in her cheeks.

"Well," said the unobserving Richard to Gallatin, "I confess I don't grasp your meaning. But it doesn't matter. A good woman loves her husband, and he knows it. The rest's of no consequence. We must get him a wife, Courtney. He'd make an ideal husband, don't you think?"

"A good wife does not think," said Courtney.

Richard was amused. "But if she did?" he persisted.

"Then she'd probably think it fortunate for husbands that wives aren't independent."

Vaughan again looked puzzled. "That sounds as irrelevant as what Gallatin said a minute ago. Now will you tell us, what has it to do with what we were talking about?"

"I don't know," replied she. And she did not. She was astonished before this apparition of a thought she had not been conscious of having definitely in mind since that conversation with her mother long ago; and here it was popping up as if it were her constant companion. "It just came into my head," she went smilingly on. "You know we women are irresponsible, irrational beings, and so we don't think straight or talk connectedly."

She said good night, went up to her apartment. She was wishing now that Gallatin had not told her about this love of his for the woman across the seas. It had made her discontented—unhappy. It had compelled her to think what a patchwork of makeshifts her own life was. "Yet I ought to be contented. Haven't I Winchie? And I can't even complain of poor health or discomfort of any kind. I don't deserve my good fortune. Other women would envy me." No, they would not. She saw in remembered faces of women friends the same discontent she was hiding in her heart. A woman—a woman grown—craved more than material comfort could give, more than work or play, however interesting, more than motherhood could give—craved that grown-up, equal love without which life was like a wonderful watch with a broken mainspring. She thought of Basil Gallatin again. At least she was more fortunate than he. Suppose she, like him, loved and it were not returned. Then indeed would her heart ache.

When she saw him alone next day, she said shyly and with color high: "It seems to me you can't have told her—told her as you told me. Won't you go to her—not write, but go—and try again? Believe me, Mr. Gallatin, women appreciate love—at least, any woman who could inspire the love you give her. And if she knew, she'd love you—she couldn't help it."

She feared she had intruded. But when he at last spoke, his tone was not the tone of one who is offended. "Thank you, thank you," he stammered. "But— I assure you it's hopeless. She is not for me."

"Oh!" Courtney shrank. "She cares for some one else. I—I'm so sorry I spoke. I——".

"No—no," he said; "it was friendly. It was—like you."

This began their real friendship. And she needed friendship just then. What he had told her put her in a mood where all her occupations were in vain, and all the wisdom she had gathered from books and from thinking about things as they are, and all the patiently, slowly acquired stoicism of the matrimonial routine. Her heart was clamoring as it had not since those first months of her discovery that love was delusion and that she must learn to live without it. She wished Gallatin had not told her; she wished he had never come. And at the same time she felt that through the sadness he had brought there had come into her life a pleasure she would not wish to give up—the sympathy between him and her, based on their knowledge each of the other's secret. She felt very proud of his confidence, of his friendship. Also, there was the fascination that always issues from a great emotion, even though it be seen but in mimic on the stage. This great emotion of his was a vivid actuality. It made a smile upon his features heroism; it made a look of sadness tragedy.

He helped her in the gardens often now. Richard, making some secret experiments, did not want him at the laboratory. Sometimes he and she worked together at changing color schemes or improving mass effects or vistas. Again each worked alone, perhaps at some surprise for the other. It was after a morning of hard labor in opposite ends of the grounds that she said when they met at the house: "Richard's not coming up, so Nanny has to take him his dinner. And Lizzie's away and Mazie not well. I'll wait on you."

"Let's have a picnic," suggested he, "out under that big elm."

And with Winchie helping they carried everything to the rustic table and proceeded to have one of those happy-go-lucky meals that make the blue devils put their tails between their legs and fly away on their forks. Winchie, let eat what he pleased, forgot his dislike of Gallatin—at least so far that he only frowned occasionally as Gallatin and Courtney talked the most hopeless nonsense with the keenest pleasure. When Basil's face was animated it was never homely; when he smiled it was always handsome. For the first time since he came he lost all constraint, and the sparkle of girlhood came back to her. They stayed out there nearly three hours, and it seemed no time at all. Nanny, sour and scowling at the impropriety of such conduct in a married woman—one married into the ancient and rigid house of Vaughan—took away the dishes and linen. But the hint so plain in her dour looks went unnoted. It was a shower that broke up the party, sent them scurrying to the house, he carrying furious and protesting Winchie. She punished Winchie for his rudeness by sending him up to his bedroom to sit alone and think down his temper.

"You oughtn't to have done that," said Basil, when the boy, defiant even in obedience, disappeared.

"It's the only way to make him remember. And I can't whip him. I'm too selfish, even if I didn't know it was equally degrading to him."

"He can't help not liking me," persisted Basil. "We're not to blame for our likes and dislikes."

"No. But we are to blame for giving way to them." She was arranging freshly cut flowers in vases and jars in the sitting room.

"Yes, for giving way to them," said Basil thoughtfully, after a long time.

"To what?" asked Courtney, who had forgotten.

"Our feelings."

"Oh, I remember."

"You're right about that." Basil was speaking with an effort. "For example, if a man were to—to fall in love with a married woman, he'd be a—miserable cur if he told her. Those last few words came explosively.

"Gracious!" Courtney beamed mischievously at him from behind a gorgeous spread of half blown roses. "You are fierce! Well, that's settled. If he heard you, he'd never dare tell her."

She saw his face, and it flashed over her that it was a married woman he loved. Yes, of course! Why had she not guessed it at once! And he was saying these harsh things to make it impossible for himself to yield to the impulse. The smile left her eyes. He was at the window with his back to her. She looked tender sympathy. "Poor boy!" she thought. "And I saw to-day how happy he could be, and how happy he could make a woman.... Perhaps she does love him. What a sorrow that would be! And utterly hopeless!"

He turned abruptly. "Will you be my friend?"

She came straight up to him, put out her hand. "Indeed I will," she said.

He took her hand, pressed it. Then he drew back with his hands behind him. "You are a good woman," he said. "Good through and through. I want you to help me fight a battle I'm having just now. I thought I'd won it. I haven't. But I will!"

"I understand, I think. It is hard. But you are strong and honorable. You— The woman— She is already—" She paused, looked at him inquiringly.

"Yes—God help me!" he cried, turning away.

His cry could not have reached a more responsive heart. After a pause she said: "If she doesn't love you, it'd be useless to tell her."

"Worse! It would mean I was a cur."

"And if she does love you, it'd be wicked to tell her—to add to her unhappiness."

"If you were in my place— Suppose I could be with her—could go and live near her——"

"Oh, no; you oughtn't to do that! You ought to spare yourself and her that."

"But suppose," he urged eagerly, "suppose she didn't care for me—never would—and I could keep my secret——"

"But you couldn't! And she might grow to care."

He sat in a big chair by the window, stared moodily at the floor. "It seems to me I *can't* do that!" he said at last. "I don't love her as men usually love. She means infinitely more to me than that. And, loving her as I do, I'm in no danger of telling her. And it would make me almost happy so much of the time, and a better man— yes, a better man—to be near her. What you say I ought to do—it's like turning a man out into the desert without food or drink—to wander—on and on——"

"I know, I know," she interrupted, her small, sweet face all tenderness and distress. "Oh, I'm not competent to advise. You mustn't ask anyone. You must do what you think is right."

"Right!" he echoed forlornly.

She who had eaten of the husks that went by the name of right hadn't the heart to urge them on him. She returned to the table, to the arranging of the flowers. Without looking up he went on: "I haven't told you quite all. There's another thing. I—I'm engaged."

"Engaged!"

"Don't look at me that way. I can feel it, though I'm not seeing. You can't think less of me than I think of myself. But let me tell you. The girl's a distant cousin of mine. And her grandfather, who was crazy about families, left her a fortune on condition that she married me. He left an equal sum to me on condition that I marry her. But there's this difference: What he left her is all she'd have—every cent. I've got enough without his legacy to me."

"And you— Oh, it's dreadful, isn't it?"

"We're not in love—not in the least. But I've given her my promise, and she'd be penniless if I broke it. She's nineteen. We've got till she's twenty-one. She's abroad now."

"The letters I've seen in the mail—they're from her?"

"From her," replied he. "How can I marry when I love another woman?"

"I see," said Courtney. She was sitting now, her hands full of roses and listless in her lap. "Then you've no more right to love this woman than she has to love you.... Oh, I don't know what to say!"

"Don't think I'm trying to shift part of my burden to you. I'm not. But I felt if I could talk it out loud with some one who was sympathetic I'd see the way better. And I do." The expression of his eyes thrilled her; it was so manly, so honest, so resolved.

"What have you decided—if you don't mind telling me?"

"To go to Starky—-that's my cousin—her real name's Estelle, but she detests it—I'll go to her and we'll marry."

"No—no!" cried Courtney. "Whatever's right, that isn't. Oh, you don't know. She has a right to love. You're cheating her—cheating her!"

"But I can never give her that."

"You may——"

"Never!"

Courtney shook her head slowly, lifted the roses, buried her face in them, inhaled their perfume deeply. "Then—you mustn't marry her," she said.

"You don't know her. She cares for money—the things money buys—more than for anything else in the world. It's the way we bring 'em up in the East."

"Believe me," cried Courtney, solemn in her earnestness, "that's not true. There isn't any woman anywhere who doesn't put love first. Go to your cousin—yes. But go and try to love her."

His eyes suddenly blazed upon her. "Love her after—" he began impetuously. He reddened, his head sank. "After the woman I—" He muttered confusedly, "I can't talk about it," and hastily left the room by the door-window nearest him.

She sighed sympathetically, rose, moved slowly toward the vase she had only half finished. Midway she halted. That look of his had just penetrated to her. "Oh!" she gasped. And she wheeled round and stared with blanching cheeks, as if he were still standing there before her with his secret betrayed in his eyes. "Oh!" she repeated under her breath. How her mistaken romancings about his sadness had misled her woman's instinct! For now, like steel filings round a magnet, a swarm of happenings since he came ranged round that telltale look of his—where they belonged.

# Chapter 7

Basil was last in to supper, came with his nervousness plain in his features. His uneasy glance at her met a smile of ingenuous friendliness that could not but reassure. Richard was there, absent-minded as usual, and unconscious of them both. They were unconscious of him also, Basil no less so than she, for he had long since acquired the habit of the household. No one spoke until Richard, having finished, lighted a cigarette and fell to explaining to Basil an experiment he had made that day. He was full of it, illustrated his points with diagrams drawn on the yellow pad which was never far from his hand. Courtney, relieved of the necessity of trying to look natural before Basil, was able to turn her thoughts again to the subject that had been occupying her steadily from the moment she discovered his secret.

If Gallatin could have seen into her mind, he would have been as nearly scandalized as it is possible for an infatuated, unsatisfied lover to be. For even where a man feels he himself has the right to revolt against exasperating musts and must nots of conventional morality, he is unusual indeed if he honestly approves any such revolt, however timid, in a woman. Man is the author and guardian of that morality; in the division of labor he has imposed upon woman the duty of being its exemplar. Thus, though human, she must pretend not to be; she must stifle if possible, conceal at any cost, her human fondness for the free and the frank. For Courtney there was double attraction in this love of Basil's—because it was love for her and because she was lonely—how lonely she had never realised until now. There is the loneliness of physical solitude, the loneliness for company—and a great unhappiness it is, especially to those who approach the lower animals in lack of resources within themselves. Courtney had never suffered from this; she had never cared for "just people." Then there is the loneliness of soul solitude, the loneliness for comradeship—and who suffers from this suffers torment. It may lull, but it will surely rage again, and it will never cease until it is satisfied or the heart itself ceases to beat. This was the loneliness of Courtney Vaughan. "If he," thought she, "were bad, and I, too—no, perhaps not exactly bad, but—well, different— less—less conscientious—how happy we might be! That is, of course, if I cared for him—or could make myself believe I did—which is impossible." She lingered over this impossible supposition as over a sweet, fantastic dream. She dropped it and turned away, only to return to it. And thinking of it filled her with the same tender sadness she got from love stories and love songs. "I would not if I could, I could not if I would, but—" Love! Into the silence of that void in her life had come a sound. It was the right word, but not the right voice. Still, there was joy in the right word. And she would not have been human had she bent other than kindly eyes and kindly thoughts upon the man who pronounced that word of words. Long since—from her first notion that he was hiding a romantic secret—his real self had begun to receive from her imagination the transfiguring veil of illusion. The discovery that she herself was the secret certainly did not make the veil thinner. A strong imagination flings out this beautiful, trouble-making drapery always; not quite so eagerly if there has been sad warning experience, but none the less inevitably. It would be many a day, if ever, before Courtney could again see Basil Gallatin as he was in reality.

As she sat there, silent, all but oblivious of her immediate surroundings, she was awakened by hearing him say, in reply to something from Richard: "But I'm afraid I'll have to—to change my plans—and—go away." It was said hesitatingly, with much effort.

"Go away!" cried Richard. Courtney could not have spoken.

"I'm afraid so."

"Not for good?"

"Probably—in fact, almost certainly."

"Why, man, you can't do that!" protested Dick. "You can't leave me in the lurch."

"Oh, I want to keep my interest. It's simply that I can't stay on, myself."

"But I need you now as much as I need the capital. Why, it'd upset everything for a year—perhaps longer. I couldn't easily find a competent man I could trust."

Basil repeated in a final, dogged way, "It's impossible for me to stay."

"Is there anything unsatisfactory in——"

"No—no indeed. My own affairs entirely, I assure you."

As he had finished supper, Vaughan took him out on the veranda, where Courtney heard them—or, rather, heard Dick—arguing and protesting. Presently she drifted into the sitting room, sat at the piano, let her fingers wander soundlessly over the keys. What should she do? What was best for him—for her—"and there's Richard, too, who needs him." Why should he go? How would it help matters? True, she had declared that to be the right course; but then she was merely theorizing, merely talking the conventional thing. This was no theory, but actuality, calling for good common sense. It was not the first time she had found the facts of life making mockery of the most convincing theories about it. Presently she felt that Basil was in the window farthest from her, was watching her—probably with the same loving, despairing expression she had often seen without a suspicion that it was for her.

"Where's Richard?" inquired she, not looking in his direction.

"In the library."

"You've upset him dreadfully."

"I'm sorry. But things will soon adjust themselves." He advanced a step, was visible now in the half darkness, looked pallidly handsome in his becoming dinner suit. "A few weeks at most," he went on, somewhat huskily, "and I'll be the vaguest sort of a memory here."

She was glad her back was toward him and that the twilight had darkened into dusk. Of course, he did not really love her. It was simply another case of a man's being isolated with a woman and his head getting full of sentimental fancies. Still—While his love was not real, and therefore its pain largely imaginary, the pain no doubt seemed real, and the love, too. So she was sad for him—very sad. As soon as she felt sure of her voice, she said: "Won't you please light the big lamp for me? I wore a négligée this evening because I wanted to sew. I'm making a suit for Winchie—like one I saw in a French magazine."

He lit the lamp beside the table where she worked in the evenings when she did not go to her own room. "Anything else?" he asked.

"Only sit and talk to me."

"I couldn't talk this evening."

"Then sit and smoke."

She began her work, he smoking in the deep shadow near the window. She could hardly see him; he could see every wave and ripple in her lovely hair, every shift of the sweeping dark lashes, every change in that sweet, small face, in the wide wistful mouth. Even better than playing on the piano, sewing brings out the charm of delicate, skillful fingers. She did not need to look at him to feel his gaze, its longing, its hopelessness. And never before had she thought of him in such a partial, personal way—the way a woman must feel toward the man she knows loves her, even though she only likes him.

She had made up her mind what to do, how to deal practically with this situation. But she had to struggle with her timidity before she could set about the audacious experiment she had planned and resolved. She had long had the frankness of thought that is inseparable from intelligence. The courage to speak her thoughts was as yet in the bud. "Do you mind my speaking again of what you were saying this afternoon?" said she as she sewed industriously.

"No," said he.

"I've been thinking about it. At first I was startled—very much startled. But I soon began to look at it sensibly. I want you to stay. Richard wants you to stay. There's no reason why you shouldn't stay and conquer your delusion."

"It's no delusion."

"Real love is always mutual. So yours must be delusion." She was pointing a thread for the eye of the needle. "You've led a very—very man sort of life, haven't you?"

He shifted uncomfortably, then confessed: "You know the standards for men are different from those for women."

She smiled, threaded the needle. "Yes, I know. I don't understand, but I know. You needn't explain. I don't want to understand. It doesn't interest me. As I was about to say—" Her courage failed her, and she sewed a while in silence. At last she dared. It was with no sign of inward disturbance, but the contrary, that she went on: "You've been shut in here too long. Go to your old haunts for a few days. You'll come back cured."

She had practiced saying it, this advice which she believed wise and necessary in the circumstances. She said it in calm, matter-of-fact fashion; and it was the less difficult for her to do so because, in thought at least, she had long since emancipated herself from what she regarded as the hypocrisies of modesty, and had taught herself to look at all things rationally and humanly. She knew her frankness would not please him; so she was not surprised when after a pause he said roughly, "I don't like to hear you say that sort of thing."

She laughed pleasantly, put quite at ease by his impertinence. "And I don't in the least care whether you approve of me or not. You men seem to think you've got a sort of general roving commission to superintend the propriety of women."

"I beg your pardon."

"Certainly. Give me that pair of scissors—on the stand in the corner."

He rose, issued from the deep shadow. She could now see into what confusion her words had thrown him. The hand that held out the scissors was trembling. He moved to go upon the veranda. "Please," said she. "I'm not nearly done. Won't you sit down?"

He seated himself.

"You see," she went on lightly, busy with her hem again, "I know your awful secret."

"You've no right to laugh at me," muttered he.

"I'm not laughing at you.... I'm only looking at it in a friendly, practical way.... I want to help you.... Why are you going away?"

She sewed on, feeling his emotion gather behind his self-control. The stillness was unbroken. A light breeze, cool and scented, came fluttering in at the open windows to play with the soft brilliant hair that grew so beautifully round her temples. In a low voice, so low that she scarcely heard, his answer at last came: "Because I love you. I love you and I am not a cur."

Her needle missed its way into the cloth, pierced her finger. She put the wounded finger in her mouth. When she looked toward him she was smiling. "Still you've not answered my question. Because you think you care for me—that's no reason why you should go.'

"I can't control myself. I—" He made a gesture of helplessness. "I can't think of you as—as married. You seem like a girl to me—free. I keep forgetting."

"It doesn't seem to occur to you that I might be trusted to remember."

"I know," said he humbly.

She held the garment at arms' length, eyeing the hem critically. "No, you don't. You're like all the men. You fancy weak woman can always be overborne by man, big and strong and superior."

"You wrong me."

"Why else should you talk of going away?"

"Because it's torment to me to be near you—to———"

She stopped sewing, looked at him with anger in her deep green eyes. "Then your feeling is just what I thought."

"It is not! It is love!"

Again she sewed a long time in silence. It was very calm there, in that quiet room with its flowers and tasteful, gracefully arranged furniture, and the single lamp like a jewel shedding all its radiances upon her small industrious figure. "Then tell me," she said in her sweet, gentle way, without looking up or pausing, "what do you want that you cannot have? You can see me as much as you like. You can talk as freely as you like. You can count on sympathy, on friendship. And, if you want to, you can keep right on loving me in that exalted way you profess. Nobody's going to hinder you."

She sewed on in silence, he motionless watching her, perplexity in his honest, rather boyish face. After a while her voice broke the silence. "Love!" She laughed with raillery that did not sting. "My dear friend, don't you see I was right? Go away for a few days and——"

"For God's sake, don't suggest that again."

"Then don't say it's love that makes you want to leave and upset everything." She put the needles, thread, and thimble into her workbox, rolled up the little suit, rose. "It's always the same story," she said, sad rather than bitter. "A woman means only one thing to a man. Yes, I think you had best go."

"You're too severe," he cried. "It's true there's such a thing as passion without love. And I'll admit that I, like all men have felt it often—have lied to myself as well as to the woman—and have called it love. But it's also true there's no love without some passion—at least, *you* couldn't hope to inspire it. And though in your innocence you may think so, you'd not want to have less than all love has to give—if you loved."

Her eyes, large and softly brilliant, were burning into the darkness beyond the open window. "I'm not innocent," she said. "And I try not to be a hypocrite. If I loved, I'd want all."

There was a long silence, she at the window gazing out into the gathering night. Then he said: "You were right. It was not love that made me feel like flight. I can conquer that feeling. Will you let me stay?"

She turned slowly. In the look she fixed on him there was doubt, hesitation. "You've made me a little uneasy—a little afraid."

In his eagerness he sprang up. "Don't!" he cried. "Don't send me away. I'll never speak of love again. You've taught me my lesson."

"I do want you to stay," said she. "It'd seem very lonely here with you gone. For I've come to depend on you as a friend. It hurts to find you seeking your own selfish pleasure under the pretense of a feeling for me."

He winced—not because he felt scandalized by her candor, but because he felt convicted by it. "How well you understand men!" he exclaimed. "Better than they understand themselves."

"In that one way I do," was her reply, an arresting hardness in the deep voice that was usually altogether sweet. These last few days she was understanding a great many things about the relations of men and women—or, perhaps, was letting herself realize that she understood them.

He lowered his eyes, that he might not read her thoughts, that she might not read the same thoughts in his own mind. "You often make me think of the lake out there," said he. "There's the surface one sees at a glance. Then there's a little distance below the surface, that one sees when he looks intently straight down. And then there's fathoms on fathoms where all sorts of strange things—strange thoughts and feelings—lie hid. Sometimes—for an instant—one of them shows or almost shows at the surface."

"When one lives alone a great deal, one gets the habit of living within oneself—don't you think?"

"I suppose that's it—partly. A brook couldn't hide very much—and most people are like brooks or ponds. The ones that seem to have depth seem so simply because the water's muddy."

She looked admiringly at him; and her admiration of his originality and insight did not lessen when he added, "At least, so a friend of mine used to say." He returned to *the* subject. "Then—I may stay?"

Her face brightened. In her eyes as they looked at a smile slowly dawned. Quickly all her features were responding, especially that wide, expressive fascinating mouth. "I hope you will. But—no more dreariness!"

"I hate gloom as much as you do." He glanced round the room—at the harmonies of woodwork and walls and furnishing, with here and there bright flowers always in the restraint of those of gentle hue. "As much as you do," repeated he. "And that's saying a great deal. How *do* you manage it!—house and garden, always gay yet never gaudy—and such variety! Is there no end to your variety?"

"Oh, one's a new person every day, isn't one?—and different."

"*You* certainly are. But no one else I ever saw." He colored furiously at his finding himself, without intending it, upon the forbidden ground. She had turned away, and was leaving the room—the safest course, since it enabled her to hide her pleasure in the compliment that peculiarly appealed to her, and also seemed to give him a sufficient yet not harsh rebuke.

Her aversion to restraint was perhaps stronger than is the average woman's—certainly had more courage. She had been too thoroughly trained in the conventionalities not to have the familiar timidity as to action, so strong in all conventionally bred people, so dominant over women. But the "unhand-me" spirit of her time was finding outlet in thought and feeling. Reflecting much in her aloneness, she had reached many audacious conclusions about life and the true meaning of its comedy drama—that meaning so different from what we pretend, from what usually passes as truth in history, philosophy, and literature, based as they are upon man's cheap hankering for idealistic strut. The audacities of thought that occasionally showed at her surface in speech or commentary of smiling eyes and lips were conventional in comparison with whole schools of deep-swimming ideas and fancies that kept hours of aloneness from being hours of loneliness. Physically, her passion for freedom showed itself in her dislike of tight or stuffy garments. She could pass her hand round her waist inside her closest-fitting corset. Her liking for few clothes and for as little yoke and sleeves as custom allowed came not from the thought for the other sex that often explains this taste, but from aversion to restraint.

As usual, the first thing she did that night, when she was alone in her rooms, was to rid herself of all her clothing and put on the thinnest of thin white nightgowns, almost sleeveless, and cut out at the neck. She thrust her feet into bedroom slippers, braided her long hair with its strands of red almost brown, with its strands of brown almost gold. She turned out the light, threw open all the long shutters screening her windows, to let her bedroom fill with warm, perfumed freshness from lake and gardens. She stepped out on the balcony to take the breathing exercises that kept her body straight, her chest high, her bosom firm as a girl's, and her form slim and supple. The fireflies were floating and darting in the creepers and the near-hanging boughs. The slight agitations of the air stole among the folds of her gown and over her neck and arms like charmed fingers. There was no moon; but she did not miss it in the dim splendor of the thronging stars.

"Aren't you about ready to come in?"

She startled, suppressed a scream. She turned. Richard was standing in the window. Her blood which had rushed to her heart surged out again and into her brain in an angry wave. She hated to be taken by surprise. It was on the tip of her tongue to cry furiously, "I detest being spied upon." But she had resolved soon after Winchie was born never to speak angrily to him, never to let him hear her speak angrily. The habit restrained her now, as it had scores of times. Instead, she said: "Why, how did you get in? I'm sure I locked my door."

"So you did," replied Dick in the cheerful unconscious way that so irritated her in certain moods. Not always could she bear with composure his masculine assumption that whatever pleased him must delight his wife. "So you did," said he. "And it's still locked. But there was the window from the front balcony into your sitting room—and the door from your sitting room to this room. You see, I was determined to find you."

His tone of laughing tenderness helped her half to guess, half to make out his expression. Usually she accepted without a protesting thought the whole of the routine of married life. But to-night she grew hot with a burning blush of imperiled modesty as he advanced toward her. "Don't," she said; "I'm doing my exercises."

"No—you were dreaming. Of what?" Then, without waiting for an answer about a matter of so little importance, "Gallatin tells me he has decided to stay on—if he can arrange it—and he seems to think he can. So I'm feeling fine. You don't know what a jolt he gave me at supper. Did you talk with him about it?"

"Yes."

"Urged him to stay?"

"I tried to show him he ought to stay."

"Ever so much obliged."

She stopped in her exercises to say quickly: "Oh, I didn't do it for you. I did it for myself."

"Why, you dislike him."

"He's some one to talk with—some one that listens and answers. And—I don't dislike him."

Richard laughed. "That's right. Try to make the best of it. Well, if you're not coming in——"

"Not for an hour or longer."

"Then—good night. I must be up early. I think I'll sleep down at the Smoke House. I'm so glad about Gallatin—just as much obliged as if you'd done it for me. And I believe you did." He put his arms round her to kiss her good night. As soon as his lips touched her cheek she drew away, disengaged herself. "What's the matter, Courtney?" She had long since learned that for all his absent-mindedness and ignoring of things that didn't directly interest him, he became as sensitive—and as accurate—as photographic plate to light, the instant his attention happened to be caught. "What's the matter? Why do you draw away?"

"I don't know," replied she—truthfully, yet with a sense of being untruthful. "I seem not to like to be touched to-night."

"I don't remember you being that way before."

She went on with her exercises; he yawned and departed.

# Chapter 8

The morning after Courtney and Basil came to this clear and promising understanding, she got down to the seven-o'clock breakfast perhaps ten minutes late. She expected to find the two men and Winchie there, and was thinking of asking Gallatin to go to town with her and Winchie. When she entered the dining room, there was the table in its usual morning place, in the wide-flung door windows to the cast, and at it sat Winchie only, sunbeams sifting through the trellised morning glories to dance upon his shock of tawny hair.

"Where are the others?" she asked.

Winchie, forgetful of his teaching, had his mouth full, far too full for immediate speech—unless he gulped it empty, and that would have been breaking another rule. So Lizzie, who was just entering from the kitchen hall, answered: "Mr. Richard telephoned up at half past six, and made me wake Mr. Gallatin. They had breakfast down at the Smoke House long ago."

Winchie had climbed from his high chair and had come round to kiss his mother good morning. He was dressed for the trip to town—all white except dark blue edging round his wide collar, and a dark blue belt. His features suggested his father's and his mother's, yet were those of neither. That morning their usual suggestions of will and character were lost in a general expression of sweet good humor. He looked a sturdy bronzed cherub. After searching his mother's face with those inquiring, seeing eyes of his, he said: "Mamma's happy this morning," and resumed breakfast.

"Indeed she is!" exclaimed Courtney.

She drew the bowl of yellow daisies and pink-white mountain holly from the center of the table, and fell to rearranging them. Each blossom seemed to glide into just its right position, as if there were magic in her fingers. She could not remember when she had felt quite so content and hopeful. And her spirits rose as the day advanced. On the way to town she stopped at the Vaughan farm across the highroad to inquire into a slight falling off in quality of butter and milk. She had never seen the farm so fascinating. The very dock weed and dog fennel carpeting the barnyard had an air and a charm. And the road to town, as she and Winchie sped along in the runabout—what a shady lane through Paradise it was! In town everyone seemed so agreeable, so glad to see her. After lunch with Sarah Carpenter, she shopped, made several calls. They did not start home until late, and supper was on the table when they arrived. At the table—always in the middle of the room for the evening meal, and formally set—at the table was Richard, alone, eating and figuring on his everlasting yellow pad.

"Hello!" said he, with barely a glance away from his pencil point. "Glad to have company."

"Where's Mr. Gallatin?" asked Winchie.

"Gone," was Dick's curt answer in the tone of an interrupted man. "I sent him away."

Courtney, crossing the room, halted. A moment of horrible silence. "Gone!" she echoed hoarsely, her eyes wide, as if a monster had suddenly appeared open-jawed in her very face. "You—sent—him away!"

Vaughan, without looking up, said: "What did you say?"

With her hand on her heart, "I thought I understood you to say Mr. Gallatin had gone."

"So he has. For a few days."

"Oh!" Courtney drew a vast breath of relief. She felt a tugging at her skirt, glanced down. It was Winchie, looking up at her with an expression of terror; and she knew she must have revealed herself in her face. Her pale cheeks flooded with color. She sank into her chair opposite her husband. She could lie to herself, cheat herself, no longer. "How much Basil means to me!" she muttered. Then, in terror, she glanced round, for she felt as if she had shouted it. But Vaughan was at his unending calculations. Only Winchie saw. *Only* Winchie! There was a look in his great gray-green eyes, a look of the accusing angel, that made her hang her head while the dark red burned upon her whole body.

"He'll be back Thursday or Friday," continued Vaughan, tossing the pad into the window seat, a dozen feet away.

"You sent him on business?" inquired she, to make conversation.

"He wanted to go to Pittsburg, so he told me. I guess it's some girl. I suspect our 'dressy' friend of being a ladies' man. He takes too much trouble about his clothes—and silk underclothes! Anyhow, I let him go."

She sat there, the food untouched, her blood pounding at her temples, at her finger ends. For she was remembering her advice to Basil when she was trying both to persuade him to stay and to deceive herself as to why she intensely wished him to stay. And now, on her advice—on the advice of the woman who loved him—he was journeying—even as she sat quietly there at supper in respectable calm—he was journeying to his "old haunts"—to some woman—he who belonged to her! Such a wild tempest raged in her that she wondered how she could sit motionless, why she was not walking the floor and crying out. With another woman! Oh, the vileness of men! "And I was beginning to care for him!" she said to herself. "He's like the rest—worse than most. How many men are there who'd dare talk of love to a woman like me, and then go jauntily away to a low woman?"

She went upstairs immediately after supper, shut herself in. She moved calmly about; she took her exercises; she read for several hours before turning out her light. But beneath a surface that could have been no more tranquil had she been observed and on guard, chaos reigned. One tempest succeeded another—anger against Basil, against herself—disgust, scorn, jealousy—and, before she slept, she had seen that in reality all these moods were jealousy under different forms. The following morning, when the coast was clear, she slipped into his room, knelt by his untouched bed, cried upon its pillow. This humility soon wept itself out, however; she flung herself into her work. "Nonsense! I don't care for him. It's simply pique and outraged friendship. How coarse men are!"

"What's the matter, mamma?" said Winchie, who was following her about the garden, looking after insects and dead leaves. Than his there never was a keener eye for signs of the red spider.

"Why, dear?"

"You treat the flowers as if you wanted to hurt them."

"Your mamma is in a very naughty humor this morning."

"And you were so happy yesterday. Is it because Mr. Gallatin's gone away?"

Courtney, flushing deeply, looked hastily round. "Sh! You mustn't say those things!"

"Why not?"

Already she was teaching the boy to conceal! "I didn't mean that, Winchie," said she. "You are to say whatever you please—as always."

"I don't want you to like Mr. Gallatin. *I* don't like him."

"Why not?"

"Because he likes you."

"You wouldn't want anybody not to like your mamma, would you?"

"No." A long silence. Then: "But he looks at you exactly like papa does when he's really seeing you."

Courtney's skin burned. The same story—always the same! "Well—dear—I'll not like him."

"I hope he won't come back."

The suggestion set her heart to aching with loneliness. "I have no shame and no pride," she said to herself. "What a contemptible creature a woman is!" But these sneers availed her nothing. As she sat at table—dinner and supper—his vacant place gave her a sense of bereavement not unlike death itself.

Another night of wakefulness and of the subtle and varied torments known only to those blessed and cursed with vivid imagination. What if he should not come back! That was the final and crudest twist of the rack. Next day, it was all day long as if the silence and darkness of the night were still suffocating her. The house, the grounds seemed a desolation of despair. What if he should not come back! A drizzling rain fell, and she sat miserably by the window, unable to sew, unable to read. And at the first sound from the piano—the melancholy notes her fingers instinctively struck—she sprang away as if a hateful ghost had breathed on her. It was only Wednesday; he would not be home until the next day—probably not until Friday—perhaps not then.

She put fresh flowers in vases in all the rooms every day. That day she filled the vases in his sitting room with the best. And she lingered among his belongings, that promised his return. In the drawers, his fine tasteful shirts and ties; in the closets, those attractive suits, silk lined, agreeable to the touch, varied and always tasteful in pattern. She went back to his books—to the poetry, of which he was particularly fond. The volumes fell open naturally at poems that glorified the lofty, the spiritual side of love. Then, like a scorpion, scuttled across the page of Browning's "Last

Ride" what Winchie had said—"He looks at you like papa does." She shuddered, was all dread and foreboding again. Was there no such thing in man as love for woman, but only its coarse and lying counterfeit?

She heard an outside door open noisily. She darted along the hall and down to the angle of the stairway, to the landing from which the drive-front entrance could be seen. She leaned over the balustrade, looked. She drew back, stopping the glad cry that rose to her lips; for it was Basil. With features composed she leaned forward again. His soft hat and his rain coat were dripping; evidently, in his eagerness to arrive, he had crossed the lake in an open boat, instead of coming round by the road in a closed carriage. He was gazing toward the sitting-room door with an expression that thrilled her—and at the same time gave her the courage to treat him as her self-respect and her ideas of decency in a man dictated.

"Back already?" said she in a pleasant, indifferent tone.

He turned, looked up at her, his face alight. "How are you?" he cried. "It seems an age."

"We didn't expect you for several days yet," she went on, descending. When she reached the hall, he was waiting with extended hand. "It *is* good to be here again!" said he. "It was worth going, for the pleasure of getting back."

She shook hands, smiled friendlily, continued on her way to the sitting room. He hesitated, an uneasy look in his eyes that did not escape her. He put his hat and coat on the rack, followed her. "I *am* glad to be back!" said he.

She laughed, friendlily enough, but her baffling manner only increased his uneasiness. "We're glad to have you," was her polite reply. "If you want to go to your room before supper, you'd better hurry."

"I've been doing a great deal of thinking while I was away."

"Really? That's good."

"I see you've changed your mind—as I felt you would, when I thought it over. Your first impulse was to be lenient. But when you fully realized what a dishonorable thing it was for me to do—to——"

"Don't you think you'd better go up before supper?"

"Not till I've said one thing," replied he doggedly.

"Well?"

"I want you to know that you can trust me never to repeat my offense. I'd go to Vaughan and tell him and apologize——"

"And, pray, what has Richard to do with it?" inquired she coldly.

"I understand," he hastened to protest. "I'm not going to speak of it to him. It might put unjust suspicion of you in his head——"

There she laughed outright at him. "You are making yourself perfectly absurd," she said, and turned away to go into the dining room.

When he came down, the others were at table. Dick, figuring on his yellow pad, glanced up, rose, greeted him with unprecedented cordiality. "Why, when did you blow in?" he exclaimed.

"A few minutes ago." Gallatin glanced at Courtney. The quiet mockery of her absent gaze made him red and awkward. "I—I—got through—so—I—came," he explained with stammering lameness.

"Naturally," said Dick. He had taken up his pencil. "Make yourself at home."

Gallatin's glance fell on Winchie frowning at him. "Howdy, Winchie?" said he.

The boy made a curt bow, resumed his supper. He was permitted—or, rather, under Courtney's system of training him to think and act for himself, he permitted himself to eat only certain simple things, and very little of them—and he was wonderfully sensible about it. When he finished he kissed his mother good night, made his salute to his father and, almost imperceptibly, to Gallatin, and went upstairs. Gallatin nerved himself to several efforts at beginning conversation with Courtney. Each time, as he glanced up, he was checked and flung back into embarrassed silence by seeing in her absent eyes the same disconcerting mockery. After supper, Richard hurried away to the library. When she showed that she was going upstairs, Gallatin detained her. "One moment, please," he pleaded humbly. "What have I done to offend you?"

Courtney flushed. But the raillery came back instantly. "I'm not offended. I'm amused."

"At what?"

"At you." The smile broadened charmingly. "So you've had a successful trip?"

"Yes—in a way."

"And have come back completely cured."

"I want you to be my friend—if you will. I repeat, you can trust me now."

Her eyes sparkled dangerously. "It's fortunate I understand men—and have a sense of humor."

"I know I deserve any punishment you choose to give," said he. "And I'll take it. Only—I want to stay on here—and to have your friendship."

She studied him critically. Her expression would have been trying enough in its penetrating judicial intelligence for the least self-conscious of men. It utterly disconcerted Basil, bred in the fashionable world's incessant consciousness of self. But in his desperation he withstood her look, returned it with eyes that were appealing yet not abject. It pleased her that he was not abject. "After all, you went on my advice, didn't you?" said she in a friendlier tone. "And you've been most manlike—have shown yourself to be just what I thought you. So I'm really unreasonable." She gave him her hand. "Yes, let us be friends."

"And you forgive me?"

She smiled queerly. "That's asking too much. I may—in time. Just at present— you've made me feel horribly cheap and—common."

He hung his head. "If you knew how I've suffered for it," he said. "I was afraid you'd send me away—would never see me again."

"Let's not talk about it," cried she, angry at her own weakness in not meting out to him what he apparently expected and certainly deserved. But she was not so angry that she held to her purpose of going upstairs. Instead, she sat at the piano and began to dash off the noisiest pieces she knew.

# Chapter 9

The friendship now throve like Courtney's best-placed flower bed. She had always been healthy; so she had not a touch of "temperament"—which is the misleading romantic name for internal physical conditions anything but romantic. Most of those who have mentality have also imperfect health through neglect of physical needs; and the somberer shades, the grays and blue blacks, made the more melancholy by imagination, usually canopy their lives. But with her it was not so. Always healthy in body and in mind, she now irradiated perfume and color like the rose that is getting just the right sun and rain.

Late in that summer there were several weeks when one perfect day followed another like a child's dream of fairy-land. Vaughan wished to work alone, dropped completely out of their life, was forgotten. Every day, all day long, she and Basil were together, he helping her at the pastime that kept house and grounds beautiful. She was one of those human beings who abhor disorder; if anything went wrong it was righted at once. If a knob came off a door or a plant withered, she could not rest until the imperfection was remedied. It kept her incessantly occupied, but the results were worth the pains they cost. Her imagination, stimulated by Basil, planned many changes in grounds and gardens, changes that would bring the place still nearer the landscape artist's three ideals—contrast, variety, bounds concealed. And she and Basil together carried out these alterations.

Then there were the leisure hours, as full as the hours of toil. They—with Winchie—strolled in the woods on the farm, across the highway, and picnicked under the trees beside the brook, or in the shadow of some gigantic fern-covered rock left on a hillside by the retreating glaciers of the ice age. Or, they went out on the lake, Winchie fishing, she and Gallatin talking in low tones or happy in sympathetic silence, with the boat moving languidly where the shadows of the great weeping willows were deepest, its keel troubling the dark clear waters hardly more than a floating leaf.

She was fond of talking, he of listening. And she had so many things to say—the things that had been accumulating in those five years when she had said little, had read and thought much. When Basil did talk it was usually of what he had experienced in his wanderings over Europe and Asia. And, as she had been everywhere in fancy through her reading, she drew him out with questions that made it hard for him to believe she had not actually viewed with her own eyes. He seemed a wonderful person to her, he who had lived in the world's half dozen great capitals, had wandered all over the earth and had seen everything. Her comments astonished him, made him ashamed, and privately reverent of her "woman's intuition. No wonder it's considered better than brains."

"I wish I'd had some one like you along when I was chasing about," said he. "It was usually horribly dull, and I went on at it chiefly because I was always hoping something interesting would turn up. Now, I see it was turning up all the time. You have a light way of looking at things. A man sees only the serious side."

"Oh, it couldn't be dull—not anywhere on earth," insisted she.

"No—not with—that is, with somebody like you along." An awkward silence; then, "and I don't see how you ever learned so much without having experience."

"I don't really know things," confessed she. "I just *seem* to know. As a matter of fact, I'm frightfully innocent."

"That's the beautiful part of it," said he with enthusiasm.

"I hate it!" she cried.

"Oh, no," protested he.

"Yes, hate it," she insisted. The chief pleasure in this friendship with him was that it gave her freedom to be herself, to be frank. She would not let him spoil it for her, as Richard had in their early married days spoiled even the times of closest intimacy with formalism and restraint. "I want to know—I want to *live*," she went on, with glowing, eager face. "I've always felt proud it was the woman who had the sense to eat the apple. I detest innocence. I love *life*!"

"Oh, you don't mean exactly that."

"Just that."

"Even—sin?" This, not an inquiry, but an argument proving her beyond question in the wrong.

But she replied undauntedly: "It seems to me, the only way to learn is by doing things. And doesn't that mean making mistakes—sins, as you call it? Life's a good deal like gardening. You have to do it wrong first in order to learn how to do it right."

"That's all very well for a man. But——"

She was giving him one of those disconcerting eerie glances from the mysterious eyes. "I've got to *live*, and in the same world you have. Also, I've got to bring up a boy to live in it."

"I must say," confessed he, "I don't see just how to meet that." And she accepted the answer as evidence of his broad-minded sympathy. She did not realize that he was anything but convinced, but was simply admitting the "light cleverness" of her reply and was too eager about standing well with her to combat her "queer ideas."

The interruption to the delights of this friendship came before she had nearly exhausted his novelty, and while she was still as uncritical of him as a starving man of the cooking. However, in any circumstances it would have been long before she could have made any accurate judgment of him. She had become his partisan; and a generous nature takes the most favorable, the always too favorable, view of a personality to which it is attracted.

Until that summer Richard had been, for a young man, remarkably careful about regularity and exercise. At the very outset of his task, away back at Johns Hopkins, seven years before, he had realized that he was in for an investigation of all known elements in every possible combination—that is, for a long and hard struggle for about the most jealously guarded of nature's secrets—the origin of heat. And he knew that, if he was to win any victory worth while, he must resist the temptation to overwork, and must make health his first consideration. And although he had small liking for physical exercise and was as little fond of the grind of regularity as the next man, he had kept to his rules for himself with the same inflexible firmness that characterized him in all his serious purposes. But Basil's coming with the additional money he had needed, and the help, too, tempted him beyond his resistance. In exercise, as in everything else, there is system or there is nothing. Before Basil had been there a month Richard was breaking his rules; and soon the whole system went by the board. All summer he had not exercised, and he ate at any hours or not at all. Such a reversal of a long-established routine could not but create an immediate internal commotion. There were no physical surface signs; he looked the same as always; but his temper became uncertain. Where he had been simply absent-minded he was now irascible in it. Without reason—except the internal physical turmoil he himself did not feel or suspect—-he would burst from abstraction to attack Gallatin or Courtney or Winchie or one of the servants, or to rave against everything and everybody. And this new Richard appeared at just the time when it would stand out in sharpest, most odious relief—most dangerous contrast to the even temper of Basil Gallatin. Under the stimulus of her friendship with Gallatin, Courtney had got back much of her former gayety. Again she was overflowing with jest and laughter, with the joy she seemed to have absorbed from the bright things that grew or flitted and flew in her gardens.

The change in Richard came rapidly, yet was so gradual that its cause escaped them all. It is not in human nature to be inexhaustibly patient even with the vagaries of an obvious invalid. Where the illness is unsuspected, patience with its victim soon turns to gall. This new development in Richard's character—for Courtney and all the others assumed it was character—changed her passive, almost unsuspected resentment and indifference into dislike that could easily deepen into aversion.

He was disagreeably reminding her of his existence; he was saying in effect "Look at me!" She looked. She had bowed to fate, had accepted a loveless life of duty. She had done her part loyally. She had made a home, had kept it in order, had submitted whenever his physical necessities began to distract him from his work. Yes, she had accepted all the degradation without a murmur. And when love had come to her unsought, had tempted her, she had put the temptation aside. In order that his plans might not be upset, she had taken the hard instead of the easy way to combat this temptation, had let Basil Gallatin stay on. And what was her reward? Whenever Richard spoke, it was to say something disagreeable, to be as nearly insulting as a well-bred man could become.

"It's perhaps fortunate for Richard," reflected she, "that Basil showed the true nature of his love in that trip to Pittsburg. For what do *I* owe Richard Vaughan? Is there any woman anywhere who does not in her heart feel she'd be justified in doing *anything*, when her husband has treated her as mine has treated me?" And the obvious answer—that her husband was the normal husband, that it was she who, expecting what the conventional and customary marriage relation did not contemplate and did not provide, was in the wrong—this answer seemed to her no answer at all, but an insult to her intelligence and her self-respect.

Because of Vaughan's rages Gallatin got into the habit of rising from the table as soon as he finished and leaving the Vaughans to themselves. Courtney, with the sex charm subtly seducing her to seek and exaggerate merits in Basil, was deeply moved by this thoughtfulness; for it increased her humiliation to have him there when Richard lost control of himself. One evening, as they finished supper, Vaughan was suddenly infuriated by the stealthy fiend of indigestion that is the chief cause of humanity's faults of temperament, from morbidness to acute mania. He burst out at Gallatin—sprang from absent-mindedness with flaming eyes like a madman from ambush. "You messed everything to-day!" cried this unsuspected and unconscious invalid, sicker far than many a one in bed with doctors and nurses. "You simply raised the devil. Another day or so like it, and I'll not let you come into the shop."

Gallatin made no reply.

"I suppose you're cursing me," fumed Richard. "That's the way it always is. The whole world's mad on the subject of self-excuse. Somebody else is always to blame, and criticism is always an outrage."

"Not at all," said Gallatin, and Courtney knew his self-control was wholly for her sake. "I was stupid to-day, Vaughan. It was wholly my fault. I know I came near blowing up the shop and sending us both to kingdom come——"

An exclamation of terror from Courtney halted him. She was pale, was looking with frightened, questioning eyes from one man to the other.

Vaughan blazed again. "There you go!" cried he to Gallatin. "Now, she'll think I'm at something as dangerous as a powder factory—when, in fact——"

"Yes, indeed, Mrs. Vaughan," interrupted Gallatin. "It was my stupidity that made all the danger. Really, we do nothing that ought to be dangerous."

"That's not true," said Courtney quietly. "I know the truth now. And I never thought of it before!" She could not understand how she had been so unthinking; it was another, an unexpected measure of the cleavage between Richard's life and hers.

"You'd better confine your attention to things you understand," said Vaughan. "It was all Gallatin's folly, I assure you."

"That's the truth, Mrs. Vaughan," said Gallatin earnestly. "The whole truth."

She said no more, but her face showed she did not believe him. Gallatin, depressed and remorseful, went out on the veranda, strolled down toward the lake. Vaughan sat on, pulling savagely at his cigar. He was enraged because his outburst had caused the disclosure of the secret he had intended to keep from her, had given her a false idea which, as she was a woman, a creature of notions and whims, nothing could ever correct. He forgot his fine philosophy about self-excuse, and turned his rage from himself to her. "It's really all your fault," he exclaimed, glowering at her.

Winchie, seated between his father and mother, took up his knife and raised it threateningly against his father, his gray-green eyes ablaze.

In another mood Vaughan would have been secretly delighted, would have gravely accepted the rebuke and made apology to the boy and to Courtney. But the devil—the realest devil that torments spirit through flesh—was in him that night, was on the prowl. He pointed his cigar at the infuriated child. "What's the meaning of this?" he demanded.

"Winchie," said Courtney, in a low, firm voice.

The boy's eyes shifted from father to mother.

"Put down that knife, go upstairs and go to bed."

Son and mother looked at each other fully ten seconds; the boy lowered the knife, laid it on the table, descended from his chair, marched haughtily from the room. When he was gone Vaughan said: "You should have made him apologize to me."

Courtney did not reply. She was pulling out the bows the flowing tie she was wearing under the loose collar of her shirt waist.

"I'll have Lizzie bring him back."

"No," said Courtney, and her eyes met his. "You will not interfere with Winchie. I do not interfere with your work."

"But you do!" Richard burst out. "It's your interfering that's making Gallatin so worthless."

She shrank back in her chair, hastily veiled her eyes. Now it was the cuffs of the shirt waist that were engaging her attention.

"You dislike him, I know," Vaughan went on. "But why do you treat him so badly?"

No answer. She could hardly believe that it had been so long since Richard had noted her and Basil. Besides, when had she ever treated him in a way that could be called badly?

"I am sure you treat him badly. Why?"

No answer.

"I asked you a question. Politeness would suggest——"

"Not in this family," said Courtney, cold and calm, her slim fingers touching her hair here and there.

"All I've got to say is, it's no wonder Gallatin's becoming useless at the shop. He must feel his position acutely. I can conceive of no reason why you should subject a gentleman—and my guest—to such indignity."

Courtney looked as if she were sitting quietly alone.

"Has he been making love to you?" demanded Vaughan.

Her eyelids fluttered, but it was the only sign she gave.

"Some time ago I observed he had a way of looking at you that was most loverlike."

Still no answer, and no sign.

"Even so, you could deal with him tactfully. He is a gentleman."

"You said that before," observed she, elbows on the table, her chin on the backs of her intertwined fingers, her gaze upon the bowl of old-fashioned yellow roses in the center of the table.

He glowered at her. "So I did," said he. "Now I say it again, and perhaps you will be able to grasp it. And I want you to treat him as a gentleman should be treated. So long as he is my guest, so long as he conducts himself like a gentleman, you must be courteous to him."

No answer; no change.

"Do you hear, Courtney?"

"Yes."

"What do you intend to do?"

Up went the long lashes and the deep green eyes burned coldly at him. "As I choose," said she. "And I may add, I will not put up with your bad temper any longer. At the next outburst from you, Winchie and I leave this house. I will not be insulted, and will not have my boy ruined by his father's bad example."

Richard's eyes softened; he lowered them, the red mounted. After a silence he said "Excuse me" without looking at her, rose and went to the veranda. When she finished giving directions for the next day to Nanny and was going upstairs, he was still walking up and down, head bent, hands behind his back, sternness in that long aristocratic profile. An hour later, as she sat at her desk in her own sitting room upstairs, she heard his voice at the door into the hall.

"May I come in?" he asked.

"Certainly," replied she. Her back was toward the door.

"I want to beg your pardon."

"Very well," said she, her voice cold and even. She did not realize how much this meant from a man who had not the apologizing spirit or habit. And if she had realized, she would have been no more appreciative.

"You do not accept it?" said he, ruffled at once, and feeling that she was now the one in the wrong.

"I do not care any thing about it, one way or the other."

He was silent for a moment, then: "I hardly blame you," said he, with a great air of generous concession. "I've been out of temper, rude—disgracefully so—for some time. I'm sorry." And he stood looking at her expectantly, more complacent than penitent.

"I see you think a few words are enough to make up for all you've done."

"What more can I do? It's not a bit like you, Courtney, to——"

"And what do you know about me?" inquired she, turning half round and looking calmly at him over her shoulder. "It's quite true," she went on, "that I have no means of support but what I earn here as your housekeeper and—wife. But, I——"

"Courtney!" he cried in a tone of imperative rebuke.

"A few plain words—of truth—seem to shock you more than your own conduct."

"Such language from you! But you did not realize what you were saying."

"I did. I meant just what I said."

"That is not language for a wife to use to a husband."

She rose from the desk and, without looking at him, went into her bedroom, closing the door behind her.

She was working in the garden beneath the west windows. She moved among the flowers, as restless and graceful as any other of the elves always hovering about blooming things—bees, humming birds, butterflies. It was a rare chance to study the marvels of pose of which the human body is capable. Now she was stooping, now kneeling; bending forward, backward, to one side; or, erect and stretching upward, to relieve a tall rosebush of a dead leaf or spray. And the lines of her figure, ever changing, were ever alluring. Her arms, too—and her neck—how smooth and slenderly round, and how intensely alive! Her whole skin seemed aureoled with invisible, tremulous, magnetic waves. She was wearing a big pale-green garden hat; her hair was perfectly done, as always—as if it had taken no time or trouble, yet so that it formed a delightful frame for her small, delicate face, and splintered and reflected every stray of sunlight that dodged in under the brim. Her short skirt revealed slim, tapering ankles and small feet. There are feet that are merely short; then there are feet such as hers—exquisitely small—not useless looking, but the reverse. The same quality of the exquisite was in her figure. She was small, but she was not short. Her smallness enabled a perfection nature never gets in the long or the large. She made largeness suggest coarseness. Women of her form send thrilling through their lovers the feeling of being able completely to enfold and to possess.

All alone and thinking only of the flowers, she entered one of the narrow paths that led toward the veranda. She stretched upward to re-curl a refractory tendril. Both arms were extended, her head thrown back, the rosy bronze face upturned—pathetic, yet laughter-loving mouth, eyes of deep, deep green. Like one awakening from a profound sleep she slowly became conscious that she and Basil Gallatin were gazing into each other's eyes with only the trellised creeper between. And his look made her heart leap. She straightened herself, colored, paled, stood trembling. The next thing she distinctly knew, he had come round to the lawn at the edge of the garden in which she was working.

"How you startled me!" she said, in a careless, casual tone.

As he did not answer, she glanced at him. He was standing with eyes down. And his look made her vaguely afraid.

"Are you going to help me to-day?" she asked, resolved to brave it through.

"I can't stand it!" he cried, his voice trembling with passion. "I love you. I must go. I shall go as soon as Vaughan comes back. Until then I'll keep to the other part of the grounds."

"Why not just do it, and not talk so much?" she demanded, suddenly angry.

"If you had ever loved," said he humbly, "you'd understand. But I didn't intend to say these things. I came to tell you Vaughan's away. They telegraphed for him to hurry to Washington—something about the duties on a lot of new instruments."

"How long will he be?"

"Several weeks, perhaps. He's going afterwards to Baltimore, and then to Philadelphia and New York. He left word with Jimmie about sending a trunk after him. He had just time to catch the express. He asked me to explain to you."

Nanny appeared at the drive-front corner of the house. He said to her: "Oh—Nanny. I've been upstairs packing a few of my belongings. Will you have them taken to Mr. Vaughan's apartment at the shop?"

"Jimmie says Mr. Vaughan locked everything up down there, and took the keys, and said no one was to go near it while he was away."

Basil hesitated, but only for an instant. "How forgetful he is!" he exclaimed with a smile. "Of course I've got to sleep there—as watchman. Well, I'll force the stairway door. You can telephone over for a locksmith this afternoon or to-morrow. He'll make a new lock and key."

Nanny departed, muttering. She did not like disobedience to the head of the house of Vaughan; but, on the other hand, she would have liked it much less had Gallatin stayed on at the house with Mr. Richard not there. Gallatin turned to Courtney. "Would it be too much trouble to send my meals to the shop?" he asked, in a constrained, formal tone that deeply offended her.

"Nanny will attend to that," replied she, eyes cold as winter seas.

"Thank you. If you should need anyone—there's the telephone to the shop. I'll re-connect it."

"You needn't bother."

"There have been several robberies round here of late, and———"

"As you please.... Thank you."

He looked at her as wistfully as a prisoner at the fields of freedom beyond his cell window. She seemed impatient to resume work; he went reluctantly away. She stood gazing after him until he disappeared in the shrubbery at the far eastern edge of the lawns. Then she sighed and glanced at the unblemished sky as if she thought it was clouding.

Three uneasy, tedious days and two wakeful nights. In the third night, toward one o'clock, she tossed away her book, put out her light, and opened all her shutters as usual, to air the rooms. "If I opened his door and window, I might get a breeze," she said to herself. "It's terribly close." She crossed the hall, entered the room Gallatin had occupied, raised a window, and leaned upon the sill—it was the small window beyond the end of the balcony, and so did not extend to the floor. The sky was clear; the moon was hidden by the house. Stillness—peace—beauty—beauty of view and of odor—the lake with its dark banks, trees tossing up into the blue-black sky and shimmering with moonlight—perfumes of foliage and flowers and of the fresh-cut grass in the meadows beyond the highroad.

"It's as if everybody in the world were dead except me," she murmured. She listened again to get the weird effect of utter absence of sound. This time she heard the faint plaint of a cricket, appealing for company in its blindness and solitude. Then—her nerves became tense. From the balcony, which ended just a few feet to her left, came a stealthy sound—like a step. Softly she crossed the room—the hall—her own room, to the high-boy. She took from its top drawer her pistol. She returned to Gallatin's bedroom—noiselessly unlocked the shutters over one pair of the long windows opening on the balcony—unbolted one of them and held it ajar. Yes, there was some one on that balcony. Several of the neighbors had been robbed; now, it was their turn. The pistol was self-cocking. Taking it in her right hand, she drew back the window with her left, stepped out. She thrust the pistol into the very face of the man.

He sprang back. She saw what looked like a knife in one hand—nothing, apparently, in the other. At the same instant she heard him cry "Courtney!"

The pistol dropped from her nerveless hand to the balcony floor.

"It's I!" Gallatin exclaimed. "I heard a second-story window go up very softly—I was walking and smoking in the path. I came—climbed a pillar—and——"

"O God! God!" she sobbed. Down she sank to the floor, her face buried in her hands. "My love! My love! And I almost killed you!"

He knelt beside her. "Dearest—" He put his arm round her. Instantly he drew away and sprang to his feet. Up she started, gazing wildly round. "What is it?" she exclaimed. "Where?"

"Nothing—nothing," was his confused answer. But already she had felt a thrill from where his arm, his hand had been, and understood.

A stifling silence. He said: "I must go now. I'm sorry to have disturbed you." And with his conventionality that was of instinct he lifted his hat and made a dignified bow. In her hysterical state, she did not miss the grotesque humor of this; she burst out laughing. She leaned against the window frame and laughed until she had to wipe away the flowing tears. He stood staring blankly at her, with rising offense, as he, always sensitive about himself, suspected she was laughing at him. For his sense of humor was not nearly so keen as she had been deceived into thinking by his store of jokes and songs, of odds and ends of amusing cleverness, all entirely new to her, and therefore seeming practically original with him.

"What is it?" he said stiffly, when she was somewhat calm. "I should like to laugh, too." It seemed to him characteristic indeed, but most untimely, this display of her utter incapacity for seriousness.

"Hysteria—reaction—and your everlasting good manners," replied she. "Is there anything on earth that would make you forget you are a gentleman from Philadelphia?"

"Nothing but you," answered he bitterly. "Good night."

"Wait a second—please," she pleaded. And—why, she could not have told—she went on, to her own surprise, "The other day you said you had changed your mind and were going."

"Yes."

"Isn't that—cruel? I've learned to—to depend on your friendship."

He did not answer immediately. When he did, his voice betrayed his agitation. "I'm going because my manhood demands it. It may be weakness, but if I stayed I should—should go all to pieces."

"I can't argue against that. But there's one thing: As you're going, I want to be able to feel that there's no blot on our friendship. I've been condemning you unheard. Tell me——"

She paused. He felt how embarrassed she was. "What?" he asked gently. "Anything you wish to know?"

"Did you go to—to Pittsburg because—because—I sent you?"

He did not answer; it was too dark to make out his expression.

"I told you," she went on, speaking rapidly, as soldiers advance at a double quick, where if they advanced at ordinary pace they would have time to think, to be afraid, to turn and fly, "I told you to go back to your old haunts and cure yourself of—of your fancy for me.... You went?"

"You could suspect that!"

"If you did, don't lie to me. Say so, and I'll never think of it again. I'd understand. I'd—I'd—forgive."

"There is no woman for me but you," he answered, drawing a step farther from her and putting his hands behind his back. "I went because my aunt telegraphed for me. I came as soon as I could get away."

She clasped her hands and pressed them against her bosom. She leaned toward him, eyes like two of the few large stars in that summer night sky. "I am so glad," she murmured.

"Why did you suspect? How could you? Why did you care?"

"I was—jealous." The confession was almost inaudible.

"Courtney!" His arms impulsively extended.

She waved him back. "Go—go! I am upset—hysterical. Forget what I said. We are friends again. There is jealousy in friendship, too. Good night."

He hesitated. There she stood, all in that flimsy white—her coils of soft fine hair about her small head—her arms, her throat, her face tantalizingly half revealed in the dimness. "Courtney—do you love me?"

"No—no—not that," answered she, softly, hurriedly, pleadingly. "But I like you—and I'm a woman—and—and that tells the whole story. Good night, Mr. Basil." She held out her hand.

He did not take it. "I dare not touch you—to-night," he said. "I can't be trusted—nor can you."

"No," she assented, letting her hand drop. She drew a long, deep breath, and he also—a draught of that intoxicating air, surcharged with perfume and moonbeams and the freedom of the midnight outdoors.

"We are friends—through and through?"

"Yes." His reply was in the same low, hushed voice as her question.

"That is so much—so much." Their nerves like their voices were tense from the restraint of the passionate emotions damming up higher and higher within.

"And I'll see you at breakfast—and thank you for coming.... Good night, Mr. Basil."

He bared his head. She did not feel like laughing now at his "everlasting good manners," but was shivering, with hot tears in her eyes. He said "Good night, Mrs. Courtney."

Slowly she went in at the window of his room. Just as she was about to push the bolt, she opened it again. "You must come in this way," she said. "I'll let you out at the front door."

"No, I'll go as I came."

"Nonsense!"

"If any of the servants——"

"You make me feel guilty—when I'm not. Come!"

He entered the room. Both began to close the window. Their hands touched, hesitated, clasped. She was in his arms, his lips were upon hers. A long kiss. Her form relaxed; she drew her lips away to murmur, "Hold me. I'm—faint." Again their lips met, and he clasped her to him until he could feel the wild pulsing of her blood against his face, against his chest, against his arms—could feel it in every part of that small form, so utterly within his embrace. "Don't," she gasped. "It is too much—too much."

"I love you—I love you. You are mine—yes, you are, Courtney! There is nothing but love."

She gently released herself, swayed, leaned against the casement, looked up into the summer starlight. Again he seized her, and again his lips found hers. Her head dropped upon his shoulder. A sound—one of those creakings that haunt the stillness of a house in the night hours. She startled, stiffened, shut her teeth upon a scream.

"It was nothing," he said. He, too, was rigid, with every sense alert for danger.

"What have we done!" she exclaimed. They stood silent, facing each other, overcome with shame, burning with longing. "Oh—Basil!"

He took her in his arms. But she pushed him resolutely away. "No—not again," she said. He looked at her; she gazed up into the sky. "Love!" she murmured. "Love! And I—must not."

"I forgot—forgot!" he cried. "O God—Courtney—I love you more than honor." And he opened the other the door windows, rushed past her, vanished round the corner of the house. She sighed, shivered, stepped out upon the balcony, stood at the rail until she saw a dark form rapidly cross the lawns toward the shrubbery densely inclosing the Smoke House. She looked all round—sky—lake—woods. "It is so lonely," she sobbed. "So lonely!"

# Chapter 10

Ten minutes before breakfast time a knock at the hall door into her bedroom. She knew who it was that could not reach above the lower panels. "Come in!" she cried. Winchie entered—stopped short on the threshold.

"Good morning, Mr. Benedict Vaughan," said she, nodding at him by way of the mirror before which she was arranging her blouse at the neck. And he knew she was in a particularly fine humor.

"Have we got company? Who?" he asked.

"No. Why?"

"Aren't you going to take me for a walk after breakfast?"

"Of course. Don't we always go?"

"But it's raining."

"I know."

"Wouldn't it spoil that dress?"

"One'd think you had a sloven for a mother. Don't I always dress?"

"But that's a long skirt. And you're not putting on a shirt waist."

"I'll change after breakfast."

"Oh." This, however, contented him for a moment only. He eyed her critically as she made one insignificant little change after another, displaying a fussiness quite unusual. "I guess we're to have company—maybe."

"Not at all. We never have people to breakfast. What *are* you puzzling about?"

"Why didn't you put on the rain dress?"

Courtney's delicate skin was showing more than its normal color. She shook her head laughingly at him—this child whose questions were forcing her to see a truth she was striving might and main to hide from herself. "You don't like this dress?"

"Yes, I like 'em all. It isn't the dress, exactly."

"Then what is it?"

"I don't know. It's—something. It made me think company right away." The bar of music from the gong came floating up from below. "There's breakfast!" he exclaimed. "Are you 'most ready?"

"Quite," replied she, with a last look at profile, back hair and back of skirt with the aid of a hand glass.

"Maybe there'll be company," said Winchie as they started.

"I'm sure there'll be corn muffins," said she. "I smell them."

"If there's hash, may I have a little?"

"A little."

The descent was slow as Winchie's legs were short. She listened at every step, but could hear no sound of the kind she hoped. At the sitting-room door she glanced round. He was not there. "He's in the dining room," she said half to herself.

"Who, mamma?"

90

Courtney startled, flushed. "What is it, dear?" she stammered guiltily.

"Has papa come?"

"No, I was thinking of Mr. Gallatin."

Winchie drew his hand from hers. But she did not note it; for they were at the threshold of the dining room, and no one was there but Lizzie. She and Winchie sat, but she did not begin. A moment and she went to the telephone in the hall, took down the receiver of the private wire. Soon she heard in Basil's voice, "Hello. What is it?"

"It's—I."

"Oh." Then silence.

"Did you hurt yourself last night?"

"No, not at all—thank you."

In a constrained voice: "I thought you were coming to breakfast."

"I felt it was better not to."

"Oh!—good-by." And she hung up the receiver.

Back in the dining room, uneasy under Winchie's serious steady gaze, she winced at his first remark: "Mr. Gallatin's company. There's you—and me—and the rest's company." After a pause, doubtfully: "Except papa. He's not quite company, I guess."

"Do you want some of the hash?"

"You said there wasn't to be company."

"Please! Please!" she cried. "You'll give me the headache."

"You said I was always to say what I had in my brains."

She bent over and kissed his hand. "And so you must."

"Do you say everything that's in your brains?"

She reddened again. "Everything Winchie'd understand," replied she. "After a while, when you grow up, you'll find a lot of things in your mind that it'd be of no use to say because nobody would understand—a lot of things you won't understand yourself."

"There is those in, already," said he solemnly.

She laughed. "No doubt."

As she did not encourage him, he addressed himself to the hash, which was the kind he liked—brown and not too dry, and with the potatoes in little cubes. She poured her coffee, just touched one of Mazie's famous corn muffins as she slowly drank it, and gave herself up to the clear and calm daylight reflections that make comment so cynical and so severe upon what we do and say and think under the spell of night. She put on a waterproof hat and suit, leggings and boots, and issued forth for a two-hours' tramp with Winchie, who was dressed in the same fashion. When they got back at ten, she felt she was not the same woman as the one who had the adventure with the burglar on the balcony. She saw Winchie into dry clothes and settled at his rainy-day games—then out she went again. She walked rapidly along the path to the Smoke House; was soon rapping at the heavy iron door of the laboratory. She rapped again and again, turned away angry, was almost back at the edge of the shrubbery when she remembered that Richard had locked the laboratory, that Basil could not possibly be there.

She hesitated, returned to the Smoke House, knocked at the door of the stairway leading up to the suite. No answer. She opened it, went upstairs. At the top she paused, called, "Anybody here?"

Basil appeared in the doorway of the sitting room. He was in a dark-blue summer house suit, a cigarette in the corner of his mouth. His face was very red; his eyes did not meet hers. "Lizzie straightened up and left about half an hour ago," said he.

"I came for a look round," explained she, admiring, without seeming to do so, his elegant and fashionable suit, the harmony of its color with his soft négligée shirt and flowing artist's tie. But then she always liked the way he dressed, the way he wore his clothes. "I come once a week in the morning to keep Lizzie up to the mark," she went on. "You're down in the laboratory at that time, so you haven't known what a model housekeeper I am."

He did not stand aside for her to enter.

"I also had another reason," pursued she. "Please don't choke up the doorway. I'm coming in."

He bowed, stood aside. She entered, glanced round the sober but not somber room with its walls, ceilings, floor, and furniture of walnut. It was a comfortable place and beautifully clean. "Jimmie attends to the floors?"

"Every week."

She glanced into the adjoining room—kalsomined walls and ceiling, a white oak floor, a big chest of drawers, a big mirror, a big table and chair, a roomy brass bedstead. "Any complaints?"

"Everything perfectly satisfactory," he assured her.

"Now for my other business—my real business," said she, disposing herself in one of the window seats. "You may continue to stand, if you prefer; but it would please me better if you sat."

He seated himself stiffly at the table desk. Her eyes were dancing with amusement at his overelaborated formality. It made him seem such a boy, made her feel vastly wiser and stronger and older than he.

"Why didn't you come to breakfast?" she inquired in a most businesslike tone.

"I made up my mind not to see you again until Vaughan returned."

"And then, to go away?"

"Yes."

"Why?"

"I prefer not to answer that."

"Why not?"

"It's true Vaughan and I are not exactly friends. Still, I've been disloyal. I shall be so no more."

She clasped her hands round one knee, looked at him with half closed eyes. "I do not like to be regarded as part of some one's else belongings," said she. "I belong to myself."

"I wish to God you did!"

"You attach too much importance to what a woman says and does on impulse. I was much upset last night. I said and did things that seem absurd to me in daylight."

"I am just as absurd, as you call it, in daylight as I was in moonlight."

She flinched, controlled herself, made an impatient gesture. "Don't say those things, or you'll spoil everything," she half pleaded, half commanded.

He strode to a window across the room from that in which she was sitting. "Everything is spoiled. I've simply got to go."

"No." She shook her head slowly. "You will stay, and we'll be friends again, as before."

"If I could only wipe out last night!" he cried, and he wheeled upon her.

She caught her breath. "Do you mean that?" she asked impulsively.

He stopped short, faced her, but his eyes were down. "No, I don't," replied he. "And that's the devil of it."

"Why?"

"If I honestly regretted last night, I could stay."

"Why do you lie to yourself?" she asked, crossing the room toward him. "You have no real intention of going."

His gaze sank. "I shall try to go," he muttered.

She laughed—after she had returned to the safer distance of the window seat. "What a passion for hypocrisy you men have. 'I shall try.' You hope that last tiny rag of a remnant will cover your real purpose."

"You think I am a dishonorable dog. I don't wonder at it."

"No, I don't. But I do think you are taking yourself entirely too seriously. You don't want to go, do you? And I don't wish you to go. And Richard doesn't want you to go."

"He'd compel it if he knew."

"But he doesn't know. Maybe, if I knew some things about you, I'd want you to go. Maybe, if you knew me thoroughly, you'd be eager to go. As it is, we all want things to stay as they are."

"Last night was a warning."

"Yes," she hastened to assent. "Let's heed it. Let's go back to friendship and not wander. My friend, you're letting your mind hang over just one subject, just one side of the relations of men and women. Isn't there more to me than—that?"

"Courtney!" he protested.

"Then let's be friends. Let's put aside what we can't have. Let's take and enjoy what we can. Let's not talk or think about—about love—any more than one frets about not being able to visit the moon. We've been finding life happy these last few weeks, with that subject never mentioned. Why not again? Are you too weak? Am I too uninteresting?"

"I tried once before and failed."

"But now that we've looked the situation straight in the face—now that we're both on guard—don't you think we can do better?"

"I don't know," he confessed. "I'm afraid to try—aren't you?"

Her eyes held him, they were so mysterious. "Not so much as I'm afraid not to try," replied she slowly.

He dropped into his chair again, sat staring at the blotting pad on the desk.

"Had you thought," she went on, "what would happen if we owned ourselves beaten and fled from each other?"

He presently lifted his eyes, looked at her in wonder. "And that never occurred to me!" he cried. "Why, our only chance now is to stay here and fight it out. If we shirked and tried to escape—" He paused.

She nodded gravely.

"If I went away, it'd only be to come back—desperate. And you——"

He did not finish his sentence. They sat silent a long time. "It would be horribly lonely with you gone," said she in an absent, impersonal way. "And loneliness breeds such wild longings."

A long silence. Then she rose. "Come up to the house and help me with those plans for a kitchen garden under glass," she suggested.

He nodded without looking at her, as if to show her that he understood all and accepted what was beyond question the less dangerous of their alternatives. "As soon as I dress, I'll be there," said he.

"I forgot. I must change, too. In an hour?"

"Less."

They shook hands in an emphatically comradely fashion, and she went. The former conditions were restored. They would not permit them to be interrupted again. They would demonstrate that, with a thousand, thousand other things, interesting, amusing, to talk and to think about, they could bar out love and keep it out.

An hour over the plans, then they had dinner, laughing and joking together like two children. They did not heed or even note the gloom of Winchie and old Nanny—she was waiting, as it was Lizzie's day out. Winchie sat mum and glum, eating in the deliberate way Courtney had taught him and never lifting his jealous eyes from his plate. Nanny—middle-aged, homely, prim with the added sourness of those who have never had the least temptation to be otherwise—Nanny glowered at Gallatin every time she came into the room. She had disapproved of him from the outset and had made no secret of it. This gayety of his, in the absence of the head of the house of Vaughan, changed that dinner for her into a Babylonish revel. She was shocked at Courtney's taking part, but was not surprised. What was to be expected of the weak and frivolous younger generation of her own sex, mad about adorning the body, scornful of the idea of "settling," and incredulous as to hell fire? Her anger concentrated on Gallatin. He was a man; he seemed a serious, moral man. Yet here he was, leading on the vain, weak woman—he a guest of Mr. Vaughan's—trusted by him—put upon his honor. "It's enough to bring Colonel 'Kill back a-harntin'," muttered she into the oven.... Early in the afternoon it cleared gloriously. Outdoors, the two trespassers upon ancient propriety giddied into still higher spirits. And after supper! They banged on the piano and sang "coon" songs and became so hilarious "that you'd think the settin' room was full," said Jimmie to his aunt.

Nanny scowled at the blue yarn sock she was knitting with wrinkled, rheumatism-knotted fingers. "Such goings-on!" she growled.

"Why not?" demanded Jimmie. "Where's the harm? And I reckon Mrs. V. knows how to take care of herself."

"Who said she didn't?" snapped Nanny.

Toward nine Courtney and Basil went out on the veranda. It was a perfect August night. The honeysuckle in great masses upon the rail was giving forth an odor that quieted them like pensive music. Under the trees and among the bushes the now pale, now bright lamps of the "lightning bugs" shone by scores and hundreds. There was a moon, sailing high and almost full. She thought she had never been so happy in her life. At former happy times there was in her no such capacity to appreciate and enjoy as experience had now given her. And what an ideal companion Basil was—so much the man of the world, wise, experienced, yet simple and amazingly modest. And how marvelously they fitted into each other's moods! She had never thought to find a human being with just the right combination of qualities—one who could be serious—always in an interesting way—and also as light as the lightest.

"Look at those elder blossoms," said Basil in a low voice, as if louder tones might break the spell and dissolve the beauty, delicate, fragile, unreal.

Elder bushes were the outer wall of the eastern shrubbery; their flowers, soft, feathery mats, deliciously sweet to smell, looked at that distance and in that light like a wall of snow. Courtney and Basil descended from the veranda, strolled across the lawn. She lifted her head, seemed to drink in the beauty with her whole face, and to exhale it in a newer, subtler loveliness and perfume.

"How sweet the boxwood hedge is after to-day's rain."

As they neared the water's edge, all other perfumes yielded to the powerful, heavy, sensuous odor of the locust blossoms, in white clusters above the bench on which they presently sat. They were silent, gazing across the lake where, in contrast to the darkness and silence of their shore, lay the town, a shimmer of light, a murmur of confused sounds mingling pleasantly. Down the lake, far out beyond the edge of the heavy shadow flung by the trees, a boat was coming, the man rowing, the girl playing the mandolin and singing. The tinkling of the mandolin and the fresh young voice floated over the waters to Courtney and Basil. She drew in her breath sharply, with a sense of alluring danger hovering. The boat drew nearer; the sounds were clearer—clearer, more tender, more moving. The mandolin tinkled. The free, sweet young voice sang: "I want you—ma honey!—yes I do! I want you—I want you——"

She clasped, clinched her hands in her lap. Basil started up. "I can't bear it!" he cried. "I can't!"

"No—no!" she exclaimed, and her strange look suggested a soul drowning. "Go—go quickly!" And drawing her white shawl about her shoulders, she fled into the house.

# Chapter 11

"Where's Mr. Gallatin?" asked Winchie, as he and his mother were finishing breakfast next morning.

"At the Smoke House, I guess," replied she. There was a far-away look in her eyes, and their lids were heavy. Although Lizzie had been unusually unsuccessful in arranging the flowers, she left the bowl untouched in the center of the table—a solid mass of carnations which she could have changed into a miracle of lightness and grace.

"Is he coming to breakfast?" asked Winchie.

"No—at least, I suppose not. How'd you like to go to grandpa's?"

"Will Mr. Gallatin go?"

Courtney's cheeks flushed. "No," she said.

"Then I'd like it—for a while."

"We are going to-morrow," said Courtney. "To-morrow morning."

"Is grandpa sick?"

"No. Nobody is sick."

"Then why?"

Courtney's face wore a queer smile. "We'll help grandma and Aunt Lal and Aunt Ann put up fruit and jam and preserves."

"Will we stay long?" inquired the boy anxiously.

"Until—until your father—gets back."

Winchie looked much downcast. "Why?" he asked.

"Why not?" said Courtney. "And now, you'll help me pack and I'll help you."

It was a busy day, as there were many things to arrange besides the packing. Gallatin did not appear at the house all day, and Courtney did not expect him. Toward ten that night the packing was finished and everything ready for an early departure. Courtney went downstairs and out across the moonlit lawn. Slowly, with gaze straight ahead, she strolled toward the lake, toward the summer house in the copse at the western edge of the grounds. She entered, curled herself up on the broad seat, her elbow upon the rail, her hand supporting her chin. She watched the moonlight in the ripples along the middle of the lake. From time to time, she lifted her head, strained her eyes into the encircling shadows, then resumed her attitude, mental as well as physical, of forlorn abstraction. Something less than half an hour, and when she lifted herself to glance round for the third or fourth time, she did not sink back, but slowly straightened, her breath coming quickly.

"Who's there?" she called softly, addressing the deep shadows over the path by which she had come.

No answer but the chorus of tiny creatures murmuring excitedly in every crevice and beneath every blade and leaf.

"Who is it?" she demanded, but not loudly or nervously. She stood up.

"Only I," came in Basil's voice, and he advanced and stood between the entrance pillars of the open rustic pavilion.

"Oh!" said she. And she resumed gazing over the water, but did not resume her seat.

"I saw you cross the lawn," he explained. "And I was afraid some one might intrude."

"Thank you," said she gratefully.

"You knew it was I—didn't you?" he went on.

A brief silence, then—"Yes," she admitted, and gave a little laugh.

"Why do you laugh?"

"Because I just realized that I was expecting you—that I came here hoping to see you. How one does lie to oneself!"

"Do you wish me to leave you?"

"No.... What a beautiful night it is!"

"The loveliest I ever saw."

"These locust blossoms— The perfume makes me feel languid—but not sleepy."

"I guess it is the locusts," he said. "I feel that way, too."

"I'm taking Winchie to my father's for a visit—in the morning."

"So Jimmie said."

"We'll stay until Richard comes back."

"I supposed so."

A silence. Then she: "I must go in soon," and an instant later, without realizing it, seated herself.

"I wrote to Starky—Estelle—to-day.... To ask her to fix the date for the marriage."

She shivered.

"I decided it was best for me to commit myself."

She buried her face in her hands.

"And," he went on, "you know I shall always love you—*always*! ... I say that because—in a few minutes now we'll part, and never see each other again."

With her face between her hands, she gazed at the dancing surface of the watery highway of moonlight, and repeated monotonously—"never see each other again." Then, after a moment, "How heavy the perfume of the locusts is."

"Yes," replied he, "but so sweet."

Then the thin film of surface over their emotions suddenly burst. "Never again— oh, my Courtney!" he cried between set teeth. Both had thought all day that they were calm and resigned. They knew now how they had been deceiving themselves. He flung away from her. Both knew what was coming, knew it was too late to save themselves, felt the wild reckless thrill of terror and rapture that precedes the breaking down of all barriers, the breaking up of all foundations, the free sweep of unfettered passion. So young—so young—with such a long stretch of empty years—and they never to see each other again!

"How can I live on, without you to help me?" she said.

"It'll be easier for you than for me. You have—your boy. I have—nothing." He sat down, away from her, stared into the blackness of the copse. "Nothing," he repeated. He was holding his breath and waiting for the inevitable storm to break.

"Basil!" she cried, and in impulsive sympathy reached out and touched him. "Won't it be something—to know that you have my heart—my—love?"

She felt him trembling, and there was a sob in his voice as he answered: "But when your arms ache with emptiness, you can put them round Winchie. While I—Courtney, how can I touch another woman, when it's you—you—*you*—" And his groping hand met hers, clasped it. He bent his head, kissed her hand—the back, the palm, then the fingers one by one. And they softly touched his cheek. "Basil!" she sighed.

The faint wind agitated the clusters of locust blooms; their perfume descended in heavy voluptuous waves. He pressed his hands one against each of her cheeks. "Courtney," he murmured. "My love—my dear love!" Their lips met.

"We must not!" she pleaded, her arms about his neck.

"After to-night," he reminded her, "we, who love, will never see each other again."

"Never again!" she moaned.

It was the signal both were unconsciously, yet deliberately, awaiting. He gave an inarticulate cry, caught her up as a strong wind a flower. "I've had enough of right and wrong," cried he. "You are mine! I will not let you go. I love you—I love you—I love you!" And he showered kisses upon her until she, dizzy and fainting, yet never so alive, was clinging to him, was calling him endearing names, was laughing and sobbing. And in that darkness and mad frenzy of longing and despair they could pretend to themselves that it was all as unreal as a dream—was, in fact, a dream, or at worst, impulse—irresistible, irresponsible.

He felt her heart flutter, halt in its steady, strong beat within her breast close against his. She raised her head from his shoulder, listened. "What is it?" he whispered.

"Listen."

A bird broke from the copse and with a great noise of wings against leaves blundered away to another and higher place. "A bird—that was all," said he.

"Sh—h! No. They never stir so suddenly at night without cause." She was cold, was shivering. They looked at each other, tingling with guilty alarm.

"I'll go see."

"Yes—do."

He disengaged himself lingeringly, with a parting caress of his lips along her cheek. "It's cold," she murmured. "And I'm—I'm afraid." Never before in all her life had she been afraid.

He went softly along the path until the shadows hid him. After a moment he returned to the entrance. "I see nothing," said he.

"And I hear nothing—any more," replied she. "You don't know what a queer, creepy sensation I had. It was—was—as if some one were near us."

He did not seat himself by her again. "Isn't it—very—very late?" he said hesitatingly.

"Perhaps. But come, dear. Let's forget. It was nothing. Oh, I was so happy—and now—Basil, I'm cold."

Instead of sitting and taking her in his arms he drew her to her feet. "I saw your front door open," he said. "I think you'd better go."

She flung herself into his arms. "No—no!" she cried. "Not yet."

He held her closely, but soon released her. "You had better go," urged he, and she felt nervousness and constraint in his tone, in his touch.

She laughed quietly. "What are you afraid of?"

"Nothing!" he retorted stoutly. "Still, the door is open, and some one might——"

"Why, *you're* quite cold! ... Basil, what is it?"

"Nothing—nothing at all," replied he, his arms round her again, his lips upon hers.

Presently she said: "I *thought* you were neglecting me rather long. It's a habit men have after—after a woman is entirely theirs."

"Don't say those things, even in joke," he begged, so seriously that it jarred on her overwrought nerves.

"If you take that sort of remarks in earnest," said she, a trace of resentment in her tone, "I'll be likely to believe there's something in it."

"It was so—so frank," apologized he.

"Why not speak frankly?" said she. "One of the joys of loving you is that we'll be entirely frank with each other. I'll never be afraid to show you how much I love you, or to say whatever thought comes into my mind. And you must feel that you can be your natural self always, can speak out any thought you may have, no matter what it is. All that doesn't mean much to you. But to me—" She drew a long, deep breath. "You—a man—couldn't possibly know how delicious it is to a woman to be able to be her—her naked self! ... You're not listening. You don't hold me tightly. Are you shocked?"

"No," answered he with constraint. "I keep thinking of—of—that door."

She was silent, offended.

"I wasn't quite frank with you a moment ago."

"Already!" she sighed. Then, repentantly: "I know I'm silly. But it means so much to me to feel that we—you and I—can stand before each other, just as we are. Oh, I've hidden myself so long, Basil. Your love—the great temptation of it was that it meant freedom. If I were your wife, you'd expect all sorts of conventional things of me. If you were my husband, I'd feel and you'd feel we had to live up to standards and do customary things. As it is, our love's free—free!"

He was silent.

"Basil, don't you feel that way?"

"Yes, dear," he answered absently. "But—I must tell you. When I went out—a while ago to look, I saw Nanny on the porch."

Even in that dimness he saw the terror in her face. "On the porch!" she gasped. She sprang up. "Why didn't you tell me before?" she cried angrily.

"I—I thought it might alarm you foolishly."

"I'm not a hysterical fool. Please don't forget that—again."

"Courtney!"

"Oh, forgive me—my love." When they had embraced: "Yes—I must go—at once.... Why can't you come with me? Start as soon as you see I'm at the door. But you mustn't cross the lawn. You must go round by the shadows. It would be quite safe. You needn't go back to the shop."

"Impossible!"

She was silent, waiting for him to feel how hurt she was and to reassure her. But he stood aloof, and presently asked in a constrained voice, "How long will you be at your father's?"

"At my father's!" she exclaimed. "Why, I shall not go!"

"You must," he insisted. "You've made all the arrangements."

"You can send me away—*now*?"

"Please—dear. Don't be unreasonable. If you changed your plan everybody'd think it strange."

"Everybody—who?"

"Nanny, for instance."

"Nanny? Why should I care what Nanny thinks? My first scare was only—guilty conscience. Basil, why are you so queer—so absent and—distant? Tell me—just what it is in your mind?"

She rested her hands pleadingly on his shoulders and looked up at him. In her eyes, as in his, shone the fever of their delirium. He took her hands, kissed her. "Don't be foolish," he said, trying to laugh. "I guess I am a little bit unnerved."

But she was not satisfied. "Basil—do you regret?"

"Courtney! Courtney!" he pleaded. "That's the way to tear our happiness down, stone by stone, till nothing's left but ruins. You must not be suspicious." He patted her reassuringly on the shoulder with an air of possession. "Of course I love you, more than ever."

"You say it in a tone that—that sounds like superior to inferior." She sighed. "Is nothing in the world up to its promise? Here, I thought we'd be perfectly happy— two pariahs together—two lost souls—but accepting our punishment of secret shame and hypocrisy—accepting it gladly, as it was the price we had to pay for freedom and each other. And already, in the first hour, we're almost quarreling. It must not be, Basil."

"No, dearest," he cried. "And it will not be. We will be happy. Trust me. I'm unstrung—and maybe you, too. But you know I love you—more than I ever thought. And really you ought to go in the morning—really, dearest! You need stay only two days. You can come home the second day. Don't you see we must— must—must be careful? Now that there's something to conceal, we can't act any longer as we did."

She laid her clasped hand on her breast, looked wistfully up at him. "We can't ever be free and unafraid again, can we?" said she. "It isn't just one act of—of concealment—is it?—and freedom and openness afterwards. I see lies—and lies—and yet more lies—stretching away—away—until—" She shuddered, hid her face in his shoulder. "Oh, my love!"

"I'd tell all the lies in the world to have you." He embraced her almost roughly. "All—all! And care not a rap. You—you are my god and my morality. To love you, to have you, to keep you—that's all. The rest is trash."

"Yes—yes," echoed she feverishly. "The rest is trash. We've got the best. Love!"

"And we'll hold on to it—always!"

"Must I go in the morning, when life has just begun? How can I? No—no—don't answer. I know you're right. I'll go—and ... Good by!"

She flung her arms about him. He caught up her small, warm body with its soft curves and its radiations of vivid, perfumed life. Their lips clung together. They separated, laughed dizzily. She waved her arm and darted up the path. From the shadows he watched her cross the lawn, like some creation of the summer and the moonlight. In the doorway she paused, waved to him once more; the door closed. Then he, like a thief, sneaked along the retaining walls at the lake shore—now stooping to keep in the deep shadow, out of sight of anyone who might be watching from the house—now advancing erect with stealthy swiftness—until he was able to strike into the darkness of the path to the Smoke House.

Midway in undressing his eyes chanced upon her picture, framed and hanging opposite the foot of the bed—a large photograph, with Winchie, a tiny baby, against her shoulder, his fat check pressing upon hers. Basil stood before the picture, his expression a very human and moving mingling of awe and adoration and passion. Suddenly he remembered to whom that picture belonged. "But not she!" he said aloud defiantly. Nevertheless, he flushed, hung his head, switched off the light, and sought his bed. "How can I ever face him?" he muttered. Then: "She is mine! She never was really his. I take nothing that belongs to him. I take nothing she could give, or ever did give, to him."

He fell immediately into a sound sleep—the exhaustion of nerves so long on fierce tension. But about two in the morning he started up, listened. Yes, some one was moving beneath the window. He went to it, looked down. There was Courtney, swathed in a long, dark cloak. He thrust his feet into slippers, drew on a big dressing gown, descended, and opened the door. He stretched out his arms.

She flung herself against his breast. "I couldn't go without seeing you again," she panted. "After I left you, and got into bed, I began to think all sorts of dreadful things about you. You acted so strangely. And then I felt ashamed of myself, felt I must come and beg your pardon. And—and—here I am. Are you glad?"

His laugh was answer enough. He took her in his arms, carried her up to the sitting room, set her down on the sofa. "How light you are!" he cried. "But how strong—I've seen you swing Winchie to your shoulder as if he were nothing at all. Now—please—won't you let your hair down? There never was such hair as yours."

She sat up, let the cloak fall away. The moon was flooding the room. As she sat there, with eyes sparkling and small, sensitive face shy-bold, she looked as if she had sprung to mortal life from an old folk song about loreleis and nymphs and enchanted princesses. "You floated in on the moonbeams," he declared. "I'm afraid, if I don't shut the window, you'll flit away."

"That'd not stop me," laughed she. And she began to take her hair down. Just as it was about to unroll, she paused. "Wouldn't you like to take it down yourself?"

He went round behind her, drew out the hairpins one by one, fumbling softly, lingeringly for them, keeping them carefully. Her hair loosened, uncoiled, fell about her in a shimmering veil. "Oh, my love!" he cried. "My beautiful Courtney!" And he took the soft, perfumed veil in his hands, kissed it again and again, buried his face in it, wrapped her head and his together in it.

She laughed delightedly, then drew away, looking at him with mock severity. "And where, sir, did you learn how to make a woman so happy?"

"What things you *do* say!" he laughed, just a little bit scandalized. "I might ask the same question of you."

"And I can answer it—" with a mocking smile—"without evasion. Imagination. I've so often thought—and thought—and thought—what I would be to a man I freely loved—one I wasn't afraid of scandalizing. Oh, I know I shock you—for there's a great deal you've yet to learn about women—that they're human, just like men. But you'll learn—and then I think you'll see I'm good—for I am. I couldn't be bad—hate anyone—play mean tricks, say or do mean things. Don't you wish I were tall—wish there were more of me?"

"I couldn't live through it."

"And you really—really—love me?"

He held her tightly by the shoulders, gazed into her eyes. "So much that, if you were untrue to me, I'd kill you."

"Now, what made you think of that?"

"I don't know."

Thoughtfully: "I guess it is because I'm giving myself to you when I am—am— Now, there you go, shocked again."

He laughed recklessly. "Give me time," said he, "and I'll get used to it. You say you'd rather I showed just how I felt than locked it away and pretended."

"Yes—yes—a thousand times! I don't mind your being shocked—not really." With a queer little laugh, "I'm shocked myself. Somehow I seem to delight in shocking myself—and you. Loving you is—all sorts of pleasures and pains. I want them all!"

"All!" he echoed. "Yes—all!"

Midway in her embrace she stopped him, pushed him laughingly away with, "But you weren't quite frank a while ago."

"When?"

"There at the lake."

"Why do you think so?"

"Did you ever see one of those little toy spaniels—how they quiver and shiver all the time? I'm just as sensitive as that. You mustn't try to deceive me—ever! You mustn't say or act any of those hypocrisies of what some people call good taste, either. They're not necessary with me. They'd make me feel deceived. I might not confess I knew—and then—'The little rift within the lute.'"

"I guess I'll tell you," he said for the moment deeply impressed. "Yes, I will."

"Tell me everything—*every*thing. There mustn't be any concealment—anything to lie hid away in the depths of some dark closet to rot and rot and infect the whole house." She suddenly lowered her head; and, as the full meaning of her words, the meaning she had not foreseen, reached him, he, too, became ill at ease.

Presently he said: "I didn't want to frighten you needlessly. When I saw Nanny—she was—just going up the steps of the porch."

Courtney's eyes widened and her face blanched. "You think—" she began when she could find voice.

"I couldn't tell which direction she had come from," he replied. "But it's no matter. She couldn't know."

Courtney remembered the darkness—how grateful she had been for its friendly aid. "No," said she resolutely. "She couldn't know."

"Certainly not," echoed he, as if the idea that she could were absurd. "But it made me realize how careful we must be."

"Yes," replied she thoughtfully. "Yes." And she was clinging to him, was sobbing. "Oh, my love—my love—I don't care what comes, if only it does not separate us.... Look! Look!" she cried, pointing out into the sky. "Dawn! I must fly. Where *are* my slippers!"

He found them for her, put them on, bundled her into her cloak, picked her up, and hurried downstairs with her. "I'm not so little," said she. "It's because you're so big and strong. One kiss—quick!"

He kissed her—on the lips and, as she turned to go, again on the nape of the neck. "Day after to-morrow!" he cried.

"Yes, I'll come here at nine, rain or shine."

And she ran along the path. The moon had set; it was intensely dark. Arriving within sight of the house she stopped short. There were lights, upstairs and down, shadows of moving figures on the curtains. "God!" she ejaculated. "What *shall* I do!" And for the first time the great fear—the fear a woman has when she thinks she has lost her reputation—buried its talons in her throat and its beak in her heart. Do? Face it! She lifted her head high, gathered herself together, advanced boldly. As she entered the front door she ran into Nanny.

"What's the meaning of this?" she demanded. In the same instant her courage fled and she leaned faint against the wall. "Winchie!" she gasped. "Has something happened to him?"

Nanny was standing stiffly with eyes down—a sullen figure, accusing, contemptuous. But she answered respectfully enough if surlily: "Winchie missed you and came up and waked me and Mazie just now."

Down the stairs came the boy, sobbing, shouting, "Mamma! Mamma! I lost you."

Courtney caught him up, hugged him, kissed him. "You silly baby!" she cried, laughing. "What a fuss about nothing. Put out the lights, Nannie." Halfway up the stairs she hesitated. Would it be more natural to make an explanation or to say nothing? She decided it was best, more like her usual self, to say nothing. "Put out the lights and go to bed," she repeated.

# Chapter 12

She had said nine o'clock, but it was not quite half past eight, the next evening but one, when she appeared at the edge of the clearing. He was seated in the entrance to the upper story, his gaze fixed on the opening in the trees where the path emerged. At first glimpse of her in the long dark cloak, he flung away his cigarette and rushed toward her. He embraced her, then held her off as if to reassure himself that it was really she. "Do you still love me?" he asked. "Are you *sure*?"

The emerald eyes flashed up at him. Her face, revealed in the starlight, was gravely earnest and sweet. But beneath her calm, as beneath his, there was evidently still raging the hysteria that had whirled both clean out of the realm of sanity and sense—the fever that keeps whirling the soul it seizes from pinnacle to abyss and back again. "Ever since we separated," said she, "I've been imagining I was struggling to give up our love. But as the time for me to come got nearer and nearer, I realized what a fraud I was."

"Do you love me?"

"I am here."

They sat side by side in the entrance. "May I smoke?" he asked.

"Do." As he opened his cigarette case, "Let me have one."

"I didn't know you smoked."

"Oh—a little—at college. We girls used to do it, for the sensation of being devilish. Wouldn't you like me to smoke?"

"If you wish to."

"You don't approve?"

"Well—I don't exactly like for women to smoke or use slang. Those things seem sort of unsexing. Of course, it's only an idea."

She smiled indulgently, rolling the cigarette to loosen the tobacco, as Basil did, with a great air of being an old hand at it. "I'm afraid you're narrow."

"I guess I am."

"Gracious! What you must be thinking of me!"

As she said it, she gave that little audacious laugh of delight in her freedom to be frank. But he became grave, and it was with deep earnestness that he answered, "I love you."

She, too, was grave and thoughtful now. "What a difference that does make! Then everything—anything seems all right."

"And is!"

She put her arm through his. "Here, take your cigarette. I'll not distress you."

"No—do smoke."

"I'll confess the real reason. It makes such a nasty taste in my mouth."

He tossed his cigarette into the grass. His every gesture—and hers—betrayed what a strain they were undergoing, how deceptive was their appearance of sanity.

"Now, what did you do that for?" exclaimed she.

"I oughtn't to smoke when I'm going to kiss you."

She put her cigarette to his lips. "Please," she urged, "I like you to smoke. Don't you know a woman likes everything, even the unpleasant things, that make a man different from her? ... Smoke, and tell me what you've been doing. It's forty hours since we were together."

"I've been conscious of pretty nearly every one of them," said he. "I've done nothing but think of you."

"Sad thoughts?"

"Very. But I'll not do that again. What's the use, Courtney? We've got to have each other. What's the use of struggling against it?"

"I can't realize it—I can't," said she absently. "Last night—out at father's—I got up in the middle of the night and ran and looked at myself in the glass. And—" She paused.

"Yes?"

"I could look myself straight in the eyes and tell myself what I had been to you, and not feel like hiding. Is it that I'm not doing anything bad or that I'm so bad I don't know good from bad?"

"It's love," declared he gloomily.

"I can look back now and see that from the beginning—from the day I saw you cared—I've been coming straight to you. I was lying to myself."

"I, too," he confessed. "Courtney, we've been—and are—in the clutch of a force that's stronger than we."

"I—don't—know," said she slowly. Then, with her arms round his neck, "and I don't care. If conscience tolls its ugly bell, I'll shout 'Love! Love!' so loud that it'll be drowned. I must have love—I will have love. And how can I help loving you, who are so altogether wonderful in every way? You've only kissed me once since I came."

"Twice."

"And what's twice?"

For answer he gathered her into his arms, carried her up to the sitting room. With all of her within his arms, he sat in the big armchair. "Now!" he exclaimed. "We'll be happy!"

"Yes. Oh, *what* a scare when I was here before!"

She sat up and told him about Winchie's raising the hue and cry for her. He listened with a somber countenance. When she had, finished he said, "And where's Winchie now!"

"In bed—asleep."

"But—if he wakes!"

"Why, he'll lie perfectly quiet till he sleeps again. I told him never to repeat that escapade."

"But he may get frightened——"

"You forget, sir," said she smilingly, "he's my child. He could not be afraid.... What a mournful face!"

"I'm horribly jealous of him."

"If Winchie didn't keep us apart, he never could push us apart now."

"I'm very selfish," he said despondently. "I want all—all!"

"Here we are—sad again."

He sighed. "And in a few minutes you'll have to go."

"Why?"

"You can't stay away from the house. Something might happen."

"Croak! Croak!"

He passed his hand impatiently over his face. "I'm a fool!" he exclaimed. "I must learn to be content with what I have—when it's so much—so vastly more than I ever dared hope—or—" He stared out into the darkness. The ducks among the reeds close inshore were quacking discontented forebodings of rain. "I trifle with my good fortune."

"What's the matter, dear?" she asked, her cheek against his.

"Nothing. Nothing."

"What have you been thinking while I was away? ... Look at me, Basil."

"It seems to me I can't ever look—anyone in the face again."

She understood who "anyone" was. She pressed closer to him, said caressingly: "Except me. You can always look at me, and I at you. And what more do we want?"

He did not echo her tender reckless laugh, with its threat of a storm of hysterical tears. "You have good excuse for what you've done. But there's no excuse for me."

She seemed to be shrinking within herself. He gently put her on the arm of the chair, went to the window, stood there with his back to her. "The truth is, I've been in hell since you left, Courtney—a hell of remorse!"

"Remorse! Excuse!" Her bosom heaved; her eyes flashed. "Oh, you men! What hypocrites you are! ... Tell me, do you wish to give me up?"

He faced her. "I cannot give you up," was his inflexible reply.

"Then dismiss all these gloomy ideas," urged she. "Excuse? You think I have the excuse of—of his indifference, of his tyranny and bad temper—of his——"

"For God's sake, Courtney, *don't* say those things!"

"I think them—you think them. Why not say them?"

"Yes—you are right. I am a hypocrite."

"How easily we hurt each other," she sighed. Then, "But how easily it heals, too." She went on: "We were talking of excuses. Anyone can find an excuse for anything. Only weak people look for excuses." She elevated her head proudly. "I want no excuse for what I did, for what I'm doing. I need no excuse. Do I not own my heart, my self? I have the right of my youth, of my love. Isn't that enough?"

"The right of our love!" he exclaimed, as gay and confident as he had been depressed and doubtful. "We're wasting time. Let's talk and think only of love." And he drew her down into the chair, into his arms. "Courtney—when he does come—promise me you will not—will not——"

There he halted, for the wave that passed over her as she lay in his arms told him that she understood. "You know I will not," she said. "I belong to *you*, now."

"But he may——"

She laid her fingers on his lips. "Trust me," she said. "I've planned it all. Only, that's the one thing we mustn't ever talk about." She laughed, with desperate straining to be audacious. "There is honor, even in the dishonorable."

"You—dishonorable? I, perhaps—yes, certainly. But you—you belong to yourself. It is I who will play the part of dishonor. You can be as cold and distant as you like. I must smile and pretend to be a friend." He shrugged his shoulders, laughed unpleasantly.

"That's manly!" exclaimed she, nerves instantly unstrung.

"What can you expect of—of *me*?" he replied, so down that she straightway relented.

"Let's drop this subject, dear," she pleaded. "Let's never speak of it again—and think of it as little as possible. It's one of the conditions of our life. We will admit it—and ignore it."

"How can we drop a subject that crops out, comes to the tips of our tongues, every time we look at each other? But be patient, dear. I shall grow hardened——"

"Oh, but you must not, Basil!" she cried in dismay. "*We* must not. That's our danger, and we must fight it.... Isn't it pitiful! If we were two coarse people, mere animals, merely the ordinary man and woman, why, we'd be happy and never give remorse a thought."

"If we suffer more, we enjoy more," said he, clasping her as if some power had tried to snatch her away. "When I feel ashamed, Courtney, all I have to do is to remember your hair, to feel again its soft splendor on my face, between my fingers—and I am delirious."

"Love—always love!" she murmured. "No price too great to pay for it."

They heard steps—stealthy steps—upon the walk, just under the bedroom window. "Yes, yes, I hear," he whispered, as in the darkness she clutched his arm. He went to the open window, she sitting up, rigid, wide-eyed, with bated breath. Keeping in the shadow, he glanced down. He saw a man, half hidden in the shrubbery. A moment and his eyes focused so that he saw the outline of the man's face, the angle of his head—saw that the man was peering up toward that very window. He went softly back to her. "Go into the sitting room," he said. "I think it's one of those prowlers."

"Sh-h!" she warned. "Listen— On the stairs."

Both stopped breathing and listened. It was the faintest of sounds, but unmistakable. Yes, it was a robber. He was ascending the stairway—slowly, silently, steadily, up and up, step by step. Now they would miss the sound altogether; then it would come again—nearer, softer. Their hands were clasped—were like ice, but without a tremor.

"How did he get in?" she breathed.

"Don't you remember? I left the outside door unlocked—wide open."

"Sh-h!"

"Go back into the sitting room," he whispered.

"No—I stay here with you."

The awful sound, so faint, so relentless, was in the hall. "Go!" he commanded. "You'd be in my way, dear. If I need you, I'll call."

She saw that he was right—that at least he must not feel hampered. She pressed his hand, glided into the sitting room. Suddenly she almost cried out. "Is the bedroom door locked?" she called in a hoarse undertone.

He made a silent dash for it, to lock it. Too late. It opened. He could see nothing in the black hall. He made a forward leap, right hand clinched, left hand open and ready to inclose a throat. His fist thrust past the man's head, but his left fingers closed upon the throat, and his weight bore the man to the floor. But the prowler was not taken wholly by surprise. Basil instantly realized how fortunate it was that he had got the initial advantage. The two grappled; a short, sharp struggle and Gallatin felt the form under him relax. He took an even stronger hold on the throat, planted his knee squarely in the chest. "I've got him!" he cried to Courtney. "Go! Go!"

But he triumphed too soon. With a tremendous effort the prowler tore Gallatin's fingers from his throat. "Good God, Gallatin—is it *you*?" he gasped.

"Vaughan!"

Gallatin dropped all to pieces. But Courtney was instantly herself—and more. On went the lights, and she burst out laughing. Gallatin rose, staggered over to the window seat. Vaughan, not without difficulty, picked himself up from the floor, gazed savagely from Gallatin to his wife. She kept on laughing, more and more wildly, laughed until she fell into a chair, sat there laughing, with the tears rolling down her cheeks. "Was ever anything so ridiculous!" she gasped. And she looked from one to the other, and went off again.

Vaughan, straightening his collar and coat and waistcoat, appealed to Gallatin. "What's the meaning of this?" he demanded.

By way of reply Gallatin stared at him, as if debating whether or not to renew the attack.

"What does this mean, Courtney?" Vaughan said to her sharply.

"That's what *we'd* like to know," replied she.

"Why did Gallatin——"

"Serves you right," interrupted Courtney. "Why did you come prowling round here? Why didn't you go home?"

Vaughan looked sheepish. "Well, I wanted to make sure everything was all right here."

Courtney smiled with resentment in her raillery. "You were more anxious about your workshop than about your wife and child."

Vaughan reddened. "Oh, I knew everything was all right at the house," he stammered. His glance fell upon the tumbled bed. "Why!" he exclaimed. "Some one's living here!"

Gallatin, startled, was standing up with his hands clinched. But she had no fear. She did not feel guilty toward this man, who was nothing real to her; and she knew enough about him to know that his absolute belief that good women were good, and could not stray even in thought, made it impossible to tax his credulity. All that was necessary was boldness. "Mr. Gallatin is living here," said she composedly.

"Gallatin!" exclaimed Vaughan. "Why, I locked the whole place up." He wheeled on Basil. "How did you get in here?" he asked. "Didn't I make it plain to you from the outset—didn't we have a distinct understanding——"

"Richard!" interrupted Courtney sharply. "Mr. Gallatin is here because I sent him here."

Richard concentrated his angry attention upon her. "You! What right had you———"

"You will not address me in that tone," said she haughtily. "You come back home, like a thief in the night. You give me a fright. You half kill Mr. Gallatin, and then you begin to quarrel. I repeat, Mr. Gallatin is here because I sent him."

"I thought it best to live here while you were away," said Gallatin stiffly. He did not wish to throw upon Courtney the whole burden, yet he hardly dared speak, as he could not see how she hoped to extricate herself and him. In his guilt, in his ignorance of such a character as Richard's, he was amazed at her having hope. He thought her courage superhuman.

Vaughan glanced, half amused, half disdainful, from one to the other. "Are you two still disliking each other? I had forgotten that."

"You are mistaken," said Gallatin. "I do not dislike Mrs. Vaughan."

But Vaughan did not hear. "What on earth—" he suddenly ejaculated, staring at Gallatin, then at Courtney—"What on earth were you two doing here in the dark?"

Gallatin grew white as chalk. But Vaughan was looking at Courtney. "We weren't in the dark," said she, with never a tremor of eye or voice. "We were in the sitting room." As she spoke she threw open the door between the two rooms. Gallatin gazed into the sitting room like a man seeing a miracle. The lights there were all bright. The instant she had heard her husband's outcry, she had turned on the lights in both rooms, the buttons being on either side of the same wall just beyond the door frame; and she had closed the sitting-room door before the two rose from the floor.

"Come in here," she said, leading the way. "I kept getting more and more afraid at the house," she went on in rapid, easy explanation. "It was very lonesome—there were several robberies in the neighborhood—and Nanny and Lizzie and Mazie sleep so far away from my rooms. I took Winchie and went home for a couple of days, but it wasn't convenient for me to stay there—and so dull! I came back to-night, and strolled down here after dinner to make my peace with Basil—" Here she made a mocking bow to him—"and to ask him to please come up and guard the house. How well you're looking, Richard!"

"I do feel bang up," said Vaughan, "except here—" He touched his throat where Gallatin's fingers had closed in. "The trip was just what I needed. I went to a specialist in New York, and I serve notice on both of you that I've turned over a new leaf. I'll take regular exercise again—and stop grinding away all day and all evening. The great discovery of the fuel that will make it as cheap to be warm as to be cold can wait. Perhaps it'll come the sooner if I keep in condition."

"That's sensible," said Courtney. "And you must live at home, and let Mr. Gallatin stay on here."

"It's good advice. I'll take it," assented Vaughan promptly. "Being here tempts me to work when I ought to be resting." He threw a good-humored look at Gallatin. "I guess you're not likely to succumb to that temptation, old man."

"Not I," said Basil, with the first sickly hint of a smile.

"Gad, it's good to be home!" Vaughan was gazing at Courtney now, in his eyes the proprietorial look, bold, amorous. "She's looking well—eh—Gallatin?"

Basil did not answer. He was glowering at Vaughan, and biting his lip, and his fingers were twitching.

Courtney rose. "Let's all go up to the house," proposed she: "You'll come, won't you, Mr.—beg pardon—Basil?"

Gallatin stared coldly at her. Her "superhuman courage" now seemed sheer brazenness to him. "Thanks—no," said he in a suffocating voice.

"Hope I didn't damage you, Gallatin," said Vaughan with the rather careless solicitude of man for man.

"Not in the least," replied Gallatin curtly.

"Oh, come now, old man," cried Richard. "Look at my throat." He inspected it himself in the mirror ruefully. "If I can forgive you, you ought to forgive me. Come along, Courtney."

He took her by the arm, smiling at her, she mustering a return smile. Basil was looking intently at her, with an expression of cold fury. When he caught her eye he sneered. She, already at the breaking pitch, could not endure that contempt. She looked piteously at him, gave a low cry, sank upon the sofa, fell over in a dead faint.

Basil gazed stupidly at her. Vaughan dashed into the bath room, reappeared with a wet towel, rubbed her temples and her wrists with it. She opened her eyes, looked round—saw Basil. "Take me away!" she sobbed. "Take me away!"

Her husband gathered her into his arms as if she were a tired child. "Good night, Gallatin. See you in the morning," he said, and strode out with her.

Gallatin fell into one of those futile rages that are the steam of the strife between a man's desire and his courage. "It's my love for her," he assured himself, "that keeps me from following him and taking her from him." He found small comfort in this, however; for, he suspected it was only part—a minor part—of a truth, the rest of which was altogether to his discredit. He sat, he leaned, he stood at the bedroom window overlooking the path. Again and again he fancied he saw her, a new and deeper shadow in the shadows beneath the trees. Whenever the wind stirred a bush there, his fanciful hope made it her cloak. He knew it was impossible for her to return; but he could not give up. He did not leave the window until dawn. Then, he lay on the bed, exhausted, wretched, burning with hate for Richard, with rage against her, with contempt for himself.

# Chapter 13

Toward eight o'clock came Vaughan, in high spirits. Basil, stiff and sore, was still lying on the bed.

"Sure you don't want breakfast?" said Richard. Then, getting a view of his partner's face: "You *are* a sight! I beg pardon, old man. I've got a few marks, myself. But— *You* must have the doctor."

"No, thanks," was Basil's surly answer. "I'm all right."

"But you ought to do something for that eye—and that cheek. I sure did give you some hard punches." As this sounded as if it were—and was—not without a certain pride, he added: "The worst you gave me are hidden by my clothes—except these finger marks. What a stupid thing for me to do! And poor Courtney's quite done up this morning. Really, old man, you'd better let me send for the doctor."

"I'll telephone for him," said Basil. "I want to be left alone."

"Beg pardon. I've done nothing but apologize ever since I got home. Well, I'll go to work. Don't bother to come down to-day. I shan't need you."

Gallatin muttered "Selfish beast," as soon as Dick was clear of the room. And it was undeniable that Dick's pretense of sympathy had been rather more offhand than such pretenses usually are. He had never had to conciliate and cultivate his fellow beings in getting a living, and had been brought up indulgently by Colonel 'Kill and Eudosia. Thus he was candid in his selfishness, often appeared worse than would a man who was in reality more selfish, but was through fear or training, less self-revealing. However, Basil was not one with the right in any circumstances to be censorious of such undiplomatic conduct; for he, too, had been born and bred to wealth and security, and had been "spoiled" by a worshipful family.

Not for a week did he dare show his face. Dick called twice a day—did all the talking—always about the chemistry into which he had plunged with freshened energy and enthusiasm. Usually he apologized for Courtney's not coming—"She still feels weak and upset," he would say, "and wants me to make her excuses. I tell her you'd refuse to see her even if she could come."

When Basil's face and complexion were once more about normal, he waited until Richard was at work downstairs, then adventured the path to the house. He found Courtney in the sitting room, in a négligée, sewing; Winchie was building a lofty house of blocks on the veranda just outside for her to admire. He scowled at Winchie; Winchie scowled at him and, when his back was turned, made a face at him. "Good morning, Mrs. Vaughan," said he coldly. "I've come to pack my traps." In a lower tone that was menacing, he added, "I want to see you."

She laid aside her sewing, a strained expression in the eyes that shone wistfully in her pallid face. The boy dropped the block he was putting into place and stood up. "Go on with the house, Winchie," said she. Then to Basil, "You may come right upstairs."

She preceded him into the study on the left of the upper hall—the study that had been his, and was now Richard's. He, following, closed the door, advanced toward her with lowering brow and angry eyes.

"It's very imprudent to close the door," said she, calmly returning his gaze. "Nanny is at work across the hall."

"Did you break your promise to me that night?" he demanded.

"I'll answer no question—not even from you, Basil—when it's in that tone."

"First you want me to open the door, so that I can't speak out," sneered he. "Now you evade.... You admit your degradation. I knew why you were keeping away from me."

"That was not my reason," she stammered, with lowered head.

"You lie! You are doubly false. You have no shame. Now I understand why you said those bold things—why you acted so free—as no innocent woman could. You—expert!"

Her eyes were milky like a tortured sea; her face became ghastly; she trembled so that she had to steady herself at the back of a chair. "Basil!" she exclaimed. "No, it's not you. What we've suffered since he came has driven you mad. It has almost crazed me."

"Answer me!" he commanded fiercely. "Did you or did you not break your promise to me?"

Suddenly she drew herself up, and with the sad dignity of guilt that has been expiated she said: "I ask you to pity me." And she stood there, pale and haggard, a statue of wretchedness.

His fury could not hold against that spectacle—and she, the proud, asking for pity! "It's I who should be ashamed," he cried. "How I have suffered! What a coward—what a cur I am!"

She rushed to him. "Oh, my love! What we've been suffering has only made you dearer to me, dearer than ever! There's no bond like suffering."

He was about to take her outstretched hands when suspicion flamed into his eyes again. "How easily you twist me round your finger!" he said roughly. "Now, there's your making me move down to the shop. Why should you want to get me out of the house when, if I were here, we could see each other all the time?"

She showed no resentment, felt none. "It's natural you should suspect me," said she. "I'd suspect you in the same circumstances. I see now how absurd it was to dream of happiness founded on lies. No happiness for us—not even joy now and then. If we didn't love each other, we might be happy. But we do love, and misery is all we can expect. I'll tell you why I wanted you down there." She paused, went on with veiled eyes and bright red in her cheeks. "As I said to you, even dishonor has its honor. I didn't want us meeting here—with my boy—and his—so near."

Basil looked as if he were about to sink down under his shame and self-contempt. "Forgive me. What a hound I am!" he muttered.

"As for my free actions and free speech——"

"Courtney!" he begged, seizing her hands. "Don't speak of that."

"I must explain," she insisted gently, freeing herself. "I'll always explain everything to you. As I told you, I wanted to be free with you, perfectly free. So I said and did the things any woman who loved would think and feel, but most women hold back for fear of spoiling a lover's ideal. I didn't want you to idealize me, but to love me just as I was, just for what I am."

"And I do—I do!" he cried, trying to draw her into his arms.

"Yes, you do, I believe," answered she, insistently drawing back. "I know you truly love, and you know I truly love. I know you are a man any woman would be proud to have love her, and you know I'm not a low or a bad woman. Yet, see how it turns out.... Basil, we must give it up!"

"Give it up!" He was bristling with suspicion at once.

"You must go away."

He laughed scornfully. "That is your kind, considerate way of dismissing me. What vanity! I shall suffer no more than you."

"Not so much," she answered sadly.

"I shall go away and marry."

"You can't make me jealous now, Basil. Not after what you've been to me. I mean just what I say. You must go, and I'll try to be to my husband all a wife should be. If you'd been through what I've been through—that night and since— you'd understand. Basil, do you remember how I lied, how I laughed and cheated— like an 'expert,' as you say. Oh, you must have despised me! If you had done what I did, had done it as fluently, I'd have loathed you."

"And what about me? Didn't I stand there, a contemptible coward, and let him take you away?"

"What else could you have done?"

"Shown myself a man!"

"And ruined me—and my child? Oh, no, dear. You love me too well for that." She startled, listened. "He's coming," she warned, flying to the door. She opened it softly to its full width, advanced composedly into the hall, saying in her usual voice, "Then Jimmie'll take your things down about four o'clock."

Richard, on his way up, had reached the head of the stairs. "Oh!" he exclaimed. "Here you are! I asked Winchie where you were, and he said he didn't know. So I've been hunting all over the place for you. I want you to take a walk with me."

"Certainly," said she tranquilly. "I'm talking business with Basil. Go down and help Winchie finish his house, and we'll take him along. I'll come in a few minutes."

"All right!" said Dick cheerfully. He shouted out, "Hey, Gallatin, how's your grouch?" and descended the stairs, laughing as he went.

As she reëntered the sitting room, she said, with the quietness of the emotions that are too deep and too terrible for tumult, "Am I not 'expert'? How long do you think we could keep this sort of thing up without becoming—I tell you, Basil, looking within myself as I've lain in the dark, I've realized it takes decent people— people with nerves and imaginations and sense of right and wrong—to become frightful, if they once get on the down grade. Did you hear what he said about Winchie?"

"Yes," muttered Basil. He was at the desk, his elbows on it, his hands supporting his head.

"Winchie knew where I was. Why did he lie to his father? Already a liar!"

"I must go. You are right— But, Courtney—you must get a divorce."

"I've thought of that. On what ground? And how can I leave him alone—take Winchie away from him?"

"You must get a divorce."

"I think so, too," assented she. "But I will not lie to do it. I'm done with lies. I'll tell him."

"No—let's go to him together." Basil's face lighted up, his manner became enthusiastic. He thought he saw a way to redeem his manhood put in pawn for this sin so dear yet so detestable. "Together!" he exclaimed. "He is generous and broadminded."

She shook her head. "Men are not generous and broadminded where women are concerned—the women they look on as theirs."

He colored and glanced guiltily at her. But it was plain that she had not in mind his own exhibition of the male attitude toward the female. His memory of it helped him to appreciate the folly of his proposal. But he would not give in at once. "I'd not suggest it, if he really loved you. But——"

"If he really loved me, he'd have felt the truth long ago. If he really loved me, he'd wish me to be happy—would give me up. But then—if he had really loved me, none of this would ever have happened. No, Basil, it's because he doesn't love me, because it's only passion that takes and gives nothing, that uses and doesn't think or care about the feelings of its creature——"

Basil, horror-stricken by this bald candor, ashamed for her, stopped her. "Let's not talk about it," he pleaded. "As for the divorce, I leave it to you. You know best how to deal with him."

His manner and its cause had not escaped her, with nerves keyed up to the snapping point. Once again he had raised in her heart the dread lest their love would not mean the perfect frankness, the perfect oneness of which she had dreamed. Did a man always demand and compel concealment and pretense in the woman? But she thrust out the doubt. "I'll do what seems best," she said to him, avoiding his eyes and speaking with constraint. "I don't know Richard very well. You see, we never got acquainted. He's like most men. They don't want the woman, but only the outside.... He's so wrapped up in his work that I think I can free myself."

He took her hands, gazed into her eyes. "Yes," he said, "you do love me. You feel that we belong to each other, just as I do. So when I'm away I'll know you are coming—as soon as you can."

"As soon as I can," she replied. And the expression of her eyes, meeting his steadfastly, and the deep notes in her sweet voice thrilled him with a new sense of her love and of her constancy. This woman had not given in whim; she would not change in whim.

"I will go—to-morrow," he said. "The sooner I go, the sooner I shall have you. Will you come to-night to say good-by?"

"Don't ask it, dear. I mustn't ever again—until I'm free."

"In the summer house, then. For a few minutes. We can't part like this."

"Yes, I'll come."

Along the hall from the foot of the stairs sounded Richard's imperious, impatient voice. "I say, Courtney! Do hurry!"

"I can't go for a walk with him now," she said, half to herself. "I'll make some excuse." She looked at Basil, he at her. In their eyes was a sadness beyond words and tears. And what would it be when he was really gone? "I mustn't linger here—I mustn't!" she cried. "And don't come near me when he's around. I can't control myself."

They clung together for an instant, then she fled.

She made vague household matters her excuse for not taking the walk. She did not see Richard alone until late that afternoon. She was in her and Winchie's big bathroom, which she also used as a dressing room. As she sat at the dressing table there, in petticoat and corset cover, doing her finger nails, he walked in. "May I come?" said he, already in the middle of the room.

She glanced at him, or, rather, in his direction, by way of the mirror and went on with her polishing. But she was not resentful of the scant courtesy of this intrusion. In the beginning of their married life she, through love, had confirmed him in his life-long habit of considering only himself and of expecting himself to be considered first. Now, indifference was making her as compliant as love had made her. And it was just as well. An attempt to assert herself would have seemed to him a revolt which pride and duty made it imperative for him to put down. The man a woman has spoiled through love, or the woman a man has spoiled, must be born again to be got back within bounds.

"You don't ask how I happen to be home so early—nearly an hour before supper," said he.

"It *is* early," replied she absently.

"I've made up my mind not to kill myself with work and no exercise, and to give more time to my family. I had a chance to look at myself—at my way of life—from the outside while I was in the East. And I'm going to try to live a more human life, though it'll not be easy to work less, when Gallatin's leaving me."

Until he spoke Gallatin's name she had not heard a word. We are all surrounded at all times in our customary haunts by a multitude of unchanging objects, animate and inanimate. We become practically unconscious of them so long as they maintain the same relative position toward us. We notice only changes, only those changes that are radical. Richard had long been to Courtney a mere familiar part of her environment—as she of his. She could look at him without seeing him, could answer him without having really heard. She could submit to his caresses without any sense of them. This unconsciousness was not deliberate; it was far deeper, it was habitual. At Gallatin's name, however, she began to listen.

"Yes, he's going," said Richard.

She inspected the nail of her right little finger. "Is he?" she asked, head on one side critically and emery slip poised.

"For good. And I'm not sorry. He's of less and less use to me at the laboratory. His mind isn't on it." There Richard laughed.

"I thought you felt you couldn't get on without him," said she, searching in a box for an orange-wood stick.

"That was some time ago. I suppose you're glad he's going."

"Why?"

"I know you don't like him. You've been very good about it, and I appreciate your being polite to him. But I can see that you dislike him."

She glanced in the mirror, arranged a stray of hair. "You are mistaken."

"No, I'm not. You've got the good woman's instinct to please her husband, and you think you've conquered your dislike. But you haven't."

"How you understand women," said she placidly. "But then there isn't much to understand about a woman—a good woman."

"Oh, you underestimate yourself," said he generously. "You're a very clever little lady—in your own charming feminine way. I often admire it."

A ghost of a smile flitted about her lips; but she seemed more intent upon her nails than upon his half-absent compliment.

"To confess the honest truth," he went on, "I've never liked Gallatin myself. I know he's a good sort— But— Well, he has no depth. He has a stock of education and a stock of manners, just as he has a stock of clothes. But it's all of some one else's make; nothing of his own, except a pleasant, amiable disposition. And he lacks purpose. However, all these things—especially lack of purpose—would only recommend him to a woman. Women are so frivolously constituted that purpose is a bore to them."

"Any more of a bore than it is to most men?" inquired Courtney.

Vaughan laughed acknowledgment. "Anyhow, I couldn't warm up to him. He's going, but he keeps his partnership—at least, for the present."

"Has he gone?"

"Of course not! He'd hardly be so rude as not to say good-by to you. Do you know why I think he's going?"

"Didn't he tell you?"

"He says a business letter came at noon to-day. And no doubt it had something to do with it. But mere business would hardly take him off in such a rush. At first I thought it was a hurry call from some idle female for him to come and amuse her. All bachelors get them, and Gallatin's just the sort of gander to respond. But on second thought I suspected he's flying because he's in love with you."

Courtney, conscious that his eyes were on her face, smiled.

"It's natural that you, being a good woman, shouldn't notice it."

"Women sometimes think a man's in love with them when he isn't," said she. "But the woman never lived—good, bad, or both—who didn't know when a man was in love with her."

"Well, I may be mistaken. But he had a queer way of acting. Why, only this morning he was lowering at me like a demon." Vaughan laughed. "Poor Gallatin. But he'll pull through all right."

"No doubt," said Courtney.

"Sometimes—now and then—a man or woman in love, and staying in some dull place, where there's nothing to do but brood, does go under, with love one among the contributing causes," pursued Richard. "But not a city person. And Gallatin's going to New York." Something in her expression made him hasten to say: "Now, please don't get angry. I apologize. I admit my joking was somewhat coarse. Naturally it grated on your modesty. Really, I was only joking. I know he's going for business reasons. Then, too, he has a grouch for me because of the fearful punch I gave him. No, he—any man who has led a free life as long as he has—could no more appreciate a good woman—a woman like you than—than—a drunkard could appreciate a glass of pure, clear, sparkling spring water."

Courtney gathered her manicure set together, swept it noisily into the drawer. "Go out, and let me finish dressing," said she in a low voice between her set teeth.

And he departed, saying: "What a relief it'll be to have Gallatin off the place—to have it to ourselves again."

She sat motionless with her eyes down. Presently she lifted them, saw her reflection in the mirror. She gazed in horror. She had relaxed the instant he left her alone, and now all her anguish was in her features. "A little more of this," said she, "and I'd be an old woman." She passed her hands over her face, looked into her eyes. "Spring water" flashed to her mind. Her eyes wavered and sank; her skin burned. But her hungry heart clamored defiantly.

When she reached the dining room her husband and Basil and Winchie were already at the supper table. As they rose, Basil did not lift his eyes; her husband gave her a glance of greeting. But Richard, the married man of five years, did not really see her face as it then was, but the face that had long been fixed in his mind as hers. To have seen her as she was, he would have had to be startled out of matrimonial myopia by some shock. There was no arresting change flaunted in Courtney's features; youth has no wrinkles and hollows in which the shadows of emotion can gather thick and linger. She simply looked tired and not well. Her eyes were veiled; but in her skin there was a lack of the ruddy tinge beneath the bronze, and in her hair, which was with her an unfailing index to health or to spirits, there was a suggestion of the lifelessness that is in the last wan autumn leaves the dreary winds of November spurn. In tones that seemed to them more unnatural than they were, she and Basil exchanged the commonplaces necessary on such an occasion. Winchie watched her sympathetically. Presently he dropped down from his chair, came round to her. He put his arm about her neck, drew her head toward him, kissed her tenderly, and whispered, "Mamma is sick."

She kissed him, whispered: "Yes, dear, but you mustn't say anything."

Winchie went back to his place. The conversation was wholly between the two men, the subject being, of course, chemistry. After supper Courtney pleaded a headache and, having uttered the formulas prescribed for the parting and having heard from him the formulas embodying his part in such an exchange, withdrew. Instead of being agitated, she was in truth as calm as she seemed outwardly—and numb. She saw Winchie to bed, occupied herself mechanically for an hour, then sat at one of the windows of her front room looking out toward the lake. When she thought at all, it was of trifles; most of the time, during those two hours of waiting, she did not think, but listened to the beating of her blood as it made the ringing in the ears that climaxes the oppression of an intense silence.

At length Richard came up. He glanced in at her. "How's the headache?" he inquired, laying a caressing hand on her shoulder.

She moved; his hand fell away. "No better," replied she. "Good night."

"You'll feel all right in the morning," he said. He kissed her crown of hair and departed toward his own rooms—those that had been Basil's.

She heard him stirring about, first in his study just across the hall, then in his bedroom. Half an hour, and she went on the balcony, to the corner of the house, to see if his lights still showed. All his windows were dark. She returned, listened at his door. No sound. She stole down the stairs, unlatched the lake-front door, went out. She strolled across the lawn, in full view—for the moon was rising. At the edge of the shadows made by the bushes round the summer house, she halted.

"Basil!" she called softly.

He came from the summer house and stood before her. "It's safer to stay here," she said. "We can watch the house."

He made no protest. He took her hands, drew her to his breast. Never before had he touched her without feeling the glow and surge of passion; now he had no sense of her physical beauty, of her physical charm, only sense of the being he loved.

"Forgive me the horrible things I said, Courtney," he murmured. "It wasn't I that was speaking. It was the beginnings of what I was fast becoming."

"I know, I know," she answered. "Kiss me, dear."

Their lips met in a caress of tenderness. When she spoke again she said: "Dear love, I never felt before how much you care."

"I never realized before. I'm beginning to realize. You won't be long about arranging the divorce?"

"You must not get impatient—or misunderstand—if I'm longer than you expect."

"I'll not misunderstand."

"There's Winchie, you know. I must have Winchie."

"Yes, indeed. You'll accomplish it," he said confidently. "Be careful not to tell him too much. Even if he doesn't really love you, there's his vanity. And that's often stronger in a man than anything else."

"I'll not forget what's at stake.... He suspects that you love me."

"I was afraid so, and this evening I told him I was engaged. He looked astounded."

"I can tell him that I love you, and he will think— No—no—what am I saying? Lies, always lies! ... I'll do the best I can, Basil."

"I know you will."

"You see now I was right in feeling you must go?"

"I felt it, Courtney, the moment we three stood together there in my room—though I wouldn't admit it to myself. If I stayed, there'd be a crime, or a scandal that'd spatter you with mud and brand you with shame. It simply could not be otherwise."

"I haven't told you the real deep-down reason why I felt you must go."

"No," he said. "Your real reason was the same as mine."

"Because it was all so vulgar and—and cheap?"

"Cheap—that's it!" he exclaimed. "Cheap!"

"I could stand it," she went on, "to commit and to have you commit, big, bold sins, scarlet and black. I might even glory in it. I wasn't a bit ashamed that first night. I think I even got a sort of joy out of defying all I'd been brought up to believe was moral and right and lady-like. But— Not when we stood there, like two caught sneak thieves."

"That was it, Courtney," eagerly assented he. And he went on, in a tone in which a less love-blinded woman might have detected an accent of repentance for masculine thoughts of disrespect: "No wonder I love you! How happy we shall be, when you're free. How good and pure you are—and innocent. It needn't be long—in this State—need it?"

"I think not," she laughed. "Being a judge's daughter, I ought to know. But I don't."

"Look there!" he exclaimed, gazing toward the house.

She turned, saw a figure at the east corner of the house, apparently looking toward where they were standing. The figure moved. "Nanny," she said under her breath. "I must go."

He caught her to his breast; for an instant they clung together, then with a last lingering handclasp, she left him, to emerge from the deep shadow of the trees and stroll back across the lawn. Presently she pretended to catch sight of Nanny, halted, changed her course, went toward her. "What is it, Nanny?" she asked.

Nanny turned without a word, started to go back toward her kitchen.

"Nanny!" said she sharply.

The old woman stopped, turned.

"What do you mean by not answering me when I speak to you?"

"I didn't know as you expected an answer," replied Nanny, sullen and cowed, but insolent underneath.

"I asked you what you were doing here?"

The two women looked straight into each other's eyes. "I just came out to get a breath of air—like you," said Nanny. "I don't see as there's any harm in that."

"Certainly not," said Courtney. And she resumed her stroll, back and forth across the lawn for three quarters of an hour.

She did not come down to breakfast. About nine o'clock Richard, at the Smoke House, called her on the telephone.

"Gallatin cleared out on the midnight express," said he. "Now, what do you think of that?"

"Why?"

"He left a note saying good-by and explaining that he found he could make better time."

"Well?"

"Don't you think it a little queer?"

"No."

"Anyhow, he's gone. I feel better already. Don't you?"

"I can't say I do."

"Well—I'll see you at dinner."

"Yes—good-by."

She returned to her sitting room, all in a glow. Basil had gone because he, sensitive and honorable, wished to spare himself the hypocrisy of a farewell handshake with Richard—"and to end the suspense," she added. "The suspense!" And she struck her hands against her throbbing temples.

A few days and there came from New York a crate of orchids, with only his card. "That's what I call decent and very handsome," declared Vaughan, roused to enthusiasm by this attention. "I must say I rather miss Basil, now that he's really gone. Don't you?"

"Yes," said Courtney.

"Which means no. Don't even these orchids soften your heart? Think how he used to let you work him. Oh, women! women! Orchids cost a lot of money, don't they?"

"Some kinds."

"When you write thanking him, do put cordiality and friendliness into the note."

"Very well."

She sent eighteen closely written pages—a line about the orchids, the rest an outpouring of love and longing—a sad letter, yet hopeful—and ending with the injunction that it be left unanswered. "You must not write until you hear from me," she said. "And that will be soon—soon, my love, my Basil!"

Next day Dick asked, "Have you thanked Basil for those flowers?"

"Certainly."

"I wish you had let me see the letter. I'll bet you made it all frost. You don't know how cold you are, Courtney. Sometimes you chill even me, well as I know you.... I guess I'll write Basil a note, too—and let him see that we did appreciate his thoughtfulness."

"As you please."

# Chapter 14

Five days since the letter to Basil, a fortnight since he went, and the first move toward freedom not yet made. Each day added its strength of loneliness and longing to the resolve that became the guiding purpose of her life when she sent him away. But she must restrain her eagerness, must compel herself to wait upon opportunity—upon the favorable gust of event or emotion. To be tactless and abrupt would mean defeat; for, hard though it was to realize, she must keep ever in mind that Richard had legal right over Winchie. Moral right she denied not only because he was as much a stranger to Winchie as to herself, but chiefly because a child belonged to its mother. Indeed, if she had not been brought up in a legal family it would not have occurred to her that in any circumstances she need disturb herself about having Winchie. There was nothing of pose or effusiveness about her love for him; it was that deep and utter love which is not conscious of itself, but simply is. She and the boy were as much part of each other as when his being was still hidden within hers. She knew that she and Winchie were one; but she also knew the man-made law. So in seeking her freedom she must move carefully. Sometimes she felt she must be dreaming; it simply could not be possible that in arranging her life she must take into account a person so utterly alien and apart as this nominal husband of hers.

She had rarely seen him since Basil left. He was exercising—walking or rowing on the lake—very early in the mornings. But he spent the whole day at his work. When he occasionally came to dinner or supper, he was deep in his problems, was as unconscious of his wife and child as his child was of him. Courtney was no longer unconscious of him. As before, she did not see him when she looked at him, did not listen when he talked, answered, if answer was necessary, by a sort of reflex mental action that never involved her real mind. But she had the sense of his presence—as keen when he was out of sight as when he sat working or in a deep abstraction before her eyes. And she was constantly revolving how to begin the revolt—for she saw more and more clearly that it would be regarded by him as a revolt against womanliness, against duty, against honor, against decency, would burst upon him like thunder from clear sky, no matter how adroitly she might begin. Until then his ideas of woman had impressed her only in a vague, general way. She had avoided thinking them out or hearing them from his own lips because she knew definite knowledge would only make the struggle to be a wife to him as far as she might the more painful, the more humiliating. But now, piece by piece, his conception of womanhood and woman's place fitted itself together in her mind from stray sentences dropped by him from time to time in their five years. Every day she recalled some forgotten or ignored remark that added to the completeness of the record—and to its discouragement. As to the position of woman in the scheme of things, he was untouched of any modern idea. He was just where his grandfather had been; and Colonel Achilles Vaughan had been where the whole world had been since the Oriental contempt for women reconquered Europe under the banner of the Cross.

In one of the last warm days she half sat, half lay in the hammock on the lake-front veranda, apparently idle, really with a brain as industrious as a beehive. Gradually, however, the beauty of the scene—summer dying like a lovely woman whose mortal disease only enhances loveliness—stole in upon her and won her for the moment. She looked at the wonderful colors far and near, she drank in the last potent draughts of summer's perfume. And suddenly she thought, "I would be divorcing all this, too!" These gardens that she had created; the house that she had made over. Why, these things were part of her very soul. The same life throbbed in them that throbbed in her boy and in herself—her own life blood! The place was in Richard Vaughan's name just as she herself was, just as Winchie was. But it was not his; it—all that made it individual—was hers!

Most of us pass through the world, leaving little more trace of our individuality than a traveler leaves in a hotel room. But Courtney had the creative instinct powerfully developed. She even never dressed in exactly the same way, no matter how simple her costume or how often she wore it; and her clothes were so individual that Richard the absent spoke of hats and dresses she had worn several years back. And this place—it was like the picture the artist keeps by him and touches and retouches. Also, she now realized for the first time how profoundly domestic she was by nature. Not by chance had she avoided the life of the gadabout and meddler which is chosen by so many women when they find themselves mismated, and so, without hope of the normal life. She had always classed herself with the flyabout sort of women rather than with the domestic sort; she had fallen into the common error of taking as representative of the domestic type those dreary rotters who sit at home inert and slovenly simply because it requires less effort to stay at home than to dress and issue forth. Now she saw that she was domestic, was a home-maker and a home-lover; and she understood a deeper depth of her unhappiness—the unhappiness that comes from being cheated out of one's dearest desires; for how incomplete must be any home without love of husband and wife. And she understood why, as she made her surroundings more and more like her dreams, her longing for love had grown apace; she was like the bird that builds its nest, and has nothing to put in it.

She had built this nest; now she must abandon it. Heavier and heavier grew her heart, as she thought of the years of thought and toil she had invested, as she looked about at the results. She rebuked herself almost fiercely—in terror of the weakness to which these lamentings might tempt her; in shame at the disloyalty to Basil. "I'm utterly selfish," she said to herself. "I'm shrinking from making any sacrifice at all." There she stopped short in a kind of terror. "Sacrifice"—what a strange word to use—what an ominous word—and how clearly it warned her that delay was eating out courage, was strengthening her natural woman's inertia. Sacrifice! She began to picture what the new life would be—perfect sympathy, companionship ever closer and closer, how she would grow and expand, how Winchie would thrive in an atmosphere of ideal love—and Basil and she would together create a place, a home which would be incomparably lovelier than this.... "Yes, I must establish my life on its permanent basis." Her life must be straightened out, must be settled right. Until it was based right, nothing could be right; mind and heart would always be uneasy, and from time to time in a turmoil. "Nothing is settled," her father often used to quote, "until it's settled right." He was thinking of large affairs, but the thing was just as true of the affairs of private life. Her and Richard's relations, her and Basil's relations, and therefore her and Winchie's relations, were awry, all awry. There had been successive adjustments; they had one after the other fallen to pieces—because "nothing is settled until it's settled right."

That very evening, it so happened, for the first time Richard made a remark that gave her an opening. "Why don't you stay down in the evenings?" said he. "It doesn't disturb me for you to play and sing in the sitting room when I'm in the library."

"The last few times I did it," replied she, "you slipped away to the shop."

He reddened, laughed guiltily. "Did I? Well—perhaps in certain moods——"

"Oh, I'm not complaining," she assured him. "I've got used to our leading separate lives—long ago.... I like it as much as you do."

"Separate lives," said he reflectively. "It's true, we don't see much of each other. Husbands and wives rarely do, when the man amounts to anything, or is trying to amount to anything."

"Unless they work together."

"And that's impossible where people are of our station."

Our station! Her lip curled and her heart protested. How could a human being with a human heart talk of a station too high for love—love that was the soul of life.

"Also," continued he, reflective and absent, "it's out of the question where the husband is pursuing an intellectual occupation." Even had he not been merely thinking aloud, it would not have occurred to him that there was any slur in a statement of an elementary axiom as to the different spheres of the two sexes. "And," he went on, "it's unnecessary to married happiness, as we've proved. You had an idea once—do you remember?—"

"Yes—I remember."

"If I'd let you have your foolish, impulsive, romantic way, and you'd been at my elbow down at the shop, where I get irritable and cranky—we'd not have made our present record—would we?"

She shivered. "No," she said faintly.

"Five years with hardly a misunderstanding, and not one quarrel."

His words, his manner—complacent, content—calmly possessive—dried up her courage and her hope. But she held to her purpose. She said, "We're not interested enough in each other to quarrel."

He laughed, assuming she was jesting. "That's it! That's exactly it."

"I was speaking seriously. It's the truth. We care nothing about each other."

"Courtney!" he admonished. "Aren't you carrying the joke too far? I don't think you realize how that sounds."

"I realize how it *is*."

He looked at her curiously. "Why, I thought you were joking."

"Not in the least."

"How pale your face is. And what a strange expression round the mouth—and your eyes are circled. Are you ill, dear?"

"Absolutely well. It's the strain of getting ready to say these things to you." She saw he was observing her like a physician studying a patient. "No, I'm not insane, either," said she good-humoredly.

"What's happened to upset you?"

She put one knee in a chair, leaned toward him over its back, her elbows upon it. Said she, "It isn't a matter of to-day, but of five years—or, rather, of four years."

He straightened up in his chair. She imagined that his grandfather, old Colonel Achilles, must have looked like that at the same age. "What *are* you talking about?" he demanded.

"About our failure as a married couple," replied she, meeting his gaze with calm courage.

"Failure!" exclaimed he. "Why, our married life is ideal. I wouldn't have it changed in the least particular." He nodded his handsome, powerful head. "Not in the least particular."

She had expected him to say something like this. But the actual words, spoken with sincerity and conviction, stopped her. Her road had ended against the face of a cliff with a precipice on either side.

"I want to be free," she said desperately. "I must be free!"

"Free? You *are* free."

"I mean free from marriage," explained she gently, "free to make my own life."

He reflected, looked at her, reflected again. She saw, as plainly as if his thoughts were print before her eyes, that he had decided she was a spoiled child in a pet, that he was trying to find some kindly, effective way of humoring her. But to take her words seriously, to meet her on a plane of equality—the idea had not occurred to the grandson of Achilles Vaughan, and could not occur to him. Anger boiled up in her, evaporated. She laughed.

He glanced at her quickly. "Oh, you were joking!" said he in a relieved tone.

"That wasn't why I laughed. It was to save myself from doing something ridiculous—shouting out, or upsetting the table, or running amuck."

"No matter. It's clear to me that you're not yourself this evening—not at all."

"Richard," said she slowly, "I know it's hard for you to believe a woman's not a fool. I don't expect you to credit me with intelligence. Perhaps you might if I were a big, fat woman with a loud voice. But I'm not. So, assume I'm as silly a fool as—as most women pretend to be, to catch husbands and to use them after they're caught. But please assume also that, whatever I am or am not, I want my freedom. And try to realize that we women are living in the twentieth century as well as you men— and not in the tenth or fifteenth."

His expression was serious and respectful; he was not one to fail in polite consideration for the feminine—the wayward, capricious, irrational feminine with which stronger and rational man should ever be patient and gentle. But she saw that he was in reality about as much impressed as he would have been by a demand for the open cage door from a canary born and bred to captivity and helplessness. He came round the table, put his hands tenderly on her shoulders, pressed his lips in a husbandly caress upon the coil of auburn hair that crowned her small head. "You're tired and nervous to-night, dear," said he with grave kindness. "So we'll not talk about it any more. Go to bed, and get a good night's sleep. Then———"

She rose, found herself at a disadvantage standing before one so much taller, sat down in another chair. "Yes, I am tired and I am nervous. But I'm also in earnest. Why, if we weren't strangers, you'd realize. You'd have felt it long ago. Can't you see I'm nothing to you or you to me that is, nothing especial—nothing that ought to satisfy either of us?" She was trying to speak with serious calmness; the very effort overstrained her. And his face—its expression was so hopeless! She was speaking a language he did not understand, was speaking of matters of which he had not the faintest glimmer of knowledge. Her voice broke; she steadied it. It broke again. She began to sob. "This life of ours is a degradation. It's like a stagnant pool—it's death in life. I can't stand it. I want love—want to give love and get it! My whole being cries out for love! I'm dying here of the empty heart. I must go. I ask you to be just—to give me my right—my freedom———"

It was his expression that stopped her. He was not listening to her words at all. He was simply waiting for her to talk out her hysteria, as he thought it, so that he could begin to soothe the agitated child. She threw out her arms in despair.

"Go on, dear," he urged. "Say all you want. You'll feel better for it."

The cliff, with choice between turning back and leaping over one of the precipices on either side—the precipice of flight to Basil in secrecy and dishonor, with Winchie, or the precipice of a divorce with Winchie taken away from her. She buried her face in her arms and burst into wild sobs. With Winchie taken away from her! If she fled, he would follow, would take Winchie. If she divorced him, he would take Winchie. It was hopeless—hopeless. There was no escape. Sobbing, she ran round and round her prison's outer court to which she had penetrated. It had no gates—none! He waited until she was quiet, except that her shoulders heaved occasionally. "Poor dear!" he said tenderly. "Poor child!" And he took her in his arms. She felt physically and morally too weak for the least struggle. She lay passive against his breast, her heartache throbbing dully. He carried her upstairs, laid her gently on the sofa at the foot of her bed. "Now you feel better, don't you?" said he, bending over her and smiling sympathetically down.

She gazed at him with forlorn, hopeless eyes, then rested her head weakly against the cushions in the corner of the sofa.

"Of course, I understood that what you were saying a while ago was only a nervous mood. But it gave me a shock, too. I know now what was the matter."

She grew cold, rigid. Did he suspect? Would he take Winchie?

"I admit I've been neglecting you lately. Gallatin's leaving put a lot of work on me. And, too, I read an article that gave me a silly scare—made me afraid I'd be anticipated in one of my discoveries if I didn't push things. But even if I was negligent, I can't see how you could get the notion in your head that you weren't loved any more." He sat down by her on the sofa, kissed the nape of her neck. "I'll make up for it," he murmured. "Why, it'd be as impossible for me to stop loving you as for you, a good woman, to stop loving your husband. The idea of *you* talking divorce!" He laughed boyishly. "You and I—divorced! What a naughty child it was! It seems dreadful that those pure lips could be sullied by such a word. But it never was in your heart. A woman like you, a woman I trust my honor to, and trust my boy to, couldn't think such things."

His words and manner, all tenderness, were for her reminders of the Vaughan prejudice and the Vaughan will and the Vaughan pride that lay behind; the clang of iron doors, the grate of brass keys in steel locks. She, back in her cell and prostrate on its floor, felt she must indeed have been driven out of her senses by heart hunger to imagine she could get freedom and Winchie from Richard Vaughan. How love and hope had tricked her!

"Asleep, dear?"

"No."

"You don't doubt my love any longer, do you?"

She moved restlessly.

"Still cross?" He took her in his arms in spite of her struggles, began to caress her. And she who had never resisted did not know how to resist now—did not dare to resist, so cowed was she by fear of losing Winchie, so utterly was she despising herself—"nothing but a woman." She endured till reaction stung her into crying out in anguish: "For God's sake, Richard! I am so miserable!"

"I'm sorry," he said contritely. "I thought you wanted it." He rose at once. "Would you like to be left alone?"

"Please."

"You forgive me for neglecting you?"

"Anything!" she cried. "Only go. If you don't, I shall—" She pressed her lips together tightly and drew all her nerves and muscles tense to keep back the avowal that was fighting for exit.

"I'll give up my work until you feel better."

"No—no. I don't want— Go—please go! For Winchie's sake—for mine—for your own."

He did not attach enough importance to her words to note them and inquire. When the door closed behind him, she drew a long breath—not so much relief that she was alone, as relief that, before seeing how useless it was to try to escape, she had not burst out with the whole truth. A turn of the wind of emotion before he spoke of Winchie, and she would have told all! Even after he had reminded her— yes, even until the door closed between them, she might still have been goaded by her despair or by his manner into precipitating the cataclysm——

"For he'd never have let me see Winchie again!" And—what else would he have done?—what would he not have done? She put out her lights and, without drawing aside the portière, softly opened Winchie's door and entered. She dropped down by his bed, slipped her hand under the cover, delicately warm from his healthy young body. Her fingers rested upon his breast over his heart. That calm, regular throb of young life beat upon her spirit like the soft, insistent rain that soothes the storm-racked sea.

Winchie! If she had lost him! If she had brought disgrace upon him! She drew her hand away lest its trembling should waken him. The room was pitch dark, but she could see him lying there, his tumbled fair hair against the white pillow, his round cheeks flushed with healthy sleep. She sat on the floor beside the bed, listening to his breathing. She had gone down to the gates of the world and had led him through them into life. Claim upon him she had none—for he owed her nothing, and if his lot were not happy he would have the right to blame her. No, he owed her nothing; but his claim upon her was for the last moment of her time, for the last thought of her brain, for the last drop of her blood.

"If it were not for Winchie," she said to herself, "I'd go to Basil. I'd leave here to-night. I owe nothing to Dick. While his way of looking at life is not his fault, neither is it mine. And as it's his way, not mine, he should suffer for it, not I. But for Winchie I must stay—and live and make this house a home."

Never again would there be the least danger of her being goaded into telling Richard and defying and compelling him. No delirium, not even a fever like a maniac loose in the brain and hurling all its tenant thoughts helter-skelter through the lips, could dislodge that secret. It was sealed with the great seal of a mother's love.

When she came down to breakfast, Dick was at one of the long windows, back to the room, hands deep in trousers' pockets. At her "Good morning," he turned quickly. Before he answered, he noted her expression, and his face brightened. He kissed the cheek she turned for him as usual, and they seated themselves. In came Mazie with the coffee; it had the delicious fragrance that proclaims fine coffee well made, the fragrance that will put the grouchiest riser into an amiable frame of mind. Then she brought the spoon bread and an omelette—not the heavy, solid, yellow-brown substantiality that passes for omelette with the general, but a light and airy, delicately colored thing of beauty such as a skilled cook can beat up from eggs the hens have laid within the hour.

"Feeling all right this morning?" asked Dick when Mazie had gone out.

"Perfectly," replied Courtney, her smiling eyes like the dark green of moss round where the spring bubbles up. She was rearranging the flowers in the bowl.

"Sleep well?"

She had not slept at all. She evaded his question by saying: "I was very much upset last night, wasn't I?"

Dick made a gesture of generous dismissal. "Oh, I knew it was only a passing mood," said he, helping himself liberally to the omelette. "Everybody has moods. Do give me some of that coffee."

Strange indeed was the expression of that small, quiet face. What a chaos a few blundering words from her a few hours ago would have put in place of this domestic content of his! "I want to say one thing more," said she, "and then we'll never speak of last night—or what led up to it."

"Yes, dear?"

"We talked a lot about ourselves—and I was thinking altogether of myself, I find. But the truth is, Winchie's the only important fact in our lives. We don't belong to ourselves. We belong to him."

"That's not exactly the way I'd put it," said he hesitatingly. "Do try this spoon bread. Mazie's a wonder at making it. Do try it."

"Not just now," said she. "No, I know you wouldn't put it that way. Put it any way you like. But it must be Winchie first, last, and all the time. We must see to it that he has the right sort of example—from you—from me—from us both."

Dick nodded approvingly, and when his mouth was said: "There's no disputing that. Where is he, by the way?"

"He'll be down in a minute," replied Courtney; then went on unruffled: "If you and I had had love before our eyes in our homes when we were children——"

"But I did. And I'm sure your father and mother were an equally fine example——"

"No matter," interrupted Courtney. Then she said, in a tone that revealed for the first time how profoundly moved she was: "The point is I want you to help me make a home—of love for Winchie."

"By all means!" exclaimed Dick heartily.

He stirred his coffee thoughtfully, looked at her with puzzled eyes; and she saw that his keen, analytic mind, usually reserved wholly for his work, was curiously inspecting her words and her manner for the meaning that must be beneath so much earnestness about a passing anger over a few days of neglect. She said no more—and was glad when Winchie came rushing in to turn the current of his thoughts. As he was leaving for the shop, he hunted her out in the library to kiss her good-by—a thing he had not done in several years.

She colored, made an effort, kissed him.

"I'm sorry for my negligence since Basil left me in the lurch," said he cheerfully. "And you're sorry you flew into such a fury about it. And it's all settled—and forgotten?"

"We—make a fresh start," replied she.

"I'll come and take a walk with you before dinner."

"No—no. Please don't. You mustn't change abruptly." She stopped, confused to find herself already shrinking from the new course she had so highly resolved. "Yes—do come," said she.

"Oh—I forgot. There's one thing I simply must attend to to-day."

"Then—to-morrow."

"Yes—to-morrow we'll make the start—the fresh start."

"Very well," said she, relieved—for she felt she had done her duty.

Instead of going out immediately for a walk with Winchie, as was the habit, she lingered about the house, keeping herself busily occupied. She must write Basil. What she said must be final, for she owed him the truth. And she must not say much; a long letter would give him hope, no matter what words she used, and would harrow him in the reading and her in the writing. At last she put on hat and even gloves for the walk, sat hastily down at her desk, wrote: "I cannot. I belong to my boy, not to myself." She wished to add, "I shall try to forget. So must you, for my sake—" and also some word of love. But with the two sentence she halted her pen. She read what she had written—"I cannot. I belong to my boy—not to myself." She folded the sheet, sealed it in an envelope, addressed it. As she reached for the stamp she called Winchie. They went out together, and she mailed the letter in the box at the edge of town. Well, it was settled—once more. Was this final? "Nothing is settled until it's settled right." And she said to herself that this settlement was undoubtedly right—that is, as nearly right as anything ever is. Yes, it was settled—but her father's uncompromising axiom continued to reiterate its clear-cut, unqualified assertion.

"Why did you sigh, mamma?" asked the boy.

"Did I sigh?" said she, trying to smile as she looked down at him.

"Yes—and you haven't been listening as we came along. You didn't hear what I said about the dead whip-poor-will I found on the lawn—did you?"

"No," she confessed. "But I'll listen now."

She found herself wondering at her calmness. "Perhaps," reflected she, "my fright about Winchie conquered my love. And how deep the roots of my life are sunk into the soil of this place! Still—I don't understand it. It doesn't seem natural I should be calm." There flashed before her mind a picture—herself flying disheveled—coming forward with laughter and jest—and lie—with the sting of forbidden kisses still upon her face—the thrill of forbidden caresses— And she flushed crimson as the autumnal maples above her head, and glanced guiltily down at Winchie—and saw that he was trying to pretend not to see.

# Chapter 15

Long before Dick got caught up with the particular piece of work that postponed their "fresh start," Courtney's "queer mood" and his own resolution were shelved in one of those back closets of his memory where reposed in darkness and dust matters relating to his family. He forgot nothing; his was not the forgetting kind of mind. Everything was stored away somewhere, under its proper heading, ready for him if he should happen to need it. But for that especial matter there came no demand. His happy married life had resumed its unrippled course. He worked, with allowance for exercise—usually a long walk or a row on the lake in the very early morning, before breakfast. Courtney occupied herself with house and garden. She was building a vegetable greenhouse with a small legacy from an aunt; also, there was the household routine of a multitude of time-filling, thought-filling, not to be neglected details for keeping things smooth and orderly—and there were reading and painting and music—and there were callers and visits. She even began to be philosophical about the almost daily evidences that her husband regarded her as an inferior. All men felt that way toward women. The very men who never made a move without consulting their wives thought themselves superior intelligences, and their wives mere possessors of a crafty instinct, in common with the lower animals, an instinct that was worth availing themselves of, as long as it was right there in the house. No, she was a silly supersensitive, she told herself, to be disturbed by such a ridiculous universal masculine weakness of vanity. As husbands went, Richard was about as good as any—better than most.

The evenings they spent together. A charming picture of family life they made each evening during that rare, exquisite September. The big log fire in the sitting room; he at the desk, she reading or sewing, or, less frequently, playing and singing softly. She had never been lovelier. The slightly haggard look was becoming to her young face, and the weariness of the eyelids also, and the pathos of her mouth so eager to smile, and the milky emerald of the eyes, like seas troubled so deep down that the surface was only clouded, but not ruffled. Sometimes she let Winchie stay with them an hour or so. Then the picture was complete—the boy playing on the floor before the fire, making what he called drawings at the table, always between his father and his mother, always nearer his mother, near enough to put out his hand and touch her and make quite sure of the reality of her lovely presence. Yes, she assured herself many times each day, the struggle was over; the pain would grow less and less, would pass—for the question of her life relations was settled—"and settled right."

This until mid-October, when the bleak rains inaugurated what promised to be a worse than the previous winter. On the fourth successive day indoors, as she sat at a drawing table in the upstairs sitting room, she suddenly lifted her head, thrust back the table, flung down the pencil, and rushed to the window. The lawns were flooded. Bushes and trees were drearily fluttering the last wet faded tatters of autumnal finery. Decay—desolation—death— "Will he never come! Will he never write!" And the secret of her calm, so carefully guarded from herself, was a secret from her no longer.

It had been a farce—the six weeks of resignation. One of self-deception's familiar farces; those farces that finally make old people cynical in spite of themselves about the reality of disinterested goodness, of self-sacrifice, of anything except selfishness. A farce—nothing more. That was why she could write a brief farewell and send it off with merely a pang and a sigh. And ever since she had been confidently waiting for something to happen. Something? What but his coming—coming to give her again the love that was life and light to her, the love she could no more refuse than a drowning man can withhold his hand from clutching the rope though the devil himself toss it. And once more her father's maxim, "Nothing is settled until it's settled right," began to thrust itself at her—mockingly now, as if deriding her self-deceiving attempts to found her life upon conditions to which mind and conscience had agreed, but not heart. And heart, the most powerful of the trinity that must harmonize within a human being or there is no peace—heart had suddenly torn up the treaty of peace and declared war. And war there was.

About seven that evening Dick knocked at her bedroom door. "May I come?" he called.

"Yes—if you won't stay long," was her reply in a listless tone.

He entered, looked surprised when he saw her propped up in bed with her supper tray in her lap. "Are you ill?"

"No."

"You didn't come down to supper."

"No."

"I don't think I ever knew you to do this before."

"No."

"Your voice sounds—strange—tired."

"I am."

"You don't exercise enough, I guess. And there's little for you to do about the house—with Lizzie looking after the flowers and Nanny such a good housekeeper and Mazie such a splendid cook. We're getting the benefit of my aunt's toil. She built up such a splendid system that it runs itself—and there's really not enough for you to do. You ought to——"

"Won't you take this tray—take it down with you?"

"Don't you want me to sit a while?"

"Don't let me interfere with your work."

"Oh, there's no hurry."

"I'm sure you want to be at it."

He took the tray from her lap, put it on the floor beside his chair. She reached for the book on the stand at her elbow, opened it, seemed to be waiting for him to go. He glanced round uncertainly. "What a charming room this is," said he. "That pale brown paper with the panels made by broad violet stripes— Let me see—was this one of the rooms you did over?"

She was reading.

"Yes of course. In my aunt's time— You'd have admired her, and she'd have been invaluable as a teacher. But then she taught Nanny; and Nanny's been very good about teaching you, hasn't she?"

No answer.

He laughed. "We've got a rather bad habit of not listening—haven't we?"

"Oh—I don't mind."

He glanced at the tray. "Why, you didn't eat anything!"

"No."

"Are you quite sure you're not ill?"

"Quite."

"Well, if there's anything I can——"

"Nothing, thanks."

He went to the bed, bent over and kissed her. "Good night."

"Good night." She was reading again; and his thoughts returned to his work as he closed her bedroom door behind him. If he had looked in on her an hour later, he might have seen that she had not yet turned the page she pretended to begin, to get rid of him—or, rather, to help him go where he really wished to be. And he would have distrusted her assurance that she was not ill. For her eyes, wide and circled and wretched, were staring into space. She was indeed ill—ill of loneliness, of heart-emptiness, of that hope deferred which maketh the heart sick. And the rain streamed on and on. The sight of it by day filled her with the despair that lowers and rages. The sound of it monotonously pattering upon the balcony at night changed her despair from active to passive, from vain revolt to lying inert in the wash of inky waves under inky sky.

The sympathy between her and Winchie was so close that they were like one rather than like two. He had early discovered her sensitiveness to the weather, but never before had he seen her frankly downhearted. He did not annoy her. He watched her furtively, his little heart aching. He spent most of his time near the west windows of the upstairs sitting room. From them, now that the trees were almost bare, he could see part of the Donaldson's roof—the part topped by a weather vane. He knew that so long as the vane pointed east the rains would pour down, and his mother's low spirits would continue—that when it should veer to the west the rain would cease and the sky clear.

Day after day he watched, his hopes rising as the vane veered now toward the north, now toward the south, and falling again as, with a jerk, it flirted back into the eye of the east. That vane was the last thing he saw as the darkness closed down in the late afternoon; it was the first thing he looked at in the morning, dashing to the window the instant he awakened. The change came in the night, when it finally did come. As he awakened, the difference in the light, in the feel of the air told him that all was well once more. But he made sure; he hurried to one of his windows, turned the slats of a blind, looked at the vane. Then, with a shout, he darted to her door, beat upon it, crying: "Mamma! Mamma Courtney! The wind's west—the wind's west!"

She understood, opened the door. She had made her face bright. "Thank you—thank you," she said, with a catch in her voice, as she knelt and took him in her arms. He put one of his small hands on each of her cheeks, kissed her, then looked into her eyes. His face fell. She could not deceive him; it had not been the rain.

The wind was in the west; her mood veered—but to another futility. She watched for the postman. She startled and ran to the window at every crunch of wheels on the drive. She was agitated whenever the telephone bell rang. At night every suggestion of sound from the direction of the window made her lift her head from the pillow to listen; and often she would fly to open a shutter and lean out into the darkness. She would not go to Wenona, lest he should come while she was away. She never left the house for a walk without telling the servants just where she was going—"and if anyone comes, send for me."

Never before had she surrendered to the somber mood; she had always met it by taking up some one of the things at hand that interested her, and working at it until health and youth and hope reasserted themselves. But this time she could find nothing to build upon; it was all quicksand, slipping away and leaving her to sink. She no longer cared about her surroundings. She had always seen to it that the servants she had so thoroughly trained in a modern system she had carefully worked out did their duties, and did them well. Now she let the servants do as they pleased—and they soon pleased to do very poorly—as poorly as the average human being does, unless held rigidly from his natural tendencies to slovenliness and shirking. She had always done the buying for the kitchen, and had herself selected at the farm the things to be sent over. Now the good old days of Aunt Eudosia returned, with the farmer sending whatever gave him or one of "the hands" the least trouble, and with Nanny accepting from the storekeepers what they chose at their own price. The bills went up; yet the meat was often tough, the chickens and game inferior, the butter and eggs only fair, instead of the very best. Canned vegetables appeared on the table when fresh vegetables were still to be had. The coffee was capricious. The table itself was carelessly set; napkins were used several times, instead of only once; tablecloths did not always go into the wash with the first spot. Lizzie and Mazie lost no opportunity to cut down the amount of work they would have to do on wash and ironing days.

In the living rooms, upstairs as well as down, there was no longer the beautiful order that had made the interior a pleasure to the eye and so comfortable. A chair had only three casters; a door was losing its knob. A window curtain had broken away from its rod at one corner and was hanging down. Several cushions had rips in them that would soon be rents. Winchie's ravages remained unrepaired—and unrebuked. The flowers in the vases were not fresh every day, and were arranged by a servant's heavy hands. Window gardens and baskets and hothouse suffered from alterations of drought and deluge, and showed it. The red spider was rarely interrupted in his ruinous feasts. Where order has been perfect, brief neglect produces unsightly disorder. The house was becoming like most houses—

indifferently looked after by women who know little about housekeeping as an art and feel "above" the endless petty details that must be attended to, no matter what the enterprise, if there is to be success. The work of changing the library to a winter conservatory had, like the vegetable greenhouse, been begun, and abandoned midway.

From the house the blight spread to herself. It is well-nigh impossible for a person who has been bred from birth in personal order and cleanliness to become really slovenly and dirty, unless beaten down into the hopeless wretchedness of extreme poverty. But Courtney had lost interest in herself, just as she had lost interest in the house. She got herself together "any old way" in the mornings, took to breakfasting in bed. Sometimes she dressed for supper, and sometimes she came in working or walking clothes or in the négligée she had been wearing all day. Sometimes her blouse was buttoned in the back, oftener it was partly open. Wrinkled stockings had been her especial abhorrence, as she was proud of her slim tapering legs; now she habitually went the whole day without garters. She read much, and always novels. Formerly their pandering to "spirituality," to "culture," to all the silly and enfeebling sentimentalisms had bored her. They had offended her sense of what was truly ideal—for, even thus early in her development, she had a strong suspicion that "idealism" was not a mode of life but a strut, and that "idealists" were not above but beneath usefulness. Now she took novels as a drug fiend his dope. Anything to escape reality—the ugly facts which her negligence was making uglier day by day.

She was in the way trod by so many women who, married and safe, cease to compete and deteriorate physically, morally, and mentally. And she knew it. She had too much intelligence to delude herself, as some women do. Instead of being angered when evidence of her plight thrust at her, she found bitter satisfaction in it. "I'll soon be down to the level of those 'good' women Dick regards as models," thought she. And she read on at her novels.

And still she continued to hope, though she constantly assured herself that hope was dead and buried. It was nearly Christmas; he had been gone more than four months—a hundred and thirty days. No word from him, no sign. "It's over," declared she. "It was just physical attraction, nothing more. And he got enough." This lash upon pride and vanity stung. But the pain seemed to ease another and fiercer pain, and she scourged on. "He got enough. In New York he found fresh attraction—not hard for a man with money and free." Yes, he had used her, despising her the while—how she writhed as she rubbed the coarse salt of these taunts into her wounds!—had used her, despising her the while, had cast her away, like the butt of a smoked cigarette. "And why shouldn't he use and despise and drop me? Could anyone have been 'easier' than I was—I, poor fool, with my dreams of love, and my loneliness and credulity? Well, anyhow he ought to be grateful to fate for having given him a distraction in this dull hole." ... What vanity had been hers, to imagine she could win and hold such a man as he—man of the world, experienced, clever. What colossal vanity! "Really, I deserve all I've got. I'm just like the rest of the women—a vanity box, a mirror and a powder puff, silly and empty—a fool for men to flatter and wheedle and laugh at.... What a poor, dependent thing a woman is! Dick's right; we're worthless except as pastimes. Don't we always despise and trample on a man who takes us seriously? We feel he has dropped down to our level."

She dissected, one by one, the "good" women over in the town and in the big houses along the south shore—their inane lives, their inane pastimes, their inane conversation. What animal grossness concealed by manners and a thin veneer of education, just as their costly clothes concealed the truth about their neglected bodies. What lazy ignorance beneath those pretentious fads for "culture" or religion or charity. And the men, too—through their passions dominated by these women. Not an idea—not an aspiration—just hunting and money-making and eating and drinking—catering to crude appetites. Slavish conformity to the soddening, mind-suffocating routine prescribed by custom for the comfortable classes. Fit associates, these men and their women. The nauseating hypocrisies and self-cheating about virtue and piety and "pure family life!" A pigsty of a world, if one looked at it as it was, instead of at its professions and pretenses. "I'd rather be the dupe of my own honest folly than the dupe of the world's cheap frauds. At least, I aspired. And now that I've fallen back into the muck, all bruised and broken, I don't lie to myself about its being muck.... And what can I do for Winchie? If I teach him what he ought to be, I'll unfit him for life in the world. If I fit him for life in the world, I must teach him to pretend, to cheat, to lie, to trample and cringe. If I teach him the truth about women, he'll become a rake. If I don't, he'll become their dupe. If I teach him the truth about men, he'll shun them. If I don't, they will debauch him."

A wound always constructs a cover, to protect itself while it is healing. The wounded heart of an intelligent man or woman usually protects itself with the scab of cynicism. For the last few years Courtney had shared with Wenona's few progressive, restless young married women that reputation for thinking and saying startling things which anyone at all free in thought and speech soon gets among conventional people. Now she became a mild scandal. Wenona appreciated that it was the fashion in these degenerate days, the mark of the "upper class," to indulge in audacities of every kind. Also, whatever a Benedict and a Vaughan did must be just about right. But sometimes, when she was in a particularly insurgent mood, her callers went away dazed.

They wondered what her husband thought of such disbelief in everything that men, themselves disbelieving, held it imperative for women to believe—women and children and preachers. The fact was he knew nothing about it. Conversation between him and his wife was confined to the necessary routine matters, and never extended beyond a few sentences. They saw each other at table only; then Winchie did most of the talking, or it grew out of and centered round things he had inquired about. Richard and Courtney neither acted nor felt like strangers. That would have meant strain. They ignored each other with the easy unconsciousness that characterizes an intimate life in which there is no sympathy, no common interest. When Richard talked about his work, as he did occasionally, merely the better to arrange his thoughts, Courtney did not listen. When Courtney and Winchie talked together, Richard did not listen.

"You saw the news in to-day's paper?" said Richard at supper a few days after Christmas.

As he continued to look expectantly at her, she roused herself from her reverie, slowly grasped his question. "I didn't read to-day's papers," answered she.

"Well, Gallatin's engagement's announced—from Philadelphia."

She nerved herself for the reaction of inward turmoil which would, she felt, certainly follow such a blow. To her amazement no reaction came. She felt as calm as if the news had been about some one of whom she had never heard.

"Why, you seem not to be interested."

"Oh, yes," replied she indifferently.

"I remember, you didn't like him."

It almost seemed true to her. Or, rather, that she had never cared about him one way or the other.

"And he so mad about you," continued Richard with raillery. "I'll never forget the looks he used to give you—or the ones he gave me, either. Well, it's all over now. He's evidently cured."

"Evidently," said Courtney. She looked calmly at him, shifted her gaze. It happened to fall upon Winchie. The boy was frowning jealously into his plate. She colored. She never had the slightest self-consciousness about Basil with Richard, but only with the boy. However, the reminder soon passed in marvel at her amazing tranquillity. How could she be thus calm in face of such a blow? Had she really conquered her love? Had this sudden, unexpected news of his perfidy killed it all in an instant? Had she never loved him?

Richard had been talking, and she had been so absorbed she had not heard. Now he was holding a letter across the table toward her. Mechanically she reached out, took it, fixed her eyes upon it. "And Mrs. Torrey says," Richard was explaining, "that we ought to ask Cousin Helen here—for a few months at least—until she gets over her father's death."

"Wenona's no place for a girl in search of a husband."

"A husband!" exclaimed Richard. "Who said anything about a husband?"

"Now that her father's dead, with nothing but a small life insurance, she's got to marry."

"Yes, I suppose so."

"That's what Mrs. Torrey's saying between these lines." And she handed the letter back.

"Mrs. Torrey's a fine, noble old lady. Such sordid ideas never'd enter her head."

"Mrs. Torrey's a woman."

"And a good one—and so is Helen," maintained Richard. "Marrying's about the last idea in her head at present."

"I believe that is the theory—among men who know nothing about women."

"She's doubtless almost prostrated with grief."

"With anxiety, perhaps. Not with grief. Not for a worthless old drunkard."

"You forget, Courtney. He was her *father*."

Courtney lifted her eyebrows. "So much the more certain she detested him. She had to live right up against him."

Richard leaned forward slightly, to add emphasis to his rebuke. "I repeat, Helen is a good woman—a woman with a sense of duty. She must have loved him."

"Why repeat such twaddle?" inquired Courtney, unimpressed. "What has duty to do with hearts?"

Dick looked strong disapproval. "What is the matter, my dear? You're not talking in the least like yourself."

"You always make that same remark," observed Courtney, "whenever I say anything that does not suit you."

"Are you irritated by the prospect of Helen's coming? If you don't want her——"

"I am not irritated about anything. As for Helen, I care not a rap one way or the other."

Winchie had finished. He kissed his father, then his mother good night, and went upstairs. Richard came out of a deep study to say, "It's a pity Gallatin isn't free and here—if Helen comes."

"It would have made a good match," said Courtney judiciously. "A splendid living for Helen."

"I wasn't thinking of Gallatin's wealth," protested Richard, reddening. Then he laughed, "At least, not altogether."

"The living's the main point in marriage."

"What an unpleasant mood you're in."

"I? I never felt more amiable."

"Have I said anything to offend you?"

"Not a thing." She rose languidly. "You're still the model—not a single redeeming fault."

She stretched herself with slow, lazy grace. "But you," said he, "are a bundle of redeeming faults and vagaries—a bouquet of them." And he was about to kiss her.

She flung away from him with flashing eyes. He stared, amazed. "How you startled me!" she exclaimed, quickly changing her expression from fury to half-laughing irritation.

"Miss Caprice!" And his gaze was soft and brilliant.

There was a virgin coldness in her manner that puzzled and abashed him. "How I hate this body of mine, sometimes!" said she. "An admiring look makes me angry, and a kiss seems an insult. Come to me with your love when I'm old and ugly. Then, perhaps, I'll believe it."

And she strolled out of the room and upstairs. The instant she had her bedroom door locked, she knew why she had come away—knew she had been obeying an instinct warning her secret self that she could not many minutes longer endure the strain. "But really I am calm," she insisted. In the same second her wound opened and was aching and bleeding and throbbing, unhealed. "I can never forget—never!" she cried. "Was it only this body of mine he cared for? What does it matter? Even the little he gave was more than I had to give. I ought to have been more humble about giving—I who had so little. And what happiness he gave me in exchange! No—not happiness, but more than happiness." Her eyes strained into the night. It was so dreary—so lonely. "Basil!—Basil! I'm dying for you—dying from the core out!"

She flung her windows wide. The snow came whirling in. The wind was moaning among the branches. Somewhere, far away, a bell tolled. Silence, utter solitude, a stretch of white snow under a black sky, and the chilling cold. "Come to me!" she cried. "I am so cold—so lonely—so hungry! And I love you."

Even where a woman cannot doubt that her lover has forgotten, there are times when memory—of his vows so convincing, of his caresses that seemed the inspiration of her charms alone—makes her defy certainty and believe. And Courtney had no real reason to think him either false or forgetful. They had been torn apart when their love was still hungry and thirsty, when even the long calm that precedes satiety was still far in the future, when they were so absorbed in loving that they had not yet had time to begin to get acquainted with each other's real self. It was doubt of him that was forced, belief in him that was natural. "If he were not so strong, so honorable!" she cried. "Ah, if he were only where I could tempt him!"

Even the thought of Winchie now lost all power to check her; he was too much like part of herself. She seemed as placid in her slender youthfulness as those handsome matronly women who suggest extinct volcanoes covered with flowers and smiling fields. Beneath her manner of monotonous, emotionless calm she was battling with the temptation to take her boy and fly from that cold desolation of loveless loneliness, to fly to him. If Richard had not been absolutely apart from her life, absolutely out of her thoughts she would have hated him. As it was her rage fretted at the impersonal barriers and bonds that held her—not Richard, but conventionality and, above all, lack of money. "If only I had money!" she cried again and again.

But she had nothing—her clothes, a few dollars that must be paid out for expenses already incurred. "If I went to him, it would be to become his dependent, just as I am Richard's. Oh, the horror of being a woman! Bred to dependence; bred for the market; bred to tease some man into undertaking her support for life. There is the rotten spot in my whole life. If Richard had ever deigned to speculate as to what was going on in my head, he'd never have dared touch me. He'd have feared I was his only for hire. But would he care? Doesn't he expect me to be true because he supports me? Isn't that what marriage means, beneath the cant and pretense? Yes, I'm simply part of his property, and the pretenses that gloze it over only make it the more revolting. Oh, if men had sensibilities, and if they knew what women thought!—why we smile and flatter and stay on, in spite of neglect and insult!"

She felt that, if she should go to Basil, the day would come when their love would die of this poison exuding from the basic fact of their relations—his sense of his rights because of her dependence; or, her fear of losing or impairing her living; or, her feeling that since she took bread she must give body—all she had to pay with. Richard thought he could afford to be neglectful; and when it suited him to give passing attention to his property again—to walk in his garden and eat a little fruit from his tree—he thought he had a perfect right to do so. If Richard was thus, if all men believed thus, why fancy Basil an exception? Basil, in time, when passion cooled, would hold her in the same light disesteem. If a man lost his virtue, even hypocrisy did not go beyond a half smiling shake of the head; if a woman lost her virtue, she was "ruined." Ruined—that is, a worthless wreck. "No, I shall not go to Basil. No doubt, he still cares—in a man's way of caring. But he holds me, the unfaithful wife, cheap enough. If I were to lose reputation also, were to be unable to give him the pleasure of trespassing on another's property, were to be merely a ruined woman, living off him, he'd soon treat me like the slave that I am. No, I'll not change owners.... If only I had money!"

What, then? She had seen all along that she was like one sinking in the ooze of a marsh—softly, inevitably toward suffocation. "If I stay on here, I'll become like the rest of the settled, disillusioned married women. I'll become a chronic sloven and—as my disposition isn't toward fat, squatted good nature—a shrew. A slovenly shrew!" Why not? What had she left to live for? In a few years Winchie would be away at school—then in some city at profession or business—and married and out of her life. "I might as well give up. Why not?"

There seemed to be no reason. But our conduct in its main lines is not governed by reason, but by instincts that impel us even against will. When Richard had failed her at the outset of their married life, she had sunk; then her temperament of hope and energy had forced her up again in face of deepest discouragements. So now, while there was no reason why she should cease to sink, should begin to struggle, while Basil's announced engagement assuring a speedy marriage seemed just the thing to make her sink on, she began to rouse herself and to look about her. For the second time her longings and energies had lost their stimulus, their inspiration, their vitalizing center. And that center is to an unselfish nature as necessary as queen bee to swarm which clusters about her, labors for her, and renews through her. With human beings such as Courtney Vaughan longings and energies rarely die upon the corpse of their inspiration. After a while they fly upward, as did hers, and begin to circle in search of a new clustering center, a new reason for living and working on. "I can't stay here," she kept repeating. "I must go somewhere. I must do something. Where? What?" How settle her life problem so that it would be "settled right," and she could have peace and happiness? She found no answer. But she kept on thrusting the question at herself. It was as significant of her character as of her trend of thought that her cry "If only I had money!" changed to "If only I could *make* money!"

# Chapter 16

They were at supper, Dick reading the paper, Winchie busy with bowl of rice and milk, Courtney listening to the storm that shrieked in baffled rage after each vain assault upon the house. Her whole being was quivering with the pain that never pierced her more acutely than when she was in the presence of Basil's vacant place at the table. Winchie, without looking up, broke the silence: "We shan't go, mamma, shall we, unless it clears up?"

Dick, turning the paper, happened to hear. "Go where?" he asked.

"To grandfather's."

"When?"

Courtney said: "Winchie and I are going to-morrow."

"Impossible," said Dick. "They'd think you were crazy."

"Perhaps I am," Courtney replied. "Anyhow, we're going."

"Why?"

"I need a change."

"Put it off till spring." And he resumed the newspaper as if the matter were disposed of.

"No. To-morrow," said she, not in the least aggressively; but her tone was of unalterable determination.

"Or, if you must go somewhere, why not Saint X? You can visit Pauline Scarborough or the Hargraves—and bring Helen March back with you."

"I prefer the farm."

He laid the paper down. "You're not serious?"

"Quite."

"Now, my dear—" he began. His tone was one he had unconsciously adopted from his grandfather. He used it whenever he, as head of the family, confronted an "irrational, feminine caprice."

"What's the use of reasoning with me?" interrupted she. "Didn't your grandfather teach you that women can't reason?"

"I'm willing for you to go to Saint X. But——"

She looked significantly toward Winchie. Dick took the hint, went back to his reading until they were alone. Then he resumed: "I'm sure you'll not persist now that I've pointed out to you——"

"If you wish me to keep my temper," interrupted she, "you'll not use that wheedling tone. I'd feel I was degrading Winchie by speaking to him in a way that belittled his intelligence."

Dick looked astonished. "I had no intention——"

"I know—I know," said she appealingly. "It doesn't matter. I really don't care anything about it.

"But you'll not go when it's so clearly a folly to——"

"I am going," said she. "You ought to be grateful that I have such inexpensive whims. Most of us silly women——" She paused, with a lift of the long, slender eyebrows. How absurd to gird at him whose opinions interested her as little as hers interested him!

He revolved what she had been saying, presently reddened. "I thought I had explained to you," said he, "that the laboratory is very expensive. I know I don't give you much. I've had to cut down the household allowance because I feel sure Gallatin will be withdrawing his capital. But just as soon as I——"

She was even of temper again. "You remind me of old Hendricks," interrupted she pleasantly. "You know, he made three people toil for him all their lives, with no pay and mighty poor board and clothes—on the promise of a legacy—and they died before he did."

But Dick was offended. "It seems to me," said he, "in view of what I'm doing at the shop——"

"Please don't," she cried. "You're trying to make me out an ingrate, who doesn't appreciate how you're toiling just for wife and child. Now, what's the fact? Isn't your work your amusement?"

"Of course, I like it, but——"

"Weren't you doing the same thing before you had a family? Wouldn't you be doing it if you should lose them? Isn't it your pride that you work solely for love of science?"

He looked disconcerted assent.

"Then the fact is, you spend most of your income on your own amusement, as much as if you drank it."

He reflected. "That never occurred to me before," said he. "Possibly I have viewed it too one-sidedly. I must think it over and see."

She shrugged her shoulders. "Pray don't, on my account."

He made no reply, put forward no further objections to her going, though the next morning developed a driving sleet. As she and Winchie were about to get into the carriage he asked; "How long will you be gone?"

"Until I feel better."

"If you are ill, you must not go in this weather."

She looked at him strangely. "If I were dying I should go," was her slow reply.

He hesitated, studied her small, resolute face, her fever-bright eyes, with a puzzled expression. "I suppose it's best to give a woman her way in her whims, so long as they're harmless," said he aloud, but to himself rather than to her. She finished wrapping up the boy, went out to the carriage, and got in. He lifted Winchie in, tucked them both carefully, bade them a last good-by, his expression grave and constrained.

In those fifteen miles through the searching cold, over roads like fields deep plowed and frozen hard, she debated how best to carry out her main purpose in going to that dreary farm—how to take her father partly, perhaps wholly, into her confidence so that she might get his help—for help she must have. Her mother was now impossible—quite demented on the subject of religion latterly through the long steeping of mind and heart in a theology whose heaven was hardly less formidable as an eternal prospect than its hell, and whose hell was a fiery sea canopied by shriek and stench of burning multitude. The old maid sisters had neither experience nor judgment, only bitterness. To them it would be inconceivable that a married woman, with a husband who supported her in comfort, could be other than blissfully happy. But her father— He had been a man of affairs, judge. He had lived and read and thought. She had heard her mother rebuke him for expressing "loose" opinions; probably he was concealing opinions even more liberal and enlightened and humane. Perhaps he could give her practical advice—or at least sympathy.

But, arrived at the farmhouse, she had only to look into those four countenances to see that she was among people who knew no more of the life of the present day—or indeed of the real life of any day, even of what they themselves actually believed and felt—than deep-sea oysters in their bed know of Alpine flowers. Even her father— In this remote desert he had lost what knowledge of life he formerly possessed. She was now developed enough to realize that he in fact never did know much about life, that his was a book education only. She had journeyed for help in vain; she was still alone, dependent wholly upon her own courage and resource.

"Don't you wish we hadn't come, mamma?" said Winchie when they were in the room assigned them.

"No," she replied truthfully. She was watching the hickory flames in a calmer mood than she had known for weeks; at least she had got away where she could think, could get an outside point of view upon the posture of her affairs. "No, indeed," she went on to Winchie leaning against her knee and looking up at her. "No, I feel better already."

"Then I guess I can stand it," said the boy with a sigh.

"You don't know about the hill where we can coast."

As he had never coasted, this did not lighten the impression made on him by the gloomy farmhouse sitting room, its walls and ceilings covered with somber paper, by the shriveled grandparents, with deep-sunk, lack-luster eyes, by the sharp, sour faces of the two old maids. But next day, when the sun came out and the farmhands beat down a track on the long hill, Winchie found the situation vastly improved. Flat on her breast on a sled, with the boy breathless and happy upon her back, she initiated him into the raptures of "belly-buster."

"Why, mamma, you look like a little girl, not a bit grown up," cried he after they had been at it all morning and were tugging up the hill for one last, magnificent rush down before going home to dinner. And she did indeed seem to be a sister of Winchie's, one hardly in her teens. Of course, the short skirt and her smallness of stature helped. But it was in her cheeks, in her eyes, in the curve of her lips as she showed her white teeth in the happiest of smiles.

"I *am* a little girl," declared she. And before starting out with him after dinner she did her hair in two long braids that hung below her waistline.

They coasted every day; they took long sleigh rides, long romping walks; they hunted rabbits, went fishing through the ice, were uproarious outside the house and in—the latter to the scandal of the three women of the family, who regarded such goings-on as clearly forbidden in the Scriptures. Even Sunday wasn't so bad as might have been expected; for it snowed too violently for Mrs. Benedict to take them to the church where her favorite doctrines were expounded, and they slipped away to the glorious outdoors. In a sheltered hollow under a shelf of rock they built an enormous snow man, with a top hat of bark. They ate what Winchie regarded as the most wonderful meal of his life at the cottage of one of the farmhands. Never before had he seen such brown brownbread or such molassessy molasses or eaten off such big, strong dishes that there wasn't the least danger of breaking, no matter what you did to them. And he was fascinated by the farmhand's wife and daughter, both acting their company best and eating with the little finger of each hand stuck straight out. And in a box in the corner of the room where they ate was a most exciting brood of little chickens, chirping and squeaking. And in the midst of dinner a huge, hairy, black dog suddenly snatched a piece of meat from the farmhand's plate and retired to the kitchen with it. "Ain't he a caution?" said the farmhand, and Winchie thought he certainly was.

Courtney was like those who put out to sea, leaving their troubles at the one shore, not to think of them until they touch the other. All around were the white hills, and there seemed to be no beyond. She abandoned her plan of studying her situation. She stopped thinking; she ate and slept, and played with the boy, and pretended that she was the little girl she looked, home from school for the holidays, and half hoping somehow something would happen so that there wouldn't be any school any more. She did not think, but she hoped. How? What? Where? She did not know; simply hope, that can burst the strongest grave despair ever buried it in.

Well along in the second week, toward the middle of the afternoon, she and Winchie were on the long hill, rounding out one more happy day. She was as happy as he. When all is lost save youth and health, what is really lost? She on her breast on the sled and he sprawled along her back, his arms round her neck, they shot down the steep with shouts and screams. They stopped, all covered with flying snow, in a soft bank beneath which the zigzag fence was deep buried. They rolled in the snow, washed each other's faces, stood up—were within a few feet of a man in a fur-lined coat almost to his heels. They stared, astounded. Then Winchie's face darkened and hers grew more radiant still as the tears sprang to her eyes.

"Basil!" she murmured, Winchie forgotten. "Oh—*Basil*!" And all in that instant the misery of those months of despair was gloriously transformed into joy.

"Courtney!" he cried. "How beautiful you are!"

He was extraordinarily handsome himself at that moment. Love is a matchless beautifier; and if ever love shone from a human countenance, it was shining, irradiating from his just then. With Winchie jealously watchful they shook hands. "Aren't you and Winchie going to speak to each other?" she asked. And Basil, with reluctance and some confusion held out a hand which the boy very hesitatingly touched.

"I'll pull your sled to the top for you," Basil offered. "Get on, Winchie."

The boy planted his feet more firmly in the snow. "We were going home," said Courtney.

"Get on, Winchie," cried Basil friendlily. "I'll haul you."

"I'm going to walk," replied the boy sullenly.

Courtney understood. "Get on, Winchie," said she. "I'll pull it."

The boy obeyed. The rope was long, so Basil felt free to speak in a lowered voice. "Seeing you—hearing you—touching you— O my darling! my Courtney!"

She forgot where she was, who she was, everything but love. Love! The road danced before her. The cry of the chickadees, the twitter of the snowbirds, the call of Bob White from the fence sounded like supernal music in her ears. The blood tingled and dizzied her nerves. Love again! "You care—still?" she murmured.

"Care? There's only you for me in all the world."

She caught her breath, like the swinger at the long swing's dizziest height when it halts to begin the delirious descent. "Love!" she murmured. "Love!"

"And I know you love me," he went on. "I've never doubted—not once. I've tried to doubt, but I couldn't. Up before me would come those dear eyes of yours, and—Courtney, there isn't a kiss—or a caress—hardly a touch of the hands you and I have ever lived that I haven't felt again and again."

"Don't!" she pleaded, her eyes swimming. "Don't, or I'll break down. My love—my love!"

"I don't know what would have become of me," he went on, "if I hadn't known you'd send for me—yes—in spite of your note. I expected it, for I knew you wouldn't be able to come. The more I thought, the clearer I saw. Not to go any further, there was the boy." He glanced round at Winchie; the angry gray-green eyes were fixed upon him. He glanced away, disconcerted. But he forgot Winchie when his eyes returned to her. "Beautiful! Beautiful—little girl," he murmured, his look sweeping her small, perfect figure to the edge of her short skirt. "I like your new way of wearing your hair."

She blushed. "I did it to make me feel young. I've been feeling so old—old and tired and lonely."

"Thank God, you sent for me."

"Sent for you! A hundred times a day in thought." She laughed aloud, sparkling like the ice-cased boughs in the late afternoon sun. "A thousand thousand times in longing—every time my heart beat."

"Oh, it is so good to be with you!" He drew in a huge draught of the clean, cold, vital air. "Does the sun anywhere else shine on such happiness as this? But I've been mad with happiness ever since the word came."

"The word? What word?"

"Vaughan's letter. I knew you got him to write it."

Courtney stopped short. "I!" she exclaimed. "I don't know what you mean."

"I got a letter from him three days ago. He asked me to take another quarter interest in his work—said he needed the money, as he found he'd been using more of his own in it than he could afford with justice to his family——"

"Oh!" cried Courtney sharply.

"What is it?" asked Basil.

She was looking straight ahead. "Nothing—nothing. Go on." And she started to walk again.

"Your cry sounded like pain."

"Did it? Go on."

"I assumed you had at last succeeded in making the chance for me to come back. So, I telegraphed I'd accept, provided he'd let me work with him again—and that I'd be on at once to talk things over. I took the first train—and here I am."

"Yes, here. That's another mystery to explain."

"Nothing simpler. The station man at Wenona told me you were visiting your father. I jumped at the chance. I can say I thought you all were here. Anything more?"

"I saw the announcement of your engagement."

"It's broken. I couldn't marry her—couldn't have done it in any circumstances. So, I gave her what she was losing by our not marrying. And I'm free. You want me to stay?"

He spoke indifferently about the money he had given up, and he evidently felt indifferent. She would have been hurt had he acted otherwise. At the same time it was a measure of his generosity and of his love, a sordid but certain measure. She regarded that payment as a sort of ransom—his ransom for the right to come to her. "That was his price for the right," thought she. "He paid it without a second thought—would have paid any price. My price for the right to be his may be harder. But I must pay, too—as generously as he."

He was watching her anxiously. "Courtney, I can't go away!"

"You mustn't," replied she. Then a reason—the reason—the solution of her life problem—came to her as if by inspiration. "It's my only chance to be a good woman. That sounds strange, doesn't it?"

"Not to me. I understand. If you hadn't sent for me soon—" he checked himself.

"What?"

"You didn't know that my coming here last spring—and loving you—cured me of the drinking habit. I know, it's stupid and disgusting. I used to loathe myself when I gave way. But it's the only resort in loneliness. And if I realized that you were lost to me, what would I care?"

She nodded sympathetically. "I was going all to pieces, in another way. I was sliding down as fast as Winchie and I were coasting the hill back there. I was going the way of all women who have no love—grown-up love—in their lives. I know now, the reason I used to keep myself together and built myself up and looked after things was because I was waiting and hoping for love, and was expecting it. Love is all of a woman's life, as things are run in this world—at present."

"And quite enough it is, too," said he.

"No," disagreed she. "But let that pass. If I went back to—to that life—alone, I'd be going to ruin. And I'd probably drag him and Winchie down with me. A woman of that unburied-dead sort drags down everybody about her.... You've only to look round, in any station of life, to see those women by the scores. Some few are saved by children—not many and they are of a different nature from me—from most women, I think.... If I don't go back, I either go to you disgraced, a shame to my family, a lifelong stain on my boy here, a miserable, afraid dependent of yours.... No, don't interrupt; I've thought it all out.... Or, I'd plunge into a life of social dissipation. If possible, that sort of woman is worse for herself and for her husband and children than the domestic rotter. A chattering, card-playing gadabout. Possibly I might remain true to my husband, but— If the world weren't the fool it is, it would have discovered long ago that there are worse vices than—" As always when she forced herself to say frank, merciless things, she looked straight into his eyes with defiant audacity—"worse vices than ours."

"But—" he began, shifting his gaze and coloring.

"Oh, yes, it is. Don't make any mistake about it. But I know lots of 'good' women—liars, gossips, naggers, petty swindlers of their husbands, envious, malicious, spiteful—lots and lots of so-called good women beside whom I'd feel white as this snow."

"Rather!" exclaimed Basil.

"So—if you'll go with me—I'm going home—to make it a home—to be a good mother—to give Richard at least his money's worth in care and comfort and—" She looked at him with eyes suddenly solemn—"and that is all, Basil—all. It's all I can give him, all he has the right to.... I'm going home to be a good woman, if you'll come and be there too."

"There's only one life for me—to be as near you as you'll let me."

A long silence. Then she again, sadly: "I don't know how it will work out. But— what else is there for us? We're not heroes. We're human. We must do the best we can. Together we may survive. Apart, I at least will perish—and destroy those near me. I suppose I'm all wrong. But"—with a sigh—"I'm doing the best I can."

Silence again. Then he, deeply moved: "I'll try to be worthy of you, dear."

"Worthy of *me*? For God's sake, don't say those things. There isn't any pedestal I wouldn't fall off of and break to bits.... Basil—" wistfully—"you don't care for me in just a physical way—do you, dear?"

"I care for you in every way," he answered. "Courtney, I never believed I could respect a woman as I respect you. You know, men aren't brought up really to respect women—or themselves, for that matter."

"Then—couldn't we try to—" She lowered her head, faltered—"couldn't we live as if we were engaged only?"

"Why should we?" he cried.

"I know it's only a fancy. But fancies count more than facts.... I'd feel less the—" She faltered—paused.

"Yes—yes—I understand. And— Well, it doesn't do a man any good to be pretending friendship and smiling in another fellow's face, when all the time— I'll try, Courtney— But—it won't be exactly easy."

Her gaze burned for an instant on his, then dropped. "I should hope not!" murmured she.

They, absorbed in each other, moved so slowly along the road that Winchie, silent, motionless, sullen, upon the sled they were trailing as far as the rope permitted, was stiff with cold. But he did not murmur. By the time they reached the door of the farmhouse, Courtney and Basil had it all planned. He was to leave immediately after supper, was to go at once to Vaughan, make the arrangements, reinstall himself. She was to come home in three or four days—unless Vaughan sent, asking her to come sooner. He dined with the family at the farmhouse, made himself so agreeable that they were all pleased with him—even sister Ann whose bitterness over her failure at what she secretly regarded as woman's only excuse for being alive, took the unoriginal disguise of aggressive man-hating. At six o'clock he drove away in the starlight with a merry jingling of sleigh bells that echoed in Courtney's happy heart. The cold was intense; but she felt only warmth—that delicious warmth that comes from within. She stood on the little front porch, with the stars brilliant above and the snow white and smooth over hill and valley. She watched the swift dark sleigh—listened to those laughing bells, their music growing fainter and fainter—but not in her heart. She was so happy that the tears were in her eyes and the sobs in her throat. It was for her one of those moments in life when she asked nothing more, could imagine nothing that would add to joy. Love again!— and oh, what exalted love, to warm the heart and fill it with light and joy, to brighten every moment of life, to guide her up and ever up.

Winchie, standing beside her and looking up at her rapt face, tugged angrily at her skirts.

# Chapter 17

When the mail cart on the third afternoon failed to bring a letter from Richard, she decided that prudence had been satisfied, that she need wait no longer. Toward four she and Winchie set out, snuggled deep in furs and straw in the rear of a huge country sleigh. The roads were perfect; the snow was like a strand at low tide, rolled smooth and firm by the broad tires of high tide's billows. The big horses, steaming as if they were engines, flew as if they were a wind. But her impatient heart was always far ahead, fretting at their laggard pace.

They dashed into the outskirts of Wenona. The journey was ended except the mile and a half round the curve of the lake. She became all at once serenely calm. Life her real life—was now about to begin. It was far from the life she would have chosen, had she been prearranging her own fate. However—who could live an ideal life in such a topsy-turvy world? Nature and conventionality ever at war; right and wrong, not two straight paths, one up, the other down, but a tangle, a maze, a labyrinth. One must often travel the path of the wrong in order to reach the path of the right; and keeping to the path of the right often meant arriving in a hopeless network of blind alleys of the wrong. She was in the confused state about right and wrong characteristic of this era of transition that has seen the crumbling of the despotism of dogma, and has not yet received, or created, a moral guidance to replace it. "Life is a compromise, unless one lives alone and miserably and uselessly," thought she. "My life's to be a thistle with fig grafts. I'll do the best I can with it—Basil and I. With him to help me—his strength and character and self-denying love—with him to help, all may go well. Is my compromise—Basil's and mine—worse than those almost everyone has to make? If so, then they ought to educate women differently, and change marriage."

And when the sleigh reached the drive-front porch, making a dashing and musical arrival, she was in a mood of moral exaltation that might have stirred the enthusiasm of a saint—that is, a saint ignorant of the foundations of that mood or the processes by which it had reared itself skyward. Saints who are wise in the ways of humanity do not interrogate too closely the glitter and lift of moral temples; they know humanity has only humble materials with which to build.

The doors opened wide and, in a flood of bright warm air, redolent of the perfume of flowers, out came Dick to welcome them. "I *am* glad!" cried he. Because of the peculiar relations long established between them—relations such as must exist in some degree between a husband and a wife before the triangular situation can ever even threaten—because of these peculiar relations, she had not anticipated and did not feel the least embarrassment. She was not defying or ignoring her husband; she had no husband. After he swung Winchie to the porch he turned to do the same service for her. But she had quickly disengaged herself from the robes and was standing beside him. He looked into her face, fully revealed by the pour of soft light from the hall. "Your trip certainly has done you good," said he.

"Thank you," replied she absently, presenting her left cheek for the necessary formality of the occasion. Her attention was wholly elsewhere.

In the hall before her there had appeared two people, hanging back discreetly, so that they would not intrude upon the family reunion. Basil, she expected. The woman beside him so astonished her that she forgot to be glad to see him. *Who* was she? This tall, slender girl with the proud, regular features, the attractively done dark hair, the big, honest brown eyes? She glanced at Basil, standing beside this lovely girl and making a laughing remark; her feminine sight instantly noted how the remark was received by the girl—the flattering glance and smile a marriageable woman rarely wastes upon anything from one of her own sex or from an ineligible man. And through Courtney shot a pang that dissolved her structure of moral uplift as a needle thrust collapses a toy balloon. Who was this woman?— this *young* woman—this *tall* woman—this *handsome* woman—so pleased with Basil Gallatin?

"Aren't you surprised to find Helen March here?" Dick was now saying.

Helen March! So, that scrawny, raw-boned girl, all freckles and pimples, and unable to manage her mouth, the Helen March she had seen three years before and had not seen since—so, that prim and homely gawk had developed into this stately creature! Prim, still—unless that expression was the familiar maidenly pose to attract wife hunters. But certainly neither homely nor awkward. She even dressed her hair well, and wore her clothes with quite an air. All this Courtney saw and felt and thought in a few twinklings of an eye—for in such circumstances a woman's mind works with the rapidity of genius, and with genius's grasp of essential detail. Helen was advancing.

"Don't you recognize me, Courtney?" she asked. The voice was one of those honest, pleasant voices that disarm the most cynical pessimists about human nature—the voice that makes the *blasé* city man fall to dreaming of taking a country girl to wife.

"*Now* I do, of course," said Courtney sweetly. And the two embraced and kissed.

To do this, Helen had to bend, as she was more than a head the taller. She bent with not a suggestion of condescension in manner or in thought. Nevertheless Courtney, for the first time in her life painfully sensitive about her stature, flamed and was resentful—and in her scorn of her own pettiness felt tinier within than without. True, Helen's figure was commonplace, the bust too high and ominously large for her age, the hips already faintly menacing, the waist and arms somewhat too short for the great length of leg. True, her own figure was—certainly better. Still, Helen had that advantage of height—could look at Basil level-eyed, could make her seem—short! And this Helen here to stay indefinitely!

There was pathos in the slow, sweet smile Courtney gave Basil as their trembling hands met in what seemed to the others a formal greeting. She turned away with a sigh. Just as she, the thirsty, the desert-bound, was all ready to rush forward and drink—the mirage vanished. Was it to be always so? Was life to be ever a succession of mirages, vanishing at approach, only to reappear and revive hope—and cheat again? Through her mind flashed the memory of the first one—an indelible memory, always for her symbolic of vain expectation: A fourth of July when she was a very small child—how she awakened at sunrise, rushed to the window to find sky clear and world radiant and ready for the picnic that was to be her first great positive joy; how she was dressed in her best, in wonderful new white frock, in white stockings and shoes and white bows covering the top buttons, shimmering sash of pale green, and bows of pale green on her braids; how, just as she descended in all her glory to issue forth, down came the rain—in floods—and no picnic, nothing but stay at home all day and weep and watch the downpour. "It was my horoscope," thought she, as she stood there in the hall too sad for bitterness over her spoiled home-coming. "Is it fate? Or, is it somehow my fault? My fault, I suppose. I must be asking of life something no one—at least, no woman—has the right to expect."

She was near the library door, with Winchie on its threshold staring round big-eyed and crying, "Oh, mamma Courtney. Look!" His eyes were no more wondering than her own. She had been too disheartened to make the library over into a conservatory that year; now, here it was transformed into a conservatory—the carpet up from the hardwood floor, plants beautiful for bloom or for foliage or for both in boxes, in jars, in pots—everywhere. A conservatory like that of former years, but more elaborate.

The others were laughing and watching her face. So she exclaimed "I am surprised!" in the indefinite tone the listener can easily adapt to his expectations. But she was not pleased—far from it. Another fierce pang of jealousy. She, modest about her own abilities, did not realize that the room lacked just the finishing touch of her exquisite taste. To her it seemed better far than she could have done. Why, she hadn't been needed, or missed even! Things went on as well in her absence as when she was here. And near her, side by side, were Basil and Helen—how she could feel them!—so well matched physically—and he fair, she dark. And Courtney had not that self-complacent, satisfied vanity which shelters so many of us from any and all misgivings and doubts.

"Helen did most of it," explained Vaughan. "She's a trump, you'll find. Look out, Helen, or we'll make you do all the work."

"Cousin Dick proposed it and really carried it out," protested Helen in her school-teacherish or collegiate speech and manner. "And Mr. Gallatin was invaluable in showing us how you had it last winter. We wanted to get it exactly the same."

Courtney turned brilliant, grateful eyes on Basil. "So, you remembered, did you?" she ventured to say, sure her meaning and her tone would pass the others safely.

Basil flushed. "You can judge for yourself," said he.

"I'm so overcome I don't know what to say." Their smiling, friendly faces, all bent upon her, made her natural generosity burst forth like April's unending green at the first warmth of the sun. Her eyes filled. "Thank you—thank you all!" she cried.

"I am so—*so*—happy!" And she kissed Helen again, ashamed of her mean impulses toward one whose aloneness and poverty commanded kindness and consideration and help from another woman, especially from a woman who had known the bitterness of dependence and aloneness.

Good sense and decent instincts, having driven off jealousy, held the field—not without occasional alarms and excursions, but still decisively. It was the merriest party that had gathered about the mahogany dining-room table since Colonel 'Kill imported it from beyond the mountains, along with sundry novelties in those parts, in that early day—carpets and curtains and window glass, wall paper and carved beds and crystal chandeliers. In Colonel 'Kill's time the atmosphere had been genial but austere; Aunt Eudosia, during her brief reign between his death and her own, had maintained his traditions reverently; and Courtney had struggled not altogether with success, though bravely and resolutely, against the atmosphere that lingered on after all her brightening changes. But that night, the spell was broken. Dick put aside his chemistry; Basil and Courtney forgot him and their burden of deceit. Helen belied her mourning which, as Courtney had shrewdly guessed, was mere formality anyhow. Everyone was gay, even jealous little Winchie, devoting himself to Helen, determined to make her love him. And Courtney was gayest of all; was not that vacant place at the table filled once more? Her heart overflowed with joy and her lips and eyes with laughter each time she looked in that direction and saw—*him*! Everyone was gay except old Nanny, listening sourly to the merriment that came through door and hall into kitchen and sounded like a burst from a ballroom whenever Lizzie was passing in or out. "Poor young man!" muttered Nanny to her dishes and pans. "If he only knowed the whited sepulchre he's living amidst, what a holocaust there'd be." She did not know what holocaust meant, having got merely its vague sense from a sermon; thus, it gave her a conception of anarchy and chaos far beyond the scope of words she understood.

Courtney's emerald eyes, dancing and laughing though they were, scrutinized Basil. Not that she really suspected him; she simply wished to fortify herself against the folly and the unhappiness of suspicion—as women look under a bed before getting into it. Having fortified herself, she concentrated on Helen—Helen, the homeless, the unmarried, the eager to be married. There the results of her scrutiny were not so satisfactory. Basil would have called Helen's manner mere civility; and perhaps, in strict justice, it was nothing more. But Courtney the woman, judging Helen the woman, saw the hidden truth beneath the surface truth—saw that Helen was not without an instinct for a possible customer for the virtue so carefully nurtured against the coming of an opportunity for it to expand in the garden of matrimony with the flower and leaf and fruit of wife and mother. Courtney judged fairly, conceded that Helen was the reverse of forward, was using no arts, no subtleties. But the candidate for matrimony showed in her charmingly receptive and appreciative attitude toward the young man. The danger which Courtney foresaw and feared lay in the fact that Basil and Helen were both attractive. To Courtney it seemed a question of a very brief time when, without any effort whatever on her part, Helen must fall in love with him. What then? A well-bred, pretty woman in love is always more and ever more attractive to the man she centers upon. And Helen was free—and could be honorable throughout!

As Courtney undressed for bed, these reflections, so forbidding of aspect, faced her whichever way she turned. "I like Helen," she thought, "and it's decent and right to give her a home. If I were what I ought to be—ought to try to be—I'd give her every opportunity to win Basil. She's got to have some one to support her. I'm provided for. It's mean of me to stand in her way." She found some cheer in the reflection that, while most women would straight off hate Helen and look on her as an impudent interloper, she herself had generosity enough to be just in thought at least. "But I'm human," said she. "Helen has got to go. She doesn't love him. I do. She doesn't need him. I do. She's got to go!"

It was her habit to sit on the rug before the fire in her sitting room, and do her hair for the night; then she would sometimes stretch herself out flat upon her breast and read by the fire light or watch it and dream or think. She was lying that way, head pillowed upon a book and face toward the fire, when Dick opened the door, glanced in, entered. So absorbed was she that she did not know he was in the room until he spoke.

"It's like what Nanny would call a special providence, isn't it?" said he, seating himself on the sofa parallel to the fireplace but well back from it. He had a long dressing gown over his pajamas and was smoking a last cigarette.

"Special providence? What?" inquired she without turning her head. His entrance had not interrupted her train of thought. Her answer was, as usual, a reflex action from her surface mind.

"Why, Basil's coming back."

No reply. She was not thinking of Dick's statement of Basil's return as coming from him but as if she had herself begun to revolve it of her own accord.

"And Helen's being here."

A restless shiver. She was unconscious of Dick's presence. She was gazing absorbed at the proposition: Helen is here.

"It's just as we wanted it," he went on.

The lithe, delicately formed body grew tense. "Speak for yourself," she said curtly.

Richard received this rebuff in silence. "I know you don't like Basil," said he at length. "And, it's true he was a tank and a tear-about at college——"

There he stopped, shamefaced. He forgot he had told her about Basil; he felt it was undignified and unworthy gossip now that he had matrimonial designs upon him. "That slipped out," he said to her apologetically. "I never intended to tell you. Anyhow, he has dropped all that sort of thing, and I don't believe he'll ever turn loose again.... I wonder why that girl broke the engagement. He tells me he's free, and I suspect he wanted to come back because he's pretty badly cut up.... You will be nice to him, Courtney?—and help him and Helen along? They were intended for each other—height—contrast of coloring——"

Courtney sat up impatiently, turned her back to the fire to warm it, clasped her knees in her arms. She was conscious of him now, vaguely, unpleasantly conscious, though the ideas he had suggested still held most of her attention. Gradually she became uncomfortable; no, it was not the cold. Her wandering glance happened upon Richard's face. His expression— That was it! Not cold, but the sense of being looked at by eyes that had not the right. She blushed furiously from head to feet, had an impulse to snatch the rug about her and dart from the room.

"You are—*beautiful*!" he exclaimed, rising. "I was just contrasting you with Helen March this evening. She's undoubtedly handsome. Has height, and go, and, for a girl, really a surprising amount of——"

Courtney was not listening. She was thinking of her oversight in not locking her doors into the hall.

"Of charm—aside from the freshness that's about all there is to most girls, I imagine."

She must be careful not to irritate him, not to rouse him to the vigilance that nothing can escape. What a luckless beginning of a new life!

"And you're so well now—so alive——"

"I'm all but dead," she declared, pretending a yawn. "I must go to bed." She sprang lightly up. "Good night," she said. And to take away the sting—for, his slight wince showed her there was sting—she stood on tiptoe, hands behind her and face upturned.

His lips touched her cheek hesitatingly; fired by the contact, he took her in his arms and kissed her. She did not draw away; an instinct of prudence, not a deliberate thought, restrained her. She flushed from head to foot, her modesty wounded, her pride abased. "Good night," said he, lingeringly.

"Good night," she echoed, turning away to screen the fire.

Half an hour later all the lights in the house were out. She had gone to bed, but not to sleep. She suddenly sat up, gazed eagerly toward the window giving on the small veranda. It was open for the night; the shutters were latched, however, and through them came intensely cold air and some faint light. She thought she heard a tapping at the shutter—that shutter she had so often thrown wide in the hope that Basil had secretly returned. She listened. After a long wait, again the tapping—so soft that only the attention of an expectant listener would have been attracted.

"Basil!" she murmured. "I must have been expecting him."

She was about to dart to the window when there came a thought like a blow in the face flinging her back and making her cover her head. First the one man; now the other. "God!" she muttered. "How they will degrade me, between them."

No, it should not be! She grew angry with Basil. At the first opportunity, breaking his promise, trying to tempt her to become what he could not but despise. *That* was what he called *love*! And how poorly he must think of her! ... She uncovered her head, listened. No repetition of the sound. She ran to the window, opened the shutter. No one! Yes—the snow on the rail had been disturbed. She leaned out. Snow—the black boughs—the biting midnight air—stars—the crescent moon with a pendant planet—the distant muffled sound of a horse stamping in its stall. She closed the shutter, went shivering back to bed—heartsick with disappointment.

# Chapter 18

When she at last went to sleep it was like a ship going down in a storm. But she slept nine hours without a dream; and she awakened in that buoyant mood with which perfect health of body will triumph over whatever heaviness of soul. Her troubles seemed largely fanciful, were certainly anticipatory; she would push steadily forward, and all would be well.

When she descended, the two men had breakfasted and gone, and Winchie was out on the lawn playing at snow man with the Donaldson children and their governess. Helen, still at table with coffee and newspaper, greeted her so honest of eye and of voice that she was altogether ashamed of her thoughts of evening and night before. Also, Helen did not look especially well in the mornings. Sleep swelled her face, her eyelids; her skin inclined to be cloudy; her hair hung rather stringily about her brow. And in négligée the defect of too much bust and too short waist seemed worse than it was. "I must see that she gets a proper corset," thought Courtney. "Like so many women, she doesn't realize that corset is three fourths of the battle for figure." She studied Helen with an artist's eye and an artist's enthusiasm for bringing out the best, the beautiful. "Yes," she said to herself, "Helen can be made a perfect wonder for looks. I *must* try it." And then she knew she had never really intended to send Helen away. She who had suffered so much from the tyranny of dependence—it would be impossible for her to exercise that tyranny over another. "I don't want to send her away. But if I did want to, I couldn't, no matter what happened. I might think I would, and try to compel myself to do it. But when it came to the pinch, I'd remember—and I couldn't. No other human being shall ever know through me the sort of humiliation I bear."

She was ashamed of her fears about Basil, too. "As if he hadn't known lots of women. As if our love were just the ordinary thing that passes for love. And Helen'll help brighten things up—this house must not and shall not be gloomy." Then too—and this idea she did not definitely express to herself—Helen would give her and Basil more freedom by pairing off with Richard when they were all together.

Still more cheering were the thoughts that came from her mail. From the bank's monthly statement she learned that Richard had for the first time fixed an allowance sufficient for the position she was expected to maintain. There is a minimum amount on which a family can live in a certain style; every dollar below that means pinch, every dollar above it luxury. Courtney had at times been hard put to keep from going into debt. Many a woman, bred as she had been, as most American women are—with small practical knowledge, with only the silly useless "education" the usual school and college give, with no notion of values or mistaken notions, with contempt for realities and reverence for inanities—has in the same circumstances become hopelessly involved. But whatever the shortcomings in Mrs.

Benedict's system of bringing up her children, she had certainly inculcated a horror of debt. And as human life and character are grounded upon material things if they have any substantial foundation at all, this dread of debt had been and continued to be one of the main factors in Courtney's development. It is amazing how far a single cardinal *real* principle, such as a fixed aversion to debt, will go toward keeping any human being straight, toward bringing them back to sense of the just and the right, when they have been swerved by emotion or irresistible gale of circumstance. But in human affairs all the truly great powers are forces so quiet and move so close to the ground that their existence is unsuspected; or if pointed out, it is denied and scouted, and some windy fake of philosophy or politics or superstition is hailed as the god in the machine. Instead of going into debt and playing the "refined, cultured lady," Courtney had set about learning to economize without privation or meanness or tawdry pretense, acquiring the supreme art of living—the getting of its full value for every dollar. It had been a hard schooling; she began to realize how valuable, how invaluable. With this additional allowance Richard was now making, she saw what wonders of improvement she could work—she who had been getting out of the smaller income what many women in Wenona, spending four and five times as much, had not got. Certainly, the sky was brightening.

"If you haven't taken a dislike to me," Helen was saying, "and are going to let me stay a while, I'll make myself useful. In fact, I'll not stay if I don't. I must pay my way, and I can't pay in money."

"Whatever you like," said Courtney, "if you'll only stay. We want you. We need you."

Helen never forgot the warmth that cordial genuine tone sent through her. She didn't try to put her thanks into words, for there are no words for such real and deep feeling. She simply looked at Courtney—a look that more than rewarded her. After a moment she went on in an unsteady voice, "I could help—with Winchie. I took a course in kindergarten work at Tecumseh—and in housekeeping, too. They really teach things—real things—there. Then, I sew beautifully—the finest kind of sewing."

"So I see," said Courtney, looking at the sacque Helen was wearing. She did not like the sacque, because she did not like flummery and elaboration—and Helen had the poor girl's weakness for both. But she did admire the quality of the work that had been put into it.

"You must let me do some sewing for you. Do you like fine underclothes?"

"Crazy about them."

"I knew you were," said Helen who, judging by Courtney's dress and light way of talking, had already clearly and finally made up her mind that the verdict of "serious people" as to her cousin was just—a sweet, light, pretty creature, fond of dress and all the frivolities. "Just you wait! Mrs. Hargrave up at our town brought back some things from Paris—perfectly wonderful! All the women were excited about them. Well, I know how to make them—and where the goods can be got. Not expensive, either."

"I'll get the material," said Courtney, "and you can make some for both of us."

"Then I took a course in fitting. Don't judge by the things I wear. I somehow can't fit myself."

"It's the corset," said Courtney.

"I suppose so. I could never afford to have them made—or to buy the best ready-made kind. But I can do well for others. I can teach your dressmaker how to behave herself. That'll save you a lot of time and worry, won't it?"

"And work. Now, I have to remake most of my things."

Courtney began to respect Helen. The evening before, the girl, bent upon making a favorable impression, had been a wholly different person. She had seemed to Courtney stuffed to bursting with the familiar, everywhere admired and nowhere admirable "idealism" that chokes thought with cant and cumbers action with pretense. She had displayed a disquieting fondness for the "cultured" drivel about art and literature, about morals and manners, that destroys sincerity and simplicity's strength, and creates the doleful dreary lack of individuality characteristic of the so-called educated classes throughout the world. Courtney had always had the courage to confess that these honored frauds seemed to her ridiculous and wearisome. She assumed that Richard's and Basil's admiring attention, as Helen "showed off" after the manner of young girls, was politeness—or tribute to Helen's good looks. Now that she had discovered real virtues in Helen, she was not alarmed; for, she had learned that men are not interested in such virtues in young women but only in surface charms that stimulate their sex illusions. "It'd take a man who had been married at least once to appreciate Helen," thought she.

By the time Courtney finished breakfast, she had explained her plans and Helen had made many intelligent suggestions. They lost no time in getting to work. The morning flew, dinner was ready before they had given it a thought. Yes, Helen was a genuine addition, was just what she needed. "Yet I've no doubt Basil'll think her stupid once he gets used to her beauty and her sweetly pretty romantic pose for the matrimonial game."

Dick and Basil came, and the merry party of the night before was repeated. Courtney noted with pleasure that Dick and Helen had taken a fancy to each other. Without her realizing it, this was a thorough test of her absolute apartness from him; for, many a woman who is not in love with her husband, who actively dislikes him, will yet be furiously jealous of him—and by no means entirely from the sordid motive of fear lest his being attracted elsewhere will end in lessening her own portion of the income. Dick showed that he thought Helen, tall of stature and serious looking, an appreciative listener to his discourses on chemistry; and Helen's manner was indeed well calculated to deceive—a man. After dinner Dick led her up to his study further to explain some things they had been discussing. Winchie hurried away to resume play with the Donaldsons, their governess having come for him—and Courtney and Basil were free.

"It seems too good to be true," said Basil. "How much better this is—in every way—than what we've been condemning each other to.... Courtney, I did a very indiscreet thing last night. I came to your window—climbed up by a ladder Jimmie had forgotten to lock up in the woodshed."

Courtney, rosy red, lowered her head.

"I don't wonder you're angry. I'll never do it again. When we have such happiness as this, we must do nothing—*nothing*—to endanger it. And I want to say, you were right about—about what's best for us. The very resolve to try has made everything seem entirely different. I'm not ashamed when I look at Richard. I can meet his eyes. And with your help I think I can wait patiently—and hope! ... Don't you think it possible those two might fall in love?"

She was startled, then fascinated by the idea. "Why not? If they only would!"

"It's just possible—barely possible." They sat silent, reflecting on this new hope. Presently Basil went on, "They're both very serious minded. And Miss March would be a real companion for him. She's thoroughly intellectual, has quite a remarkable mind—more like a man's."

At "intellectual" Courtney thought he was joking. She began to smile, rather reluctantly—for, she did not like to laugh at so sweet and honest a girl as Helen, even with one so near to her, so like another self. Then his expression warned her that he was in earnest, that he really regarded Helen's "cultured" conversation as an indication of intelligence, did not see that it was merely education of an elementary and commonplace sort—the sort the colleges, those wholesale dealers in ready-made mental clothes, dressed out all minds in, so that usually one could tell a college man just as one could tell a ready-made suit. It was at her face to laugh at him. What an instance of woman's good looks blinding susceptible man to the truth about her internal furnishing, as different from the real thing as a hotel parlor from the drawing-room of a person of taste and individuality. But she did not laugh; that would have seemed meanness toward Helen—and Courtney, no lenient critic of her own character, rather suspected herself of a sly ungenerous envy of Helen's stature.

"Yes," pursued Basil, "Miss March has a remarkable mind. But I'm afraid there's no hope—about her and him. You see, she's not at all that sort of girl. She'd rather die than commit any impropriety—that is, I mean of course," he stammered, "she's horribly prim."

Courtney would have thought nothing of it, had he not stumbled and hastened on to explain. But that agitated, apologetic embarrassment changed "she'd rather die than commit any impropriety" from a commonplace into a tribute to Helen which was a slur upon herself. For her love's sake she resisted the temptation to pretend not to have heard or felt. "You like that sort of thing in a woman, don't you?" said she, with a lift of the eyebrows, those deep notes in her voice ominous.

"In Miss March—yes," blundered he. "That is, in a young girl." He halted, burst out desperately, "You're always suspecting me of not respecting you."

There began to gather in Courtney an emotion that terrified her. It was not anger; it was not shame. It seemed, rather, a sort of dread—though of what she did not know—did not wish to know. "Please, no protests," she said hurriedly. "Let's drop the subject."

"I do respect you," he said, doggedly. "But if I didn't"—there, he looked at her—"I feel for you something that's so much more than respect—I love you."

She drew in her breath sharply, and her eyes gleamed and glistened as they opened wide. She had a way of opening her eyes upon him that made him feel as if he were standing on a high place and about to plunge dizzily into the sea at the call of a mermaid. The silence that followed was interrupted—rudely it seemed to them—by the return of Helen and Dick.

"I need somebody in addition to you, Gallatin, to help out down at the shop," said Dick, "and Helen is going to try."

"If Cousin Courtney is willing," said Helen. "She may need me here, as I told you."

Courtney had been standing with her fingers on the edge of the chimney-piece, gazing between her arms into the fire. She slowly turned and regarded Richard. Basil and Helen working together!

"Oh, no, she doesn't need you here," asserted Vaughan. And catching Courtney's eye, he glanced from Basil to Helen and winked.

Courtney seemed not to see. "Helen doesn't want to go down there," said she. "Richard imagines, if people listen politely to his talk about chemistry, that they're as interested as he."

"Really I'd like it," said Helen, a good deal of nervousness in her enthusiasm.

"She could try it anyhow," urged Vaughan. "We need some one—don't we, Basil?"

"Yes," said Basil. "You remember, I suggested you ought to ask Mrs. Courtney to take a hand."

"Courtney!" Vaughan laughed gayly. "She has no fancy for anything serious. Now, Helen is masculine minded."

"Not a bit," declared Helen, much agitated by such an accusation, in presence of an eligible young man. "I'm so much a woman that I'm what's called a woman's woman."

"Helen prefers to stay here," said Courtney. "So, I think *I'll* try."

Richard stared and frowned.

She smiled at Basil. "Richard is getting broad minded," she went on slowly, selecting her words. "A short time ago the idea of a woman in that laboratory of his would have upset him quite. I remember, when we were first married, I made the most desperate efforts to get him to let me help. He was finally quite rude about it." She spoke with no suggestion of resentment; and, indeed, that time seemed so remote, so like a part of another life or another person's life that she felt no resentment.

"I'm sure—we'll—both—be glad to have you," stammered Basil. He was confused before the instinct-born thought that those few apparently simple words of hers, so quietly and so good-humoredly spoken, were in fact the story of the matrimonial ruin he had found when he came—and was profiting by.

"I'll come down to-morrow," Courtney went on. "Helen can look after things here."

Helen could not conceal her relief; when the men were gone she said: "I'm so glad you got me out of that. Dick would have discovered what a stupid I am in about one hour, and he'd have despised me. I'd hate that, as I think he's wonderful. How proud you must be of him. Of course, Basil is very sweet—and *such* a gentleman—and how well he does dress! But Dick— They're not in the same class."

"No," said Courtney.

Just then Vaughan came hurrying in. "I forgot something I wanted to say to you, my dear," he began. "Come in here——"

Helen took the hint and hastened away. Vaughan went on, "Why on earth didn't you help me?"

Courtney looked interrogative. She felt a curious impersonal anger against him for having blunderingly interfered in her affairs.

"Didn't you see," explained Richard somewhat irritably, "I had it all fixed to bring those two together?"

"How dull of me!"

"It's not too late. All you have to do is back out and send her."

"And have her exhibit herself before him at her worst. And get him sick of the very sight of her." Richard began to look foolish. Courtney went on in the same tone of light mockery: "If you want a girl to marry a man, or a man a girl, you mustn't let them see too much of each other. If possible, make it hard for them to get at each other." The emerald eyes were mockingly mirthful now. "No such love-inducer in the world as holding two people apart. And when two can see each other freely—to their heart's content—and satiation—why—" She finished with a shrug, her eyes looking straight into his.

"All right. You women know each other best," said he, uncomfortable, without being able to locate the cause.

"Helen will stay at home, like the homebody she is," pursued Courtney. "And I'll come to help you. I've had it in mind for several days."

"You're not in earnest about that!" cried Vaughan in alarm. "Why, what'd you do there? You'd be in the way."

"More than Helen?"

"Frankly—yes," said Richard bluntly. "As I said before, serious things interest her. You know, I dislike that sort of thing in a woman—am glad to see that you've gotten entirely over it, as I knew you would. But I could have put up with it—for a while—to help Helen to a good husband and Basil to a fine wife. It wouldn't have taken long—at least, I thought not. I admit I was probably wrong, and you right."

"Well—now that I've said I'd come, I'll come," said Courtney. "Helen'll take most of the detail here off my hands."

"If you really want to come—" said Dick, reluctant. "I suppose—after what I've said— Well, you can come for a few days."

Courtney was looking into the fire. Not for a "few days" but for as long as Basil worked with those dangerous chemicals. If anything happened—they would be together. Richard was looking at her; but he thought it was the fire light that was giving her the strange, somehow terrible expression which yet enhanced her beauty and her charm.

"How serious you look," said he. "Really, quite tragic—in that light."

"Yes, it must be the way the light falls," replied she. "Or is it because I've mislaid my pet powder rag?"

Next morning as soon as Courtney dispatched her household routine she went down to the Smoke House and appeared before Richard in his laboratory for the first time since that morning after the homecoming, long, long ago in that other life. With a platinum rod he was slowly stirring some fiery mixture of a dark purple color in a big iron crucible. She saw that the fumes were poisonous, as his nose and mouth were protected by a respirator. As on the previous visit she stood silent in the doorway watching him. She had long since passed the stage of comparisons and contrasts; and her mind was altogether upon the present and the future, as an intelligent young mind is extremely apt to be. So, she was not thinking of that previous visit, but was simply interested in what he was doing—in his work, which she had now resolved, with an experienced woman's determination, to make her own work also, no matter what opposition she might encounter. Her achievements in house and gardens, in bringing up Winchie, in breaking through the barriers of moral convention so powerful round a woman born and bred as she had been— these feats had wonderfully developed her will, had replaced shyness and timidity with quiet self-confidence.

When the contents of the crucible cooled and he took off the respirator, she spoke. "I see you've run up a partition."

He glanced at her with a frown—not severe but irritated, as at the persistent naughtiness of a sweet and charming child. "Oh, you've come—have you? ... Yes— the partition gives Basil and me each his own shop. I like to work alone, whenever it's possible."

She advanced calmly, indifferent to his unfriendliness. "Then you don't want me to help *you*?" She put all her diplomacy of tone and manner into that little speech. She knew how much depended upon this "entering wedge"—this getting tolerated within those walls.

"What a whimsical creature you are!" Dick was still vexed, but half laughing, too. She was so delicate and graceful, so fascinating to the eye; and she seemed to him absurdly, quaintly out of place there. "Basil!" he called. "Gallatin!"

Gallatin, in a blouse, rubber apron and gloves appeared from the other part of the shop.

"Well—here's the—the 'prentice," said Dick. "You're not busy nowadays. Take charge of her."

"It'll be a great pleasure, I'm sure," he stammered. He looked about as uncomfortable at sight of her as had Richard. Demurely she followed him into his compartment. As the partition did not extend to the ceiling, they had to content themselves with an exchange of eloquent glances. Then, taking the tone of gentleman chemist to not overbright and densely ignorant lady visitor at a laboratory, he began to explain to her the names and uses of things, and to demonstrate how to use them.

For the entire morning he talked and illustrated, thoroughly enjoying himself at making a fine impression with his display of superior knowledge. He told her little she did not already know. But she was not so tactless as to spoil his pleasure or hurt his vanity. She listened and tried; and when he complimented her on her quickness in learning, she showed delight at being praised. In the afternoon he allowed her to practice his teachings unassisted—set her at weighing a little nitrate of potassium precipitate in the gold and ivory and aluminum balances. She had done this sort of things a hundred times, but was meek under his elaborations of cautioning and explaining.

"I worked a lot in laboratories at school," said she ingenuously, when his guidance became a little tiresome. "It's beginning to come back to me."

He smiled in a way that reminded her of Richard. "All right. Do the best you can," said he. "We'll not expect much of you for the present. I'm afraid you'll soon give up."

She looked at him. "I'm here to stay," said she, "You'll not get rid of me."

"But the work's very hard—not at all feminine."

"That suits me. For, I'm not at all feminine, myself—what men mean by feminine."

He laughed, went about his own business. As she sat at the balances, her whole mind on the needle she was watching through the reading glass, she felt herself caught from behind. She turned her laughing face upward and backward, and they kissed. "Isn't it splendid!" he exclaimed under his breath. "Yes—you must stay." It had been part of her plan of life that they should never caress. Suddenly she realized how impossible this rule was—and how foolish. On occasions—such occasions as this joy in the unexpected kindness of fate—the rule must be suspended.

"How long it's been!" he said in a low voice. "Not since early September have I kissed you—and this is almost February."

She glanced warningly toward the top of the partition.

"Away at the other end," Basil assured her, "and doing something that can't be left an instant for an hour or more."

"Well then—" She blushed, hesitated, gave him a passionate, longing look. "One more kiss—and we go to work."

He seated himself and drew her to his lap. With their heads close together, they talked—of anything, of everything, of nothing—and hardly knew what they were saying—and cared not at all. "Oh, the happiness of it," she murmured. "And we are to work side by side, too. It seems a dream. I can't believe it."

"And soon it will be spring again, and we shall be a little freer."

"Be patient until I get everything settled," she answered, "and we shall be free almost all the time. I have thought it out."

"You think of everything."

"I think of nothing but you—always you," she answered. "What have I but our love? I want to make the house comfortable, your apartment comfortable, myself attractive—all, so that love will never begin to think of taking flight."

"Flight!" He laughed softly. "How absurd! Can't you feel that I'm just wrapped up in you?"

She touched his tight encircling arms. "I can feel that I'm just wrapped up in you," she retorted. "Now, let me go. I am not to keep you from the work—or you me."

"Not just yet."

"Yes"—firmly. "You don't take me any more seriously than Richard does. But I don't in the least care. If I am serious, what does it matter whether anyone thinks so or not?" She laughed a little. "And I'm feminine enough, I'll admit, to want to be what the man who wants me wants me to be."

He was not listening. He held her more tightly, and she knew what was coming before he began to speak. "Let me come to-night, Courtney. Just this once. I simply want to be alone with you——"

"Not yet," she replied. "Don't let's tempt each other to risk years of happiness for a frightened moment." And, afraid she would yield if he kept on urging, she abruptly freed herself and sent him back to his seat.

An hour, and he came to her again. "I've been doing nothing but watch you, and you haven't looked round once."

"This work is interesting," replied she—and it was the simple truth.

"No—not once!"

"What a good example I'm setting you. I always used to like chemistry. And I was a harum-scarum girl then. Now, I see I'm going to be tremendously fond of it."

"Courtney—I can't stand—our—our compact. I simply can't. I feel as if you had thrust me out of your life. And— Have you no memory, sweetheart? Courtney, we're only human beings, after all. And we've the right. Aren't you my wife?"

"Don't tempt me, Basil," she answered with a sigh. "Do you suppose I don't feel it? Sometimes I get to thinking what might be— But I will not! You do not wish it." And she glanced meaningly at the partition.

"You are mine!" he whispered, moved by the reminder but not abashed. "If I had never known love in its fullness, I might be able to endure this cold, repellent pretense of virtue—for, it's nothing but a flimsy pretense. Courtney, if you love me——"

"Is your love only—*that*!"

"If you loved me," he repeated, "you'd not calculate so puritanically. If I weren't seeing you, dear, I could bear it. But seeing you all the time—touching you— kissing you—Courtney, Courtney, how can you make me, and yourself too, suffer so needlessly? If you really love, how can you keep me out of your inmost life—as if I were not everything to you?"

"I explained to you——"

"Explained! Explained!" he said, impatiently. "We explain and explain, but it's all sophistry. The truth is—what? That we are lovers. And, if our love is a sin, why not take all its reward since we'll have to take all its punishment?"

"Don't harass me now," she begged, agitated and trembling.

"Harass you!" He drew away offendedly. "I thought I was pleading for you, as well as for myself. If I am not, please forget what I said."

"I didn't mean that!"

"Then I may come to-night—or you to me?"

She gave him a sad, pleading look. "Not to-night, dear. Not just yet. We *must* wait till things are going quietly in a routine."

"How easily you put us off!"

"Basil!—*Please!*"

He stared sulkily out of the window. "It does sting my pride that you care so much less than I. It does make me—almost doubt."

"Not so loud!"

"You don't realize how far away he is, and how absorbed.... I take back all I said." And he straightened himself coldly and went to his own part of the room.

A moment, and she followed him. "You are offended, Basil."

"No—hurt."

She sighed. "I will come to-night."

"You do not wish to come!"

"To be honest, no. I should feel—" She hesitated. She wished to be frank; but how could she be, when he was in that mood of doubt? How could she explain again that, in some respects, she loathed the memory of the times they had been stealthily together—the alarms, the narrow escapes from discovery—the commonness of it all—like those low intrigues that get into the newspapers, to make coarse mouths water and vulgar eyes sparkle? If she tried to tell him, he would misunderstand. "Not just yet," she went on. "I'm in a queer mood—not myself. You——"

She was so tender, so loving, so deeply distressed that, in shame and contrition, he embraced her. "I'm sorry I said anything. But you'll understand. How can I help longing for you? It's your own fault—you beautiful, wonderful *woman*!"

And their first clash ended in kisses, in serenity restored, with him saying—and thinking—"How much braver and better you are than I! Yours is the love that makes a man stronger and decenter."

Her look was eloquent of gratitude and happiness. But the happiness in it was forced, at least in part, was rather what she felt she ought to feel than what she actually did feel—as is so often the case. And she went back to work with a certain heaviness of heart—and a foreboding. The slightest alarm, however fanciful, was enough to call up the specter of those months of loneliness and despair after he left. That specter haunted her, was in her mind the fixed idea that becomes an obsession. She knew that to quiet it, she would if necessary stop at nothing. "I can never give him up again. I'd do anything—anything—rather than even risk it." Pride and self-respect were all very well, but those who could put such things before love had not loved. She hoped and prayed Basil would not force her to the test. But—if he did— She sighed, and bade herself wait until that situation arose before worrying over it.

# Chapter 19

Now that the throes of birth were over, their love bade fair to be like those robust infants that almost kill mothers in the bearing but thereafter give not a moment's anxiety. Outdoors it was rivalling the previous winter; indoors—at the house and at the laboratory—there reigned mid-summer serenity. Nanny—always a shadow, though very faint indeed latterly—had yielded before her arch enemy, rheumatism, had been pensioned off, had gone to her brother's, seventeen miles into the wilderness. She would shadow them no more. Richard had come to another crisis in his researches; and a mind in the act of gestation is like a hen on eggs—solitary, brooding, best left utterly alone. He was as unconscious of Courtney and Basil as of himself; all three were, for him, simply instruments to the strange and terrible marvels of chemical action that were unfolding. Soon Basil felt about him as did Courtney—that is, lost all sense of his being related to her or to the life of the household. As they held to their compact, they experienced none of passion's inevitable alternations of rapture and revulsion. Habit is equally the friend of virtue and of vice. It was not a matter of months but of weeks when they were looking on their love as not only moral but even exalted, since they were self-restrained.

The chief factor in the tranquillity was the work. Courtney began at the laboratory solely that she and Basil might be together. Soon she had another reason—love of the work itself. Everything worth while, whether for achievement or for amusement, involves drudgery at the outset—tennis or bridge no less than a trade or an art. Although Courtney had done at school the worst part of the drudgery in acquiring chemistry, it was nearly a month before she began to enjoy. Then came the first haunting alluring glimpses of the elusive mystery which makes chemistry the most fascinating of the sciences; and from that hour forth she forgot the difficulties in the delights. She often stole in to gaze longingly at Richard's work—for, he kept the main part of the great task of finding a new and universal fuel altogether in his own hands and used the other two as mere helpers. She would have liked to work with him; and, as she understood better and better what he was about, the temptation to try to bring her skill and her knowledge to his attention became strong at times. But she was afraid that if he began to think attentively about her being there, he would send her away. No, it was best to remain hidden behind Basil, to do nothing to remind Richard of her existence.

At first Basil assumed she was toiling like another Richard because she wished quickly to get knowledge enough to make plausible her necessary pretense of interest. But after a few weeks he saw she was in earnest, or thought she was—for, he could not believe one so pretty, so charming, so light of spirit and of mind, could be deeply in earnest about such a heavy, unwomanly matter as chemistry—or about anything else, except of course love. He was fond of chemistry; but it was in the fashion of most men's fondness for serious effort—to get excuse and appetite for idling. However, partly through pride, partly because her enthusiasm was contagious, he buckled to and worked as Richard had never been able to make him.

"Really, you needn't crowd yourself quite so hard," said he to Courtney, when his own energy began to flag.

"I've got to choose between being a drag and a help. Besides—" She glanced down with the shy, subtle smile he had learned to recognize as a cover for something she meant very much indeed—"don't you find that being occupied is a great aid?"

"I'd not have thought it possible to live as we're living—and be happy."

"You are happy?" As she asked this, she scrutinized his face in woman's familiar veiled fashion. She was always watching, watching, for the first faint dreaded sign of discontent.

"So much so," answered he, earnestly, "that I'd be afraid to change anything."

She saw that he meant it, that he felt it with all the intensity of the fine side of his nature. And she breathed a secret sigh of relief. She said: "Every day—time and again—I say to myself, 'If only this will last!'"

"It will!" declared he.

And, pessimist though she had been made by disappointment on disappointment in small things and large her whole life through, she began to hope that this would last, that the worst of her life was perhaps over, that her life problem was settling and settling right. The watchdogs of presentiment are like their much overrated animal prototypes. They bark at everything, that they may get credit for usefulness if by chance they once do happen to vent their nerve-racking warnings in advance of a real peril. Even presentiment called its dogs off duty.

She had been brought up among people who imagine they see the operations of natural law in the artificial conventions of morality that differ for every age and race and creed, really for every individual. She had long discarded as superstition the creed of her parents; but she had not been able wholly to uproot all the ramifications of beliefs dependent upon that creed for vitality. Thus, she vaguely felt a relationship of effect and cause between her sufferings in the autumn and early winter and those fear-shadowed, shame-alloyed but ecstatic moments of joy in the summer. And in the same vague way, there seemed to her some sort of connection between their present happiness and their self-restraint. She would have, quite honestly, denied, had she been accused of harboring such a "remnant of superstition." Nevertheless, it was the fact. However, she did not analyze or reason about her happiness. She simply accepted and enjoyed it—and forgot the foundations on which it rested.

And the days—the long, long days that only people who live in quiet places have—moved tranquilly and happily by, swift yet slow. The weeks seemed to be flying, and the days went very fast; but each hour presented its full quota of sixty minutes for enjoyment. In those dreadful days of the previous fall she had wished every hour that she was living in a city, because in the city a thousand resolute intrusions compel distraction, make the moments seem to fly, whether the heart is heavy or light. Now, she was glad with all her heart that she was living and loving where there were no distractions, where each moment could be lived as a connoisseur drinks his glass of rare old wine drop by drop.

One day late in April she and Richard, it so happened, were alone for a few minutes before supper. He abruptly emerged from his abstraction to say, "Basil and Helen are getting on famously."

She startled, then lapsed into her usual isolation when alone with him.

"I expect there'll be a marriage before the summer is out."

"Yes?" said Courtney, absently.

"Well, it's a good match. They're both comfortably shallow. They're fond of the same kind of harmless pretenses. They look well together.... I hope they'll stay on with us—at least until the first baby comes."

She shivered, rose abruptly. "Supper must certainly be ready," said she.

"Then," pursued Dick, intent upon his train of thought, "they might get the Donaldson place. The Donaldsons want to sell."

She smiled ironically. "I suppose you've spoken to Donaldson about it."

"Not yet. But next time I see him, I'll give him a hint. He might sell to some one else."

Basil now came in. "Sell what?" he asked, to join in the conversation.

"Oh, nothing," answered Dick. "Courtney and I were discussing the Donaldson place. Donaldson wants to sell, and we thought we might get neighbors we didn't like."

"Richard suggested," said Courtney, in her most innocent manner, "that you might buy it."

Dick looked alarmed. Basil, with his eyes on Courtney, promptly said: "Maybe I will. It's second only to this place. And I shall always live here."

"Richard thought it would be a good idea for you to settle there when you and Helen marry," said Courtney, with a smile only Basil could understand.

If anything, Basil looked more confused and nervous than did Richard; he laughed hysterically. "Really—really—that's very attractive—if—" he stammered.

Just then Helen, out of hearing on the lake-front veranda, happened to call, "Oh, Mr. Gallatin!"

"Yes," he answered, and hastened out to join her. Richard stared helplessly at his wife. "Now, why did you do that?" he demanded.

"What?"

"You certainly are the most thoughtless, frivolous person! I never knew you to be serious about anything—except something that was of not the least importance. I must remember to be always on guard when I speak before you."

"Yes, you ought to be careful. I'm not intellectual, like Helen. But I was forgetting; now you say she's shallow, too."

"All intellectual women are shallow," said Dick. He was ashamed of his heat of the moment before. "And I never said you were shallow. You ought to be glad you have no intellectual tendencies, but are a bundle of instincts and impulses, as a woman should be. I guess you didn't spill the milk, after all. If Gallatin loves Helen, a little break such as you made won't scare him off."

"No indeed. When a man's in love, the sight of the net doesn't frighten him. He helps to hold it open so that he can jump in deep."

Courtney intended to tease Basil, the next time they were alone. But it slipped her mind until nearly a week later. Basil had got into the habit of going out for a stroll and a smoke every morning about ten. She never went with him, because she did not wish to interrupt her work to which she could give only the mornings, as the time for gardens and growing things was at hand. One morning it so chanced that her task of the moment was just finished when Basil moved toward the door. "I'll go with you," said she.

He hesitated, looked disconcerted.

"Oh, if you don't want me," laughed she.

"Indeed I do," he hastened to say. "Only—usually you don't."

They went out together, walked up and down the wide retaining wall of the lake, beyond the Smoke House. Presently Helen appeared, on her way to the apartment over the laboratory. Now that she had charge of the housekeeping, it was part of her duties to look at the apartment and see that Lizzie was keeping things clean and was making Gallatin comfortable. At sight of Basil and Courtney, she stopped short, colored painfully. She answered their greetings with embarrassment, went with awkward haste in at the apartment entrance.

"Helen's extremely shy," said Courtney.

"She *is* difficult to get acquainted with," replied Basil. His manner might have been either absent or constrained.

"I'm afraid I haven't given you much chance," said Courtney, merely by way of saying something.

"Oh, I know her pretty well," Basil hastened to protest. "There's a lot more to her than one sees at first."

"Indeed there is," said Courtney, warmly. "I've grown very fond of her—fonder than I ever thought I could be of another woman. I don't care much for women. They're so small toward each other—because they're all brought up to be cutthroat rivals in the same low business—husband-catching. But Helen isn't a bit small. She has a real heart."

"And real intellect, too."

Courtney's smile was absolutely free from malice. "That's just what she has not," she replied, for she talked with perfect frankness to him, her other self. "I suppose the man never lived who could judge a good-looking woman. Women don't always misjudge men. But men always fancy beauty means brains, if the woman's heavy and serious—and not downright imbecile."

"I shouldn't call Miss March imbecile," said he. "Or even heavy."

"Now don't be cross because I hinted that women could fool you," teased Courtney. "And I didn't mean to suggest that Helen is imbecile or heavy."

"She knows an awful lot," said Basil. "She often corrects me—in little slips about authors and poetry, and so on."

Courtney could hardly keep from showing her amusement that Basil should be impressed by what was really one of Helen's weaknesses. For Helen, like so many who have small or very imperfect knowledge, attached as great importance to trifles of worthless learning as a college professor; she became agitated if anyone showed lack of knowledge of some infinitesimal in etiquette or grammar or what not, just as fashionable people sweat with mortification or distend with vast inward derision if some one, however intelligent, however capable, appears among them in an out-of-style garment or uses an expression not in their tiny vocabulary. Courtney was striving tactfully to open out a less ignorant point of view to Helen. And here was Basil showing that Helen's weakness was in reality a strength, highly useful in dealing with men.

Courtney said: "Helen is a fine, sensible, capable girl—about the finest I ever knew. And she has genuine sweetness and good taste."

"She does dress well," said Basil warmly. "If she had the means, she'd be stunning."

"Could be, but wouldn't be," replied Courtney, perfectly just and good humored, but perhaps a little weary of hearing another young woman's praises in her lover's voice. "She'd 'settle down' if she married. She's resolutely old fashioned—hates to think or to exert herself. She'll make a fine, old-fashioned wife for some man who likes to be mildly bored at home and wants his fun elsewhere. This reminds me. Richard has you and her married—wedding in the fall—baby next spring."

Basil flushed at this teasing.

"You don't seem enthusiastic."

"I don't care to hear a good young girl spoken of so lightly," said he, with some stiffness.

And now Courtney colored. After a moment she said, apologetic without knowing why: "Perhaps I shouldn't have done it. But I always feel free to speak out to you any stray thought that drifts into my head—without choosing my words."

Helen now reappeared, cast a peculiar glance in their direction, blushed rosily, hastened away toward the house. "She'd better be careful how she blushes at sight of you," said Courtney smiling, "or you'll be thinking she's in love with you."

"Nonsense!" protested Basil, again unaccountably irritated.

"How solemn you are to-day, dear. And, why shouldn't she fall in love with you? I can see how a woman might."

He did not respond to her glance. He stared straight ahead, answered awkwardly, "Helen and I are simply good friends."

The phrase jarred upon her a little. "Simply good friends." As she repeated it, she remembered suddenly, vividly, the beginning of their own love. They too had been "simply good friends." The phrase kept recurring to her, dinning disagreeably in her ears. She frowned on herself; she laughed at herself. But it continued to ring and to jar. "I certainly have a nasty jealous streak hidden away in my disposition," she said to herself. "I mustn't encourage it."

During the next few days every time Helen and Basil were together, she caught herself watching them for signs—"Signs of what?" she demanded of herself. But in spite of herself she kept on watching. That specter of the dreadful days without him—that specter so easily called up—began to glide about in the background of her thoughts, rousing those fears before which she was abject coward.

Helen had the young girl's usual assortment of harmless little tricks. Her favorite was to note when a man made a remark which she thought he regarded as clever, to go back to it after a moment or so, and repeat it and laugh or admire according as it had been intended to be amusing or profound. She was constantly doing this—with Richard, with Basil, with every man she met. The time came when the overworked trick began to get upon Courtney's nerves, especially as Helen, being entirely without humor and a close-to-shore wader in the waters of thought, was not always happy in her selection of the remark. Still, her intentions being of the best, Courtney endured; and at times she got not a little secret amusement from seeing how Basil and even Richard were flattered by the trick, never suspecting, even after Helen had again and again laughed or admired effusively in quite the wrong place. As she watched Helen and Basil now, the only "sign" she saw was this clever-stupid subtlety of Helen's for flattering male vanity—Helen practicing it on Basil, Basil purring each time like a cat under the stroking of an agreeable hand. This certainly was not serious. She laughed at herself with a reproachful "You don't deserve happiness—trying to poison it with contemptible suspicion." And the specter faded, and she no longer heard the sound of rain beating, of rain drizzling, of rain dripping through days and nights of aloneness and despair.

Spring was smiling from every twig. The birds, impatient at winter's reluctant leave-taking, had arrived before the young leaves were far enough advanced to cover them. So, every tree was alive with them, plainly in view, boldly about their courting and nesting, like lovers who, despairing of finding a quiet place, march along the highway embracing in defiance of curious eyes. One morning, half an hour after Basil went out for his habitual stroll and cigarette, Courtney changed her mind and decided to join him. She looked along the retaining wall. No Basil. She walked up and down, noting, and feeling in her own blood, the agitations of the mightiest force in the universe—those agitations that in the springtime set all nature to quivering. Ten minutes passed—fifteen—half an hour—nearly three quarters of an hour. Still no Basil. She decided he must have gone up to his rooms and fallen asleep. She resisted the temptation to go and waken him, and went slowly toward the laboratory doors. Just as she was about to jump from the wall, out of the apartment entrance came Helen, her face aglow, her eyes sparkling, all the austerity gone from her regular features. "How pretty she looks," thought Courtney. "I wonder what's delighting her so. One'd think she was in love and was loved. There never lived a sweeter, more unselfish girl. Nothing petty in her. She even has a nice way of being prudent about money."

Helen did not see her, went quickly up the path and into the wood between the Smoke House and the lawns round the house. Courtney resisted the impulse to call because she had already been out of the laboratory too long. As Helen disappeared among the trees, Courtney was astounded to see appear at the apartment door—

Basil! On his face a contented pleased expression, as if he were reflecting upon something highly agreeable—Helen's face—his face—Courtney stood for an instant like a flaming torch planted upon that wall—a torch with a white-hot flame of hate.

As Basil was taking a last puff at his cigarette, she darted into the laboratory and sat at her case. When he entered, she was just where she had been at his going out. "Still at work!" he cried.

"Still at work!" said she. She forced her lips to smile, but she did not dare lift her fluttering eyelids. She looked calm and, as always, sweet; but in those few minutes all the sweetness of her nature had transformed, as the thunderstorm changes milk from food to poison. And the remembered horror of those days of desolation goaded her toward a very insanity of fear and jealousy. That smile on Helen's face—then on his.

He stood behind her. If she had had a knife she would have whirled round and plunged it into his breast and then into her own. But she had not; also, this was twentieth-century and conventional life. She sat rigid, intent upon the flame of the blast tube she was using.

He bent and kissed her neck. "Sweetheart!" he murmured.

The fixed smile became a distortion, as she lowered her head.

"The spring—outdoors," he went on in the same low caressing voice. "It's hard to bear. It seems so long—so long—since—" His pause finished the sentence better than any words.

Long indeed, thought she; a singularly patient and restrained lover; strangely respectful.

"There are more kinds of happiness in love than I imagined," he went on. "But do you never—never———"

"Please," she interrupted. She found her voice could be trusted; she ventured to test her eyes. She looked up at him, taking pleasure in veiling her hate behind a smile. She strove to make the smile sweet and tender. She felt that she was succeeding. "How homely he is," she thought. "And I love him—ugly and a traitor. I love him, and I'll keep on loving him—for, he's all there is between me and misery."

Richard called them into the front compartment, and the three worked together at the big retort the rest of the morning. It was a strange hour and a half. She seemed to be two distinct persons—no, three. One was hating Basil and Helen—a being that seemed to concentrate all that is venomous and malignant. One was watching with interest and excitement the awful processes by which calm liquids poured together suddenly became violent, colorless liquids a marvelous radiance of exquisite color, heat became infinite cold and cold became heat that consumed hard metals as if they were bits of fluff. The third personality within her was aloof and calm, and watched her other two and wondered at them.

At dinner time she and Richard walked to the house together, Basil stopping at the apartment to tidy himself, as usual. "Well, how do you think they are getting on?" she asked carelessly.

"I can't tell," replied Richard, "till I've got several other reactions."

171

"Helen and Basil, I mean."

"How should I know? All right, I suppose."

"Didn't you tell me, a week or so ago, you thought it was a match?"

"Of course it's a match," said he, as if there weren't a doubt about it.

She quivered at this pressure upon the thorn that was pricking and festering. "Why are you so positive?" she asked.

"You know as much as I do. He goes out to meet her every morning, doesn't he?"

Every morning! To smoke! In a series of internal explosions whose flames scorched her soul she traced the progress of that smoking habit of his. With an outer calmness that amazed her she pursued her inquiries. "Are they—affectionate when they're alone?" she asked.

"How?" Richard's mind was back at his experiments.

She repeated her question in a voice that was under still better control.

"I've never seen them but once—one day when he was helping her balance herself at the edge of the wall—she was pretending to look down into the water at something—the old trick."

Courtney laughed. "The old trick—yes." She laughed again.

"It's all settled, no doubt," declared Richard. "And good business!"

Courtney hurled a glance of fury at him. "Unless he's making a fool of her."

"Oh—absurd. He's a gentleman."

"Gentleman. That sounds as if it meant a lot, but does it?"

Richard wished to think of his work uninterrupted by this trifle of a love affair. "Why not ask her about it? She's no doubt dying to tell—if you give her the excuse of opening the subject."

Courtney went up to her balcony, seated herself in a rocking-chair. She rocked and thought, thought, thought—getting nowhere, motion without progress, like that of her chair. She did all the talking at dinner that day. She took the relations of men and women for her subject and shot arrows of wit at it. As Winchie was having dinner next door with the Donaldson children, she did not need to restrain herself. She was mocking, cynical, audacious. Basil stopped laughing and stared at his plate. Helen, all blushes, looked as if she would sink under the table. Richard remained calm—he was not hearing a word. Basil's gloom and Helen's shocked modesty delighted Courtney, edged her on to further audacities. She looked from one to the other, smiling, jeering at them—and she rattled on and on, because she felt that if she stopped scoffing and laughing, she would spring at him or at her. She had the longing to do physical violence, like one in the torment of a toothache.

Richard and Basil had not been gone many minutes before she began on the unconscious Helen. A sigh gave her the opening. "Unhappy?" she said.

"No, indeed," answered Helen. "If anything, too happy. You know what this life here means to me."

"But you must find it lonely."

"Lonely! Not for an instant."

"We've had almost no company this winter and spring. I must hunt up some young men for you."

"I don't want them, as I've often told you." Courtney remembered that she had, and muttered, "What a blind fool I've been." Helen went sweetly on: "Beside such men as Richard and Mr. Gallatin, the ordinary young man is anything but interesting."

"Still, you must marry. And you've got the looks to make a first-rate bargain."

Helen looked gently disapproving of this frank mode of stating the case. "I could never marry for anything but love."

"Of course. But, being a well-brought-up woman, you'll not have difficulty in loving any proper candidate."

"I'm well content."

Courtney bent low over the scarlet and pink and white tulips in one of the window boxes. Content! This woman who was stealing her lover—this woman who was thrusting her back into the despair of those loveless, hopeless days when Basil was gone and the icy rains poured on and on upon her desolate life! She controlled herself, repeated vaguely: "Content? Impossible unless you've got your eye on a likely man. No single woman ever was since the world began."

Helen blushed consciously.

"Who is he?" teased Courtney. She had seen the blush, and her nerves were twitching. "Who is it?" she repeated softly. "Basil?"

The blush deepened.

"I thought so!" exclaimed Courtney with laughing triumph. "You've yielded to his fascinations, have you?"

Helen paled and her lip trembled. "Please don't," she faltered. "Don't joke me about—about him."

Courtney turned hastily away to hide the devil that gleamed from her eyes; for she felt that her worst suspicions were confirmed. "Tell me," she said, as soon as she could find voice, and could make that voice gay with good-humored raillery, "how long has this—this idyll been going on?"

"Really—you're quite mistaken, dear," pleaded Helen.

"How long have you and he been keeping those trysts?"

"You're quite wrong. We've met by accident," protested Helen. "We just happen to meet." She hung her head. "I'll admit I—I arrange to go to look at the apartment about the time I know he comes out to smoke."

Courtney was all smiles. "And he arranges to come out to smoke about the time he knows you're going to the apartment. How—delicious!"

"Do you think he does it deliberately?" inquired Helen eagerly.

Courtney was amazed at the girl's skill in duplicity. She began to wonder how far they had gone. But her face was bright and innocent as a poison locust bloom when she said: "You sly child! What were you and he doing in his apartment to-day?"

"Oh!" cried Helen, covering her face with her hands.

Courtney's features were distorted with fear and fury; the specter was stalking and leering. But her voice sounded soft and seductive as she urged: "Go on, dear. You needn't be afraid to tell me—everything."

Helen lifted her flaming face. "There's nothing to tell," cried she. "When you asked me that question, something in your tone made me feel as if I had done a—a wickedly indiscreet thing. But it was all so harmless and accidental. I came earlier than usual, and he was getting the cigarette case he'd forgotten."

"Highly probable!" exclaimed Courtney, apparently much amused. "And so, you could make love to each other at your ease."

"Courtney!" Helen started up, horror-stricken. "Can you think I'd let him lay the weight of his finger on me?" And she burst into tears. "Oh, *what* have I done!" she sobbed. "And it seemed perfectly innocent."

Insane with jealousy though she was, Courtney could not but be convinced. "Don't take it so to heart, my dear," said she. "Tell me all about it."

"And you could suspect me! But I deserve it. If I'd been really a good woman, I'd not have thought of him until he had spoken to me."

"Dry your eyes," said Courtney, calm and practical. "How far has this gone?"

"Not at all," declared Helen. "We've never said a word of love to each other."

"Is that the truth?"

"As God is my judge."

"Not a kiss—no hand-holding?"

"Nothing."

"Only looks?"

"Sometimes—I've hoped—from the way he looked—" She sighed. "But I'm afraid he meant nothing."

Courtney studied her ingenuous face as a bank teller a note that is under suspicion of being counterfeit. Yes—Helen was telling the truth.

"Do you think he cares?" asked Helen wistfully. "He seems to like to talk with me. And he's very eloquent about sentimental things. He talks and he acts like a man in love. But—at times I feel as if it were with another woman."

Courtney buried her face in the urn of violets. And next to her feeling of enormous relief at the clearing of Basil from the worst charge against him was gratitude that she would not have to try to play the tyrant—try to send Helen away.

"It may be some bad woman's gotten hold of him," continued the girl reflectively. "He may be chained by a love he's ashamed of."

"That sounds like a weekly story paper."

"I know there's *some* weight on his conscience," maintained Helen.

Courtney looked strangely at her and laughed. "When people look and talk remorse, they're only boasting. He's trying to make himself interesting, my dear. He wants to thrill you with the story of his life—some commonplace adventure he exaggerates into an epic drama." She laughed again, most unpleasantly. "Heaven deliver me from these 'My God! How she loves me' men!"

"He's not like that—not at all," protested Helen. "But—oh, I wish I knew whether he cared for me. I don't know *what* to do! I've given him every opportunity—" She stopped short with such an expression of horror at her slip that Courtney laughed outright. "I don't mean I've done anything forward or unladylike—" stammered Helen.

"He's a man of the world." She pinched Helen's cheek. "He reads that innocent little mind of yours like an electric sign."

Helen was hysterical with dismay. "You think he's laughing at me?"

"And getting ready to—to amuse himself."

"Courtney!"

Courtney nodded and smiled.

"He never could think so lightly of me. Never!"

"Lightly? He sees you are in love with him. Why should he suspect you of being calculating?"

"Calculating? I don't understand."

"Unwilling to give except for an annuity—for life support."

Helen's honest brown eyes were big and round. "What do you mean?"

"What I say," was Courtney's reply. And in a, to Helen, appallingly matter-of-fact way, she went on to explain. "And what I say is simply the sense under all the nonsense about marrying. You want to marry, don't you? You're looking about for somebody to support you and your children, aren't you? You say you love our homely, fascinating, well-to-do friend Gallatin. But not enough to go very far unless he'd sign a life contract. Didn't I hear you say one day that you didn't think it proper for people even to kiss until the preacher had dropped the flag?"

Helen gazed at her with an expression of sheer horrified amazement that delighted her. "How can as sweet and pure a woman as you talk that way?"

Courtney laughed gayly. "Because she's neither sweet nor pure. Because she's got intelligence and experience. I just wanted to show you that while you were pretending to think about love—ideal, romantic, unselfish love, you were really planning for food, clothing and shelter."

"But I don't want to hear such talk!" cried Helen. "If I'm deluded, why, let me stay so. You are so frivolous, Courtney! Don't you believe in love at all?"

Courtney reflected. "I don't know whether I do or not," she finally said.

Helen looked at her with sad sympathy. "And I thought you were happy!" she sighed.

"I am," rejoined Courtney. "And I purpose to remain so."

"But you are worried about me? You think Bas—Mr. Gallatin is not a fit man for me to marry?" The tone betrayed her anxiety, the importance she attached to Courtney's judgment; for, while Helen's conventional mind told her that Courtney was a "light-weight," like all lively, laughing persons, her instinct made her always consult her before acting in any matter from a man to what hat to wear with what dress. "You think he's—not nice?"

Courtney felt Helen's nearly breathless expectation; she did not answer immediately. When she did it was from the farther side of the room, with her attention apparently on a window garden of hyacinths. "Be careful, my dear.

Remember, your primness is your chief asset. If he thought—or hoped—you were—loose——"

"Loose!" Helen trembled, looked as if she were about to faint.

"It's ridiculous the way we women exaggerate the value of our favors," philosophized Courtney.

"I wish you wouldn't make that kind of—of jests, dear," pleaded Helen. "I know you don't mean a word of it. You feel just as I do—that a man couldn't do enough to repay any good woman for giving herself to him."

"Or a woman do enough to repay a man for giving himself to her," retorted Courtney. "The account's even, or the whole thing's too low to talk about. Still— you don't understand—you can't. And so long as men think a woman the grander the more conceited and selfish she is, you're as well off, believing as you do.... As to Gallatin——"

"I don't care anything about him!" cried Helen. "What you've been saying has given me such a shock." She paused, then went on in a low, awful tone, "Courtney, I must tell you that I was alone with him in his sitting room for over an hour!"

"When?" asked Courtney, sharply.

"To-day—what we were talking about."

"*Only* to-day?"

"Never before!" exclaimed Helen. "And never again."

"Then—perhaps—only perhaps, mind you," mocked Courtney, "I'll put off speaking to Richard about it—and writing Mrs. Torrey."

Helen could not see any humor in the situation. "Do you honestly believe, Courtney," she asked in deep distress, "that he could have thought of me as if I were—were a—a—*bad* woman?"

Courtney's eyes were most unpleasant.

"I see you're disgusted and angry with me, dear," said Helen, in tears again. "I know it was unwomanly of me to think of him when he'd said nothing. But I—I couldn't help it. I *will* help it, though!"

"You think you can?"

Helen showed she was astonished and hurt. "Do you imagine *I* could care for a man whose way of caring for me was an insult?"

Courtney counseled with a vase of jonquils. "No, I suppose *you* couldn't," she replied. "You don't know about wild, free—*fierce*—love— Do you?"

Helen's expression was of one appalled. "How can you talk that way?" she asked. "You're very strange to-day. You're not at all yourself."

"Self!" exclaimed Courtney, scornfully. "What is my self? What is your self? What is anybody's self?"

She no longer had the delusion of free will that makes us talk about bettering the race by "changing human nature from within"—the delusion that the individual is responsible, though obviously the social system and the other compelling external conditions move the individual as the showman his puppet. She, helpless in the whirl of strong emotions, was beginning to understand why, at the outset of her married life, instinct had bade her arrange all the circumstances round her and

Richard so that they would be compelled to live the life in common, the life of the single common interest that holds love captive as the cage the bird. She was beginning to realize how like water self is in the grip of circumstances—how self is mill pond or torrent, pure or foul, or mixture of the two, according as circumstance commands. These demon impulses—they were not her self. Self was amazed onlooker at its own strange doings—was like helpless occupant of the carriage behind the runaway team.

When Helen spoke again, she showed that her thoughts were still lingering longingly where they must not, if Courtney was to be rid of the demons. "But if a man loves a woman," said Helen, "why shouldn't he be glad to give her honorable marriage?"

Courtney hesitated, dared. "She might be already married."

"Courtney!" And her horrified eyes told Courtney she had caught the intended hint that Basil was in love with some married woman. "It isn't possible!"

"Haven't such things happened?"

"Yes—but— No married woman a nice man would notice would ever think of another man than her husband."

"I don't know about a 'nice' woman," said Courtney, slowly. "But I can imagine that a *human* woman—if her husband neglected her, and chilled and killed her love——"

Helen was not listening, was not aware that she had interrupted as she said, "Do you think Mr. Gallatin could be in love with some married woman—of—of our class?"

"I suspect so," replied Courtney, gazing calmly into her eyes.

"I'll not believe it!" cried Helen. "I'll not believe it!"

"You're like all girls. Because your own head's full of marriage, you think every man who's polite to you, or flirts a little to make the time pass more agreeably, is about to send for the preacher. Now, frankly, has Basil ever made love to you?"

"No," admitted Helen. "But—" She halted.

"But what?" came from Courtney sharp and arresting as a shot.

"I *feel* he is fond of me," confessed Helen.

Courtney laughed harshly. "All men are fond of all good-looking women—especially in the spring. Don't be a fool, Helen."

"But a married woman has no right to him!"

Courtney flushed, and her eyes flashed. "And how do you know? And what right have you to judge? Are you God?"

"No, but——"

"No!" cried Courtney. "How do you know what he—his love may mean to her? How do you know but what it may be the one thing between her and despair and ruin? You, with your timid, proper calculating little love! Why, if the woman cared enough for him—needed him so—that she sacrificed self-respect—honor—truth—all—all—for love—what could you give him to replace it? And what are your needs beside hers?"

Helen's face grew hard as these words that outraged every principle of her training poured recklessly from Courtney's lips. "I'm astounded at your defending a bad woman," she said. "You're *too* generous, Courtney. You'd feel differently if she were taking Richard away from you. But, I'm not in love with Basil. I see you know things about him. I—I—despise him. I pity him, of course, for he might have been a nice man. But I couldn't love him. I'm glad you told me. I might have engaged myself to him."

Courtney's far from sane eyes twinkled at that last ingenuous bit of maidenly vanity. Helen went about her work, and she departed to the greenhouse. "She'll stop loving him as easily as she began," said she to herself. "What does her sort of women know about love? They're faithful to whatever man they marry, as a dog's faithful to whoever feeds and kennels it.... Basil Gallatin is mine! And no man—nor no woman—shall come between us."

She had not forgotten Basil's expression as he stood in the apartment entrance, after his *tête-à-tête* with Helen. "Now—for what's in *his* heart," she said. "I must know just where I stand." She recalled how she had used to say, and to think, that if a man was not freely a woman's—freely—inevitably—without any need of being held by feminine artifice—no self-respecting woman could for an instant wish to detain him. And here she was, ready to make any sacrifice to hold this man. Truly, fate seemed determined to compel her to give the lie to everything she had ever believed, to abase every instinct of pride that had plumed or still plumed the haughty front of her soul.

Richard asked Helen up to his study after supper, to take dictation of an article he was doing for a scientific magazine; thus, Courtney had a chance to explore Basil. She was seated beneath the tall lamp, a big hat frame on her lap, ribbon and feathers on the small table. She knew he was watching her over the top of a newspaper; and she was not insensible to his extremely flattering expression—nor, perhaps, to the advantages her occupation gave her in the way of graceful gestures, effective posings of the head and arms as she studied the effect of different arrangements of ribbon and feathers. She glanced directly at him; he glanced away, confused—the frightened zigzag of a flushed partridge.

"Well?" said she. She felt more lenient toward him, now that she had discovered his innocence of overt treachery, at least; and the way he was looking at her when he fancied her quite unaware was certainly reassuring. Also, she realized now that she herself was largely responsible for these errant springtime thoughts of his—she with her struggling to keep both love and self-respect. "Well?" she repeated, when he did not speak. "What guilty thought did I almost surprise?"

"No guilty thought," replied he. "I was loving you—terribly—just then. I was thinking—how impossible it would be for a man who loved you ever to wander."

"That's very nice," said she, with a mocking smile. "So you have been—looking over the fence?" And she went on with bending the brim of the hat frame to a more graceful curve. She was placid to all appearances; but once more the great dread was obsessing her.

"Not at all," protested he. "What fence? At whom?"

"The fence of our compact—perhaps."

He sighed impatiently.

"Ah—well—" She laughed, eying the result of her shaping, the hat frame at one angle, her head at the opposite angle—"there's Helen."

He looked grave reproach at her, altogether absorbed in trying a long plume against the frame in different positions. "Do you think, dear, it's quite respectful to Helen——"

"Your thoughts couldn't harm her," interrupted she—that is, she interrupted him, but not her work. "If men's thoughts smirched women, what an unsightly lot the attractive ones would be!"

"Where did you get such ideas?" he exclaimed, trying to conceal how her frankness had scandalized him.

She worked on calmly. "By observing and reading and thinking—and feeling."

He drummed uneasily upon the arm of his chair with the tips of his fingers. At length he said with some embarrassment, "It's hardly necessary for me to say that I have the highest respect for Helen."

"Yes—and I also know she's very—very pretty."

"Yes, she is pretty."

"You respect her. You like to talk with her. You think she is physically attractive."

Stiffly, "I have never thought about her in that last way."

"Then, that's probably her chief charm for you," observed Courtney, placid and reflective and industrious. "When we think we don't think about things that are worth thinking about, the chances are we really haven't been thinking about anything else." With a smile and a shake of the head that might have been for the plumes which refused to please her, "I'm afraid you're falling in love with Helen."

"No," replied he judicially—and how he would have been startled if he had seen her veiled eyes!—shiny green and cruel as those of a puma stretched in graceful ferocity along the leafy limb that overhangs the path. "No, I'm not the least in love with her. But I do like her. Her seriousness is very pleasant, now and then. If I did not love you, I perhaps might have grown to care for her, in a way. But—beside you, Helen is—tame."

"I shouldn't call her tame—" encouragingly.

"Well—perhaps not. She sometimes suggests a person who could be waked up."

"That's a temptation, isn't it?" she asked. And she looked straight at him over the top of the plumes. She wished to see all.

"No," said he, positively. "To be quite frank I'd never give her as a woman a thought—if I weren't—" He stirred uneasily, burst out in confession. "You were right a while ago. Men often don't understand themselves. But we'll not talk about that."

There was such love and tenderness in the gaze meeting hers that all the squalid thoughts her mind had been fouled with the whole day washed away like the dust and dirt on the leaves and petals of her flowers in a sudden rain.

He said with a gentle, manly earnestness that thrilled her: "There's only the one woman for me. And—I want our love to be what you wish. And it shall be!"

She lowered her head, the tears welling. The others interrupted, and Helen sat beside her advising about the hat. When it was finished, she made Helen try it on. They all admired, and it certainly was becoming. "Now, you try it on, dear," said Helen.

"No, don't take it off," Courtney answered. "It's for you, of course." And she kissed her and, laughing away her thanks, went upstairs. She sat down at her dressing table and, with elbows resting on it and face supported by her hands, gazed into her own eyes. "If you do not wish to lose him," she said slowly aloud to her grave face imaged in the glass, "you must take away from him temptation to wander. A door is either open or shut. A man—a man worth while—won't stand at the threshold long. He comes in or he goes away. Basil does not realize it, but that other side of his nature will compel him to go away—unless—" Compel him to go away? She was hearing again the monotonous fall of those icy rains, was feeling again the monotonous misery of those days without love and without hope. She must choose. Choose? "The woman doesn't live—doesn't deserve to live—who'd hesitate. There's no choice. There's simply the one way."

Well—since it must be so—what would be the event? Would she lose him anyhow? Would she merely be putting off his going? Would her complete yielding end in disaster of some kind, as she had feared? Or, wasn't it possible that, while most people were tangled and finally strangled by the web of their own deceit, a skillful few could use it dextrously to snare the bright birds of joy? ... She stood up, stretched her arms, swayed her slim supple figure gently. "He shall have no reason for letting one single thought wander. He shall be mine—all mine! I'll take no more risks." She continued to sway gently, her eyes closed. A look of scorn, of disgust came into her face. She shuddered. "How hideous it is to be a woman! Always slave to some man! Gold fetters cut as deep as iron, and they're heavier." She stopped swaying. "I can see how I might come to hate my master in trying to hold his love.... Love! To keep our love warm, we have to bury it in the mire."

# Chapter 20

Because of the light the tables in the inner laboratory were so placed that Courtney and Basil worked at opposite sides of the room with their backs toward each other. As ten o'clock approached her agitation increased; but the only outward sign was frequent stolen glances at the clock on the wall between the windows. When the hands pointed to ten, her heart fluttered; for, she heard him push back his chair and knew he was rising from his case. He stood at the window toward her side of the room. As he was gazing out over the high sill, she was free to look at him—at his back, at the back of his head. She felt the struggle raging in his mind. Her hand, blundering among the burettes and bottles on the glass shelves before her, tilted a test tube from its support. It fell, broke with a crash on the porcelain surface of the table. She gave a low scream it would have been loud had she not, swifter than thought, clenched her teeth and compressed her lips. He startled violently.

"Good God!" he cried and his tone showed that his nerves were in the same state as hers.

"Beg your pardon," she murmured, mechanically apologetic.

If he heard, he gave no indication of it. He continued to stand motionless at the window, staring out over the lake. She tried furtively to get a glimpse of his profile, but could not. At ten minutes past ten he moved. When she saw him about to turn, she bent over her work—pouring calcium lactophosphate into a small agate mortar as if any relaxing of attention would be calamitous. He was standing at the end of her table, was looking down at her. It took all her self-control to refrain from looking up to see what was in his eyes. He was bending over her; his lips touched her hair—the crownlike coil of auburn on top of her head. She tingled to her finger tips; she knew she had won, knew he had thought it all out and had seen that his meetings with Helen were in the direction of disloyalty to the woman he loved. She looked up at him now. At first his expression was guilty and embarrassed, but the radiance of love and trust in her eyes soon changed that. He became very pale as his glance burned into hers; he turned away, and she felt that it was because he feared lest in the rush of penitent passion he would confess things it was unnecessary and unwise to put into words.

"Why, it's ten o'clock," said she carelessly. "Aren't you going out to smoke?"

A pause, then he answered "Not to-day" in a boyishly ill-at-ease way that brought a secret tender smile to her lips. She liked these evidences that it was impossible for him to conceal himself from her because any attempt to do so made him feel dishonorable.

"It's beautiful outdoors. I'll go with you."

"No, not just now, Courtney. I—I—that is, I think I'd best finish. Vaughan may need all four of the sulphates any moment." And he sat down before his case and began to fuss with evaporating dishes and crucibles.

"This is the first day you've missed in I don't know when," said she. It was just as well he should know she had begun to take note of his habit; that knowledge would strengthen his resolve to avoid in the future appearance of of evil and temptation thereto. "You've been very regular for weeks."

"It's a waste of time," he replied, after a pause. "You're right, uninterrupted effort's the only kind that counts." And both went to work.

But Courtney did not overestimate her triumph. Often day completely reverses the night view of things. But now, in the fancy-dispelling day more clearly than in the fancy-breeding night, she saw she must remove the temptation. If she had been a small or a stupid woman—or both, for the two qualities usually go together—she would have laid all the blame upon Helen and would have sent her away—and in vanity as to her power over him would have imagined herself once more perfectly secure. But the impulse to blame Helen and to get rid of her did not survive the second thought. It was not Helen's fault, or Basil's; it was nature's.

Looking back on those months under the compact she saw how she had let foolish vanity and still more foolish hope befog and mislead her intelligence. To remove Helen would avail her nothing. The law of his nature would continue to press him on; and sooner or later, in spite of love for her, in spite of loyalty, in spite of constancy, he would be swept away from her. The compact was a beautiful ideal, but it was not life—and, so, it must yield. "I must be all to him, or I shall soon be nothing to him." And that afternoon she fixed her resolution—after thinking the situation out sanely—as sanely as she could think in those days. For she, completely possessed by her need of Basil, was like all the infatuated. That is, she was in a state not unlike those demented persons who seem to be, and are, quite sane and logical and self-possessed, once you get beyond the fixed delusion which determines the posture and outlook of their entire being.

On the way to dress for supper she glanced in at Helen's open door. The girl was sitting near a window giving upon the small west balcony, her attitude so disconsolate that Courtney was at once striving with a rising wave of pity and self-reproach. "Helen will soon get over it," she reassured herself; and good sense reminded her that a young girl has not the experience of love which teaches the experienced woman to value it and makes her unable to do without it. "The love-sickness of a young girl, especially prim, unimaginative girls like Helen, isn't really personal; it's little more than a longing to be flattered and to get married and settled." But such small progress as head was making against heart was lost when Helen looked at her with a pathetic attempt to smile.

"Where have you been all day?" asked Courtney, eyes sinking before Helen's. She felt a most uncomfortable contempt for herself.

"In Wenona—lunching and shopping with Bertha Watrous."

Courtney entered, seated herself on the bed. Despite her lovelorn condition, Helen winced. "You old maid, you," laughed Courtney, rising. "I never saw any woman anywhere, not even old Nanny, not even my sister Ann, so opposed to sitting on the bed."

"I've been brought up to think it was—wasn't right," apologized Helen.

"Wasn't ladylike, you mean," said Courtney. She disposed herself in the window seat. "What are you blue about, dear?" She knew she was not intruding; Helen liked to confide her troubles—and people of that fortunate temperament were cured by confiding.

"I'm not blue," declared Helen. "I've simply been thinking of what you said, and if anything I'm angry."

"Oh—Basil? Did you see him to-day?"

"I did not." Helen tossed her head. "I went about my work as usual—went to the apartment. If he'd been lying in wait I was ready for him. But he wasn't."

Courtney understood what this really meant, though Helen didn't. Probably Helen would not have believed she had in fact lain in wait for Basil, even had Courtney pointed out to her the obvious meaning of her action. She was of the large majority—who do not know their own minds, who cannot explore them with a guide however competent, who when shown their own motives hotly and honestly deny. "Basil was busy to-day," Courtney explained. "Some sulphates Richard was in a hurry for."

Helen looked relieved. But, still not in the least aware of her own state of mind, she went on, with a toss of the head: "Well—whenever I do see him alone, I'll make him realize I'm not the sort he thinks. The more I look at it, Courtney, the more convinced I am that he was simply leading me on."

"Now, Helen!" laughed Courtney.

Helen colored. "I admit," she said, shamefacedly, "I got what I deserved for being so—so forward."

"That's the truth—you were forward." Courtney's tone made this necessary thrusting home of the painful truth gentle but not the less insistent. "We must never fool ourselves, dear. We women can't afford to."

Studying Helen, so clearly fascinated still by the idea of winning the young eligible from the East and redeeming him, Courtney realized that if the girl was to stay on there in peace she must be made to see the absolute uselessness of angling. So long as she thought of Basil as a possibility, however remote, so long would she be in danger of falling utterly and miserably in love with him. Yes, Helen must be cured—but how? There was no way. Not until Basil was married would Helen cease to hope. "For her own sake, I ought to send her away," Courtney was thinking as the two sat there in silence. But Helen had no other place to go. True, she could go out and make her own living as a teacher—Courtney envied her the training and the certificate that were practically a guaranty of independence. But Helen abhorred independence, looked on a woman's working, away from the shelter of domesticity, as the Hindu looks on loss of caste. No, Helen must stay on, might as well stay on.... An impossible situation. And from this unanticipated quarter came one more imperative reason for making Basil wholly her own. He must be in such a state of mind that he would do nothing to encourage Helen's hope to put forth even the feeblest of its ready sprouts.

Courtney rose and moved toward the door. "I must dress." She leaned against the jamb, her cheek upon her crossed hands. "Well, my dear, remember the rhyme about the lady who went for a ride on a tiger, and how, when they came back, he had the lady inside."

"You're laughing at me," reproached Helen.

Courtney's eyes were fixed dreamily upon vacancy, a strange sad smile about her lips. "I am not laughing," she said slowly. "Or, if I am, it is not at you.... Not at you, but at—" She could not tell Helen that she was drearily mocking her own entrapped and helpless self. "Take my advice, child. Don't *ever* lead a tiger out for an airing."

Yes, Helen should stay on, as long as she wished to stay. "And hasn't she as much right here as I—just the same right?"

At two o'clock that night, as Basil was leaving, he said—"You've hardly spoken since I came. Is it the darkness?"

"Yes—the darkness," she replied in the same undertone—the doors were very thick, but instinct made them careful about speech.

"I never knew you to be so silent—or so strange, now that I think of it." He held her by the shoulders. "Courtney, did you want me to come to-night?"

She clung to him. "Do you love me, my Basil?"

"How queer your voice sounds. Are you frightened?"

"No—no, indeed."

"Dear, you're not telling me——"

"It's nothing. Just a—a notion. There won't be so much of it next time. And still less the next time. And soon I'll be quite accustomed."

"Yes, I'm sure there's not the least danger," said he, wholly misunderstanding.

# Chapter 21

One afternoon she was reading in the hammock on the balcony before the upper sitting-room windows—the sitting room she shared with Helen and Winchie. She heard some one in the room, glanced up—Richard was before her. "Glad to find you alone," said he. "Do you realize it's several weeks since we've exchanged so much as a single word in private?"

"Something wrong at the shop?"

"No. I came especially to talk with you. How'd you like to go away for a week or so—to the sea or the mountains? We might take that trip through the Great Lakes."

"I'll see."

"You've been working very hard down at the shop. And by the way, you've caused an amazing improvement in Basil's work. He doesn't make those stupid mistakes any more. He used to make them every day. Yes—you've worked hard—and well."

She had no pleasure in these incredible compliments from Richard the difficult to please in chemistry. It was too disquieting to have him thus watchful and interested.

"Let's start at once," he proposed.

"Oh, I couldn't do that. I hesitate to leave here—when everything's at its best. In the fall—or next winter——"

"I see you don't want to go—with me."

His tone compelled her to look at him. His eyes—grave, searching—were fixed upon her. Instinct suddenly warned her of danger—what danger or where she could not see, but the warning was imperative. "Indeed I do," protested she, with a deceptive show of interest, though her skin burned as her fundamental and incurable honesty cried shame upon her—as it always did when she, compelled by her circumstances, could not avoid the lie direct. "But," she went on, "you can't expect a woman, with a household like this on her mind, to drop everything and fly at a few hours' notice."

He reflected, nodded. "That's true. Though, really, the servants are so experienced they'd go on just as well. My dear old aunt was thorough."

There was a little bitterness of hurt vanity in her smile of recognition at this ancient notion of Richard's about her part in that household. She felt that the *tête-à-tête* had already lasted too long. "Was Winchie in there?" she asked.

"I didn't see him," replied Dick.

She moved toward the nearest sitting-room window.

"What's the matter?" he cried, irritated. "Where are you going?"

"After Winchie. I haven't thought of him for an hour. Helen's away—at the Foster picnic——"

"The boy's all right. Sit down here and——"

But she was gone. She did not slacken her speed until she was safely clear of him. This new development of his threatened to become an annoyance, thought she; however, it couldn't last much longer; she would continue to keep out of his way; the laboratory would take hold of him and she would be once more forgotten and free. Meanwhile, she would avoid him.

And soon he did become once more absorbed, and resumed his accustomed shadowy place in her life—seen yet not seen, heard yet not heard, present yet absent; neither liked nor disliked, but unknown and unheeded—the place of many and many a husband in a marriage that seems happy and successful to the very servants in the household, to the husband and wife themselves. One evening he abruptly left the table. She saw, but did not note, his departure. When supper was over and she and Helen and Basil strolled into the sitting room, Basil took advantage of Helen's being apart to say to Courtney, "What's wrong with him?"

"I'm sure I don't know," replied she. "Nothing, I guess."

"Didn't you notice? He was staring furiously at you, and left in a rage."

She shrugged her shoulders. That night she was in one of her reckless moods, was nervous, excited, with eyes the more brilliant for the circles round them. Richard appeared in the farthest of the long open windows. He frowned at Basil, said sharply to his wife, "Courtney, I'd like to speak to you out here a moment."

"It's chilly there," objected she. "Come in." And she went toward the piano.

Dick entered. His long aristocratic face was stern and his eyes glowed somberly. "Then let's go into the library," said he, in a tone so positive that from him it sounded like a command.

She hesitated, reflectively caressing one slim tapering arm. "Very well," said she, and passed into the hall, he standing formally aside at the doorway. In the library, she faced him with eyes half closed and chin thrust up and a little out. "Well?" she inquired.

As he looked at his sweet frivolous little child of a wife, his manner softened toward that of one rebuking a child's trespass. "I want you to go upstairs and wrap up your shoulders—or change your dress."

She glanced down. The bodice did not cover the upper curve of her bosom, had no straps across the shoulders or on the arms. In the back, it dipped almost to the waist line. She looked at him with a quizzical expression. "I'm quite warm enough, thanks."

"You understand me," said he, more severely.

She gazed straight into his eyes before answering. "Yes, I do. But I prefer to pretend not to."

"I've spoken to you about my wishes in this matter before. Do you know what made me notice your—your nakedness? Pardon me for putting it that way, but I see I must speak plainly."

Her face expressed faint, contemptuous indifference. "I cannot talk with you. Your ideas of women ought to be buried in the grave with your grandfather. I do not dictate the cut of your clothes. You will not dictate mine." And she moved toward the door.

He put himself between. "I saw Gallatin looking at you with an expression—" He made a gesture of rage—a quiet gesture but significant. "I don't blame him. It's your fault. You've no right to tease a man who can be nothing to you. I speak frankly because——"

"Gallatin has seen thousands of women in just such dress as this," interrupted she. It enraged her to hear her lover's feelings for her, in which flesh was mere medium between spirit and spirit, thus leveled to the carnality of his own passion. "You," she continued icily, "read your own poisonous, provincial primness and—and vulgarity into his look, no doubt."

"You are an innocent, pure-minded woman, Courtney," said Richard, with more gentleness. "You follow a fashion, thinking of it only as a fashion. I assure you, that sort of fashion is devised in Paris by cocottes for the one purpose. If you knew men better, you'd appreciate it."

She appreciated the penetration of this remark, puncturing the pretentious haughtiness of her protest. She was surprised at his reasoning so shrewdly about a matter she would not have suspected him of having given a thought. But she must not let him interfere in her personal affairs. "Whatever its origin," said she, "it's the conventional fashion for women. I shall continue to wear it." And she looked into his eyes pleasantly. Now, it struck her as amusing, the anger of this alien, about the exhibition to others of what he regarded as his own private and personal treasure. Just one stage removed from the harem, such an idea as his. "And," she went on, aloud, "if your satrapship commands me to wear a veil over my face and muffle my figure in a loose black bag, I shall make the same reply. You can't realize it, but the old-fashioned ideal of good, pure woman was really something to be handled with tongs and disinfected."

"You're talking of things you, being a good woman, know nothing about."

"At any rate I know a mind that ought to be quarantined—when I smell it." And she made a wry face and started to leave the room. When she had got as far as the threshold, he cried, "Courtney!" and his tone told her that he had caught sight of the reverse view of her costume—the unimpeded display of slender dimpled shoulders and straight smooth back almost to the waist line. She pretended not to hear, went on to the sitting room. Yielding altogether now to the imp of the perverse, she displaced Helen at the piano and sang the maddest, most melting love songs she knew. Basil tried to keep to the far part of the room; but gradually the enchantment compelled. Forgetting Richard—though he had seen him glowering and fuming from the darkness of the veranda—he leaned upon the end of the grand piano. His eyes were down, but his burning face and his trembling fingers as he raised or lowered his cigarette proclaimed how the deep passionate notes of her voice were vibrating through him.

It was somewhat later than usual when she went upstairs. As she pressed the button just inside her bedroom door and the light came on—a soft pale violet light that seemed to permeate rather than to shine—she saw Richard in the window. His back was toward her and he was smoking so that the odor and the smoke would not come into the room. He threw the cigarette over the balcony rail and turned. The instant she looked at him, little as she knew of his character or noted his moods she saw she had gone too far. But she held a calm, undaunted front. "How you frightened me," said she, in a tone that had no fright in it. "I'm horribly tired. I must stop eating desserts. They wear one out." She stifled a yawn, took the small diamond sunburst from the front of her waist and laid it on the bureau. She seemed all but unconscious of his presence; in reality, by way of the bureau mirror, she was watching him as a duelist an adversary. "I shall fall asleep before I can get into bed."

"I shall detain you only a moment." His grave, exaggerated politeness did not decrease her inward agitation. "I simply wish to tell you," he went on, "that, as you seem determined to persist in your own mistaken way, I shall be compelled to ask Gallatin to stay away from the house in the evenings."

Her impulse was to smile disdain at the infantile futility of this. And the smile did come to her lips, and lingered there to mask the feelings that came surging with the second thought. For she instantly realized how helpless she was. This man had no part in her life nor she in his; yet he could impose his will upon her absolutely because he could take Basil away from her—not merely for the unimportant evenings, but altogether. He could make it impossible for Basil to remain—could do it by a mere word to him. And she who fancied she had provided against every possible contingency had never even thought of this, the most obvious peril, and the greatest! Faint, she leaned upon the bureau, spreading her arms so that she seemed to be merely at ease. "But why tell *me* about it?" said she to him. "Why didn't you simply say it to him?" She smiled contemptuously. "And what will he think?"

Dick's calm vanished. "I don't care a damn what he thinks," he cried. "At least, he'll not be sitting round watching you half dressed."

She drew herself up haughtily. "Good night," said she.

"I was out on the veranda," Dick rushed on. "I saw him. He forgot Helen—forgot decency—honor—everything—and leaned there, giving himself up to a debauch. Yes, to a debauch! And *you* are responsible. Not he—not at all. You, alone. At least, anger doesn't make me unjust. And I will say too, you were innocent in the matter—like a willful child. Good pure women don't appreciate——"

"But *I* do," interrupted she. "I'm not the imbecile Aunt Eudosia sort you admire so much."

"I tell you, the man's in love with you," cried Richard.

She all but staggered before the shock.

"Yes, in love with you. That's why he came back here."

As steadily and indifferently as she could contrive she went to the sofa, seated herself. "Why, you yourself told me he was in love with Helen."

"I was mistaken. How could he be in love with her, when you're about? A man always takes to the best-looking woman."

She laughed with friendly conciliating coquetry. "I'm afraid you're prejudiced."

"I saw it this evening. The way he was listening to those love songs!"

"Are you sure he was thinking of me?"

Richard did not answer.

"Perhaps Helen's equally sure he was thinking of her."

Under cover of the talk she—hardly knowing what she, or he, was saying—darted this way and that, seeking an escape from the horror closing in upon her. She felt like a hiding slave, hearing the distant bay of the bloodhounds. How escape? How throw him off the scent? Was there only the one way?

"No, he cares nothing about Helen," Richard was saying. And clear and soft in his voice now was the note she dreaded. "At least, he didn't this evening. How could he when you were there? Courtney, you simply can't understand. You're modest and pure minded and innocent——"

"Then it was only this evening?" she interrupted. "I was hoping you had real reason for flattering me."

"Flattering you!"

"Certainly. Wouldn't it flatter you if I were to tell you Helen was in love with you? She's in love with somebody, by the way. It must be you—how could she think of any other man when you were about?"

Dick half smiled.

"And I must begin to tear my hair and foam at the mouth, I suppose," continued she. She rose, stamped her foot, in melodramatic imitation of jealous fury. "Helen shall keep to her room in the evenings! Do you hear, sir? When I think of the times I've let you take her up to your study—alone!—under pretense of working! You—with your shirt sleeves rolled up and your collar open!"

"You silly child!" Dick was amused now.

"But I don't blame Helen. How could she help it—with you leading her on——"

Dick laughed. "That's very shrewd," said he. "I own up. I guess I was having a jealous fit. But you'd understand if you could see yourself as I see you." And he clasped her.

"No—no!" she gasped.

Completely possessed by his mood he was too much the man to have the power to see that her mood was different. Holding her tightly, he said: "I do believe you acted that way this evening just to make me jealous. I admit I seem neglectful. But I love you, just as I always did."

She was struggling to escape as strongly as she dared—more strongly than her instinct of prudence approved—more strongly than her physical self desired, for she realized with horror that his mood was hypnotizing her will.

"Listen, dear," he said. "I've got a confession to make. While I was raging up and down on the veranda, all sorts of devilish thoughts came to me—suspicious——"

She ceased struggling.

"I got to thinking how long we've been living apart—and how, every time I made advances, you seemed to evade——"

She felt herself growing cold. He must have felt it, too, for he hastened on: "Please, little girl, don't get cross. I didn't *really* suspect. I'm not so ridiculous. I know a good woman could no more be false even in thought to her husband—than a nightingale could change into a snake."

It was pounding, pounding at the walls of her brain that he was on the very verge of the discovery; that unconsciously he was fighting against a suspicion which too long-pent passion was thrusting at him ever more pointedly. Another repulse, another jealous fit, and—five lives overwhelmed in ruin.

She lay quiet in his arms.

In those next few days she was whimsical, capricious, fantastic. Richard, once more wholly the man of science, was as unconscious as mountain peak of storms in the valleys far below. Basil and the others, but particularly Basil, watched her with a kind of dread. "I need a change—in fact, I must have it," she announced at the supper table. "Helen, let's go to Chicago and shop. The things in Wenona are hideous this spring."

"I need a change too," Richard startled them all by saying, "I'll go with you—and Helen can take care of the house and Basil—and Winchie, if you'll leave him."

"I don't want to be left!" cried Winchie. "You wouldn't leave *me*, mamma?"

Courtney did not hear. She was looking at Richard as if his words jarred upon her savagely, goaded her to the verge of outburst. She had been feeling toward her husband as she would have felt toward an inanimate object which had bruised her when she by accident stumbled heavily against it. She did not seek the source of this feeling, or let it disclose itself to her. She simply felt so; and when he spoke of going, it seemed as unthinkable that she should let him go as that she should leave Winchie behind. When she had herself in hand, she said: "This is a shopping trip. No men wanted or allowed."

"Not even *me*, mamma?" pleaded Winchie.

"Except you," said she.

And the two women and Winchie went the following day, to spend a busy fortnight in the Chicago shops buying for all three and for the house. As Courtney had limited means and exacting taste, the labor of shopping was hard and tedious, especially in those vast modern stores. For there the satisfaction of having everything under one roof is balanced by the vexation of the search for the needle of just what one wants and can afford through the mountainous haystack of what one does not want or cannot afford. The toil almost prostrated the two women—and poor Winchie who had to drag along since there was no one at the hotel to whom Courtney would trust him. But she felt more than repaid, not so much by her purchases, though she was on the whole content with them, as by the complete change in her point of view.

The atmosphere of the city is wholly different from that of such a place as Wenona. In Wenonas, the individual is important; the sky seems near, and its awful problems of the eternal verities—life and death, right and wrong—thrust at every one every moment of day and night. In a city, the sky yields to brick and stone; men see each other, not the universe; the eternal verities seem eternal bores, and life, of the day, of the hour, tempts with its—"Since you are mere maggot in rotten cheese—tiny maggot, one of billions—tremendous cheese—since you are to die to-morrow and decay and be forgotten—since you can fret and fritter all your years away over life and death, over right and wrong, without getting a hair's width nearer solving them—why not perk up—amuse yourself—do as little harm as is consistent with getting what you need, and have all the fun there is going? Don't take yourself solemnly!" The city's egotism is showy, but shallow; the country's, hidden but profound.

Viewed from Chicago, all the beauty, all the possibilities of happiness in her life in that lovely place on the shore of Wenona Lake stood out as in the landscape of a master painter; and all that fretted and shamed her and shot her joys with black thread of foreboding seemed the work of her own tainted imagination. "I'm harming no one," she now argued. "I'm free—Richard freed me when he made me realize I was to him not a wife but simply a carnal incident. And I am helping to make life there peaceful and even happy. The trouble with me is I'm still under the blight of my early training—a training in how to die, not in how to live. True, I do lead a double life. But how few human beings do not lead double lives of one kind or another? And where am I worse than thousands who long but have not courage or chance? Isn't it better to live in deceit with a man one loves than to live in deceit with a man one loathes?" If she and Basil were found out, they would be classed with the rest of the vulgar intriguers. But that did not make them thus low; it was not their fault that the world saw only coarseness for the same sort of reason that a man in green spectacles saw everything green.

She came back as much improved in mental health as in dress—and certainly the new clothes were a triumph. Also, her sense of self-respect seemed to be restored—"and whether I'm right in my way of looking at things or am deceiving myself, I'm certainly much the better for feeling I'm right."

They brought part of the spoils of the city with them, but most of it came by freight a week after their return. Courtney and Helen were almost as excited as Winchie—and Winchie was quite beside himself—when the great packing cases and crates were opened, and the treasures of dresses and underclothes and "stunning" hats and fascinating shoes and slippers and parasols and blouses, and the furniture and pictures came into view from endless wrappings of paper and bagging and excelsior, of boxes round and square, boxes small and large, boxes fancy and plain. Everything, with not an exception, looked better than it had in the shop when it was bought. "You are a wonderful shopper, Courtney. These things seem as if they were made especially for us," Helen asserted. And Winchie, literally pale with emotion, screamed, "Mamma Courtney, let's go back and buy some more!"

For several days the agitation continued. Indeed, it was a month or longer before the last ripples died away, and the normal calm was restored. Helen had new clothes as well as Courtney—and never had she looked so lovely. Winchie was the most stylish person of his age in all that region. The Donaldson children had theretofore been disposed to feel somewhat superior because they had a real imported French governess; they now paid court to him and accepted his decisions about games as reverently as a company of New York men accept the judgments of any man with millions. And the new furniture and dishes, the new wall paper, the new cooking utensils, the new contrivances for plants and for cut flowers, some of which Courtney had had made from her own designs, were as successful as the clothes. Also, Courtney—and Helen too—had, through the stimulus of the city, a multitude of new ideas for house and grounds and gardens. These they proceeded to carry out, Basil assisting whenever he could get an afternoon away from the laboratory where Richard had now buried himself, oblivious of her, of them all. Altogether, May and June of that year made a new high-water mark of happiness. And when Helen, going to Saint X to visit and display her finery, returned in a self-complacent state of mind that indicated a complete cure, a complete restoration of her old-time content, Courtney felt as if the last cloud had disappeared from her horizon. Again and again during those tranquil, sparkling days she told herself—and almost believed—that at last her life was "settled right"—as nearly "right" as a human life could be.

One night when she had an appointment with Basil she found Helen still up as she was about to descend and admit him. Helen did not put out her light until nearly three quarters of an hour after the time. When she opened the lake-front door no one entered; not a sound. She looked out. The veranda empty; the lawns dreaming undisturbed in the moonlight; wave on wave of the heavy perfume of summer's flowers. But not anywhere Basil. Her trembling ceased; she darted to the edge of the veranda, everything forgotten but the supreme fact—he was gone. Gone! Why, she could not doubt; for, from time to time she had seen in his eyes the suspicion which, unjust though it was, she dared not discuss with him. Where had he gone? She must know, must know at once.

She gave not a thought to leaving the house—the dangers that made it impossible for them to meet at his apartment. She sped across the lawn, along the path through the pale splendor of the east flower garden and blossoming shrubbery, into the dark wood. And with her sped her old enemy—the specter dread of losing him—the ghost so easily started from its unquiet grave. She flitted on until she stood at the edge of the clearing, with wildly beating heart, looking up at the solitary building, gloomy in its creeper draperies. There was light from his bedroom window. She gave a quick gasp of relief. At least he was still within reach. The phantom beat of icy rains falling, falling ceased to freeze her heart.

Panting from the tumult of her thoughts rather than from the run, she knocked on the entrance door—knocked again, loudly—a third time—a fourth. She was shaking from head to foot. No answer—none. She tried the door; it yielded. She darted up the stairway, her body now fire and now ice. He was in his bedroom door, was watching her. As the light came from behind him she could not immediately see his expression; but she felt it was dark and angry. She flung herself on his breast—"My love—my love!" she sobbed.

His arms hung at his sides. He stood rigid.

"Basil! Put your arms round me. I'm cold—and so frightened."

He pushed her away.

She leaned against the door frame sobbing into her hands. Her long plaits hung one over either shoulder. She looked like a child, a broken-hearted child. "And you've been pretending to love me!"

"I do love you. That's the worst of it."

"Love!" She turned upon him passionately. "You call *that*—love? No matter what I did, wouldn't you know I'd done it for our love's sake? Yes, you know all that's I is yours—every thought—every heart throb." She was sobbing again, her arm on the door frame, her face against it. She was thinking how unsympathetic he was, how selfish and cruel—was asking herself why she did not hate him, cast him out of her life. But the very suggestion made her heartsick. Cast out him who was her life!

"I didn't mean it," he pleaded. "I was crazed with jealousy."

"Jealousy! Basil—Basil!"

"I can't help it. I'm human."

"But don't you know me? Oh, sweetheart—don't take from me all the self-respect I've got."

He seated himself, stared doggedly at the floor. There was a long, a heavy silence which he finally broke. "Courtney," he said, "we're both going straight to hell." He looked sternly at her. "We've got to get away from here."

She saw the resolve in his eyes, trembled, grew still. Then she remonstrated gently, "You'd forbid me to treat Winchie so, if I wanted to."

He continued to look straight and stern at her. "Either you go with me or I go alone."

Her knees grew weak. The room swam before her eyes. The big wave in the picture on the opposite wall swelled, lowered, seemed swooping down on her. "Oh, no—you wouldn't do that," she murmured. "No—you couldn't do that."

"I'll leave in the morning, unless you say you'll leave with me the day after."

She watched him, relentless and utterly inconsiderate, and her anger rose. "You've no right to go!" she cried.

"I must," he replied. "Do you mean to say you'll let me leave without you?"

"Yes—if you'd do it," replied she. "But you wouldn't. You'd not leave me to bear the whole burden alone. You'd not be a coward."

His florid face became crimson. He fought for self-control, gave up the hopeless struggle, flung himself down beside her. "I can't go—I can't," he cried. "But—how can I stay? It's dragging us down—down." He was almost weeping. "Courtney, you must see it's dragging us down."

For the first time she had the sense of strength in herself greater than his, of weakness in him. She caressed his fair hair tenderly. "It's only a mood, dearest—only a mood. It'll pass—and we'll help each other, and be strong. We'll look forward to the end of this. For, in a few years Winchie'll be off to school. Then—I shall be free to make my own life. I'll go away to visit—stay on and on—and gradually——"

"You must promise you will not live with him."

"I will do my best. But—I must protect Winchie—and us."

He grew red, then pale, was silent for a time. Then he said irritatedly, weakly, "But don't you see what a position it puts *me* in!"

"And me?" She said it very quietly, with a certain restrained pathos. But he sat glum and moody, thinking of his own plight.

He roused himself. "All right," he cried, in a tone of contempt—for himself and for her. He embraced her with a kind of insolent familiarity. "Then I'll stay. If I went, I'd only come sneaking back. I'm no longer a man. I'm a slave to you." And he held her at arms length and eyed her with an expression that told her he was making inventory of her charms.

"Please don't talk that way," she begged, offended and wounded by that expression in his eyes more than she dared admit to herself. "I know you don't mean it. I know you—love. I know——"

"Love—let's only talk of love," he interrupted.

She fell to wondering whether, when they were together in the dark, his unseen eyes had this look—and why it made his words and his caresses seem so different from the words and caresses of the darkness. She had never thought of it before; she hated to learn it then—just then; but she could not push away the monstrous truth that love and lust have the same vocabulary, the same gestures, the same tones, differ only in their eyes.

"What are you thinking about so solemnly?" he asked.

"I wasn't thinking solemnly," she protested with a hastily forced smile. "I was simply remembering how rarely we've been together alone—really alone—except in the dark, for a long long time."

"It's good to be able to see you," said he, and she felt like hiding in shame from his eyes. "You streamer of flame that's burning up my soul."

Her lips echoed his laugh. "What nonsense," she said.

"It's the truth," declared he. "But—burn on! I can't live without it."

The smile left her lips—it had not been in her eyes. "If I thought you——"

He stopped her mouth with a kiss. "Only love!" he commanded. "No thought."

"That's right," she cried eagerly. "No thought! Just feeling—just love. We must not think. It's the cause of our unhappiness."

And she tried to be as good as her word. "I do love him, and he loves me," she rebuked herself. "I'm unstrung—hysterical—full of crazy fancies. I mustn't— *mustn't*—fret at his way of loving. I must always think, 'What would become of me if I lost him?'" And she pretended to be in his mood; for the sake of a passion that had been, she simulated a passion that was not.

# Chapter 22

Masculine moral struggle is usually noisier than feminine—unless the woman is seeking to impress some man, before yielding of her own free will what she wishes him to fancy his superior charm and force and subtlety are conquering. Thus, woman being by nature freer from the footless kinds of hypocrisy than man, it was only in the regular order that while Courtney quietly accepted the situation and conformed to it, Basil should accept it with much moral bluster. He accused now his own wickedness, now the wickedness of destiny, and again woman's sinful charms. Still, the masculine conscience no less than the feminine is bred to be an ultimately accommodating chaperon; and Basil's conscience would soon have gone to sleep had it not been kept awake and feverish by a contrasting presence. That contrast was Helen's virginal beauty and virginal purity—both of which fascinated his overstimulated and degenerating imagination.

Helen was, as Courtney had said, a girl of the old-fashioned type. This does not mean that she was a rare survival of an extinct type, but simply that she was the girl of yesterday as distinguished from the girl of to-morrow, and from the girl that is partly of yesterday, partly of to-morrow—all three of whom we have with us in this transitional to-day. Helen had by inheritance and training all woman's ancient instincts to be a possessed and protected property. These instincts originated in the necessities and the ignorance of former societies; but they are cultivated and clung to because masculine vanity dotes on the superior attitude, and because the female very humanly finds it more comfortable to be looked after than to look after herself, to have her thinking done for her than to think for herself, to be supported than to support herself, to be strong through weakness than to be strong through strength. The male wants to pose as master. The female yields, since the usual cost to her is merely putting up with airs of superiority at which she can secretly laugh; at worst, the cost is only that intangible thing, self-respect. So, why not? Self-respect is purely subjective, unseen. It provides no comforts or luxuries. Lack of it attracts no attention in a world that sees only surfaces. So, why not sacrifice it, when it becomes inconvenient? Men do. Why shouldn't women?

Helen had no desire to be of full human stature—to be free. She wished to be a "true woman," meek servant of a lord and master, and never under the painful necessity of taking responsible thought for herself. Having no capacity or desire for comradeship with men, she denounced it as unwomanly. Her physical virtue— "purity," she called it—she regarded as her chief glory. She was glad it was still woman's chief asset in the struggle for existence; for, she could not help knowing she had beauty, and it is beauty that makes virtue valuable, though of course beauty adds nothing to its glory.

Helen certainly had beauty, nearly as great beauty as she imagined in that heart of hearts where our vanity feels free to spread its tail to the last gaudy feather and to strut as no peacock or gobbler ever dared. Her skin was white as milk, her features were classically regular, and she was now a shade taller than Basil, could almost look level-eyed at Richard. Her dark hair was commonplace in color and texture, was rather short, did not grow especially well about her brow or behind the ears; but it was thick and abundant, and the brow and the ears were charming in themselves. Thanks to Courtney's skill in devising a corset, the defect of waist too close to bust was no longer conspicuous. She had sound teeth, good arms and legs, narrow hands and feet. Her large brown eyes were of the kind that has been regarded as ideal for woman from the days of Homer singing the ox-eyed Juno, down to our own day when intelligence is trying to get a place among feminine virtues and the look of intelligence among feminine beauties. She had learned from Courtney—who knew—a great deal about dress—dress that all women talk, but only the rare exceptional woman knows.

Also, she had from her a practical training for what she regarded as woman's only sphere, the home. Courtney had taught her how to keep house with comfort, order and system. As Courtney had none of the teacher's vanity but used the method of suggestion, she fancied she had learned and was learning from herself; the more so, since she in defiance of daily experience could not credit a woman of Courtney's lively and, because light, undoubtedly thoughtless and careless temperament, with enough seriousness to be a good housekeeper. Helen there showed herself about on a level with the human average; for all but incredible is the stupidity of our misjudgments and mismeasurements of our fellow beings. There was not in her the capacity to reflect who thought out the new ideas that were constantly being put into effect, who told her what to do and who quietly and tactfully saw that she did it.

The most obvious improvement in Helen was through her unconsciously acting on Courtney's advice of delicately veiled suggestion and dropping the culture pose. She was now patterning upon Courtney's naturalness so far as she could. She had the handicap of an ingrained and incurable passion for those innocuous little tricks of manner with the men; also, she was greatly hindered by a conventional assortment of the so-called "lofty ideals." Still, she was letting much of her own natural personality appear. She was only slightly exaggerating her bent toward sweetness and sympathy. She was not quite so strenuous in advocacy of fine old-fashioned womanliness—heart without mind, purity that is mere strait jacketed carnality; virtue that, when it yields, makes lofty pretense of yielding only in reluctant tolerance of man's coarseness and of nature's shameful way of reproducing. At Tecumseh, when Dr. Madelene Ranger delivered a course of lectures on the profession all young women are candidates for—that is, on matrimony—to the girls of the senior class of the college of liberal arts, Helen was one of those who refused to attend and signed the—unheeded—protest to the faculty. She was no longer so proud of this as she had been, although she still thought she had done what ought to be right though it rather seemed foolish.

But the greatest improvement of all in Helen was the subtlest. She had come there, expecting to be a dependent, feeling and, in a sweet refined way, acting like the poor relation, harbored on sufferance. Women, trained from the outset to be dependents, easily degenerate into sycophants, like men who have always looked to others for employment and have lost self-confidence if they ever had it. But lack of self-reliance, a vice in a man, is regarded as a virtue in a woman; so, women have absolutely no restraint upon their abandoning even the forms of self-respect, once they get in the way of degenerating. Thus, Helen's relations with Courtney might easily have become what is usually seen where there is intimacy between a poor woman and a woman of means. But Courtney—not deliberately but with the unconsciousness of large natures—made this degradation impossible. It was not merely that Helen had not been made to feel a dependent; it was more—far more. It was that she had been made to feel independent, more independent than Courtney herself felt. And this fine feeling, this erectness of spirit, permeated to every part of her character, would have made a full-statured human being of her, had she had the mentality to shake off her early training as mere conventional female.

Richard frankly declared her an ideal woman; Basil secretly agreed with him. Helen became the constant reminder of his lost honor, of the heaven he had given up for the forbidden delights. He reveled in Courtney the tempest; but during the lulls his eyes turned yearningly to Helen, the serene and pure calm. Courtney represented sinful excess, Helen righteous restraint. Courtney's was love the devastator; a love for Helen would be love the uplifter. He wanted Courtney; he felt that Helen was what he ought to want. And in the lulls, with passion exhausted and needing the stimulus of contrast—he sometimes fancied that, if he could somehow contrive to assert his manhood and escape from slavery to Courtney, he would be happy with Helen, and once more noble and good. Like many another, he flattered himself that he had an aspiration to a better life when in reality he was making pretense of virtuous longing merely to whet his appetite for vice. He shut his eyes to the obvious but rarely seen—or, rather, rarely admitted—truth that a man is as he does, not as he pretends or dreams.

Before finally and fully condemning Basil—or Courtney or anyone—for anything he or she may have done contrary to our views of propriety and morality, it would be well to reflect upon the true nature of conscience—to which Basil and Courtney and all of us habitually refer all moral questions for settlement. As we grow older we are awed or amused rather than shocked—and, unless we have lived as the moles and the earthworms, are not astonished at all—by the wondrous ways in which our conscience adjusts itself to necessity—or to what overwhelming inclination makes us believe to be necessity. But in unanalytic youth such adjustments take place unconsciously to ourselves; the mind, in the parts of itself hidden from us, concocts the proof positive that what we desire is necessary and right; all we are conscious of is that we suddenly have the mandate of necessity and the godspeed of conscience. Thus, conscience in youth can be as flexible as occasion may require, yet can, without hypocrisy, be for the conduct of others a very Draco of a lawgiver, a very Brutus of a judge. This, in youth only. But— How many of us ever do grow up?

The free-and-easy mode of life at the house made it impossible for any two to be alone, except by stealth, without everyone's knowing it. As a man who since early youth had led the "man sort of life" he was thoroughly used to associating the idea stealth with the relations of men and women. However, flexible though conventional "honor" is, he had misgivings about bending it to the requirements of desire in this particular case. But as his longing for such a moral invigorator as Helen's innocent purity grew in intensity, he began deliberately to revolve contriving to see her alone again, and by stealth. His first success was accidental—callers occupying Courtney when he came seeking her. As he turned away from the house he spied Helen, seated under a maple tree sewing near where Winchie and the older Donaldson boy were playing ball. She colored faintly when he dropped to the grass near her and lit a cigarette. He so placed himself that he commanded all approaches from the house and could not be taken by surprise. "Why is it," he began, "that I don't see you at all any more—except at the table?"

The fact that he did not pursue when she began to avoid had disappointed her keenly. But it had given her a better opinion of him. It showed—so she told herself, perhaps by way of consolation to vanity—that however bad he might be he yet had redeeming reverence for purity. But she had long been weary of the dutiful struggle against his charm of the worldly and the rich for her the unworldly and the poor. So, her manner was not wholly discouraging as she said, in reply to his respectfully regretful question, "I've been very much occupied."

He watched her swift white fingers a while, then stared gloomily out toward the lake. She stole a pitying glance at him. "Poor fellow!" thought she. "He's suffering terribly to-day. That dreadful woman! How could Courtney, generous though she is, defend a creature who is simply wrecking his life?" As she had kept close watch on him all these months, these signs of his sufferings were not new to her. But never had she seen them so movingly plain. "Poor fellow!" thought she.

Presently he said: "Won't you talk to me? I feel like a—a damned soul to-day."

Helen thrilled. He looked so distinguished, was so elegantly dressed in his simple manly way, had that gloss, that sheen, which marks all the kinds and conditions of anglers for the opposite sex. "What shall I talk about?" she asked.

Her sympathetic smile, showing her excellent teeth and lighting up her dark eyes, changed for him her common-place query into a stimulating exhibit of depth of soul. "Anything—anything," he said. "You've got such an honest, sweet voice that whatever you say makes one feel better."

"What is troubling you?"

"Oh, I don't want to talk about myself."

But her instinct told her he had brought his stained soul to confessional. "It might help you," she suggested, blushing at her own boldness.

He looked gratefully at her and away. "It seems to me," said he, "you've been avoiding me. Is it so?"

Helen bent her head low over her work.

"I suppose it was instinctive," he went on. "To you, I'd seem— Sometimes I feel that, if you and I had kept on with those talks we were having last spring, things would have been different with me. However, it's too late now."

Helen's eyes filled. "Oh, no. It's never too late," said she.

He sighed and rose—Courtney was coming toward them. Helen took no part in the conversation that followed. She was pondering the few meaningless and youthful phrases he had uttered as if they were freighted with wisdom and destiny. And she continued to ponder them after he and Courtney and Winchie went away for a drive to Wenona. The more meaningless a thing is, the more food for thought to those incapable of thinking. When it is clear, it is grasped at once and the incident closes; but let it have no meaning at all, and lives will be devoted to cogitating upon it, and library shelves will groan with tomes of exegesis. Helen found in Basil's words what she wished to find—found a plain mandate of duty to help him. He couldn't be so very bad—probably not so bad as Richard was in his bachelor days, before chemistry and Courtney calmed him. And look at Richard now!

She did not know the very particular dangers for Basil in drink. But she saw that he was taking a great deal more whisky and water than formerly, and she felt that it had to do with his obviously desperate depression. Her one chance to see him, she knew, was when Courtney was occupied; for, had she not led Courtney to think that she did not wish to be left alone with him ever? She decided it was best not to tell Courtney she had changed her mind—somewhat—about him; Courtney would misjudge, would think her careless about principle, weak, love-sick—worst of all, would probably advise against her talking with him. Thus it came to pass that when Courtney was safely occupied—with callers, with Winchie, at sewing or painting or dressing—Helen put herself oftener and oftener in such a position that Basil could find her if he chose. She did not dream that he also wished to be stealthy; she thought the stealth was all on her own side—and he, seeing this, soon pretended to himself that he thought so, too, and had not the slightest sense of guilt toward Courtney. It did not take him long to find a satisfying explanation for Helen's aversion to having it known that they met alone; here, decided he, was another evidence of her modesty, her delicate sensitiveness of the good woman who can't bear being talked about lightly—and, if they talked alone where others could see, there would surely be joking and teasing and gossiping.

Once more habit gave illustration of its subtle grasping of ever more and more power. Before either was aware of it, they were meeting clandestinely with clocklike regularity. And Helen's life filled with sunshine of the most delicious warmth and sparkle. And Basil, keeping steadily on at his drinking, and never relaxing in his devotion to the sweet sin of which Courtney was the scarlet altar, reveled in those agonies of a sense of utter depravity that are about the only charm of wickedness. "I am not fit to live," reflected he with comfortable gloom, as he sat in his apartment alone drinking after an afternoon with Helen and a late evening with Courtney. Here was excellent excuse for drinking and gloriously damning himself. He did not go to bed until he had finished the bottle and the last cigarette in the big silver box on his table. Also, between spasms of self-damning he had contrived to finish a novel of intrigue that had as its villain-hero just such a devil of a fellow as he felt he himself was—or was in delightful danger of becoming.

How it ever befell he never could remember. But the day came when he, sitting with Helen in the summerhouse—the summerhouse!—found himself holding her hand. He stared at the pretty white hand, large and capable yet feminine in every curve. He noted that it was lying contentedly, confidingly upon the brown of his palm. He lifted his dazed eyes. Her lashes were down, her cheeks overspread with delicate color; her bosom, like a young Juno's, rose and fell with agitated irregularity. It was not poisonous mock morality, it was the decent human man underneath, that sent an honestly horrified "Good God!" to his lips. He laid her hand gently in her lap, stood up, thrust his hands deep into his trousers pockets. His face was red with real shame.

"I've often told you," said he, "that I'm no fit companion for a pure woman—that my life's ruined past redeeming——"

"Don't say those things," she implored. "They hurt me—and they're not so. I know *you*."

"Past redeeming," he repeated. "It's the God's truth. I must keep away from you. I've no right to see you—to care for you—to tempt you to care for me. I can't tell you—but if you knew, you'd loathe me as I loathe myself."

"Do you—do you—" Her voice faltered. But she had wrought herself up to such a romantic pitch about him, and his earnestness was so terrifying and so real to her, that she dared to go on—"Do you care for some one else?" And she looked at him in all the beauty of her romance.

"I don't know—I don't know," he answered, in great agitation—physical, though he of course fancied it moral. "Not with the love I might have given a pure woman, if fate and my own vile weakness hadn't conspired to ruin me.... What am I saying? I can't talk to you about it. Think me as bad as your imagination can picture—and I'm worse still."

She gave a low wail that came straight from her honest romantic young heart and went straight to his heart. He sat beside her, took her hand. "Be merciful to me," he begged. "At least I'm not so bad that I don't know goodness when I see it. And you'll always be the ideal of goodness in my eyes—all I once sought in love— all I once deluded myself into believing I had won."

She thrilled. Those words made her feel that he belonged to *her*. She laid her other hand on his. "Basil," she appealed, "you are young, and brave, and noble. You can free yourself—save yourself——"

He drew away, went to the rail of the pavilion, seated himself there. "No," he said. "I'm past saving. And—we must not meet any more."

"Why?" she asked.

"Because—I am not free—and never shall be."

"Is that true?" Her eyes looked loving incredulity.

"I am more tightly bound—by honor and by—by habit—than if I were married."

She gave a long sigh—of despair, she thought, but in reality of hope, for, at least he was free. Marriage was the only real bond. As for honor—what honor could there be in any tie not sanctioned by religion and society?

"What a cur I am!" he exclaimed, put to shame by her sigh and her forlorn expression.

"Please don't!" she begged. "I understand—as far as a girl could understand such a thing. And I know it's not your fault. And—even if we can't be anything more to each other, still I'm not sorry we've had what we've had. I'm—I'm—glad!"

He felt the glory of her purity beaming upon him like heaven's light on the bleak, black-hot peaks of hell. He longed to linger, and talk on and on; but his sense of honor had reached the limit of its endurance for that day. Without touching her hand he said good-by as if they were never to see each other again and went as if his heart were broken.

Thenceforth Helen let her longing for romance centre in him without concealing the fact from herself—or from him. And her castle-building had an energy it would never have had, if she had not imagined she felt it was hopeless. Nothing so dynamic as the hopelessness that hopes. Believing that he loved her, that she was his one chance of redemption, she continued to give painstaking attention to her toilet, to refresh her memory of those of his favorite poets with whom she was acquainted, to learn lines from those she knew less well, and to put herself in his way—always without forwardness. And he continued to drift—held fast to Courtney with senses so enchained that he would have fought against release like an opium fiend for his drug; fascinated also by the woman he could dream he ought to have loved, and might have loved. Two restraints he laid sternly upon himself. Not to talk of love in a *tête-à-tête* with a woman—that would be impossible. But he would see that the talk was kept to the general, that it never adventured the particular. Also, he would never again so much as touch Helen's hand when they were alone. Were he bred to be as expert at moral truth as at moral sham, he might have found a key to his true state of soul in the tantalization this self-restraint caused him to suffer. There were times when her physical contrast to Courtney was as alluring to his keyed-up, supersensitized nerves as was her moral contrast to his morbid moral sense. If he had had the intelligence and concentration necessary to candid self-analysis, he would have been startled—perhaps benefited—by the discovery that he was in the way to become one of those libertines who in all sincerity teach prayers to the innocence they are plotting to debauch.

And all the time he was drinking more and more deeply—not for the moral reasons he fancied, but for the practical physical reason that a disordered nervous system craves the stimulants that will further aggravate its disorder. Helen's father had carried his liquor badly; a little was enough to upset him a great deal. Basil was one of those men who are able to drink heavily without showing it, even to the most watchful eyes. Often, when she had not the faintest suspicion he was in liquor, he was in fact so far gone that he had to keep his surface preternaturally solemn in order to conceal the disorder of his mind.

The day did not long delay when, under the influence of drink, he suddenly seized her and kissed her. She did not resist; but the shock of the contact, instead of inflaming him, instantly restored him to his senses. He was conscience-stricken; also he saw the impossible complications he was precipitating. In shame and fright—in fright more than shame—he fled from her presence.

So far as outward effect is concerned, the action is everything, the motive nothing. But so far as inward effect is concerned, the action is nothing, the motive everything. In action Basil and Courtney were essentially the same—equal partners in intrigue. But her motive of seeking strength through love availed to hold her steady, even to lift her up; while his motive of sensuality ever less and less refined and redeemed by love was thrusting him down and down.

# Chapter 23

Richard and Courtney were walking up from the laboratory together. In his abrupt fashion Richard broke the silence with: "I wonder if it isn't Helen that's hanging back and not Gallatin. She's innocent as a baby, but her experience with her father must have taught her about that one thing."

"What one thing?" asked Courtney, startled out of her abstraction.

"Drinking. Helen must have noticed how Gallatin's mopping it up these days."

"Nonsense," said Courtney sharply. She was much irritated—as human beings are extremely apt to be, when some matter they are making determined efforts to ignore is forced on their attention.

"He was so drunk this morning that he had to go out and take the air. That's what made me think of it."

Drunk! She winced at that bald revolting word. She flamed at what she tried to think was an injustice. "This morning?" cried she. "Why, that's absurd. I'd have noticed it."

"You're another innocent. He carries a package well—always did." There Richard laughed at memories of his and Gallatin's "wild-oats" days of which he fancied Courtney knew nothing—and he would have been panic-stricken had he thought there was danger of her finding out about them. "Yes," he went on, "Gallatin's been going some for several weeks now. But this daytime drinking is a new development."

"I'm sure you're mistaken," said Courtney, her irritation showing in her color now. "You both drink at supper."

"He about six to my two. I never take more than two. And every once in a while I see Jimmie or Bill carrying a case of bottles to or from his apartments. I can understand a boy's doing that sort of thing. A boy wants to try everything. But how a grown man can keep on at it is beyond me. Still, he hasn't much mind. He never says or thinks anything he hasn't got from somebody else. But—women'd never notice that." This last sentence half to himself, not at all for her hearing.

Courtney was all a-quiver with anger. For, his shrewd observation on Basil's mentality compelled her to admit to herself another truth, indeed a whole swarm of truths, she had been hiding from herself—how Basil's conversation, when they were all together and the subject was necessarily other than love, no longer seemed brilliant or especially interesting even; how at the shop he made an extremely poor showing, was now pupil, and rather backward pupil, to her who almost daily had to cover up his blunders; how in helping her with the gardening he never went beyond either approving her ideas or offering suggestions already stated in the books; how she was constantly coming across things she had thought original with him only because she happened not to have read the books that contained them or to have known the phase of life in which they were familiar commonplaces. Angry though an untruth about anyone or anything we love makes us, that anger is as equanimity itself beside the anger roused by a disagreeable truth.

As they neared the house she quickened her pace, hurrying not so much from Richard as from her own thoughts—the thoughts his words had startled from unexpected lurking places as a sudden light sets bats to whirling. Courtney was loyal through and through; also, she clung to Basil like a shipwrecked sailor to a life raft. The stronger the waves of adverse destiny or of doubt, the fiercer she clung to her life raft. In face of the clearest proof from without against Basil, she would have shut her eyes and held fast to him. Yet with devilish malice and merciless persistence circumstances were now constantly taking her blind resolute loyalty by surprise and forcing upon her exhibitions of him as a shallow and sensual person. A proud, intelligent woman's love could reconcile itself to either of these—to a shallow man whose passion was simply symbol of deep and sincere love; or, to a sensual man whose grossness was the coarse rich soil that sent up and nourished high intelligence, fascinating and compelling. But no woman worth while as a human being could continue to love a shallow man treating her as mere "symbol of the sensual side of life" because he was incapable of appreciating any but physical qualities, and then simply as physical qualities.

It was with a heart defiantly loving, defiantly loyal, that she met Basil at eleven that night to admit him. He had not appeared either at the house or at the laboratory during the afternoon or for supper or afterwards. So, she had not seen him since Richard's "attack on him behind his back"—for, she had succeeded in convincing herself that Richard's accusations were an outcropping of prejudice against him. She felt humble toward him because she had listened without bursting out in his defense—this, though to defend would have been the height of stupid imprudence. As he entered the door she softly opened, he lurched against her, stumbled over the rug, saved himself by catching hold of her and almost bringing her down. A wave of suspicion, of sickening fear and repulsion shuddered through her. But she frowned herself down, took him firmly by the arm.

"Be careful," she whispered. "The floor was polished only yesterday."

He mumbled something affectionate and without waiting for her to close the door, embraced her. From him exhaled the powerful odor of mixed tobacco and whisky that proclaims the drunken man to the most inexperienced, to those blindest of the blind—the blind who dare not see. She gently released herself. Several times of late he had come to her in almost this condition; she had forced herself to deny, to excuse, to minimize. Now, however, it was impossible for her to risk admitting him; and also, she suddenly realized she had reached the breaking point of her courage to keep up her self-deception. "You must go at once," she said.

"Why?" he demanded in a hoarse whisper. His befuddled mind reverted to Helen as if Courtney knew about her. "What right have you got to be jealous, if I'm not?"

She did not puzzle over this remark. "Basil, you must go at once because you've been drinking too much." The danger was too imminent to be trifled with in diplomatic phrases.

He stood, swaying unsteadily, his head hanging. "If you think so—" he muttered.

She urged him gently toward the door.

"I—I beg your pardon," he mumbled. "I—I guess you're right."

He backed two steps. As soon as he was clear of the door she closed and locked it. Slowly she went upstairs, dropped wearily into bed. She lay quiet a few minutes, staring at the arc of the night lamp. Then on an impulse from an instinct that could not be disobeyed, she rose, took a dark dressing gown, wrapped it round her. She glided along the hall, descended the stairs, opened the lake-front door. Closing it behind her, she stood at the edge of the veranda. The sky was black; a few drops of rain were falling. She made an effort, ran down the steps, hurried across the lawn and along the path to the Smoke House. The entrance door to the apartment stairway was open. She hesitated, slowly ascended. He did not appear at the sound of her steps. His bedroom door was open. She glanced in. His bed was turned down, his pajamas lay ready upon the folded-over covers. But he was not there. She went on to the door of his sitting room. It too was open. At the table desk and facing the door he sat, half-collapsed on the chair, one hand round a tall glass of whisky and water, the bottle and a carafe at his elbow. Though her mind was on him, her eyes took in and forced upon her every tiny detail of the room; she had made it over that his surroundings might always remind him of her. He lifted his heavy head, blinked stupidly at her. She noted his face with the same morbid acuteness to detail—his swollen eyes, his puffy lips, the veins in his forehead, his brows knitted in a foolishly solemn expression. Never had he seemed so homely, since her first glance at him when he came there a stranger.

After a moment of dazed sodden staring at her, he remembered his manners, rose not without difficulty and stood, stiff and unsteadily swaying. "Give me some of the whisky," said she, advancing. "I feel sort of queer." She dropped to the chair he had just left and took up his glass. "May I have your drink?" she asked, and without waiting for a reply drank eagerly. Color returned to her cheeks, and her eyes became less heavy and dull. "I'm better—very much better," she declared, as she set the glass down empty.

He had seated himself lumpishly on the sofa. They remained silent, gazing out through the open window into the darkness and hearing the soothing musical plash of rain on lake. In upon them poured a freshness rather than a breeze and the pleasant odor of drenching foliage. "As I lay there thinking," she said presently, "it came to me that I mustn't let this night pass without seeing you and making it smooth and straight between us."

The shock of her appearing had for the moment beaten down his intoxication. It was now boiling up again, heating his nerves and his imagination, though he seemed sober and self-possessed. "All right," said he. "I know you didn't mean to insult me, and I'll forget it."

She gazed quickly at him in amazement, started to speak, checked herself.

"But I want to tell you," he went on, his tone and gestures forcible-feeble, "I want to tell you this business of my being shut out has got to stop. You must arrange for Vaughan to come down here to live, and for me to take his rooms up at the house."

This demand seemed to her as utterly unlike him as the dictatorial tone in which it was made. To condemn him—no, more—not to love him the more tenderly—because he was in this mood of distracted desperation would be unworthy of the love she professed. She crushed down her sense of repulsion, went to him, laid her cheek against his hair. "My love," she murmured. "We mustn't ever forget that we have only each other. We'll never let any misunderstanding come between us, no matter how blue we get." And she turned his head and kissed him.

With an intoxicated man's fickleness, he switched abruptly from anger to sentiment. His eyes became moist and shiny. A sensual drunken smile played round his heavy mouth. She saw though she was trying hard not to see. He reached round and drew her toward his lap. She gently resisted, while she was nerving herself to submit—would it not be a very poor sort of love that would let itself be chilled by a mood—a mood in which all love's warmth, all love's gentleness were needed as they are not needed when everything is pleasant and easy?

The tears of self-pity welled into his eyes. "God, how low I've sunk!" He got himself on his uncertain legs, arranged his features into a caricature of an expression of dignified command. "I want you to send Helen—Miss March—away," he said, waving his finger at her. "She's a pure woman. She mustn't be contaminated."

She gazed at him in horror. "Basil!" she gasped.

"Yes—I mean it. Oh, you understand. I'm not fit to 'sociate with her—and neither are you."

With a wild cry, she turned to fly. He lurched forward, caught her by the arm. "But we're just about fit for each other," he said. "And that's the truth—if I am drunk." He nodded at her. "I should say, 'That's the truth *because* I am drunk.' It's giving me the courage to speak out a few things that've been gnawing at my insides for weeks." And his fingers clasped her arm like steel nippers.

"Basil! You're hurting me."

"That's what I feel like doing." And in his eyes as in his fingers there was revealed the sheer sensual ferocity that drink had freed of the shame which at other times held it in restraint.

She hung her head. In a low voice she stammered, "You're making me feel there isn't any love for me anywhere in your heart."

"Love?" he said, swaying to and fro and opening and closing his eyes stupidly. "Love. Oh, yes there is. Yes, indeed. Sometimes I think not, but it isn't so. It's because I love you that I go crazy at the thought that I'm sharing you."

"*Sharing me!*" She wrenched herself free, put her arm over her eyes as if she could thus hide from herself the sight of his soul which in drunken abandon he had completely unmasked.

"Don't be frightened," he maundered on. "I'm a man of honor—'honor rooted in dishonor' as Tennyson says. I'll not go. I'll submit to it—all right. Love gives a man a stomach for anything."

She wished to fly, but her legs would not carry her. She had to stay—and listen.

"How I've been dragged down! How a woman can drag a man down! Not Helen—no—she's an angel. But those good women never are as fascinating as you others.... Love?" He beamed upon her like a drunken satyr. "Let's love and be happy. To hell with everything but love."

As she listened and looked she, for the first time since they had been lovers, felt that she had sinned—had sinned without justification. The judgment of guilt dazzled and stunned her as the sun's full light eyes from which the scales have just fallen. She stood paralyzed, yet wondering how she could remain erect under the weight of her vileness—for, her sin seemed as heavy and as vile as ever celibate fanatic asserted. When her lover moved to embrace her, she, with the motion of shrinking from him, found she had strength and power to fly. She rushed from the room, he stumbling after her, and crying "Courtney! Don't get jealous and go off mad——"

# Chapter 24

She knew the truth at last—the whole truth—what he was in mind and in heart, what his love was, what he in his inmost soul thought about her, about himself. The man who could believe he was sharing her could not but be shallow indeed, stupid, and also incapable of understanding the meaning of the word love; the man who could keep on with a woman he believed he was "sharing," must be sunk in a wallow of sensuality—and as weak as low. She knew the truth. Hearing she might have disputed and in time denied. But there was, and would be, no evading the records stamped clear and indelible upon her memory by that sensual, maudlin face. To falsify those records was beyond even a proud, lonely, loving woman's all but limitless powers of self-deception in matters of the heart. The coarseness of that self-revelation of his was the liquor; but the revelation itself was the man. He did not love; he lusted. He did not love; he despised—her and himself. He did not love—and he never had loved.

There is in every one of us a chamber where vanity and hope live and ever conspire to deceive, and if possible, destroy us. From that secret chamber she now wrenched an amazing secret. She discovered that from the beginning—yes, from the beginning—she, determined to satisfy the craving of elemental flesh and blood, had been lying to herself about Basil Gallatin. Passion had taken sly advantage of her loneliness and her longing for sympathy and companionship; it had beguiled her imagination into creating out of the very ordinary materials of his true personality the lover she had been adoring. One by one she took out and reëxamined all her memory plates of him. Now, a memory plate is like any other photographic plate; it has a surface picture and it also yields to a close scrutiny a thousand details which do not appear upon the surface. Long before she finished, she was realizing that she had all along, with the deliberate craft of self-deception, been hiding from herself the trick her feelings were practicing upon her intelligence. Basil—pleasing manners and dress, amiable disposition, animalism agreeably disguised by education—Basil had been plausible enough to pass muster with her, ready and eager to be deluded because of her craving for love. True, he had posed to a certain extent. But he was not really responsible for the fraud. The blame was hers—all hers.

But disillusion no more destroys a love longing than lack of food and drink destroys hunger and thirst. High above moans of shame over the pitiful collapse of her romance rose the defiant clamors of hunger and thirst. They had been lovers, he and she; and that fact in itself was a bond which a woman, at least a woman of her temperament of fidelity, could not easily break. She feared when he, sober and a gentleman once more, sweet and winning, came to her and pleaded for forgiveness she would forgive—would in her loneliness and heart hunger take what she could get rather than have nothing and the ache of nothingness. It is—at least, it has been, up to and into the present time—second nature to woman to depend upon a man, to select some one man, the best available, and stake everything upon him. Basil Gallatin was that man for her. And—not in novels, but in life—before any woman, however high minded, goes away to utter aloneness from a man who cares for her, he must have disclosed some traits more abhorrent than any such human traits as those of Basil. Yes—human. Was it his fault that he had not given her the kind of love she wanted? Was it not probably her fault that he had not been inspired to that kind of love? Perhaps, too, the love of any man, could it be seen in the nakedness of drunkenness, would be much like Basil's. "I'm only a woman," she said. "I mustn't forget that. I've no right to expect much." And then she shuddered; for in her very ears was the sound of those cold rains falling day and night upon her loneliness and despair.

She saw herself accepting; for, a great deal less than half a loaf is better than no bread. And if she accepted, she must adapt herself—must force herself to acquire a liking for what she must eat or go altogether hungry. She saw herself wending down and down—to the level at which he had from the beginning thought her arrived. She looked all around. Nothing—no one—to save her. For, what could she hope from Richard?—from any man? Was not Basil giving about the best man had to offer woman in the way of association? There was the Richard sort of man—an abstraction—an impossibility. There was the Shirley Drummond sort of man—a human incarnation of Old Dog Tray—equally impossible. There was the third sort of man—the Basil sort, somewhere between the two impossibilities. Life must be lived, and with human beings. Of the three available kinds of associates, was not the Basil sort the most livable? Rather Basil than being frozen to death by a Richard or bored to death by a Shirley. The conclusion seemed cynical; but there was no cynicism in the sad woman who faced that conclusion.

She did not go down to breakfast; and Basil, she learned, kept away also. When he did not appear at dinner she knew he had determined to wait until he should surely see her alone. The emotion that stirred in her because his place at the table was vacant gave her more and sadder light upon how little the heart heeds the things that impress the mind and the self-respect. About the middle of the afternoon she was at the small antique desk in the corner of her sitting room, trying to write a letter. But the charm of the day, the beauty of full-foliaged trees, of lake and cloudless sky seen through the creeper-framed window, would not let her write. As she gazed, her unhappiness calmed and all her senses flooded with the joy that laughs in sunbeams, in light and shadow floating on the grass, in flight and song of birds, in grace and color and perfume of flowers, the joy that mocks at moral struggle and flutters alluringly the gay banner of the gospel of eat, drink and be merry.

As she took her pen to go on with the letter, Lizzie appeared in the hall doorway. "Mr. Vaughan asked me to tell you," she said, "that he'd gone out and might not be back for supper."

"Very well," said Courtney, not turning round. It flitted across her mind that this was an extraordinary message for Richard to send—Richard who came and went as he pleased and sent no word when he was not coming to dinner or supper. "Where's he gone?" she asked—an extraordinary question from her to match the extraordinary message from him.

"He was in a hurry and didn't say," replied Lizzie. "I'll find out."

"Oh, no. It doesn't matter."

Lizzie went, and in her dreaming and thinking Courtney soon forgot the incident. Again Lizzie's voice interrupted—"Mr. Vaughan's gone to see old Nanny."

"Nanny!" said Courtney. She never thought of the old woman except as the memorandum of her pension check appeared every three months in the household accounts.

"Yes. She's dying. She sent for him. Such dreadful roads too."

Courtney's pen halted on its way to the ink well. The room seemed to her to have become terribly still.

"She sent him word," Lizzie went carelessly on, and her voice seemed to come from a distance, through a profound hush, "that she had something on her conscience and couldn't go without clearing it. I reckon she's gone clean crazy."

It was not fear that made nerve and muscle tense. It was not self-control that held her motionless. The peril was upon her; there was no time to waste in emotion. All along, she had pretended to herself that Nanny knew nothing, had at worst a dim suspicion. Now, she realized that she had always feared the old woman had seen and had heard. And those words of Lizzie's made it impossible for her to doubt what was about to occur. No time for terror, for hysteria or fainting or futile moaning. Her whole being concentrated on the one idea, What shall I do? Calmly she said to Lizzie, "Has he gone?"

"Ten minutes ago—maybe fifteen."

"Did he take the motor?"

"Yes, ma'am. She's near dead. He went in a great hurry."

Idle then to think of overtaking him, of bringing him back with a story that Winchie was missing, was perhaps drowned in the lake. Her mind—it had never been clearer or steadier—gave Richard up for the moment, turned to another phase. "Where is Mr. Gallatin?" she asked.

"Out on the lake. Winchie's with him—fishing."

"When they come in, please tell him I wish to see him at once." The events of last night were as if they had not been. Wounds closed up like magic; once more it was she and Basil her lover united against the whole world.

"I can call him from the wall," suggested Lizzie.

"Yes—please do." She dipped the pen as if about to go on with the interrupted letter. Lizzie went. She laid the pen down, leaned back in the chair, clasped her hands behind her head, gazed unseeingly into the huge tree almost directly before the window. The irony of it! Through Nanny whom they had forgotten! The blow was about to fall—utter ruin—the end of love—of life probably. A few hours and there would be a convulsion of the most awful passions. She looked round. Everything calm, bright, beautiful. Reason told her what was about to occur; but there are calamities which the imagination cannot picture, and this was one of them.... Should she tell Basil? "Nanny may be dead before Richard gets to her. If I tell Basil—and Richard comes, only suspicious—Basil's manner may confirm him." It was still more significant that it did not enter her head as even a possibility that Basil might be able to help her devise some plan to avert or to mitigate the blow.... In the midst of her debate whether to tell him, she suddenly gave a terrible cry, sprang to the window, her expression wildly disheveled. The thought had flashed, "If Richard hears and believes, he will *kill* Basil!"

Before she reached the balcony rail, reason took her by the shoulder, drew her back to her chair. "I must keep my head!" she exclaimed aloud. And she fought down and triumphed over the terror that had all but mastered her. At Gallatin's step on the threshold she did not turn. "Shut the door," she said in her usual voice. Then, after the sound of its closing, "Nanny, on her deathbed, has sent for him—to confess something. He's gone to her."

She heard him slowly cross the room, knew he was standing at the window. After a while she stole a glance at him. His skin was gray, his profile set; there were deep lines round his mouth. She liked his face, it was so manly; a wave of love surged out from her heart. "How long shall we have to wait?" he asked. The voice, though wholly unlike his own, had no note of cowardice in it.

"He's been gone about half an hour."

"Only half an hour!"

She saw the sweat burst out upon his forehead. She saw the muscles of his face trembling. There was agony in his eyes—not fear, but that horror of suspense which makes the trapped soldier rush upon the bayonet, makes the man on the scaffold assist the leisurely hangman.

Silence, except the chirping of the birds. A bumblebee buzzed almost into his face; he did not wince. A black-and-gold butterfly fluttered in at the window on the other side of the desk, hovered, settled upon the lid of the stationery box, rested with wings together as one. She turned her eyes from him to watch it, said absently:

"You will have to go at once."

She heard him turn full toward her. She was expecting that quick movement, but she could not help shrinking a little. However she went on evenly: "You can cross in the motor boat, take a trap at Wenona, catch the four-o'clock express at Fenton."

"I deserve that," he said, and she knew he was referring to last night.

She hesitated, went straight at it. "I'd forgotten last night since Lizzie told me about Nanny. It's wiped out. So, you need think only of going."

"What are you talking about?" he exclaimed. "I—go?"

She was ready. She turned upon him a look of well-simulated surprise. Then— "Oh!" she cried. "I've been thinking it out, and you haven't. At first glance it does look as if we ought to face it together. But as you consider it you'll see you've simply got to go."

He seated himself, took out his cigarette case, lighted a cigarette. "If I go anywhere it will be in his direction, to shorten the wait."

"Listen," said she, leaning toward him, her forearms on the desk, her hands clasped. "He'll have but one idea—to kill you. If you're here, the very sight of you will set him wild. He'll kill you—how can you defend yourself?"

"I can't. Vaughan has the right to my life."

She winced at this unconscious ugly reminder of what he really thought of their romance. She waved her hand as if brushing something away. "No matter about that," said she. "I'm thinking how to save Winchie from disgrace—and my own life. If you're here, there's no hope. If you're gone, he'll have the chance to reflect. And I shall know what to say and how to say it."

"I don't believe she knew anything."

"Basil!" His eyes shifted. "Don't you *remember*?"

Both were hearing the mad flapping of that frightened bird in the copse round the summerhouse. She shivered; he moved uneasily. "Even if she knew," he objected, "she may be dead or in the stupor of death before he gets to her."

"Then he'll hear nothing, and there's no reason why you shouldn't go. I'll say you got a telegram from your mother——"

"If he comes merely suspecting and uneasy, and I'm gone——"

"Still he'd not be sure," she interrupted. "And if he were, he'd not have the sight of you to inflame him." She rose. "There's no time to waste."

He settled himself. "I shall not go. We face him together."

The clock on the chimney-piece struck. She gave a cry, rushed to him. "Basil—my love!" she implored. "If you love me, go—go!"

He pressed his hands to her cheeks tenderly, smiled at her with the gentle tolerance of superior male for female. "I understand, dear. This is like you. But my honor will not let me go."

She released his hand, stood gazing at him. In the beginning she had urged only because she had wished to save him. But she had been convinced by her own arguments; and it amazed her that he was refusing to see what was so clear. "You—will—not—go?" she said.

"No, Courtney. I cannot."

She brushed the strays of hair from her brow. She laughed scornfully, with a contemptuous shrug. "Whether you two men kill each other or are only wounded, still Winchie and I will be disgraced. You may be only wounded—may get over it in a week or so—or you two may only have a vulgar fight—with the servants looking on. In any case *I* am done for."

He was like a horse when the spur is bidding it advance and the curb is bidding it halt. "If I stay," he cried, "you'll despise me. If I go, you'll despise me."

"If you stay you destroy me. If you go, I can save myself. Will you go or not? Oh, after last night—this on top of that— And, after last night, you can debate whether or not I'll despise you! Go, I tell you! You couldn't sink any lower than you have—and you may redeem yourself." They were facing each other, he white before her scorn and fury. "But not," she went on, "if to what you said and did then you add debating a point of cheap pose when I and my child are at stake. What a shallow, vain creature you are!"

"Do you mean these things? Or are you only pretending, to make me fly and save myself?"

"I mean every word. In spite of last night, of all it taught me, I was still hoping—or, trying to hope. But now— Thank God I had Winchie when I met you, and wasn't free to make an utter fool of myself. A man who could betray his friend for lust, and then betray his mistress for vanity!"

His eyes blazed mingled hate and passion at her. "But you'll go with me now!" he cried, in triumphant fury. "Yes, we'll take that train together. The jig's up, and, damn you, you witch, you've got to go with me."

She was shaking with fright. For the moment she could think of no answer. She was under the spell of the terrible expression of his eyes.

"If he comes looking for some one to kill, he'll kill you if he can't get us both. So—we go together, or die together, as you please."

"Very well," said she, seating herself. "Oh, how like you this is! You know that if we fly, my boy is smirched for life—and I too. You know that if I stay, I may save everything—even your life. If we went, Richard would never rest till he'd hunted us down and killed us."

"I've lost you," said he sullenly. "I don't care what happens. I feel like killing you myself." He straightened up. "Why not?" he cried. "Kill you, then myself—get it all over with."

The silence was broken by a shout from Winchie playing with the neighbor's children on the lawn. That sound compelled her to another effort. She went to Basil, laid her hands gently on his shoulders. "Basil," she pleaded, tears in her eyes, in her voice, "for my boy's sake—for my sake—go! Now that you think about it you can't but see it's the decent, the honorable thing to do. Let's not quarrel—we who have been so much to each other. Go and let us save everything."

He looked into her eyes, and she knew that if he had drunk as much that day as he did the day before, he would have killed her and himself. But she saw that he, sober, was hesitating, was moved by her appeal to his generous, kind nature, overflowing with sentimentality. "Dear," she said, "you can row out on the lake. And if everything's all right I'll hang something white on this shutter here. Then you can come back. Even if he comes home suspicious he'll not think it strange that you're on the lake late."

"But he may come to kill, and before I could get back——"

"But he will not kill me, I tell you. I'm 'only a woman.' I know him. You know, too. And if he would, how could you save me? Would I want to live disgraced?" The clock struck again. She gave a scream, flung her arms round his neck. "Save me, Basil! Go—quick!—quick!"

After the frightful things she had said to him and he to her, there was left him only the choice between going and killing her and himself. On the threshold he, with tears in his eyes, embraced her and kissed her. "God help me, I don't know what to do," he said. "I'll go. If it turns out wrong, remember how you perplexed me—and try to forgive me, dear."

He was so genuine, so manly and loving and she felt so grateful to him that her own eyes filled and she gave him her lips with her heart in them.

She stood at the window; she walked up and down the balcony. But she watched the lake in vain. Five minutes ten—fifteen, and no Basil—Winchie came with his usual rush, flung himself into the hammock. "What is it, mamma?" he asked presently.

She startled, turned on him with eyes wild. "Oh!" she gasped, her hand on her heart. "I didn't know you were there."

"Are you watching for Mr. Gallatin?"

"Why, dear?"

"Because, if you are, he came in with me a long time ago and isn't out there any more."

A silence, she trying to keep her gaze off the lake.

"I like him," the boy went on. "At least, some better than I did. He knows a lot about fishing. When papa blows himself up and never comes down any more, as Jimmie says he will some day, I think I'll let Mr. Gallatin stay on with us."

Courtney scarcely heard. She was grinding her palms together and muttering incoherently when at last she saw his boat pushing leisurely in the direction of Wenona. She drew a long breath. But as the boat glided farther and farther away, her sick heart failed her. She felt abandoned—and afraid. For, she had not told the truth when she said she knew Richard would not kill her.

Winchie stayed on, talking incessantly and no more disturbed by her inattention than babbling brook or trilling bird by lack of audience. His chatter fretted her like the rapping of a branch on the window of an invalid. But she would not send him away. If Richard should come, Winchie's being there would halt him—perhaps, just long enough. After an hour Winchie grew tired of talking and ran off to play. She did not detain him—why, she did not know—probably, because to detain him would have been to encourage a fear that must be defied if the coming battle for Winchie and reputation and life was not to be lost before it began. She must not seem to be afraid. That would be fatal. And the sure way to seem unafraid was to be unafraid.

She paced the floor. She watched the distant boat with its single occupant. She sat and tried to finish her letter. She roamed through the house. "I'll meet him in the grounds," decided she—and, compelling herself to walk slowly, she paced the road between gates and house—up and down, up and down. Back to the house again, to her room. "Yes, we'll not wait supper," she said, in answer to Lizzie's inquiry. At supper, the sound of Helen's and Winchie's voices rasped on her nerves. "Will he never come?" she muttered. And without explanation, she left the table, went again to her sitting room.

"Are you ill, dear?" asked Helen, putting her head in at the door.

"No," replied she, curtly.

Helen went, but Winchie came. "You must hear my prayer, mamma."

"Helen taught it to you. Let her hear it."

"No. She's busy downstairs, and I'm in a hurry to go to sleep."

"Then—just say it by yourself."

"It seems foolish to say it, with nobody to listen."

"Very well."

She sat on the floor beside his bed. He knelt before her, eyes closed, hands folded as Helen had taught him. She was listening—listening—listening. "If he came now—" thought she—one of those sardonic fancies that leer even from a coffin. She stayed on with the boy, getting him to tell her stories, she the while listening, listening for sounds on the drive, on the stairs—and hearing only the sound of the seconds splashing one by one into eternity. Winchie fell asleep. She kissed him, fled from his room with a choke in her throat. She composed herself, descended to the kitchen. Lizzie and Mazie were there, and as she opened one door Jimmie entered by the other.

She became suddenly weak, but contrived to say to him, "Didn't you bring Mr. Vaughan back?"

"Yes, ma'am—an hour ago—most. He got down at the gate and went to the Smoke House. He wanted to see Mr. Gallatin—said for me to send him if he was up here. But Mr. Gallatin's went out in a boat and ain't in yet. Guess he's spending the evening over to Wenona."

She closed the door, leaned weak and sick against the wall of the passageway. Richard knew! Back to her room. She walked, she sat, she lay down. She watched the clock. The moments were aging her like years. Each second was dropping into eternity with a boom that echoed in her shuddering heart. She looked at herself in the mirror. Skin ashen; lines round her mouth—the gauntness of age peering ghastlily through her youth like a skeleton with a fresh young mask over its face bones. A black band all round each eye, the eyes blazing out feverishly. "He must not see me like this," she cried. She went down to the dining room, trembling and listening at every step, like a thief. She drank a glass of brandy at the sideboard, fled to her rooms again. She took the pitcher of ice water into the bath room, emptied it into the bowl of the stationary stand, bathed her face. She pressed a lump of ice against her blue-black burning lids. "Why don't I wake?" she said, for throughout she had the sense of unreality that attends but does not lessen an impending horror.

Twelve o'clock—"I'll go to bed. I'll take Winchie into bed with me. Not because I'm afraid but because I'm lonely." She felt a great longing to live. She felt young and strong, and the look and the odor of life were delicious. If only this crisis could be passed! No matter how—no matter how! "I've the right to live!" She lifted Winchie gently from his bed, carried him to hers. The warmth of his vivid young body stole sweet and sad through her thin nightgown, through her flesh into her heart. He half awakened, half put out his arms to embrace her, murmured "Mamma"—was asleep again. She sobbed a little in self-pity, dried her tears for shame, lay down beside her boy, nestled one hand under his body.

For a moment she felt better. Then up she rose, bore him back to his own bed, returned. But as she was closing the door, she hesitated—"It's not hiding behind him. If I have him with me, it may save him from disgrace." She was about to open the door, when she turned away abruptly. "No! If I did that, I'd deserve to die. Why should I hide behind Winchie? Why should I hide, at all? I may have done wrong, but I wronged myself, not Richard. I may have done wrong. But I had the right to do wrong." She put out the light, lay down again, somewhat calmer. Suddenly she sat bolt upright in the darkness. She had forgotten all about Basil! Had he rowed back, had he and Richard met——

The hall door of her bedroom opened softly—she had intentionally left it unlocked. She sank back against the pillows. Her heart stooped beating as she listened. No further sound. When she could endure no longer, she said, "Who is it?"

Dick's voice, saying, "Oh, you aren't asleep."

"What time is it?"

"About half past one." It was Richard's voice, yet not his.

A long silence. She could hear her heart beating—the ticking of the little clock on the night stand—the murmur of the breeze among the boughs—and another sound—she thought it must be the beating of his heart.

Then he: "May I turn up the light—just for a minute?"

"I'll turn it up." She did so, and as she lay down again saw with a swift furtive glance that his face was haggard, that his eyes seemed deep sunk in black pits, and that he was gazing at the floor. And still she had the sense of unreality, of the dream that will pass.

He advanced a step or two. She felt him intently looking at her. Again that breathless silence. Then he gave a great sigh, bent over her, gently kissed her hair. "What glorious hair you have," he said. "And what a pure, innocent face. It's only necessary to see your face, to know you are good."

She wondered why her skin was not burning, why her lips did not open and her voice cry out. "But when *this* is past," she said to herself, "no more lies—never again!"

"Good night," he was saying.

"Good night," she murmured, the sense of unreality, of the passing dream, stronger than ever.

She heard him cross the room, heard the door close behind him. She leaped from her bed to lock it. As she was halfway across the room, the door opened. Mechanically she snatched from the sofa a dark kimona, drew it round her. "I forgot to turn out your light," he said. "Oh—it was the night-stand light, wasn't it?" Then she had the sense of impending disaster and— His whole expression, body as well as face, changed. His eyes seemed starting from his head. "You—you"—he stammered—"That night when I came home unexpectedly—" He flung out his arms, dropped heavily to the chair behind him. "It's true!" he gasped. "It's *true!*"

The kimona that had helped to remind him and to betray her had dropped from her listless shoulders to the floor. She seated herself on the edge of the bed, her hands clasped loosely in her lap. She looked calmly at him. She now felt as much her normal self as she had up to the moment when Lizzie brought her the news that he had gone to Nanny. She was glad the crisis had come. More—she was glad he knew the truth. "Now," she said to herself, with dizzy elation, "I'll either die or begin to live. 'Nothing is settled, till it's settled right.' My life will be settled right, at last."

He made several attempts to look at her, could not lift his eyes. As they sat there she seemed innocence and he guilt. "Nanny told me," he said, as if feeling round for a beginning. Then, after a long wait, "She said she couldn't die with it on her conscience. I thought her mind was wandering—but—somehow—I couldn't—" He broke off. Another long wait. He ended it with the question she had been expecting: "Where's—he?"

"Gone."

Another pause, longer. "I'm stunned—stunned." He stared at the floor, his head between his hands, his elbows on his knees. "So—he ran away."

"I sent him."

"I am glad. I might have—" He did not finish. "I'm stunned," he muttered.

She clasped her hands round one knee—a favorite attitude of hers—and waited. It was a time for her to be silent, to watch, to wait. A word, any word, from her might cause the explosion.

"Why did you send him away?" he asked. It was as if he were talking with a stranger about an indifferent matter.

"Because he has nothing to do with this. It's between you and me."

Their eyes met. "Nothing to do with this?" he repeated, as if trying to understand.

"It's between you and me," she repeated.

His eyes turned away, as if he were reflecting upon this. Silence again. Then he: "I don't know what to do. I know it's so, but I can't believe it. It's not like you—not at all." He looked at her. She met his gaze steadily. His eyes shifted. "Not at all," he repeated. He was still talking as if to a stranger. She understood why; it would have been impossible for any force, even such a discovery as this, to galvanize into a living personality, with a mind to think and to will, the woman who had for six years been mere incident in his busy life, "Not at all like you," he again repeated. "Yet—why did I feel it was true as soon as Nanny told me?"

She remained silent and motionless.

"Why don't you speak?" he demanded, trying to rouse himself to reality. "Why don't you defend yourself?"

So long as she did not defend, he could not attack. She did not answer.

"You do not deny. You admit?"

She was silent.

"He is safe, so long as he keeps away. You need not be afraid to confess that he took advantage of a moment of weakness." It was an offer of a defense he would accept.

She refused it instantly. "That is not true," she said.

"Yes, it is," he insisted. "He took advantage of my absence——"

"What I did," she interrupted, "was of my own free will—was what I felt I had the right to do."

His eyes lifted to hers in amazement. Again they found her gaze steady and direct. "Don't you realize what you've done?" he exclaimed. Such an expression as hers must mean either innocence or a shamelessness beyond belief.

"Yes, I realize," she answered in the same calm colorless tone in which she had spoken all her few words.

"How like a child you are," said he gently—and child-like she certainty looked, sitting there all in white, so small and lovely and sweet, with her heavy braids twisted round her little head, giving her appearance a touch of quaintness, of precocious gravity. "A mere child. You don't even understand what you're accused of. It simply can't be true—it—" He started up. "My God—if only I hadn't seen that room that night!" And she knew he was seeing what she was seeing—Basil's disheveled room—and she in it, like it. "Courtney! Courtney! How could you—how could you!" And down he sank with face buried in his hands and shoulders heaving.

She hung her head in shame. In vain she reminded herself how he had refused to treat her as a human being, how he had spurned all her appeals, how he had refused to let her live either with him or without him—would give her neither marriage nor divorce. All in vain. Before his grief she could feel only her own deceit. It might be true that he had not allowed her to be honest; it was also true that she had not been honest.

When she looked at him again, she was fascinated by the expression of his long aristocratic profile—stern, inscrutable. "I realize," he presently said, "that I don't know or understand you at all. But of one thing I'm certain—that you are not a bad woman. I've been recalling you from the beginning—from our childhood even. You never were bad. I can remember only sweet and beautiful things about you."

She covered her face with her arm. "Don't!" she murmured.

"I wasn't saying that to make you ashamed," he hastened to explain. "I can't help feeling that somehow or other I am more to blame than you. But that's aside. The main thing is, we must both do the best we can to straighten things out. Isn't it so?"

To straighten things out! Not to rave and curse and kill—not scandal on scandal, disgrace on disgrace—but—"to straighten things out." She pressed both hands to her face, flung herself upon the pillow and sobbed into it—an outburst like a long-pent volcano relieving itself of the fiery monsters that have been tormenting its vitals.

"We'll not talk of it," he went on, as the storm was subsiding, "until we're both of us calmer."

A long pause, the silence broken by the sound of her sobs which she strove in vain to suppress. Then she heard his voice gently saying "Good night." And she was alone, dazed and shamed before this incredible anticlimax to her forebodings.

# Chapter 25

At nine the next morning she appeared at the laboratory as usual. As she was passing through Dick's room, he glanced up. Their eyes did not meet. "Good morning," she said without pausing. She was in the rear room and out of view when his cold answering "Good morning" came. She went about her work, and several times she carried in to him the things she finished. He was absorbed, seemed as unconscious of his surroundings as had been his wont. It was the rule there never to interrupt; she did not break the rule. Toward noon the quiet was disturbed by the telephone buzzer. She answered. In Lizzie's voice came, "The grocery over to Wenona wants to speak to you." She knew at once that it was Basil. "Ask them to call up again about four," replied she and went back to her table. At noon she stopped work and left for the house. At the usual time Richard appeared, had dinner with them all, sat calm and silent and aloof, acting much as he always did.

In the warm part of the year, with the gardens to look after, it was her habit to spend only the mornings at the laboratory. She sent Helen to the Donaldsons with Winchie about three. When the telephone bell rang she herself answered. First came the voice of some clerk, then Basil's—"Is that you?"

"Yes," replied she.

"I'm at Fenton."

"Go to New York."

"Are you—well?"

"Never better. Some one may be listening along the wire."

"I understand. You are *sure* all's well?"

"Sure. Wait in New York."

"I understand. Good-by."

"Good-by."

As she hung up the receiver and turned round, she startled guiltily. There was Richard, just stepping from lawn to veranda, his eyes upon her. She felt as if she had been caught violating in stealth an implied compact not to communicate with Basil. Dick's expression told her that he was reading in her eyes with whom she had been talking. When they were face to face, he on the veranda, she one step up in the doorway, she said: "He wanted to reassure himself before starting East."

Dick's lips curled slightly.

"It isn't fair for me to let you think him a coward. I made him see so clearly that——"

"You were right," he interrupted. "I wish to hear no more about it."

Her eyes flashed at his peremptory tone, reminiscent of his habit of brushing her aside as merely woman. But the thought of Winchie was a talisman against any attack of temper.

"You said last night," he went on, "that this is between you and me only. You were right. So—I've wiped him off the slate."

As they crossed the lawn toward the water's edge, she felt a fear of him deeper than any that physical force could inspire. If he had threatened—had reviled—had done her physical violence, she would have met him with contempt, with a sense of her own superiority. But how deal with this intelligence? She had always known it was an intelligence; she was realizing that it was an intelligence she did not understand, was therefore superior to her own. When they reached the benches near the landing and sat, she was so weak that she could not have walked many steps farther.

"I think," he began, a quiet sarcasm in his tone that did not lessen her uneasiness, "you rather misunderstood me last night. In such circumstances, I believe, a man is expected to tear his hair and paw the ground and do violent things. I confess—" He hesitated an instant before going on—"I've had that inclination several times since I recovered from my stupor. Tradition and instinct and—vanity—are strong. I'll have to ask you to be a little careful what you say to me—not for your own sake but for mine. I have some emotional dynamite in my nature. I don't wish it to be set off. To mention only one thing, there's Winchie to be thought of. I have no desire to punish you. I feel too human myself, to play the part of judge or executioner. But, most of all, I'm determined that Winchie shall never know—which means that the world must never know."

Her clenched hands relaxed as she drew the first free breath since Lizzie told her where he had gone. Now, she felt she could face him for the struggle for Winchie on less unequal terms—not on equal terms, for he had the power to take Winchie away from her—had the power and— *How* could she prevent his using it?

"But when you came into the laboratory this morning as if nothing had happened," he proceeded, "you showed that you misunderstood me." He looked away reflectively. "I don't know just how I restrained myself."

"You were mistaken," said she. "I went because it's been my habit to go. I went just as you did."

He fixed his gaze upon her, danger in it. "You count too much on your success in deceiving me thus far," he said. "I must ask you not to do so—not to try to deceive me. Do you suppose I don't know now why you've been coming to the laboratory?"

His menacing gaze did not daunt her. She met it fearlessly. "That was the reason for a while—at first. But for a long time I've been going because I liked the work."

He studied her with those eyes that saw into everything, once they were focused properly. "I beg your pardon," he said with formal courtesy. "It's true you couldn't have worked so well if you hadn't liked the work."

"I've loved it." And her tone put her sincerity beyond question.

He glanced away. After a pause he said, "To go to the point—the future. I thought at first that I'd decide alone what should be done. Then it seemed to me I hadn't the right to act—about Winchie—without at least finding out what your ideas were."

He waited long; she did not speak.

"You feel, I suppose," he said gently, "that you've forfeited the right to speak."

She did not venture to contradict him. Anything she would say, however guarded, might anger him—and Winchie was at stake.

"As I told you last night, I know you are somehow not a bad woman. Until yesterday, I'd have said there were just two classes of women—the good and the bad. But I'd also have said that I'd have killed both you and him. I find I've got to revise many ideas I had. Just how, I don't know. I'm realizing in regard to my grandfather what I've long realized about everything else—that nothing from the past is trustworthy. The wisdom of yesterday is the folly of to-day." He roused himself from his half abstraction, said, "So—you need not be afraid to speak out whatever is in your mind."

On impulse of response to this breadth—an impulse that was yet, perhaps, not without quick feminine wit to see and seize advantage—she said, "You make me feel that I can trust to your sense of justice."

He smiled satirically. "I see you still don't understand. You fancy I'm more than human because I don't act as if I were less than human. I know you are a woman, but women have been given mind enough to distinguish between right and wrong, between honor and dishonor. And— Is it necessary that I give its plain name to what you've done—to what you are?"

"No," she said in a suffocating voice. Only her boy was saving her from bursting out.

"Then—don't try to cajole me with talk about my sense of justice. What do you ask?"

All in an instant—whether because her natural bent was for the frank and courageous or because instinct told her it was the only hopeful course with him—she resolved to act as she felt, to speak her thoughts. "What do I ask?" she repeated. "First, that you stop posing."

He flushed.

"If you really mean," she hastened on, "that you're acting as you have thus far because it's the right way to act, because the way men usually act is wrong and degrades them, why, you'll stop trying to convince me that you're giving a wonderful exhibition of gracious generosity."

"I had no such intention."

"Then why do you treat me as if I were an object of charity?"

"You can hardly expect me to treat you as if you had done something noble."

"You say I'm not a bad woman."

They looked at each other in silence. "No, you are not," he said. "You have acted like a bad woman, but you are not a bad woman."

"Then," she went on slowly, never taking her grave, earnest eyes from his, "I want you to ask yourself how it happens that the girl who, you said last night, was good, the girl who loved you when she married you, has become the woman you are condemning?"

A long silence. He looked away, looked again—and his gaze remained fixed upon her face. Then, in a low, hesitating voice: "Well—how did it happen?"

"Because you did not love me."

"You know better than that," he cried. "I've never given any woman but you a thought. I've never—" He broke off abruptly, grew angry. "But you're simply trying to improve your position by putting me on the defensive. And I ask you again not to goad me——"

"Because you did not love me," she repeated. "Your anger shows that you are trying to deny the truth to yourself. You married me on an impulse of passion. Oh, you had the usual romantic deceptive names for it—the words that make the man feel spiritual and tickle the girl's vanity. But you've shown what it really was by giving me only an incidental—carnal thought now and then. That's been our married life."

"Why did you not tell me you had these false, unjust ideas?"

"But they're not false, not unjust," she rejoined. "What do you know of me except my outside? What's my mind like? What's my heart like? What do I, a human being like yourself, think and feel? You don't know. You've lived on your grandfather's pompous old-fashioned ideal—that lust is love, if the preacher has christened it—that a woman's whole life is the good pleasure of her husband's various appetites."

She paused for breath. She was not so carried away by the tempest of her emotions that she did not note that he was listening and thinking. He presently said: "Even so, how does that excuse *you*?—you, the mother of Winchie."

She paled, and her hands clasped convulsively in her lap. But she went boldly on. "I had a heart and a mind, like you. How could a human being live the life you assigned me? When I pleaded for a share in your life you refused. When I begged for freedom you refused. What I did was my compromise between the woman and the mother. A mother isn't less a woman, Richard, but more."

He rose in his excitement; for, his keen mind penetrated to her purpose. "You want your freedom and you want my son!" he cried.

Her gaze was steady but her deep voice trembled as she answered, "I want my freedom and I want my child—the child I brought into the world—the child I've watched over from birth. Be fair—be just, Richard. What have you done for him except provide the home the law would have compelled? You've amused yourself playing with him a few minutes now and then. You've asked me to buy him a present now and then. And never even inquired whether I'd done it. Do you know his birthday? Do you know how old he is? Do you know anything about him? Why then do you call him your son?"

He had been in such struggle with his fury that he was unable to check her torrent of half-defiant half-piteous appeal. He now mastered himself sufficiently to say, "How dare you talk to me like this?"

"Because," replied she, quick as a flash, "I respect your intelligence, even if you don't respect mine. You asked me to speak freely. I've done it. Would you have preferred me to lie to you?"

He walked away from her to the edge of the lake, immediately returned and sat again at the other end of the bench. He eyed her passive figure—hands quiet in her lap, gaze upon the town across the lake. Her face was quiet, but all the intelligence and character which her gayety and small stature and young loveliness veiled from unobservant eyes were clearly revealed now. "It's a succession of blows, these discoveries that you are so different from what I imagined," said he. With bitter reproach, "When I think how I exalted, how I idealized you!"

"Did I ask you to do it? Did I tempt you by hypocrisy? ... Whenever I'd try to show you what I was, didn't you stop me or refuse to listen? And—is it true that you idealized me? Is woman as mere female—mere flesh an ideal?"

"I have told you——"

"But," she interrupted appealingly, suddenly all animation, "you spoke without thinking. Think of me as you'd think of one of your problems of chemistry. Don't let your grandfather do your thinking—or the hypocritical world—or the shallow people round us."

He was silent. Presently he rose to pace the retaining wall. As she watched him there was no outward sign of the dread that was licking at her heart like a flame at living flesh. "And what of me?" he said, wheeling abruptly upon her. "You say it was my fault that you did what you've done. Do you mean to tell me you think you're not to blame at all?"

"No, I don't think that," she answered. "If I'd been brought up brave and independent, instead of to be a cowardly dependent— Oh, the crime of it! To take a being with a mind and a heart and, simply because it's female instead of male, to bring it up so that it's unfit really to live—to forbid it to live—to make it afraid to live! If I'd been brave I'd have spoken out frankly. I'd have demanded my freedom—I'd have taken it. As it was—I broke my marriage promises—as you broke yours. It was chiefly your fault." And she went on, with flushed cheeks and accusing eyes: "I don't say it because I wish to shirk, but because I must tell the whole truth so that you won't do a cruel injustice. You promised me love and care and you gave me lust and neglect. We were joined in equal marriage. You treated me much as if I were a slave you'd bought. And I had to submit. For, I really was a kind of slave, and I hadn't the courage and the skill to go out and make my own living—and anyhow, you could and would have taken Winchie away from me, if I'd tried to do it. Isn't that so?"

She saw that he was impressed. Again he reflected a long time pacing up and down the wall. When he turned toward her once more he said: "But listen while I state plainly what you ask. You ask me to reward your treachery by letting you marry the man who betrayed me—and you cap it by asking me to let you make my son his!"

"No, Richard," she protested. "I simply ask you to let me keep my child on any condition you make. I'll promise not to see—him. I'll take Winchie and live on the farm with my people until he's old enough to go away to school. I know the law puts me at your mercy. But I don't believe you'll use your power to crush me." She was choking, was fighting back the tears.

He turned to the retaining wall, gazed into the water until she should fight down the evidences of weakness which he could not but see she was ashamed of. When he joined her again, it was to say in a voice that reassured her: "I want to do what's best for us all—especially for Winchie. It's very difficult.... When I think of the misery I might have caused, if I had believed Nanny and hadn't had time to reflect—I must not act until I've seen every side—Winchie's—yours—mine——"

The sound of the supper gong came floating across the lawn. Courtney rose mechanically and in silence they returned to the house. Helen and Winchie had enjoyed themselves at the Donaldsons, and told all about it. The strain between Dick and Courtney passed unnoticed. When Winchie went up, Courtney accompanied him. Toward ten she left the book she had been pretending to read and sat in the hammock on the balcony. The moon, huge and ruddy through an opening among the boughs, poured its flood of elfin light over lake and lawns and gardens. The soft shadows, the vague vistas, the overpowering perfume of honeysuckle and jasmine and rose combined to beguile her out of all sense of reality. "I've been dreaming—dreaming," she murmured. And what an incredible dream! No man— least of all Richard, the prejudiced, the domineering—would have acted so in real life. "A dream—a dream." It was impossible, this experience of hers that belied all she had read, all she had been taught, about the relations of men and women. She, a married woman, had taken a lover—and, instead of its degrading her, it had made her better than she had been when she thrust love out of her life and tried to live by rule of duty to husband. And now—instead of her husband's killing her or of her killing herself or of any of the various kinds of violence prescribed for such situations, her husband had acted like a civilized human being, gently, considerately, at the dictates of humanity and not at the dictates of vanity. And instead of abysm below abysm of disaster and death in punishment for religion's scarlet sin of sins for woman, there was prospect of a life in which she could profit by the experience she had gained. "A dream—a dream." Or, was a new world dawning?—a new way of living that made the old way seem a grotesque carnival of the beast in man?

As she was dressing next morning, in came Winchie. "Has papa gone away?" he asked at the threshold.

She paused with the eye of her belt at the prong of its buckle. "Why?" said she.

"I don't know whether I dreamed it. I thought it was so. I thought I waked up and there was papa kissing me. And I thought it made me sad. And he said, 'Good-by, Winchie. Take care of your mother and do what she says, and don't forget me.' And I kissed him and said, 'Can't Mamma Courtney and I go too?' And he said, 'No, dear.' And I said, 'All right. Bring me a gun, like Charlie Donaldson's.' And then I fell asleep again."

In the mirror she saw him run to the door into the hall, pick up a letter which had evidently been thrust through the crack. She turned and held out her hand. He brought it to her, spelling out the "Courtney" written on it as he came. "Go take

Aunt Helen down to breakfast," she said. When he was gone, she opened the envelope and read:

> "The important point is Winchie. I am going away to try to think it out. However, one thing is certain. There must be a divorce. In a few days I shall send you a formal notice of abandonment, and you will begin an action at once. Until we are free—perhaps so long as you are alone—it is best that Winchie stay with you. I leave him on one condition—that you keep him here, carrying on everything exactly as usual. He must see no sign of change.
>
> "Please let me know whether you accept. A line, in care of my lawyers, James & Vandegrift, will reach me.
>
> "R.V."

"So long as you are alone." Courtney felt as if the air had suddenly changed from the leaden oppressiveness of before the storm to the buoyant freshness afterwards. With the paralyzing dread about Winchie removed, she could think of the rest of the situation. She read the letter again and again. The regularity of line and word, the precision of phrasing indicated a carefully copied final draft. There was not the faintest clue to the feelings of the writer. She recalled those last two talks with him. At both she was in no condition to observe him, so absorbed was she in the things immediately at issue. But now, as she went over his words, looks, manner, she saw a personality wholly different from the Richard Vaughan she had known—or had fancied she knew. That Richard Vaughan really had no personality beyond a chemical intelligence, was an abstraction like an algebraic formula. This Richard Vaughan was a flesh-and-blood man; but—what sort of a man? And his conduct toward her, did it not mean that he had eliminated her as one empties out a test tube when the experiment ends—in failure? Did it not mean supreme indifference? Yes—it must be so. Still, no ordinary man, however indifferent to wife and child, could act in such circumstances so absolutely without personal vanity, with such obvious determination to do nothing small or revengeful. On any theory, there must be behind those curiously unemotional lines a character big, generous, incapable of meanness.

She looked at this newly revealed large personality, with a depressing sense of her own contrasting smallness. In the last few years of widening intelligence her sex vanity, so diligently fostered throughout her childhood and girlhood, had received many a rude shock from within as well as from without. But none so rude, so demolishing as this. "He's a man really worth while," thought she. "And women are too insignificant either to be loved by such a man or to love him."

She had been bred in and to the American feminine ideal—the woman graciously deigning to permit some man to support her in idleness; the man more than repaid by the honor of being allowed to support her; whatever further he might get, a voluntary largess from his royal guest, to be given or withdrawn at her good pleasure. This delusion was a distorted tradition from a bygone era—an era of conditions around the relations of the sexes that are forever past. In that "woman's paradise" women were scarce and men plenty; and there was the constancy that is natural in a narrow life of severe toil, with the intelligence too little developed to be restless or critical, with the passions undisputedly in the ascendant. This feminine tradition had been dying hard, as delusions flattering to vanity, encouraging to laziness, ever do. She had tried to keep on believing the lies she heard and read everywhere—especially novelists and preachers dependent on unthinking women for a living—the romantic exaltation of woman's love as of value star spaces beyond the value of man's love. She had tried to suppress her sense of humor and to be impressed when she heard women speak of kissing a man in reward for some service as if one of their kisses made an archangel's diadem, in comparison, a cheap bauble. She had tried not to see how intelligent men scarcely restrained the grin of insincerity as they poured out extravagances to some woman whom their whimsical passions chanced to covet. She had struggled against the disillusionizing thoughts about her own sex's private opinion of itself that would arise as she noted how often women treated lightly the man who took them seriously and all but offered themselves to him who winked as he bought or passed on untempted or cynically inquired for the inside price.

Step by step she had been thrust out into the truth that the whole feminist cult was a colossal fiction, that in the actualities of the life of this new era woman's value was precisely like man's—the usefulness of the particular combination of mind and heart, intellect and character, that made up the personality. She began to suspect that woman's ability to sway man through his passion was more often a handicap to her, and to him, than a help to either. She began to realize that learning how to use that ability wisely was the supreme hard problem the life of to-day set for woman to solve or perish. While passion sometimes had made one man for a moment slave to some one woman, or a few men slaves to any woman, it had through all time made womankind slave to mankind. And in the new era, while the slave was still willing, the master was becoming weary, was demanding something less burdensome, more companionable.

As she stood at the bureau, buckle still unfastened, eyes and mind upon those few calm, precisely pruned lines of Dick's, there came a thought that dealt a deathblow to her long dying feminine *folie de grandeur*. While it was true she had not sought nor wished Dick's interest of any kind, the fact remained that he, after living in daily contact with her for six years, had been so little affected by her personality that he was letting her go without any sign of emotion. "But I am as indifferent to him as he to me." she urged upon herself in hope of some slight consolation. She instantly remembered that it was he, not she, who had begun the indifference. And then came the stinging, blood-heating recollection that he had used at his pleasure the only part of her that had been able to impress him as valuable to a man of purpose and achievement. Nor could she dismiss him with a contemptuous "low minded and unworthy," for she knew he was neither. Squirm how she would, she could not get away from the humiliating fact—"six years of me, and not even enough physical value to make his jealousy for a single moment triumph over his sense of self-respect!"

Winchie had finished breakfast and was playing with his wagon on the veranda. Helen was still at table. "Has Mr. Gallatin gone East with Dick?" she inquired, turning rosy red.

"No," replied Courtney, not noting Helen's color. If she had, she would have suspected nothing. When Helen came home in good spirits from that visit to Saint X, after the Chicago shopping trip, and was no longer ill at ease with Basil, Courtney—eager, as we all are, to seize the first pretext to be relieved of a weight upon conscience—assumed that she had got completely over her fancy. As for Basil, Courtney trusted him absolutely.

"But he's away, isn't he?" persisted Helen, after a pause. "Lizzie tells me his rooms haven't been disturbed for two nights."

"He went day before yesterday, I believe," said Courtney. "Did you see Richard this morning?"

"Just a minute. He was hurrying for the train when I came down."

"I thought he didn't look very well, last night," pursued Courtney.

Helen, absorbed in her own agitating thoughts, failed to respond to this lead; so she put the question direct. "How did he look this morning?"

"About as usual," replied Helen. "I didn't notice any change. He had on that new gray suit. It's very becoming. When's he coming back?"

Courtney seemed not to have heard. "He forgot to give me his address. Did he leave it with you?"

"The Willard in Washington, then the Astor in New York."

"It may be I'll want to write him or something."

"I should think so!" cried Helen. "You and he write every day, don't you?"

"Not to each other," said Courtney dryly. "We never did establish the daily letter. That's one of the dreariest farces in married life. It belongs to the kind of people who think they're happy because they're too stupid or too bored to quarrel."

When she had eaten the tip end of a roll and drunk a little coffee, she went out on the veranda, sent Winchie to the lawn and asked Helen to sit with her at the western end where no one could hear or overhear. "You asked me when Richard was coming back," she began.

"It was simply a chance question," apologized Helen.

"He's not coming back."

"Not coming back!" echoed Helen. "You're going to move East?"

The emerald eyes met Helen's excited glance placidly. "We are going to get a divorce," she said.

Helen's big brown eyes opened wide. With lips ajar she stared at Courtney. Then she gave a little laugh that sounded as if the shock had unbalanced her mind and reduced her to imbecility. "A divorce," she murmured feebly.

"We both wish to be free," continued Courtney, talking in the matter-of-fact way that was the surest preventive of hysteria in herself or in Helen. "So, he's gone away. I'll stay here a while, then— But I haven't made any plans. There's plenty of time."

A long silence, Helen gazing at Courtney, at Winchie racing along the paths with his red-striped wagon, at Courtney again, at trees and lake, as if she doubted the reality of all things. "I don't know what to say!" she exclaimed at last.

"Naturally," replied Courtney, "since there's nothing to say."

"I can't believe it!"

"Why not?"

"There aren't two people better suited to each other. Why, you never quarreled."

"That's it. I love contention. He wouldn't give it to me. So—pop goes the weasel."

"How can you! When your heart must be breaking." Helen put aside her stupefaction and brought the tears to her soft brown eyes in tardy conformity to the etiquette for nearest female friend on such occasions.

"Now, dear, please don't cry. You know that I know how easy it is for women to cry, and how little it means."

Helen hastily dried her eyes. "Oh, dear! It must be fixed up!" she said in a more natural tone, genuinely sympathetic and friendly. "He doesn't mean it. I'm sure he doesn't."

Courtney laughed—rather disagreeably. Helen was confirming her own newly formed, anything but exalted opinion of herself as a human value. "I suppose it'll never for an instant occur to anyone that I might be the discontented one."

"Well, you know, yourself, Courtney," stammered Helen, "it doesn't seem likely a woman'd give up a good husband and a good home——"

Courtney's arresting smile was bitterly ironic. "Indeed it doesn't," assented she. "Give up what she married for? Not unless she was sure of a better living. Men think they marry for love—but it's really to—I'm not equal to saying why men marry. You can find the reason in Ben Franklin's autobiography, if you care to look it up. As for us women—it's the living."

"It's not true of me!" cried Helen, who had in all its amusing, or exasperating, efflorescence the universal feminine passion for drawing everything down to the personal, for seeking a compliment to herself or a reflection upon herself in any and every remark addressed to her by man or woman. "Poor as I am, I'm——"

"Never mind, dear," said Courtney with good-humored raillery. "At your age I was talking the same way. You'll find out some day that the hardest person in the world to get acquainted with is your real self. Why, there isn't one human being in ten million who'd know his real self if they met in the street." She rose to inspect the thick mat of morning-glories trellised up the end of the veranda. "And most of us, if we were introduced to our real selves, would refuse to speak to such low creatures—especially the romantic people."

"I *know* I'd not marry for *anything* but love!"

Courtney, her back to Helen, was busy with the morning-glories. "Of course," said she. "One may eat because one is fond of the dinner—of the dishes, of the way it's served, of the company, and so on, and so on. But what's the *real* reason?" She

228

turned on Helen with a mocking smile. "Why, because to live one must eat. That makes the rest incidental. A sensible person tries to take the most favorable view of the food he has to eat or go without. A sensible woman does her best to love the man that asks her."

"I wish you wouldn't say that sort of things, Courtney," Helen cried. "I know illusions are illusions, but I want to keep them."

Courtney's expression changed abruptly. The deep-green eyes looked dreamily away. "If only one *could* keep them!" she said. "But one can't." She shook her head sadly. "One can't." Then her face brightened. "My dear, it's better to throw them away oneself and get—perhaps something better—certainly something truer—in place of them. Sooner or later life will snatch them away, anyhow—and leave one quite naked." She turned sad, mysterious eyes on the girl. "You don't know," she went on, "what it has cost me, this being bred in illusions. Illusions—everywhere! Illusions for and about everything and everybody! Oh, Helen—Helen—that's what's the matter with us women. That's why we're such poor creatures—why we make such bad marriages, why we're such imperfect wives and mothers. We don't think. We purr or scratch."

A long pause, then Helen sighed. "And I believed you and Richard were happy!"

"No," replied Courtney, her smile mocking, but pain in her eyes. "But we're going to be—if we can get over what our illusions have cost us and can set our feet on the solid earth. No more lies! And the biggest lie of all is that lying can ever bring real happiness." She was standing in the long, open window. She thought a moment, then said with an energy that frightened the girl: "And I'm sick—sick—sick of perfumes that end in a stench!"

That afternoon she sent an acceptance of Richard's proposition—a "line" as he had suggested: "Winchie and I will stay on here until the divorce—and, if you so wish, so long as I am alone. I will keep Helen here, too." On the fourth morning after the dispatch of this, there came a letter from James & Vandegrift, inclosing one, unsealed, from Richard. She read the inclosure first:

> "MADAM: From this date I cease to be your husband. You may take such legal action as this may suggest.
>
> "RICHARD VAUGHAN."

She understood that Dick was simply meeting the legal requirements. But, these curt words made her tremble, made her skin burn, made her eyes sink with shame, though she was alone. A few moments and she glanced at the accompanying note from the lawyers. This sentence in it caught her eye: "As two years is the legal period in this State in actions on the ground of abandonment, you will observe that the date of Mr. Vaughan's letter enables you shortly to begin suit." She took up Dick's letter, looked at the date—August 17th, two years before. Then in a few weeks she could sue; in a few weeks more, she would be free. Free! That charmed word had no spell of exultation for her. She sank down by the window with heart suddenly faint and terror-stricken. She had been looking forward to a long time in which to plan—about Winchie, about her future, about Basil. And she would have only a few weeks. A few weeks—and her whole future to be decided—and she without experience, without anyone she could rely upon or even consult, without resources.

August 17th—why had he chosen that date? With so many serious things to think of, her mind kept swinging back to that triviality—why August 17th? All at once it flashed upon her. August 17th—that was the date when Nanny had spied on her and Basil at the summerhouse. She covered her face, and the blood surged in hot billows against her scorching skin.

Helen came, crying: "Oh, there you are. Winchie wants ice cream for supper. Don't you think— Why, Courtney, how solemn you look!"

"And you would, too," said Courtney, "if your hair had been falling out the way mine has lately."

"Don't be so foolish," reassured Helen. "You could lose half of what you've got, and still have more than most women.... Perhaps it's worry that's making it fall?"

"I—worry? How absurd."

"No, I don't believe you ever do."

"Let's have the ice cream. Chocolate. And I feel just like jelly roll."

# Chapter 26

The pause before the first decisive step toward freedom—and perhaps away from Winchie—had shrunk to a day less than two weeks.

It is mercifully not in human nature vividly to anticipate catastrophe. Death is the absolute certainty; yet no living being can imagine himself dead. And it was anything but certain that Dick would ever assert his legal right and take away her child. In her anxiety about Winchie, she had been giving much thought to Dick's character, which would be the deciding factor. And she was surprised at the knowledge of it she had unconsciously absorbed. Except among fools—who, whether they look within or without, see nothing—it is a commonplace of experience to discover that what we fancied we thought about a certain person or thing is precisely the opposite of what we really think when compelled to interrogate ourselves honestly. That is why the whole world can live and die by formulas in which it has not the least actual belief. These discoveries of our self-ignorance always astonish us, no matter how often they occur. Courtney had got many surprises of this kind in the past two years; yet this find—her intimate knowledge of her "abstract" husband's character—seemed incredible.

It wasn't strange that she should know how he took his coffee, his favorite brand of cigarettes and of whisky, that he detested cold baths and would not wear underclothes with silk in them, or, if it could possibly be avoided, starched shirts—that he hated low shoes and high collars. As a "dutiful wife" she had made it her chief business, after Winchie, to see to her legal husband's material comfort, so far as he would permit it. But how had she come by a deep conviction of his honesty, of his truthfulness, of his incapacity for meanness of any kind? Where had she got her confidence in his sense of justice—he who had alienated her by his stubborn and tyrannical injustices to her? Why did she summarily dismiss as absurd the suggestion that his recent conduct was dictated merely by indifference to her or selfish consideration for his own comfort? These high ideas of him certainly did not date from their courtship and honeymoon; for, then she had no more interest or discrimination as to character than the next young person. There was no accounting for it. She simply found that these beliefs were immovably lodged under the opinion of him she had supposed was hers—the opinion that had made her love for Basil seem as right as if she had been a girl. So, while she feared he would take Winchie away from her, with a fear dark enough to shadow her days and make many a night uneasy, she was always saying to herself believingly, "He could not do anything unjust."

One evening she fell into a somber mood. It wasn't so clear as usual that Dick would see the to her obvious injustice of separating mother and child. She left Helen, went up and stole in to sit by Winchie's bed—a habit she had formed lately. She got so low spirited that, when she heard Helen go along the hall toward the upstairs sitting room, she slipped downstairs and out into the air to wander among the flowers and beneath the scented trees. There was a thin moon and one of those faint, soft, intermittent breezes that give the disquieting yet fascinating sense of spirit companionship. She strolled to the edge of the lake; the fireflies seemed the eyes of the breeze spirits that were whispering and friendlily touching her. She saw a boat with a single occupant a few yards down the lake, close in shore. Even as she glanced, a low voice—Basil's—came from the boat: "Courtney—may I come?"

She was not startled. Before the voice she had thought, "Basil will probably be trying to see me before long." She answered in the same undertone, "Helen may be looking this way."

"If you sit on the bench down here, I can come to you. The shadow's deep enough."

She hesitated, went to the bench he indicated. The press of the immediate had been all but keeping him out of her mind. But whenever she did think of him it was as her lover. With a nature as tenacious as hers habit is not dethroned in a day or demolished all at once by any convulsion however violent. Also, the more she suffered and the lonelier she felt—not a soul about to whom she could speak or hint any part of what was harassing her—the more tender grew her thoughts of the man in whom she had invested so much. Throwing good love after bad is not a rare human weakness—and Courtney was by no means certain in those depressed days that her investment had been bad, as such investments go in a world of human beings.

He soon had his boat opposite the bench, made it fast. He sprang to her, seized her hands and was kissing them. "No—no. You mustn't," she protested, drawing away.

"Tell me all about it!" he cried. "How I suffered till I heard your voice on the telephone! I was watching the house with a glass all afternoon until dark. I was in the boat, lying a few rods up there all night. And from dawn I was across the lake watching with the glass again. So, I knew everything was quiet. But until your voice came, I was mad with dread—though I had seen you, just like your usual self, in the grounds and on the veranda hours before. But—tell me all about it."

"There's nothing to tell," said she. His recital had seemed to her as if it were of something in which she had neither part nor interest.

"He knows, doesn't he?

"Yes—he knows." And there she stopped because she never had discussed and never would discuss with anyone what happened between her and her husband.

"What is he going to do?"

"I don't know."

"But— Don't keep me in suspense, dear. Is he going to get a divorce?"

"No. I'm to get it."

"Your voice is very queer. Aren't you—glad?"

"I'm afraid about Winchie."

"Oh—of course. Does he threaten to—" Basil halted.

"No. But— Basil, you must go."

"Go? It's perfectly safe here."

"Yes. But I've no right to see you, after the way he has acted—until I'm free." All true enough; yet she could not make her voice sound right to herself. "It isn't wise and it isn't honorable," she ended haltingly.

She saw, or rather felt, him eying her somberly. "When will you be free?" he asked in a constrained tone.

"In a few months—I think."

"And then we shall marry at once." He said it in the tone a man uses when he wishes to convince himself and another that what he is saying is the matter of course.

She did not answer.

He laughed unpleasantly. "You don't seem overjoyed at the prospect."

"I'm thinking of Winchie."

"Oh!" A pause; then he asked, "As soon as you've got Winchie safely, we'll marry?"

This was a question she had not faced alone, yet. She was far from ready to face it with him. She found one of those phrases that come easily and naturally to women, ever compelled to be diplomatic. "If we both wish it then." Lightly, "You see, as I'm escaping with reputation intact, you're not bound to marry me."

"Bound?" he exclaimed. "Courtney, please don't joke about this."

"I'm quite serious—though I don't act as funereally as you do when you think you're serious."

"We love each other, and——"

"Do we?" An impulse of honesty, of impatience at her own yielding to the temptation to temporize forced her to say it, "Do we, Basil?"

"Courtney, have you—changed? Can't you forgive me for——"

"It isn't that," she interrupted, and she thought she was telling the truth. "Let's never speak of that. No—it's— Could anyone go through what we have without being—sobered?"

"That's true. It has made me love you more intensely, more earnestly than ever. What we've suffered has made us like—like the two pieces of metal the fire fuses into one."

"That *sounds* nice. But—is it so?"

"You know it is!" he cried angrily.

"No, I don't," she replied, as if she were weighing every word. "I've made up my mind not to tell any more lies, especially to myself. I don't feel as I used to feel. There's—some one between us."

"Vaughan?"

"Yes. I've a sense of obligation to him. If you had seen what I saw—how far above the little men who go in for cheap theatricals or act like mad dogs——"

To his sensitiveness it seemed for an instant that she was hitting at him, was slyly reminding him of his own conduct. But he soon felt that he was mistaken—that there was another reason why her words stung him. "It sounds as if you were falling in love with him," he said in a grotesque attempt at a voice of raillery.

"No," replied she, and her voice satisfied him. "That part of my life is over. It could no more be brought back than last year's summer."

"Winter," he corrected.

"It wasn't all winter, to be fair," said she, and changed the subject with, "But—remember, you are free—free as I am. We shan't see each other or hear from each other for a long time. It may be that you'll fall in love with somebody else———"

"Courtney, do you love me? ... Look at me. Answer."

She continued to gaze out over the lake. "Honestly, I do not know. Sometimes I think I do. Again I wonder, did I love you or was I only in love with love? It's so easy to fool oneself when one wants any thing as much as I wanted love."

"If you knew how you were—hurting me you'd not say these things."

"Would you rather I lied to you?" she asked gently.

"Yes! For, I love you and I can't live without you. You've made yourself necessary to me. We must marry as soon as you are free and have Winchie."

"Yes—we will marry, I suppose. There isn't anybody so near to me."

"Except Winchie."

"Winchie *is* me."

"I understand," he said. "It's—beautiful. Ah, Courtney, we must marry as soon as we can."

"No. I must—" She paused.

"Go on, dear. What is it that's to keep us apart?"

"I must be independent as well as free." The truth was out at last—the truth her nature as a woman of sheltered breeding was always dodging, but which her intelligence and pride were forcing her to face. "I must be independent."

"There couldn't be any question of that kind between us."

"There shan't be," replied she with energy that startled him.

"I'll settle any amount you say on you. I'll make myself your dependent if you wish."

She laughed in a sweet, tender way. Whatever his faults and failings, he certainly was generous. "Basil!" she murmured. Then: "As if that would help matters. Why, anything I got from you would only increase my dependence. No, I must be really free—so neither of us could think for an instant I was your wife because I had to be supported—or you were my husband because you felt I was helpless. We women have got to stop being canary birds if we're to get real self-respect—or real consideration."

"What queer notions you do get," said he with man's tolerant amusement at the fantasies of the women and the children. "Think of wasting such a night—and our few minutes together—discussing theories—and sordid ones!"

"Sordid! Basil, we're made out of earth and we've got to live on the ground. I'm done forever with the kind of romance and idealism we were brought up on. I'm going to build as high as I can, but I'm going to build on the ground. No more cloud castles that vanish when the wind changes. I'm going to use romance for decoration not for building stone, and cakes for dessert, not in place of bread."

He laughed appreciatively. "How clever you are! We'll get on beautifully," he said. "You're the sort of woman that never bores a man or makes him feel like looking about."

"Are you the sort of man that never bores a woman or makes her feel like looking about?"

"That's not for me to say," answered he with a careless laugh.

"It doesn't strike you as important—what a woman might think about such matters, does it?" said she, good-humored in her mockery.

"Oh, yes—if the woman's you. But let's not bother about such things. It seems such a waste of time. One kiss?"

She shook her head. "Not with Richard looking on."

"Do you *want* me to kiss you—dear?" he said passionately.

With a nervous glance toward the house she rose. "Please!" she said, in vague entreaty. "You must go."

"You haven't told me—anything—yet." He cast hurriedly about for some way to detain her. "There are your plans for being independent."

"I haven't any."

"Do sit down. I'll not touch you again."

"It isn't that, Basil. It's for the same reason that I didn't write and can't. Hasn't what he's done pledged us both to——"

"Don't say any more, Courtney," he interrupted; for he saw how profoundly in earnest she was, and respected her for it. "You're right. I'm going." He took her hand, pressed it. "Dear," he said, "do you know what it was that nearly drove me insane after you sent me away? As soon as I thought about it, I knew no harm would come to you. He's neither a coward nor a beast. But I was afraid you'd—kill yourself."

"I never thought of it," laughed she. "I'm too healthy. You ought to build your romance round some lady with the morbid ideas that go with addled insides—the kind they write novels about—only they call it soul."

He was amused in spite of himself. "It's lucky for you," said he, "that you look like a romance. If you didn't, your way of talking would discourage terribly."

"Is lying the only romance?" said she. "Can't you enjoy the perfume of a flower unless you make a silly pretense that perfume and flower are a fairy queen and her breath?"

She went with him to the retaining wall, gave him her hand, tried to respond to his loving pressure. He got into the boat. His expression in that odorous, enchantment-like dimness thrilled her. The feeling that he was going—leaving her to face the lowering future alone—saddened her, moved her to an emotion very like the love that had so often agitated her in these very shadows. And when he murmured, "Soon—my love!" she echoed "Soon!" in a voice melodious with the meaningless, impulsive sentiment of the moment. It sent him away believing. He pushed off. She watched the boat glide deeper and deeper into the shadow. A few seconds and the darkness had effaced it. She went slowly up the lawn. Before she reached the house, Winchie was again uppermost in her thoughts; to think of Basil involved puzzling over too many problems she was not yet ready to face.

That was one of the years when the warm weather stays on and on; goes for a night, only to return with the morning sun and change the hoar frost on the grass into dew; then in late October or later drifts languorously southward through the dreamy haze of Indian summer. On an afternoon midway of this second and sweeter, if sadder, summer Courtney came out of her sitting room to the balcony to rest a moment and to watch the sun set—a dull red globe like a vast conflagration of which the autumnal mists were the smoke and steam. Winchie and Helen were playing ball on the lawn, with Helen making great pretense of being unable to catch or to hold Winchie's curves and hard straights. Winchie, about to throw, dropped the ball, jumped up and down clapping his hands, made a dash for the veranda, crying "Papa! Papa!" Next she saw Helen, in confusion, turn and go in the same direction, her delicate skin paling and flushing by turns.

In the upstairs sitting room was the seamstress who made a local journal of society gossip unnecessary; as the divorce suit had been begun and was the chief local topic, the less she saw and heard, the more what she'd circulate would sound like pure invention. Courtney went along the balcony to the hall window and entered there. Winchie had just reached the top of the stairs. "Oh, mamma—" he began, all out of breath.

"Yes, I know," said she, laying her finger on her lips. "Let's go down."

And holding him by the hand she descended. Richard and Helen were in the lake-front doorway, Richard talking, Helen obviously nervous. Courtney advanced, her hand extended. "How do you do?" said she with easy friendliness.

"No need to ask you that," replied Dick. "Or the boy, either. How he has shot up!"

"We've had a great summer and fall for growing things," said Courtney. Then to Helen: "Don't let us interrupt your game."

"Yes—of course— Come, Winchie," stammered Helen.

"Just watch me pitch, father," cried Winchie. "Jimmie's taught me to curve."

"You don't say!" exclaimed Dick with an interest whose exaggeration roused no suspicion in the boy's breast.

While Richard was watching the exhibition with such exclamations as "fine"—"that's a soaker"—"look out or you'll do up your catcher," Courtney was watching him. She found no trace of the weary, tragedy-torn misanthrope of song and story. Evidently Dick had been too busy with other things to bother about himself. Instead of travel stains, there was neatness and care and not a little fashion in his apparel. Never had she seen him so well dressed—-and in admirable taste from collar and tie to well-cut tan boots. His hair was short—the way it was becoming to his long, strong face and finely shaped head. The face was not so gaunt as in those years of close application, especially the last two years when indigestion was giving him its look of hunger and sallow ill temper. The cheeks had filled out, had bronzed, and the blood was pouring healthily along underneath. It was distinctly a happier face, too. The eyes following Winchie's elaborate contortions in imitation of the famous pitcher of the Wenona Grays had an expression of aliveness and alertness that meant interest in the world about him. He had been one of those men of no age, like monks and convicts and professional students. He was now a young man—and a handsome young man.

When he turned away from the ball game, they went to the eastern end of the veranda. She sat in the hammock, he leaned on the broad arm of a veranda chair. "Well," said he, by way of a beginning, "you see I'm back."

"You've been abroad—haven't you?"

"Paris and Switzerland. I had a grand time. Fell in with some English people and we did three passes together, and then rested and amused ourselves at St. Moritz. Then—to Paris. I never thought I'd care about eating, but the Ritz seduced me. I think of nothing else. Then—London, to get myself outfitted. I needed it badly."

What he said sounded strange enough from him, from Richard the abstraction, the embodied chemistry. The way he said it was stupefying. There was lightness; there was the sparkle that bubbles to the surface of every look and phrase of a person with a keen sense of humor. Richard had plainly come to life while he was away. Said Courtney: "I suspect you've not worked very hard this summer and fall."

"Work?" replied he, with a laugh. "Not I! It was a hard pull at first, the habit had become so strong. But I determined I'd freshen myself up. Once I got away where I could take an impartial look at things, I saw I was not only not getting the right results by such stolid, stupid grinding but was actually destroying my mind—was getting old and stale. So, I locked up the laboratory I carry round inside me, and set out to learn to live—to learn to have a good time."

"And you did?"

"Once I found congenial people. At first I was afraid I'd been stupid so long that I'd lost the power to enjoy. But it came back."

As he talked Courtney's spirits went down and down. Just why, she could not have told. She certainly wished Richard well, had no desire that he should be miserable—at least, no active desire—though, of course, she was human and would have found some satisfaction of vanity in a Richard hard hit by the discovery that his domestic life was in ruins. Still, this vanity of desire to be taken tragically was not with her the passion it is in most men and women. She was far more puzzled than piqued. She could not understand how so serious, so proud a man as he could dismiss a cataclysm thus lightly, no matter how little he cared for her. She had pictured him suffering, suffering intensely; these pictures had given her many a self-reproachful pang, and of real pain too. Now— Looking at this robust, handsome, cheerful person, well fed and well dressed, she felt she had been making a fool of herself.

"Now that I come to examine you," he was saying, "you don't look at all well."

It was a truth of which she had been uncomfortably conscious from her first glance at him. "You ought to have gone away somewhere," he went on. "It's a bad idea to stay in the same place, revolving the same set of ideas too long. Mrs. Leamington taught me that. You'd like her. Your height—much your figure—fairer skin, though—that clear healthy dead white—a lot of really beautiful black hair—the kind with the gloss that's not greasy. She certainly was interesting. I didn't even mind her love of money. She simply had to have it—needed it in her business of being always wonderfully dressed and groomed to the last hair and the last button."

Richard paused to enjoy contemplating the portrait he had painted. Courtney wished to hear more. "She was in your party?"

"She made most of the interest. She cured me of my insanity for work—gave me a wider view—made me stop being a vain ass, thinking always about my own little ambitions and worries. There's a lot that doesn't attract me in women of the world. They're extremely petty at bottom, I find. But at least they do come nearer the truth with their cynicism than we quiet people with our preposterous egotism of solemnity."

Once more her vanity winced—that he should fancy he had to go to Europe and learn of a cynical mercenary of an English woman what she herself had made the law and gospel of her life for years. How feeble her impression upon him had been! True, the only chance one has to make an impression is in the beginning of acquaintanceship; and in their beginning she had been too inexperienced, too captivated with romance—too youthful to have developed much personality. Still, all that did not change the central fact—she had been futile.

"How's the divorce coming on?" he asked abruptly.

Courtney laughed—perhaps not so genuinely as it sounded, but still with real humorous appreciation. "The beautiful English woman—a long silence—then the question about the divorce—that's significant," she explained.

"She's not the marrying kind," replied he, easily enough. "She'll stay free as long as her looks and her money hold out. Then she'll marry some rich chap and go in for society.... She was an interesting woman—a specimen, so to speak. And I owe her a great deal. She taught me a few very important things—about myself—and about women.... What a fraud this so-called education is. One half of fitting a man for life is to teach him to know men, the other half is to teach him to know women. And we actually are taught only about things—and mostly trifles or falsehoods as to them."

His manner demolished her suspicion. There might have been some sort of an affair between him and this English woman—perhaps had been. If so, it was a closed incident. "You asked about the divorce," said she: "The suit was begun, but it has gone over till the next term of court."

"Was it my fault?" he asked, apologetically. "I've missed my mail for nearly two months."

Her hands, clasped in her lap, were white at the knuckles. Her eyes, meeting his, had deep down an expression that also belied her calm manner and even voice. "I didn't want to take the last steps until we had decided about Winchie."

"Winchie," he said thoughtfully, his glance wandering to the lawn. The boy and Helen were resting now, seated at the edge of the lake. "There's where marriage differs from other business. When it goes bankrupt, children are assets that can't be liquidated.... What do you think ought to be done?"

"I admit you've got a share in him," replied she. "But you can't help seeing that he belongs with his mother."

"I do see it," he declared. "If I took him, what could I do with him? Helen'll marry before long. Then— Could there be anything worse for him than trusting him to the care of strangers? ... As for his traveling back and forth between his mother's house and his father's—that's a farce that could only end in some sort of calamity to his character.... I don't know what to say. I know I could trust you absolutely to protect him from any possible—unfortunate influences—but—" And there he halted.

She saw he was expecting her to realize that he meant the disadvantages of Basil as a stepfather. It was stupefying—simply stupefying—this calm attitude of his toward such terrible things—at least, they were things he had always regarded as terrible.

"Don't be so gloomy about it," said he, as if reading her thoughts. "I find I can think a great deal more effectively when I'm not trying to act like the best examples from fiction but am simply human and natural. Courtney, the world—at least, the intelligent people in it—have outgrown the old, ignorant, swashbuckling sort of thing. Of course, it still survives, and ignorant people and vain people still try to act on the prescriptions of yesterday—and all the literature still pretends that they are valid. But the truth is, men and women are getting enlightened. And we—you and I—are doing, not what looks best, but what is best. Winchie isn't a problem in a novel or a poem. He's an actuality. And I see plainly his chances are better with you—in any circumstances—than with me." To make sure that she should understand, he repeated, "In any circumstances."

Her eyes were full of tears. "Thank you," she said humbly. "Thank you."

He shrugged his shoulders. "For what? For not being a fool?" He swung round into the chair and leaned toward her. "There are some things we've got to say to each other. I went away to put off the saying until I was sure just where I stood. I am sure now. Do you— Shall we—begin?"

"I wish to hear whatever you wish to say," replied she. "But—is it necessary to say anything?"

He leaned back, lighted a cigarette, smoked in silence. She again studied him. That changed expression—the tense, concentrated strain gone—a sense of life, of attractive possibilities in it other than chemistry, gave him a humanness, a reality he had not had for her even in their first months of married life. "Perhaps you're right," said he, rousing himself. "Why mull over the past? And our futures lie in different directions." He noted the queer, intent look in her eyes. "What's the matter? You seem puzzled."

"Nothing. I— Nothing."

"It's the change in me—in my point of view—isn't it?"

"Your—your mind certainly seems to have changed."

"Dropped its prejudices, rather," was his reply. "There's a difference. A man's mind's himself. His prejudices are more or less external—can be sloughed off, like clothes."

That was it, she now saw. He had got rid of those prejudices. The dead hand of his grandfather was no longer heavy upon him. This man, seated there before her in the vividness of youth, was the real Richard Vaughan.

"You used to tell me the truth about myself," he went on reflectively. "I had never seriously thought about women—about the relations of men and women. I simply accepted my grandfather as gospel on those subjects. My crisis forced me to do some thinking—and I believe you'll do me the justice of admitting I never would be stupid enough to act in a crisis without trying to use the best mind I had. Well—when I got away—and thought—I saw that the whole business was my fault."

"No," protested she. "There was where I wronged you. I blamed you—myself a little—but you most. That was unjust. But let's not talk about it. The past is—the past. I wish to drop all of it except its lessons. They'll be useful in the future."

"One thing more," he said. "I want to say I'm glad of what has happened."

She simply stared at him.

"That would sound strange, I suppose, to the mob in the treadmill of conventionality," he went on, apparently not noting her expression. "But I'm grateful to—to whatever it was—fate or chance or what you please—for my awakening. But for it, what'd have become of me? Like so many men who try to be masters of their profession or business, I had let it become master of me. A little longer, and I'd have been a dust-dry, routine plodder, getting more and more useless every day. No wonder the world advances so slowly. Just look at the musty, narrow rotters who do the work. They specialize. They soon lose touch with the whole. And their minds dwindle as their natures and interests narrow."

"You're not thinking of giving up your work!" she exclaimed in dismay.

"I'm here to begin again," replied he, with his fine look of energy and persistence. "But not in the old way. Not month in and month out, like a hermit—but with some sanity—and, I'm sure, with better results. That brings me to my real reason for calling. I wished to ask if you had any objection to my living and working at the shop." As the color flamed into her face, he hurried on, "I'll keep an independent establishment in every way and bind myself not to disturb you. If you like, Helen can bring Winchie down to see me from time to time—but not unless you like."

"I'll take Winchie and go to father's," said she, painfully embarrassed. "I'd not have stopped on here, but you'll remember you made it a condition——"

"If you leave, I leave also," he rejoined. His manner was emphatic, final. "I've no intention of intruding. Please forget I said anything." He rose to leave. "I'm going to move my laboratory to Chicago or New York. A few months sooner will make no difference."

She insisted that she would go—that she preferred to go—that going was entirely agreeable to her. But in the end he convinced her he really wished her to keep on at the house, to make Winchie feel it was his home—and would leave if she even talked of leaving. "I'll arrange with Gerster's wife over at the farm to feed me and keep the apartment in order. So, everything will go on just as if I were a thousand miles away."

When he went—like a caller after a pleasant hour—she was glad because she wished to be alone, free to shut herself in her room with the many strange things he had given her to think about—the many startling things. But just as she got the seamstress off for home, in came Helen, hoping that Courtney would talk of the amazing call, determined to talk of it herself, anyhow. "Forgive me for asking, Courtney," said she. "But I simply must. You've decided to give up the divorce, haven't you?"

The emerald eyes looked amused astonishment. "Why?" she asked.

"You and he are just—just as you always were."

"Indeed we're not!" exclaimed she. "Absolutely different."

"But I never saw two people friendlier——"

"That's it. That's precisely it. Now that we've freed each other, I can like him and he can like me."

Helen was not hearing. Suddenly she burst out: "Oh, Courtney! Courtney! What will become of you! You'll have no money—for you're not asking alimony. You'll only have to marry again." Courtney frowned at this frank statement of the problem she was putting off. "You know you'll have to marry again," pursued Helen, "and it isn't likely you'll do as well. Men don't care for widows of any kind—least of all, grass widows. They want a fresh, unspoiled woman."

Courtney's eyes danced. "The truth from Helen—at last!"

But Helen was unabashed. Because she was taller and graver than Courtney, she felt older and wiser. And because she loved Courtney, she felt she must do all in her power to avert the impending catastrophe through this divorce madness. "I do believe you've got no common sense at all!" she cried. "You talk wise enough— sometimes. But when it comes to acting— Courtney, women brought up as we've been simply have to be supported. And it's our right!"

"Is it?" said Courtney.

"Aren't we ladies? But you've never been poor. You don't realize what you've got to face. You don't realize it's your position as Richard's wife that makes everybody act so sweetly and respectfully toward you—and that makes you feel secure."

"Oh, yes, I do," said Courtney gravely. "I realize it so keenly that I'm afraid of myself—afraid I'll be tempted to do something contemptible. When I married, I had the excuse that I believed I loved and was loved and it's the custom for a man to throw in support with his love. But if I married again—feeling as I do—I'd—" She flung out her arms. "I don't want to think about it!" she cried. "I'll not do it! I'll not do it!"

Helen could not understand. And she was glad she couldn't, for she felt that such ideas, whatever they were, did not make for feminine comfort. She had listened impatiently to Courtney. She now brought the conversation back to the only point worth considering. "But you've *got* to marry," said she.

"No!" Courtney had the expression of fire and purpose that makes a small person seem tall. "There's an alternative. I can do for myself."

"Do what?" demanded Helen. She waited for a reply—in vain—then went on: "What could you do that anybody would pay for? Besides—you, a lady, couldn't ask for work. You don't know how I suffered when I thought I was going to have to do it. And you'd suffer even more—having occupied the position you have. What a come down!"

"Don't!" commanded Courtney. "Helen, you are tempting me."

"I'm talking the sense to you that you've so often talked to me," Helen insisted. "Unless we women have got money of our own or a man with an income back of us, we're— I'd hate to confess the truth even to another woman."

Courtney nodded slowly several times, then asked, "Don't you think it ought to be changed?"

"No!" cried Helen vehemently. "It's what God intended. The penalty of being a man is to have to work. The penalty of being a lady, and refined and dainty and untouched by low, vulgar things, is to have to be a dependent. And it's not such a heavy penalty, either. Even if one doesn't care much about the man, one isn't inflicted with him all the time."

At these plain truths wrenched by loving anxiety from the deepest and securest of hiding places, Courtney's eyes danced. She'd have laughed outright, had not Helen been so terribly in earnest—Helen without a sense of humor. However she did venture to say: "The chief equipments of a lady are a stone instead of a heart and a hide instead of a skin—is that it?"

But Helen did not see the ironic comment on her philosophy. "Well," she went on in her serious, stolid way, "I don't want responsibility. And I like to take my ease—and to have to do only things it doesn't much matter if they go undone. We women are different from men. Our self-respect's in a different direction.... Dear, can't I do something to help you?"

Courtney kissed her penitently. She always felt ashamed after poking fun at Helen whose heart was so genuinely good and kind. "Nothing, thanks. The divorce must go on. You don't understand, Helen. Believe me, if I knew that sheer misery was waiting for me, as soon as I was free, I'd still go on."

"Let me talk to Richard. I can do it tactfully."

In her alarm at this Courtney caught hold of Helen. "If you did such a thing, you'd be doing me the greatest possible injury."

"Don't be afraid, dear. I'd not meddle. But—" She looked appealingly at Courtney—"please, dear—do let me!"

"Richard and I would both resent it equally."

"But what *will* become of you!"

Her tone was so forlorn that Courtney had to laugh. "Why, I'm barely twenty-five—and I know a lot about several things—and could learn more."

"Don't talk that way!" cried Helen, tearful. "It makes me shiver. It sounds so coarse and common." She looked at Courtney as if doubtful of her sanity. "I can't make you out. It isn't natural for a lady bred and born, as you are, to say such things."

"You can't believe a real lady could have ideas of self-respect? Well, I'll admit they do seem out of place in my head—and give me awful sinkings at the heart. And—" There was a mocking smile round Courtney's lips, a far-away look in her eyes—"Sometimes I'm haunted by a horrible dread that I'm merely—bluffing."

Helen saw only the smile. "I'm sure you are, you dear, sweet, fascinating child!" cried she, greatly consoled and cheered.

"Don't be too sure!" warned Courtney, the smile fading.

But Helen was delighted to see that she said it half heartedly—that some effect had been produced by the grewsome reminders of the difference between independence as a dream or a vague longing and independence in the grisly reality of the working out.

# Chapter 27

After a few days Courtney asked Helen to take Winchie to the laboratory. "You can arrange with Richard as to future visits," she said. "And in talking with him—and with me—please remember he and I don't exist for each other. I can trust you?"

"Yes," presently came from Helen in so reluctant a tone that Courtney congratulated herself on having thought to exact the promise.

Winchie said little about his father at the supper table, but a great deal about a streak of light his father had made for him with an electrical apparatus—"clear across the room, mamma—real lightning—only there wasn't any thunder—just noise—like when Jimmie snaps the whip fast." Several times in the next three or four weeks she discovered evidence of visits to the laboratory in remarks Winchie let drop; for he said nothing direct, having somehow divined that the visits were not to be talked about. But he had not the faintest suspicion there was anything wrong between his father and his mother. He had always been used to their leading separate lives; the mere surface cleavage was too unimportant to affect him, all-observant though he was, with his natural mind which Courtney had not spoiled by false education. And the parents of the only children he played with—those along the shore—were exceeding discreet in discussing the divorce in the family circle.

In the first winter storm one of the maples near the edge of the lake, about the oldest and finest tree on the place, blew down and in its fall destroyed the summer-house. Courtney was awakened by the resounding crash. Before breakfast she, in short skirt and close-fitting jacket, went to see and to decide what should be done. As she reached the scene Dick in shaggy ulster and cap came from behind the towering mass of wreckage. She could not be certain whether his ease, so superior to hers, was due to his having seen her coming and having got ready, or to absolute indifference. "Jimmie told me what happened," explained he. "I came early, thinking I'd not be caught trespassing." He looked sadly at the great tree, with its enormous boughs sprawled upon the frozen surface of the lake. "Jimmie and I," said he, "used to have a swing in it that went out over the water. We used to dive from the seatboard."

Courtney could see the swing go up and up, high as the tree itself, then a daring boy release his hold and shoot through the air, slim and straight, to plunge into the lake. "You'd almost touch bottom away out where it's deepest—wouldn't you?" she said, her eyes sparkling.

"I've brought up mud in my hands from where it's twenty feet deep."

They stood in silence, in the presence of the fallen giant whose life had begun when the Indians trapping and fishing there were getting from the far coast beyond the mountains the first rumors of the great winged boats and the white man. "It was a grand tree," she sighed. "I'll miss it as I'd not miss many people I'm more or less fond of.... I remember that swing."

"You do?"

"One day my mother brought me along when she was calling here. I must have been about the age Winchie is now. I had on red shoes—I remember because they hurt terribly and I didn't dare show a sign for fear they'd be taken away. You lured me out to play—and put me in the swing—and made it go—the limit."

"I remember perfectly now. That was *you*—was it?"

"It was. It was," replied she. "You despised little girls and thought you'd scare me to death."

"But I remember you were game. You didn't scream."

"I guess I was too badly frightened. Do you remember how mother shrieked when she saw from the window what you were up to?"

"Do I? The whipping father gave me bent the whole business into me forever. *I* wasn't game. How I did howl!"

"I wish I'd heard!" She shivered laughingly. "I feel now how I was suffering when the swing was out over the water and high up among the boughs."

Richard was looking at her curiously. "So, that was you?" he said in an abstracted way. "You certainly didn't look scared.... Helen tells me you're planning to go East in the spring and study landscape gardening.... I see you don't like her having told me. I assure you it was my fault. I asked her point blank. She told me simply the one fact."

"It's not a secret," said Courtney, and she went on to explain, as to an acquaintance who knew nothing of her life, "I used to go to college—up at Battle Field—with a girl named Narcisse Siersdorf. She's made quite a reputation as an architect. We were good friends, and it occurred to me I might get advice from her. She's been wonderfully kind—took an interest right away. We're negotiating. I don't know what'll come of it. I've sent her an account of things I've done, and some pictures."

He looked at the slight, strong figure, at the small and delicate face, at the eyes so feminine yet for all that full of character. "Are you in earnest?" he asked.

"I've got to be," replied she.

His expression showed how he was touched by her air of sad thoughtfulness as she gazed across the glistening level of ice. "Not at all," said he. "While nothing's been said about it, you must know that as Winchie's mother——"

She interrupted him with a laugh that made the color flare into his face. "So, you thought I was hinting, did you? I don't suppose you ever will be able to understand a woman. No—I don't hint."

"I didn't suspect——"

"Be honest!"

He hung his head like a foolish boy.

"As I was saying," she went on, "I've got to do something because, when I'm free, I want to feel free. Maybe I'm flying in the face of nature, but I've a hankering for the same sort of independence a man has—not the same, but the same sort.... It isn't a bit nice, being a woman—if one wakens to the fact that she's in the same market—if in a higher grade stall—with 'those others.'"

He looked up with a frown. "That's not the way to look at it," he protested with more than a touch of his old-time dictatorial manner.

"It's the way *I* look at it," replied she, quietly. That reminder of his tyranny, added to his unconsciously contemptuous suspicion that she was hinting for alimony, had stirred all her latterly latent antagonism to him—made her doubt the sincerity—or, rather, the thoroughness of the change in him. She began to move away. "I must go tell Jimmie what to do about this tree."

"Please—not just yet," he said, red and embarrassed. "I beg your pardon for taking that tone. And I'll admit you're right, though I'd like to be able to deny it. Still, it's not your fault that you were brought up in the customary way——"

"I don't want to be reminded of that," she interrupted, rather bitterly. "In spite of all I've been through—and of the certainty that unless I free myself, I'll have to go through it again—I'm having a constant fight against my cowardice." Her face changed in an instant from grave to gay. "I'm saying and doing all sorts of things to make it impossible for me to back down. I guess telling you was one of them."

"You're not going to make any move until spring—toward this architect friend, I mean?"

"I've no reason to think—at least not much reason—that she'll take me."

"Meanwhile—why not perfect yourself in the trade you already almost know?"

"What's that?"

"I'm going to pay a man a hundred and fifty dollars a month to help me at the laboratory—exactly the work you did—and he'll do it no better, if as well."

Courtney flushed with pleasure at this praise. "Really?" she said. "You mean that?"

His expression forewarned her he was about to touch on the impossible subject. "I can't comprehend, now that it's over," said he, "how I was such an ass as to stick to the notion that women haven't brains when I had, right before me, proof to the contrary."

"Meaning me?" said she with amused eyes.

"Meaning you," replied he with a laugh. Then seriously, "And if you'll let me say so, the reason I blame myself for everything is, I've seen that my stupid ignorance of you was at the bottom of it all."

She shrugged her shoulders indifferently. "We were both brought up very stupidly for marriage. But then—who isn't? No wonder marriage is successful only by accident."

"What a confession the proverb is," said he, "—that people have to be married once, before they're fit to be married."

"Well," said she, "at least we've had our experience, and can be glad we got it young enough for it to be useful. But I must get to work." And she nodded and went briskly up the snow-drifted lawns. Not until afternoon, while she was overseeing the sawing up of the tree, did his unfinished offer come back to her. Had he left it unfinished because she had not encouraged him to go on or because he had repented of the impulse? Probably the latter, she decided; at any rate, even if he had urged, she could not have accepted. "He'd be sure to misunderstand. Men and women always do misunderstand each other—" She smiled at herself—"that is, they don't. They learn by experience that there's always the motive behind, in everything that crosses the sex line. He'd not realize this was an exception." There she mocked herself again. "At least, I think it'd be an exception. I'm not quite sure I'd not be doing it out of cowardice—to get him where I could recover him if I lost my nerve and had to. Our dependence makes us so poor spirited that, though we know we don't want a certain man, we like to have him where we could use him, 'in case.'"

Several stormy days, with no communication between house and laboratory. On the first bright afternoon, she and Winchie were entering the grounds after a walk to Wenona and back, through the still, dry air, charged with sunbeams, air like a still, dry champagne, strong and subtle. They came upon Dick clearing the snow from the direct path between laboratory and gates. His trousers were tucked into high boots and he was in flannel shirt sleeves. As they—or, rather, as Winchie—paused, he leaned on his shovel and laughed—at the fun that is merrier than any joke—the fun of being healthily alive from center to farthest tip. The sunshine was brilliant on the unsullied surface of the snow, on the ice-encased branches, and on those three health-flushed faces. "Just been to the doctor's, I suppose?" said he to the boy who was as ruddy as a rooster's comb, as smooth and hard as marble.

"No," declared Winchie, taking him seriously, "I never had a doctor in my life."

This was a good enough excuse. Dick and Courtney became hilarious over Winchie's earnestness. As Winchie had begun to play with the snow his father's labor had piled high on either side of the reappearing path, Courtney did not resist Dick's overtures toward conversation—about the skating, the air, the healthfulness of a hard winter, the ravages of the storm throughout the neighborhood. "I see," said he, "the old maple's gone. You did clear it up in a hurry. There's not a sign of its ever having been in existence—or the summerhouse either."

At that the color poured into her cheeks—the deeper, fierier red of acute embarrassment. When he realized what he had said—which he instantly did—he did not color but became pale. "I'm glad it was destroyed," he said, "glad not a trace of it remains—*anywhere*. If I believed in omens I'd look on the whole incident as a good omen—the landmark of the Vaughan home that seemed so strong and wasn't—the summerhouse that was a constant reminder—both gone—and the place where they were is clear—is ready for the new and better things."

She was listening with her head low. "Thank you," she said, in a choked voice. "Sometimes I think there isn't another man in the world who'd have helped me as you have."

"Don't you believe it," cried he, cheerfully. "Human nature's a lot better than it pretends. Thank God, very few of us are despicable enough to live up to our creeds and our conventions.... Winchie, you didn't know you came very near losing your father yesterday. He almost blew himself up."

Winchie's eyes grew big. "I'd like to have seen," said he, excitedly. "Jimmie says, when you do go, it'll be straight up through the roof and high as the moon."

"It all came of my working without an assistant," Dick explained to Courtney. "I've got one coming from Baltimore, as I think I told you the other day. But he can't get away just yet. I wish you'd consider my offer."

She felt no embarrassment. His tone prevented; it was businesslike, and polite rather than friendly.

"I need some one badly—some one I shan't have to teach. You like the work. You need the experience. A few weeks of the sort of thing I'd put you at now would fit you for a place in a first-class laboratory." A little constrainedly—"I know why you hesitate. But I assure you, that's foolish. What I'm proposing will not interfere with—with our plans for freeing each other. It's purely business—and good business for you as well as for me."

She looked directly at him for the first time. "You're quite sure you'd not misunderstand?"

"Quite," he assured her.

She still hesitated. "I want to accept," she confessed, "for business reasons. But I've an instinct against it."

He smiled with good-humored mockery. "A vanity, you mean."

She colored guiltily, though she also was smiling. Her nervous fingers were pulling the ice from a branch of a bush.

He noted that Winchie, rolling up a huge snowball, had got safely out of hearing. "Just a vanity," he went on. "Well—pitch it overboard. I make you a business proposition. I need you. You need the experience. I hope you'll accept. I can well afford to pay you what I'll pay Carter. He's tied up until January—perhaps a little later. If you'll accept, I can accomplish a lot this winter. If not, I'll be nearly helpless."

Thus it naturally and easily and sensibly came about that, a few months later, at the very moment when Judge Vanosdol was signing the decree of divorce, Dick and Courtney were in the laboratory, their heads touching as they bent over a big retort, heedless of the strong fumes rising from its boiling and hissing contents. The heat subsided. The compound slowly cleared—a beautiful shade of green instead of the black they hoped for—and confidently expected. They looked dejectedly at each other; she felt like weeping for his chagrin.

"What the devil is the matter?" demanded he, glowering at her. "Sure you didn't make a mistake?"

Her nerves were on edge, as were his. "That's right!" she said, tears in her eyes. "Suspect me."

"I'm not suspecting you," he retorted angrily. "Don't drag your sex into work. You're not a woman here. We've no time for poodle-dog politeness."

"I don't want politeness," cried she. "What did I say that could possibly make you think I did?"

"It was what you didn't say," replied he. "Why didn't you answer back? Or throw the ladle at me?"

"I will next time."

And there they both laughed.

Now, she was free—absolutely free—and with money enough of her own earning to get her and Winchie to New York and to keep them for quite a while. And Narcisse Siersdorf had written most encouraging comments on the account of her efforts at landscape gardening and on the accompanying photographs, and had offered her a clerkship at twenty-five dollars a week "as a starter." Also, Richard, as an earnest of his belief and his interest, had got her an offer of a trial position at twenty dollars a week in the laboratories of the American Coal Products Company at Chicago. She was not only free; she was independent.

The morning after Narcisse's letter came she saw Richard eying her curiously several times, as if he were puzzling over something but hesitated to question her. The fourth or fifth time she caught him at it, she said: "What do you want to ask me? Have I made a mistake?"

"No—no, indeed," protested he. "You don't make mistakes."

He had been extremely polite, no matter how severely his temper was tried, ever since the day of the little flare-up over the failed experiment. And every day it pleased her through and through, pleased and thrilled her, that his reason was fear lest she, perfectly free to go, should resign and quit, if he did not behave.

"Then," she went on to him, "why do you look at me inquiringly?"

"It's your manner," replied he. "You're acting very differently to-day from what you ever did before."

While he was saying it she divined the reason—the letter from Narcisse. The offer from the Coal Products Company had come several weeks before; but that had been got for her. This position in New York was of her own getting. And for the first time in her life she felt like a full-grown personality capable of taking care of herself. Unconsciously her whole outlook upon life changed; the change disclosed itself in her expression, in her voice, in her manner. She handed Richard her patent of nobility, the letter from Narcisse; she watched his face as he read. But she got no clue to his thoughts. As he gave back the letter without comment she said: "I'm in the way to get rid of the reason for a woman's so often wishing she'd been born a man."

"I understand," said he, and turned away to gaze reflectively out of the window.

She went into the rear room to work there. Half an hour later she returned, to find him still staring out over the lake. "I've given him something more to think about," said she to herself, with a sly smile at his back. "And it'll do him good, if ever he starts out to marry again." Yet somehow she was not fully satisfied that her guess covered the whole of what he was thinking. He was extremely puzzling, this polite, appreciative, carefully businesslike Richard.

She was impatient to be gone. She wished to try in longer flight the new wings of freedom and independence she had grown. She felt confident they would sustain her; but she could not be sure until she tried. She had decided for the Siersdorf offer. She liked the chemistry chiefly because, working with Richard at the explorations of hydrogen and nitrogen, she was moving toward a definite high accomplishment—the discovery of a source of happiness to millions—a cheap substitute for coal and wood that would banish that horror of horrors, cold, from the lives of the poor. But it would be quite another thing to work at fabricating new shades of color in dyes, new commercial uses for the by-products of coal; she would be descending from scientist's helper to plodder for a living, from lieutenant of a Columbus to mate on a tramp steamer. Not so, if she went into the Siersdorf office.

There she would remain artist, worker with the fine tools of the imagination. Also Basil's tastes lay in that direction. Fancy is not the air plant that idealists pretend. Its flowers may be spiritual but its roots strike deep into the physical. It may need the sun and the air of heaven, but it needs the soil even more. In the soil it is born; by the soil it chiefly lives. Courtney's fancy was the fancy of a normal human being in whom all the emotions are healthy, ardent, fully developed. It had no long or difficult task in blurring into vagueness whatever marred her memory of her and Basil's romance—or at least in making the blemishes for the time seem unimportant in presence of the rosy, horizon-filling peak moments of their happiness. Once more, from the quiet of her long lonely evenings—hardly the less solitary for Helen's rather monotonous company—arose the longings, the visions, the thrills. She felt that, in her young inexperience, she had been too arrogant in her demands upon life; she had asked more than she could possibly expect from a human love, more than she had any right to expect. But now she was chastened; her point of view was less wildly romantic. What would they not be to each other!—once they were together—and free from all constraint of moral doubts and conventional dreads. It was only natural that in their life of stress passion should have been uppermost, should have become dominant. It was human for Basil to feel that he was contending for even physical possession of her—and until there is physical possession, love has no substantial ground to build upon.

She was eager to be off for New York, to establish her independence, and then to begin her real life on the enduring foundation of equality and comradeship brightened by passion as a tree is brightened by its blossoms and their perfume. But, eager though she was, she could not deny her obligation to remain until Dick's assistant came. She knew now that he had spoken the literal truth when he said he needed her badly. It would be a return for his broad-minded humanity quite beneath her, to leave him in the lurch—especially when carrying on his particular line of experiments meant danger if he had to do all the work alone. She must stay until Carter came. And she was glad of this opportunity to show him that she did appreciate what he had done for her, even though he had done it not for her sake but for his own—in obedience to his sense of the decent and the self-respecting.

So, she worked steadily and interestedly on, just as if the divorce had not yet been entered upon the records of the court as valid and final. She found an unexpected additional source of interest in studying her former husband as an individuality. It is always a novel sensation for a woman with any claim to physical charm to find herself regarded impersonally—sexlessly. That is usually anything but an agreeable sensation; every woman feels the chagrin of failure when she sees that her charms do not charm—this, though she might be disdainful of and resentful of overt tribute to her physical self. Courtney, however, did not in those peculiar circumstances feel sufficiently piqued to try to assert woman's ancient right of dominion over the senses of man. She could enjoy the novelty of being treated like a man, and could study calmly the man who was thus unmindful of what is habitually uppermost in any strongly masculine nature.

At work with Richard alone, she was at last getting acquainted with him. From the beginning of each day at the laboratory to the end, she was receiving a series of vivid impressions of a really superior man—competent, intelligent, resourceful. He thought about himself never; he could not be daunted or baffled. His broad-mindedness was no longer marred by the sex narrowness that had made appreciation of it impossible to her, to any woman of her sort. He knew so much; he carried knowledge so lightly. It seemed to her, after much experience of "learned" men, that knowledge was chiefly power to bore. His knowledge was like a rapier of finest steel skilfully used in his duel with his mysterious masked combatant, the alchemist on guard at nature's secretest laboratory. She felt that he was a man out of a million; yet she had no sense of embarrassed inferiority. This general in the army of exact science, which is the true army of progress, was a democrat, marched with the soldiers afoot, was their equal. "If any woman ever does fall in love with him," thought she, "she will worship him. But—he's too impersonal. We women want something smaller—not a sun star, but a fire on a hearth."

Now that he was nothing but fellow worker to her, she could look at him with the friendly impartiality of human being for fellow being. Piecing together what she knew of his masculine side and what she could how see latent in those strong features, those intense nervous energies, she felt that somewhere there might be a woman equal to concentrating upon herself what went altogether into the duel for nature's secrets. "And unless she were a great woman, he would burn her up like a match tossed into a furnace."

This latent capacity of his for love fascinated her. There were even moments when it tempted her—was like a challenge taunting her womanhood as confessedly ineffectual. But at the laboratory she was too busy to linger over such thoughts; and in her other hours, there was household routine to compel her attention—and the plans for the great attempt.

At last Carter wrote that he would positively come in two weeks. "You've been splendidly patient with me," Dick said as he showed her the latter. "I've seen that you were eager to be gone." As she murmured a polite denial, he repeated, "Yes, eager—but not in the way to make me uncomfortable over my selfishness."

"I've rarely thought of it while I was down here," said she. "It was only in the evenings—and when I happened not to sleep very well."

"It was natural you should be upset," sympathized Dick. "Who wouldn't be, standing on the edge of the icy plunge so long? But you'll like it—and everything'll come out all right. I've discovered that you have a lot of common sense—and that's more than I can say for most men—including myself."

Another month, at the farthest, and she would be in New York, would have made the great beginning! ... Should she send Basil word as soon as she arrived? Should she wait until she got her bearings? She saw it would be wiser to wait. Everything depended on beginnings—right beginnings—and it would be the right beginning for Basil to find her as obviously master of her own destiny, as free to withhold or to give, as was he himself. Also— Coming from a small town in the West, she could not but feel strange in New York, and look provincial. "Yes, I'll wait," she decided, the instant this last reason dropped into the balance. For, she had not the vanity that underestimates the matter of looks and neglects the fact that everyone is at a distinct disadvantage in a strange environment.

One morning, about a week later, there came a ring at the telephone which was in Dick's part of the laboratory. As these calls were always for her, she rose from her case in the back room and went to answer. It was Mazie—"The hotel over to Fenton wants to speak to you, ma'am."

"Connect them, please," said Courtney, hoping her voice had betrayed and would betray nothing to the man behind her.

Soon came an operator's voice, and then Basil's. "I must see you!"

"Yes," she said. "I'll come."

"In your auto runabout—on the Fenton road to Tippecanoe—at two this afternoon. Will that do?"

"Yes. I'll be there. Good-by." And she rang off.

She turned from the telephone with a glance at Richard. He was busy with the blowpipe—no doubt had not even heard. As she was leaving to go up to the house for dinner, she said to him: "I'll not be back this afternoon."

"All right," replied he. "I sha'n't need you till to-morrow morning."

"I'll be here, then, of course."

He turned on the high stool. "You know," said he, with only the faintest suggestion of the unusual in face and voice, "there's no reason why you shouldn't see anyone you wish, at your own house."

She flushed guiltily. But her composure instantly returned, and she went on toward the door, casting about for a reply.

"I've no desire to interfere," continued he. "But—Jimmie went to Fenton on an errand yesterday, and he happened to tell me he saw at a distance a man who looked enough like Gallatin to be his twin. If you should be seen—you know how they gossip here. You could send the boy and Helen over to Wenona for the afternoon. Pardon my suggesting these things. It occurred to me you might not realize how closely you're watched by everybody, since the divorce."

She stood in the outer doorway, trying to conceal her agitation and trying to reflect.

"I appreciate you'd rather see him elsewhere—and I'd prefer you did, too. But your son has his rights—don't you think?"

"Yes," said Courtney. "I'll see him at the house."

"Thank you," said Richard. And he resumed his careful mixing of two powders in a small brass mortar.

She went, returned, stood where she could see his profile. "You give me your word of honor you'll not interfere with him in any way?"

Dick smiled without suspending work with the pestle. "Certainly," said he. "On my honor I'll not leave this room until you telephone me that I may." His smile broadened into a laugh that made her extremely uncomfortable, though it was pleasant enough.

"I didn't think you cared about me or him—or anything but your chemistry," she said in self-defense. "I asked simply as a precaution. I felt I owed it to him and to the boy."

"I laughed—you'll pardon me—because he's such a shallow pup. I never think of you two that I don't think of Titania and Nick."

As he tossed this lightly over his shoulder, she was hopelessly at a disadvantage. She was scarlet and shaking with anger. No return thrust occurring to her, she flung a furious glance into his back and departed, with about all the joy out of her anticipations of the meeting. Instead of telephoning from the house, she ascended to the apartment over the laboratory and by the direct wire there got the Phibbs Hotel in Fenton. A few minutes, and Basil was at the other end. "Come to the house here, instead," said she. "At the same time—two o'clock."

A silence, then his voice, "No. You come over."

"I can't do it. And I'd not ask you if I weren't sure. I'll explain when I see you."

"There's an especial reason why I want you here," urged he.

"And there's a more especial reason why I want you here."

"And there's an even more especial reason why I *must* see you here," insisted he. "It's very unsatisfactory, talking over the telephone, with people probably listening all along the wire. I'll come to-morrow—or late this afternoon. But you come here first."

"No—really, I mustn't," she declared. "Don't you trust me? Don't you know I'd not ask it, if it weren't perfectly—all right?"

"It isn't that, but— I can't talk about it.... I'll come." And from his tone she knew he had been decided by the fear that she'd think him afraid. And then she realized that she had made her remark because she counted on its appeal to his vanity—and the thought acted upon her enthusiasm not unlike a douche.

# Chapter 28

She was on the drive-front porch with Lizzie, making plausible pretense of rearranging the boxed evergreens. She heard the carriage turn in at the gates, though they were nearly a quarter of a mile from the house. As the horses rounded the bend she looked. But she waited on Lizzie, who was not slow to cry out with delighted surprise, "Why, there's Mr. Gallatin!"

Courtney said, "Do run in and see that the sitting room's straight." Thus, she was alone when he descended. She saw him through a mist and the hand she gave him was cold, was trembling. In the doorway, she said hastily in an undertone: "Helen and Winchie are at Wenona—Richard at the laboratory. You've stopped unexpectedly on your way south—for an hour or two."

"I understand," said he. "I can't trust myself to look at you. My love! My love!"

She flashed up at him a glance radiant with her florid fancies of anticipation. "Come into the house," she contrived to say in an ordinary tone.

As they went along the hall, side by side and talking for effect on possible listeners, she saw that he had dressed as carefully as a bridegroom. No more carefully than she had dressed, so far as she dared; still, it struck her as amusing—as suggestive of hollowness. And the voice which, as she heard it in fancy during those weeks of waiting, had been so moving, so magical—what a commonplace voice it was, and how very like affectation its Eastern intonations sounded. "That nasty remark of Richard's!" she thought. "How weak of me to let such a thing affect me." They entered the sitting room; he quickly closed the door, caught her hands, looked at her from head to foot. "Courtney!" he murmured. "I love you! I love you!"

She thrilled, lifted her eyes—dropped them. A chill stole over her. She had to resist an impulse to draw her hands away. He looked really handsome, was outwardly all her imagination had been picturing—and more. Yet— What was the matter? What was lacking? Why could she see only the weakness and coarseness— the qualities that had stood out the night he was drunk and the next afternoon when she was battling against his vanity and jealousy? "It's my nerves," she decided. "I'm under a greater strain than I realize." When he kissed her, she turned her head so that his lips touched her cheek. And immediately she released her hands. "We must be careful," she apologized.

"Why? You're free."

"Yes—but—" She paused.

"Why do you act so strange—so distant?"

"I don't know," she confessed. She felt ashamed of herself that she was visiting on him the consequences of her own folly in having let her imagination overleap all the bounds of probability in forecast. "I don't know," she repeated. "Nerves, I suppose. Or, perhaps it's a bad cold. I've felt one coming on all day. This morning I forgot to close the——"

"Aren't you glad to see me?"

"Yes—yes, indeed," she protested. "Let's sit down."

She took a chair near the table. He was thus compelled to the sofa, several feet away. "We ought to have met where we first arranged," said he, constrained, embarrassed.

"I have to be careful. You forget Winchie."

An uncomfortable silence, then he: "You've been free thirty-nine days. Yet you have not written me."

"I explained to you——"

"Didn't you feel like writing?"

"Of course. But——"

"But—what?"

"I wanted to be independent as well as free."

He looked at her gloomily. "Is *that* what you call love?"

She forced a smile and nodded.

"Do you know what I've come for? For you."

She felt herself drawing together, shrinking away from him. "For me?" she echoed vaguely.

"To marry you."

She was not looking at him; but she was seeing his face as it was when swollen and distorted by drink. She answered hastily, "Oh, I couldn't do that."

"Why not?"

"I can't marry till—till I'm independent. I've been making a lot of plans. I'm going to work early next month."

"What nonsense!" he cried. "Courtney, do you realize you've not yet said a single word of love? What is the matter? Is it our meeting in this house?"

"Perhaps. I don't know. I don't understand it myself." Why was her mind so perverse? Why did it thrust at her the things it was unjust to remember, generous and necessary to forget? Why was she critical, aloof, instead of responsive and generously glad? She went on: "It may be the cold. My nose feels queer, and——"

"We must marry, right away," he insisted, frowning upon her lack of seriousness. "We've been separated too long already."

That seemed to her to explain. But it did not remove. She said, "Not until I'm independent."

"But that means years—years!"

"Oh, no," protested she. "Not the kind of independence *I* mean. I simply want to be sure I could earn my living if it were necessary."

"But it isn't necessary. And life is so short, dearest. And at most we'll have few enough years of happiness."

"I know," said she, surprised that these truths did not move her in the least, nor his looks, his tones, so charged with entreaty she such a short time ago would have found irresistible. "But I've thought it out, and I realize everything depends on my getting that feeling of independence. I'll not risk again what I've been through."

"You know very well, that couldn't happen. As for your working, why, dear, unless a woman's been bred to making a living, it's almost impossible for her."

"Nevertheless I must try."

"If you loved me, you'd not talk like this," cried he, bitterly.

Instead of protesting, she became thoughtful. "Do you really think so?" she asked. "I wonder if that's true."

"Certainly not," retreated he, alarmed. "We love each other. But your way of acting and talking has upset me. I ought not have come here. We should have met over at Tippecanoe."

"You don't seem to see my point of view, Basil."

"I do, but it's a mere notion. A very fine notion," he hastened to add, though he could not make his tone other than grudging, "but foolish."

"It was my dependence that put me in such a frightful position with Richard. And——"

"Courtney," he interrupted, between anger and appeal, "please don't repeat that comparison of what you were to him and what you and I are to each other. It—hurts me, and it's not fair."

"Would you promise to love me always just as you do now?"

"I certainly would. I shall."

She lowered her eyes. Her heart sank.

"Wouldn't you?" he asked.

"No," replied she. "How can I—or anyone—honestly say how he or she'll feel about a person they don't know through and through—a month ahead—let alone a year—ten years—twenty? You know that's true, Basil. You're not honest with yourself—or with me."

He was silent, was watching her with sullen, suspicious eyes.

"It seems to me," she went on, "that love—real love—ought to make you careful. If we were a boy and a girl, without experience or intelligence or anything but hazy, rosy emotions——"

"You and I never will agree about love," he interrupted, impatiently. "But that's a small matter. The only point is that we love each other. Love's like a rose, Courtney. Tear it apart to see what it's made of and you lose the rose and have only withered petals."

"Yes—one kind of love. But is it the kind to build one's life upon?"

"I'm not going to argue with you. Have your way, if you will. You'll soon get enough of work—of this fantastic idea of independence, as you call it. As if I'd not be too afraid of losing your love not to respect your rights and consider you always and in every way."

"But suppose *I* ceased to love *you*—and were dependent on you——"

"I know. I know. Don't let's argue it. Go on with your plans. The sooner you begin, the sooner you'll see how foolish you are. You don't appreciate what work means—especially for a woman—the toil, the humiliations, the downright miseries—that cost youth and looks and health."

It still further depressed her to see how swiftly his words depressed her—how appalling was the lift and spread of the mountain she had been dreaming of removing with one shovel and one pair of feeble hands. "Instead of discouraging me," cried she with some anger in her reproach, "you ought to be encouraging me. I should think you'd be afraid to have a woman about who might be your wife for the sake of a living—might be making a hypocrite of herself and a fool of you."

He winced; she saw he was thinking of Richard. "That could never happen with *us*!" cried he.

"Never is a long time."

He was squirming in irritation and impatience—and was obviously afraid she would suspect the thoughts he yet could not conceal. "Please don't insist on discussing this, Courtney. Go ahead. Try your scheme. Work! I never heard of a woman at work who wouldn't do almost anything to escape."

She forced a laugh. "Then if I fail and send for you, you'll know what it means—and fly in the other direction."

"Not I," replied he with an overenergy that failed in its purpose of hiding the discomfort her suggestion had caused him. "I tell you, we love each other. That makes everything different." He laughed. "Work! Thank God, you and I don't have to work. We can love."

She sat with eyes down and fingers idly matching the corners of her little handkerchief. What a difference between work as a dream and work in the doing!—between imagining the glories of self-respecting independence and making the coarse, cruel struggle step by step up to those glories—between work as a pastime and work as a necessity. How unpractical she had been! She sighed. "I wish," said she, "I'd never realized that to be secure a woman must be independent. But—now that I've realized it, I've got to go on."

He put on an expression of pretended deep and respectful interest that made it hard for her to hide her amusement. "What are your plans?" he asked.

"I'll tell you sometime. I don't feel in the humor now."

"Something vague—eh?" And she saw that he assumed she was only pretending, after all. A superior man-to-woman smile had replaced his look of nervousness.

She waited until he had got himself comfortably settled down into this agreeable assumption, then said tranquilly, "No. I have the place promised me."

He rose impatiently. If she had needed proof as to his real opinion of women—his conviction of their inferiority, his expression would have given it. Yes, his opinion was the same as Richard's—always had been, as she could now see, recalling remarks he had made from time to time. The same prejudices as Richard; only, Basil had been less courageous—less honest. Those prejudices irritated her in Richard; in Basil they seemed laughable. But he was getting his impatience and scorn, his exasperation against her poor womanish folly somewhat under control. "Now, Courtney, can't you realize—" he began in a teacher-to-infant tone. Then, a new thought struck him. He broke off abruptly. "No—go ahead. It's just as well you should have the lesson," said he.

"Should learn how dependent I am on—some man?"

"How unfitted you are to be anything but a lady."

"I know that already," replied she forlornly. "Or, rather, I'm not fitted to be either dependent or independent."

"Then why not be sensible, and marry me at once?"

She did not answer. She could not tell him the truth; she would not tell him a lie. Anyhow, she wasn't sure what she did think.

"You will—won't you, dear? You'll not waste time that we might give to love and happiness?" And he anxiously watched her face—with its sweet feminineness that gave him hope, its mystery and its resoluteness that made him uneasy.

"It's a temptation," she said, absently. She saw herself trying for independence and failing—losing heart, self-respect—growing cynical through hardship—marrying Basil to escape— Just there, she suddenly surprised her elusive real self, saw deep into the inmost workings of her own mind—saw that she did not care for Basil Gallatin—that she had really been pretending to herself that she loved him because he was the alternative, the refuge, should her try for independence fail!

"I'll tell you what let's do," she heard him saying. "Let's get married. Then you can take that place, whatever it is. With your future secure no matter what happened, you'd work better and would be much more likely to succeed."

The appeal of this subtle proposal awakened her to her peril. It must be now or never; she must speak the truth now, or lose the courage and the strength to speak it. "Basil," she said abruptly, "I don't love you."

He stared.

"I've been lying to myself and to you. I don't love you."

"That's not true!"

"I never did love you," she replied—for, with the one truth out, the other forged to the front and made its amazing self visible. "No—I never did love you." How plain it all was, now! How strange that she should for even an infatuated moment have believed this was the man she needed, the man who needed her—not words alone, and kisses and thrills, but real need—for mind and heart and body—all that the three have to give and long to give and to receive.

He stood before her, looking down in graciously smiling remonstrance. "That's a little too much," he said tenderly. "You can't have forgotten all we've been to each other—those hours of happiness—those moments of ecstasy—my love—my Courtney——"

There was color in her cheeks, an answering tenderness in the eyes that lifted to his. "No, I've not forgotten. And as I had to learn and as there's no other way for woman or man to learn but experience, I don't regret. But we were both in love with love—not with each other. And what's more, we never could be." Now that she had flung away pretense, its veil of illusion over her sight dropped; she was seeing him as she looked at him—not his qualities that repelled, not his qualities that attracted, but the whole man—was seeing him as we see only those toward whom are amiably indifferent. She was thinking, "What a nice, well-bred man he is, but how small." Not bad, not grossly sensual, not mean—not at all mean, but the reverse. Just small.

He began to recover from the stupefaction of the convincing tones of her denial of love. He was hastily donning the costume of pose that is correct for such occasions. She beamed genially upon him and said, "Now, don't work yourself up, my dear Basil. Sit down over there, and let's talk quite quietly—and naturally."

It is impossible for anyone with any sense of humor whatever to indulge alone in paroxysms of emotion before a tranquil spectator. Basil stopped rolling his eyes and dilating his nostrils, and seated himself, in no very good humor. Her tone was not pleasant. It would have been perfectly proper for a man to use to a woman. It was impertinent, in weaker sex to stronger. "Oh, I'm all right," said he, crossly, as he seated himself. "But you'd better look out about those ideas of yours. They have a terribly unfeminizing effect on women."

"Yes—I guess they do," replied she. A puzzling, alluring combination of seriousness and humor she looked as she sat there opposite him, her elbows on the arms of the chair, her chin resting upon the backs of her linked fingers, her eyes fixed gravely yet somehow quizzically upon him. "Have you ever thought of our life together?" asked she. "Of what we'd do—between times?"

"Between times?"

"No one—not even the most ardent lovers—can make love all the time. There haven't been any 'between times' in our life heretofore, because of the circumstances. But when we were together without interruption—with no excitement or interest of danger—with no stimulus—with just ourselves—what would we do 'between times'?—and there'd be more and more 'between times' as we got used to each other."

This uninviting but obviously truthful picture sobered and exasperated him. "Haven't thought about it," he confessed. "I haven't gone into details. But I know we'll be happy. You'll step into the position you are entitled to and I can see that you get."

"The social position, you mean?"

"Certainly. And we'll enjoy ourselves."

He could not possibly have said anything that would have shown more clearly the width and depth of the gap between them—how little he understood her, how little they had in common.

"You'll be tremendously popular," he said with enthusiasm.

She shook her head slowly. "I don't think *I* could be happy, wasting my life, scattering myself among a lot of inane pastimes." She laughed a little. "You'd be horribly disappointed in me, Basil."

"I'll risk it. They'll be crazy about you in the East." He nodded proud, confident, self-complacent encouragement. "I'll risk it!"

She met his look with a quiet final "But I'll not." In another mood his proposal, his manner, his very poor sort of pride in her would have amused her. But as she listened, she remembered all she had believed about this man, all her idealizing of his mind and character. And she grew sad and sick. This small man!

He planted himself firmly before her. "Now, look here, Courtney. It's useless for you to talk that sort of thing. You don't mean it. And I'm not going to give you up. You're my wife, Courtney. The only possible excuse for what you did was that you loved me."

"On the contrary," replied she, "my only excuse is that I was swept away by my craving for love—for what Richard in our brief honeymoon had taught me to need——"

"For God's sake!" he cried. "How *can* you say such things?"

"Because they are the truth," she answered with quiet dignity; and he felt ashamed of himself without knowing why. "Basil, you don't love me as I really am. You find me shocking. And I don't love you as you really are. I find you—" She hesitated.

"Go on. Say it."

But what would be the use? The truth, all of it, any literal part of it would only hurt him, would not awaken him. By birth and by breeding and by the impassable limitations of his mind he was incapable of learning or appreciating the truth, was wedded forever to the morality that makes truth a vice and lies a virtue. So, she evaded. "I find you are like your dress," answered she, her eyes and her light tone taking the sharp sting off her words. "A charming style of your own but strictly conventional withal."

He did not fully appreciate this faint hint of the truth, but he understood enough to be irritated. "You've been doing too much of what you women call thinking. And you've become like all women who try to think."

"All women think," said she. "But very few of them tell the man what they think—until they've got him safely married. You ought to thank me for being candid in advance."

He scowled at her smile. "I'm not going to give you up," he said sullenly. "I know you better than you know yourself. You'll come out of this mood. And—dearest—remember that, in spite of your disdain, the old-fashioned woman—tender, simple, loving—is far sweeter than these thinkers—gets more pleasure—gives more."

"A baby's sweeter than a grown person," replied she, refusing to be serious. "But, Basil, the time has about passed when even a woman can stay on a baby—though most of the men and women pretend it isn't so, and a good many of them—like you and Helen—get angry if the truth's forced on you. At any rate, *I* can't be a baby anymore.... Do you know what would happen if I married you?"

The look that accompanied her abrupt question was so penetrating, so significant that he paled. "I don't want to hear any more of your truths that aren't true at all," he cried.

"I see you know what would happen. The same thing again."

"Courtney!—Good God!"

"The same thing again. As long as my craving for real companionship was unsatisfied, I couldn't be content. The same delusion that made me fancy I loved you would trap me again—or, perhaps it wouldn't be delusion but really the man I needed—the man who needed me. A mirage isn't a delusion, you know. It's an actuality that we mislocate. I'd hunt on—and on—through the desert for my oasis—until I found it."

He had not taken his fascinated gaze from her dreamy face, her eyes of unfathomable emerald. "Do you mean that?" he said huskily. "No—you can't. But you must not say those things, Courtney—you really mustn't. You'll make me afraid of you. As it is, I fear I'll have a hard time making myself forget."

"I don't want you to forget. And I've told you the exact truth because I want you to realize how unsuited we are to each other."

He walked up and down in violent agitation. "I don't understand it," he muttered. "Has some one—Courtney, do you love some other man?"

"I do not. I've seen no one practically but Richard."

He halted with a jerk. "Richard!" His eyes narrowed with jealous suspicion. "Has he been trying to win you back?"

She smiled at the idea, so at variance with the facts. "He treats me like another man."

"Then you see him?"

"Every day. I work at the laboratory with him."

"*What!*" Basil stared, dropped to the nearest chair dumfounded.

"Why not? ... Don't be so pitifully conventional, Basil. This is the twentieth century, not the Dark Ages. He knows you're here now—asked me to see you here rather than where it might cause gossip."

As he recovered, his mind, seen clearly in his features, slowly took fire. "And you pretended you were telling me the truth!" he cried, starting up. Everything else—doubt of her—doubt of himself—all was forgotten in the torrent rush of jealousy. "And I, poor fool, believed you! But I'll tell you what the truth is. You've lost your nerve. You love me as you did. But you haven't the courage to break off here. And you're sinking back to what you were when I found you. I might have known! A woman always belongs to the nearest man." He was raging up and down the room. "I've come for you. I'll not go without you. You're mine—not his. I'll show you! I'll show you!" And he snatched his hat from the sofa and rushed out.

For the moment motion was beyond her power. She saw him dart along the veranda, past the windows, take the path to the Smoke House. Terror galvanized her. She flew to the private telephone, rang long and vigorously, put the receiver to her ear. A pause; she was about to ring again when Richard's voice came: "Yes—what is it?"

"He's coming to you, Richard," she gasped. "I angered him. He's wild with rage. Promise you won't let him in."

"I can't do that." Richard's voice was calm and natural.

"Your promise to me!"

"Don't be alarmed. He doesn't amount to much, if you'll pardon my saying so."

"I'm coming as quickly as I can. Don't see him, Richard. Remember Winchie!"

"Come if you like. But I suspect you'll only aggravate him. Believe me, I can take care of him. Here he is now———"

She dropped the receiver, ran out of the house and along the path.

# Chapter 29

As Vaughan hung up the receiver and turned, Gallatin flung open the door on which he had just rapped a loud challenge. He scowled at Vaughan; Vaughan eyed him with the expression that simply looks and waits. It was evident Basil expected immediate combat, was ready for it—therefore altogether unready for the form of encounter less easy. Dick's tranquillity completely disconcerted him. He advanced a step, with an aggressive, "Well, here I am."

"So I see," replied Dick.

"You've been thinking it was cowardice that made me go away. But it wasn't. And I've come to face it out with you. You had your chance for her. You lost her. I purpose to keep her."

"Very well," said Dick. "She's free. Her affairs are none of my business." And he sat down at the long table under the windows, glanced at the electric furnace as if about to resume work.

"But she isn't free!" cried Gallatin. "You've not freed her, though she has the right to it. You're holding on to her through the boy."

Dick bent over the white crystals in the platinum tray on the shelf of the furnace.

Gallatin, exasperated, waved his fists. "I demand that you free her! If she were free, she'd come with me, for she loves me."

Dick took a metal rod from the case and began pushing the crystals this way and that carefully.

"She loves me, I tell you!"

Without pausing or looking round Dick said: "If you say that again—I'll begin to believe it isn't so. There's no accounting for tastes—especially for tastes feminine. But—" He did not finish; over his face drifted a slight smile more eloquent against Basil's deficiencies than the fiercest stream of epithet.

"I've won her," taunted Gallatin, in wild fury, yet as if restrained by an invisible leash. "I've got her heart. You might as well release the rest." As Dick seemed now quite absorbed and unconscious of his presence, he advanced still nearer. "By God, you shall!" he cried. "She belongs to me, and I'm here to maintain my rights at any cost."

Vaughan laid down the long rod with a gesture of deliberate precision and care, turned slowly toward him. His long handsome face was of a curious transparent pallor. His rather deep-set gray-blue eyes looked coldly and cruelly at his one-time guest and partner. "You evidently don't understand," said he. "There are times when one must either ignore—or kill."

Basil sneered, "Well?" said he, with intent to draw on.

"I have been choosing to ignore. At first it would have given me the greatest pleasure to kill you. Now—you are to me much like the cur that barks and snaps at passers by." He rose. "You've come here to try to make a vulgar scandal. You'll not succeed. You have nothing to lose. I can't give you your deserts without hurting my son. So——" Dick paused, seemed to be reflecting.

"You hide behind him—do you?" sneered Basil. In his frenzy he felt that one or the other must die then and there or he himself would be forever dishonored.

Dick apparently had not heard. In an abstracted way he said, to himself, not to Gallatin, "Yes, I think that will do." Again there was a pause, he thinking, Gallatin held silent and expectant by his expression. Suddenly Dick said sharply, "Yes—that will do." He moved the ladder to the south wall, mounted; he took from the high top shelf a jar of heavy glass, about one third full of dark red powder; he descended with it. "Close that door and lock it," he ordered.

Basil, from habit of association with him as assistant, moved to obey. Hand on knob and about to swing the door, he hesitated, turned. "What are you going to do?" he demanded.

"When you lock that door," replied Dick, "I shall empty what's in this jar into the bowl of water there, and in a few seconds we shall both be dead."

Basil shrank; a shudder ran visibly over his frame.

"I could kill you without killing myself," continued Dick, "and cover the scandal with the pretense of accident. It would serve you right, but—somehow it strikes me as cowardly. So—lock the door."

Basil was no coward; but he had grown yellow with fear. His hand now dropped nervously from the knob.

"Lock the door," said Dick sharply. "There's no time to lose. I think she's on the way here."

"She'll understand—and kill herself."

"Why not? Helen will take care of Winchie."

Basil's gaze wandered round, in search of another excuse. He braced himself, cried defiantly, "I refuse!"

"Very well." Dick set the jar on the table. "Then go."

"You think I'm a coward. But it's not that."

Dick shrugged his shoulders. "I know you're a coward. Everyone is. I'm as well pleased that you don't accept. I've no wish to die, particularly for such an absurd, stagy notion of honor. But I will not have a scandal——"

Just there Courtney dashed in, her expression so disheveled that it gave her the air of being disheveled in dress. Her glance darted from Richard leaning calmly against the table and, in blouse and cap, looking like a handsome workingman, to Basil in his fashionable English tweeds, standing shamefaced and irresolute near the door—so near that she had brushed him as she entered. On Basil her gaze rested like a withering blight. Her eyes flashed green fire; her every feature hurled at him the scorn that despises. "You shabby coward!" she said, her voice low and threatening to break under the weight of its burden of fury. "You who come here and try to ruin my child and me for your vanity!"

"Courtney!" he pleaded, not daring to lift his eyes. "I love you. I cannot give you up."

"Love! You don't know what it means! You weak vain thing! You found you couldn't have me on equal terms. So you thought you'd degrade me—compel me." She turned on Richard. "And you, too!" she blazed. "If you were a man you'd kill him—you'd kill us both—with some of your chemicals there—and protect Winchie by saying it was an accident."

"Absurd," said Vaughan with an indifferent shrug. His arms were folded upon his broad chest.

Trembling and blazing, she went up to him. "Look at me!" she cried, her hands on her surging bosom, her eyes glittering insanely up at him. Every instinct of prudence, the instinct of self-preservation itself had succumbed under the surge of elemental passion, of frenzied shame that she should have lowered herself to such a man as this Basil Gallatin. "This body of mine," she said in a voice of terrible calm, "it's been his—that thing's—do you hear? He has had me in his arms—me—your wife—the mother of your boy—he—that creature quaking there. And I have kissed him and caressed him and trembled with passion for him as I never did for you.... Now, will you kill us?"

He did not move. But slowly the veins and muscles of his face tightened, pushed up against, strained against the ghastly whiteness of his skin. And slowly his eyes lighted with the fires of a demoniac fury that made hers seem like a child's weak hysteria. She gazed at him, fascinated. Then, with a gasp, she braced herself and waited for the frightful death that look of his signaled. But she did not flinch, nor shift her gaze from his. To Gallatin, paralyzed, watching them with eyes starting and lips ajar, it seemed an eternity while they stood thus facing each other in silence. Then, as slowly as that expression on Richard's face had come it departed, like a fiend fighting inch by inch against being flung back into the hell from which it had issued at the call of her dreadful taunts. The face remained deathly white; but those were Richard Vaughan's own eyes that gazed down at the small, delicate face of the woman, in them a look that filled her with awe, made her ashamed, gave her the impulse to sink down at his feet and burst into tears.

"No, Courtney," Richard said, infinite gentleness in his tone. "I'm neither god nor devil. I—all three of us—will do to-day what to-morrow we'll be glad we did. One can always die. But living again, once one's dead—that's not so simple."

There fell silence. She stood before him, bosom still heaving but eyes down. Vaughan turned to Gallatin with a courtly politeness like his grandfather's. "Don't you think you'd better go—for the present at least?"

Gallatin, who had been awed also, hesitated. He looked at Courtney; his jaws clenched and he fixed sullen, devouring eyes on her. "I want to talk to her alone," said he aggressively.

"That's for her to decide," said Richard.

Courtney lifted her head to refuse. Then it occurred to her that, by talking with Basil, she might settle the whole business for good and all. With a curious deference she looked inquiringly at Richard. He shrugged his shoulders, began pushing the tray into the furnace. She let her eyes rest on Basil, said "Yes—that's best. Come on." She went out of the laboratory, Basil following her. Richard closed the door behind them. At the edge of the clearing she halted, wheeled upon him. "Well!" she began, her voice as merciless as her eyes.

He was a pitiful spectacle. His feature were working in a ferment of many unattractive emotions—jealousy, pique, fear that he was ridiculous, wounded vanity, desire to regain with her the ground he felt he must have lost. "You see now, Courtney," he said, aggressive yet pleading, too, "he doesn't care a rap about you."

"Well?" she repeated. Her tone was much softer; her nerves were calming, and her temper was yielding to her sense of proportions. Also, the man looked weak and shallow and ridiculous—not worth the while of a great emotion. Just small. "What of it?" she asked.

He scowled in angry embarrassment at her expression which neither suggested nor encouraged tragedy. "I never heard of people acting as we've acted to-day!" he cried.

"But no doubt they often do," replied she. "Everybody doesn't act—all the time—as if he were in a novel or a play, or thought he was."

"You can respect him after this?"

Her eyes had the expression a man least likes to see in a woman's when she is looking at him. "Don't you?" said she.

He reddened, and his eyes shifted. Presently he said humbly, "I—I am sorry for what I did. I was crazy with jealousy. I'm not myself—not at all."

She felt the truth of this at once. "And I'm sorry for the things I said to you and to him. I was crazy with rage."

He lifted his head eagerly. "I knew you didn't mean them, dear."

Her brow darkened. It was annoying that the man couldn't realize; for such as she now knew him to be to aspire to her seemed impertinence. "Basil," she said, "it's all over between us. Don't let your vanity deceive you. And don't force me to tell you what I think of you. Be content with knowing what I don't think."

"Be careful!" he cried angrily. "I'm not the man to stand and beg—even for you."

"That's good," said she pleasantly. "Then—we can part here and now." She glanced up at the windows of the apartment. "You've got your traps up there still. Hadn't you better let me send Jimmie to help you pack them?"

"Thank you," replied he, haughtily. "I'll be obliged if you will."

She put out her hand. "Good-by, Basil."

He clinched his fists in vanity's boyish anger. "You can think of that apartment, and have no feeling?" he exclaimed.

"None," declared she.

"I'll not believe it. You couldn't be so unwomanly."

Her look forecast a sarcasm. But before she spoke it changed to one that was soft and considerate. She felt that she was responsible. True he had posed as something far superior to his reality; but it was an honest fraud, deceiving himself first and most of all. She felt to blame for having been taken in—felt repentant and apologetic toward him. "Let's not quarrel," she urged. "Don't be harsh with me. I know you'll find love and make some woman very, very happy—one that is sympathetic and comes up to your ideals of womanhood." She put out her hand again, and friendly and winning was the smile round her wide mouth, in the eyes under the long, slender brows. "Please, Basil." He hesitated. "Don't be harsh. You know you don't love me any more than I love you. What's the use of pretenses? Why not part sincerely? ... Please, Basil."

His hand just touched hers and his angry eyes avoided her pleading glance. "If you'll send Jimmie," he said. And with a stiff bow he moved in great dignity along the path to the apartment entrance. He went even more slowly than dignity required, for he confidently expected she would come to her senses when she saw he had indeed reached the limit of endurance of her trifling. Richard had shown he wouldn't take her back—cared nothing for her. Where then could she turn but to him? And all that vaporing about independence was—just vaporing. A woman was a woman, and he knew women. So, he walked slowly to give her a good chance. But no call came—not though he lingered over opening the door and made a long pause elaborately to wipe his clean boots on the mat. He did not look until he could do so from the security of the sitting-room windows. She was not in sight. Had she followed him softly? He went into the hall, glanced down the stairs. Not there! She had gone! ... She meant what she said; she had cast him off. There was no room for doubt—she had cast him off.... He heard a step, rushed to the door. It was Jimmie, come bringing his overcoat and gloves, and prepared to do the packing. She had really cast him off.

"God!" he muttered. "What a contemptible position that puts me in!" And, for the moment at least, he hated her. If he could only revenge himself—in some perfectly gentlemanly way, of course. Once that day vanity had lured him clean over the line into most ungentlemanly conduct; his face burned from the sting of her remembered denunciations—the sting of truth in them. If he could devise a gentlemanly way—something that would convince her he had made all that agitation simply because he felt that, as a gentleman, he in the circumstances must go to any lengths to keep faith with her. Yes, that would be a handsome revenge—and would save his face, too.

He gave Jimmie the necessary directions and resumed his brooding. He searched his brain in vain. He could contrive no way of escape; he would have to leave that place like a whipped dog—yes, a whipped dog. Spurned by Vaughan—spurned by Courtney——

A step, and the rustle of a skirt. His eyes gleamed. "I thought not!" he muttered exultantly. "Well, I'll teach her a lesson she'll never forget."

He turned his back to the door, stood at the window, looking out and puffing nonchalantly at his cigarette. The step, the rustle were on the threshold. "I beg your pardon, Mr. Gallatin——"

He wheeled to face Helen. His confusion was equal to hers. "Ah—Miss Helen—I—I—" he stammered.

"Am I intruding?" she asked. There was a charming blush in her sweet, beautiful face, and her honest dark eyes showed how perturbed she was.

"No indeed—no indeed," he protested.

"Courtney sent me——"

"Courtney sent you!" he exclaimed in amazement.

"She told me all about it," Helen hastened on. "She asked me to let you know that she had told me—how you and Richard have had a bitter falling out over the work—and that you're going away, not to come back."

One look into those eyes was convincing; Helen believed what she was saying.

"She thought perhaps I might be able to help you about the packing. Can I?"

"No, but I'd be glad if you'd stop while Jimmie is doing it. I don't want to leave without saying good-by to you."

All the roses fled from Helen's cheeks. "Yes—certainly," she murmured.

"You'll excuse my being somewhat confused? The truth is I'm very much upset."

"I can't tell you how dreadfully I feel," said Helen. "Are you sure you and Richard—" She paused. Her glance stirred him like an angel face in a drunkard's dream—her face earnest, grieved, sympathetic, unable to credit anything so dreadful, so wicked as a parting in hate.

"Quite sure. It's—final. Please, let's not talk about it. It's all so—so revolting."

In presence of those clear, noble eyes of hers, the sordidness of his "romance" now once more began to stand out. What a mess! No wonder he had taken to drink. If it had been Helen and the kind of love she inspired— "But you and I will always be friends—won't we?" he said to her.

Her eyelids dropped and he saw her bosom fluttering. "I hope so," she said so low he scarcely heard. She was pale now, and drooping. "Though I'm afraid—when you get away off there, you'll forget me very soon."

His heart smote him as he looked at that tall, voluptuous figure, at that lovely face, so regular, so pure. Here was a woman, a real woman, and she would have loved him—perhaps did love him. "I know I'm unworthy of a thought from you who are so good and pure," he said. "But your kindness to me has helped me. And God knows, I shall need help." Oh, that it had been his lot to anchor to this strong, white soul! How much nobler than the finest passion was a love centering about the sweet, old-fashioned ideals. What a haven those arms, that bosom would be! He felt dissolute and sin-scarred as only a vain young man can feel those dread but delightful depravities.

"You must not despair, Basil," came in Helen's soft voice, like oil upon his wounds. And it touched him to see how, maidenly shy though she was, she yet could not resist the appeal of this opportunity to try to do good. She went on, "It's always darkest before dawn, and the more rain falls the less there is to fall."

These words seemed like heavenly wisdom delivered by a messenger of light. He sighed.

"You'll come out all right—and will escape from that—that—whatever it is—" Helen's cheeks modestly colored—"and be happy with some *good* woman who is worthy of you."

She looked so sad, so beautiful that before he knew it he, ever sympathetic with women, had said, "Some woman like you, Helen."

She turned away. He saw that her emotions were making her tremble. How she loved him! What a prize such a love would be—and how chagrined Courtney would feel—Courtney the vampire woman who had tried to destroy him, and thought she had succeeded—and was gloating over his misery. "If we'd had the chance, Helen, how happy we could have made each other! But I mustn't talk of that."

"Why not?" said she, with bold shyness. "I know that for some reason we can never be anything more to each other. But it's been a happiness—" earnestly, with tears in her eyes of the Homeric Juno and in her voice young and honest and sympathetic—"a real happiness to feel that the best of you—the part that's really you—found something to like in me."

He thrilled. Here was a woman! And a woman who appreciated him. He wondered how he could have lingered under a malign spell when such beauty of soul—and body, too—was his for the asking. "Helen!" he cried. And all his wounded heart's longing and all his wounded vanity's suffering gave energy to his cry. He took her hand; he put his arm round her. Her cheek touched his. How cool yet warm she was! How lovely and sweet! And the unsullied, untouched down! How fresh! Except her male relatives, no doubt no man but himself had ever kissed her— "Helen—Helen! God forgive me, but I can't refuse this moment of pure happiness."

She gently drew away. "Oh, Basil," she sobbed. "And I had said no man should ever kiss me until— But you—it seems different. You are so noble—so pure minded." Her eyes gazed into his with a trustful adoration that thrilled him.

"Helen—do you love me?" he cried.

Her honest eyes opened wider. "Would I have let you touch me if I didn't?"

"Yes—I know that!" he exclaimed. "How pure you are! It's like heaven after hell."

She gazed on into his eyes. A faint flush overspread her pale cheeks. She kissed him. "I love you, Basil," she said, gravely. Then all at once the color surged wave on wave over her brow, her cheeks, her neck. She hung her head, slowly drew away from his detaining vibrating arms. There is a time for lighting a fire; there is a time for leaving it to burn of itself. Helen had by the guidance of feminine instinct hit upon exactly the right instant for drawing back. She released herself, avoided his touch just when passion having captured his imagination swept on to the conquest of the flesh. At the edges of her lowered eyes appeared two tears to hang glistening in the lashes. From her bosom rose a sigh, soft, suppressed but heart-breaking.

The bright flame was leaping in his eyes. "You noble, splendid woman!" he cried, as his glance leaped from charm to charm—from delicate, regular features to sumptuous yet girlish figure. "What a jewel—in what a casket! You appeal to the best there is in me—only to the best. If I become a man again, it will be through you." And sincerity rang in his voice; for, the fire of high resolve to be a good man, to be worthy of this exalted womanhood, was burning in his blood. "Helen—will you help me? I've sinned—you never will know how dreadfully. But I love you."

Her answer was a beautiful shaft of the love light from her now wonderful eyes.

"Helen—will you marry me?"

From head to foot she trembled. All her color fled, leaving her face whiter than the milk-white skin of her voluptuous neck and shoulders. "I—love—you," she said simply.

"Then you will? Say you will, Helen. I cannot trust myself to go away without your strength to help me."

"I will, Basil."

There were tears in his eyes as in hers as he reverently kissed her hands. He had a sense of peace, of sin forgiven, of joyous return to the fold of honor and respectability. And her heart was overflowing with love, with gratitude to him and to God.

# Chapter 30

Returning to the house after full two hours, she burst excitedly in upon Courtney, who was at her easel in the upstairs sitting room. Courtney had by much experimenting found that of her several possible indoor occupations painting was far the best sedative for mind and nerves. The girl's face, exultant with pride, exalted with love, gave her a shock; for, only complete triumph could have so roused those regular, chastely cool features from their wonted repose. She had on impulse sent Helen to Basil in vague hope that they, admirably suited because each needed just what the other had to give, possibly might somehow get a start in the direction of making a match of it. She had the most convincing of reasons for believing that the heart in need of balm is the most susceptible to it. But she did not believe that Basil's heart was, at least latterly, involved; and, as she had not a glimmer of a suspicion of his stolen draughts of "moral tonic," she could not credit the story so clearly written upon those radiant features.

"You don't mean you got him!" she exclaimed, laying her brush on the rest and leaning back. And in her amazement and excitement over this sudden freakish prank of fate, out of her mind flew all the wretched thoughts over which she had been brooding—thoughts centering about her own ugly part in that scene at the laboratory.

Helen, undisturbed by this frankness of woman to woman friend, when there are no listeners, flung ecstatic arms about her and kissed her on either cheek. "I'm so happy!" she cried. "And I owe it all to you."

"Engaged?" inquired Courtney, the utter impossibility of the thing down-facing the clear evidence of its actuality.

Helen held up her left hand, displaying the old-fashioned diamond ring Basil had always worn on his little finger. "It was his mother's," she said, regarding it with an expression in the big brown eyes that would have thrilled him, had he seen. It thrilled Courtney; and no further proof of the absolute passing of Basil was needed than the unalloyed pleasure Helen's happiness gave her. "Engaged," said Helen, softly, dreamily. "And the day set—the second of June."

"Splendid!" Helen, she felt, was secure; for, Basil had the highest respect for his given word.

"And if you hadn't sent me down there, I do believe it'd never have happened. Just think!—though we've loved each other practically from the first meeting. He says it was his feeling about me that started him to struggling against that bad woman. Do you remember——"

"Yes, I remember," said Courtney. How dead it all was!—dead with the death that leaves no scar upon the heart, only a lesson in the memory. How could it ever have seemed living?—and immortal!

"Oh—of course you remember. You knew about her."

"Not much about her," replied Courtney. Pensively, "Really, nothing at all."

"I'm sure I don't want to know anything. The less a good woman knows about evil, the better.... I think recently he must have almost succeeded in breaking away; for, to-day I'm sure he was hesitating at the parting of the ways—whether to go back to her or not. And my coming there decided him. Isn't it beautiful?"

"Like a fairy tale," said Courtney, taking up her brush and eying critically the little landscape to which she was giving the finishing touches. "But, my dear, I don't think you ought to tell me these things."

She felt selfish in saying this; Helen had inexperienced youth's irresistible craving to confide, and was simply bursting with simple and innocent vanity over having achieved the double triumph of both spiritual and worldly advantage. But Helen was not to be suppressed or even discouraged. "Oh, yes," replied she. "He asked me to tell you we are engaged. I think he knows you've heard about that woman who was dragging him down, and thought you could advise me whether he was a fit man for me to marry. You see he feels he's been very bad."

"Men always like to think that," said Courtney. "But as long as they think so, they're not. No, he isn't bad, as men go. He wants to settle down. And he will settle down—with you." She was looking at the landscape but her quizzical eyes were seeing the pair of them a few years hence, contentedly yawning at each other, leading the conventional life of the well-to-do that swathes them body and mind in soft, indolent fat.

Helen had only half listened to Courtney, as she cared as little as the next woman about her lover's past, and knew for herself that he was high-minded and of the noblest instincts. She halted her own and Courtney's musings with an absent, "I feel that way about it, too." She moved nervously about the room, from time to time casting an appealing glance at her absorbed friend. Finally she burst out desperately: "There's something I want your advice about. I don't know whether I've done right or not."

"Yes?" said Courtney, encouragingly.

"I hadn't told you but—the fact is—while I was on that visit to Saint X, I—I became engaged to Will Arbuthnot."

Courtney looked laughingly at her over the suspended brush. "Oh, Helen—Helen!"

"But let me explain, dear," begged Helen, cheeks scarlet and eyes down. "When I went up there—and until just a few minutes ago—I thought—" Her faltering voice died away altogether.

"Thought there was no hope of getting Basil," said Courtney, with no censure, with only sympathy. She resumed touching up the picture to ease Helen's embarrassment. "Go on."

"I thought he was hopelessly in the power of that bad woman. So, I put my feeling for him out of my heart.... I know you're laughing at me. You're so cynical, Courtney. But a girl has got to do the best she can. And it's getting harder and harder for a poor girl to marry—that is, to marry a man with anything. And brought up as I've been I have to have nice surroundings. I want a good home—and—and—

children—and they must be educated properly—and able to keep their place in our station of life."

"Certainly," reassured Courtney. "You did the practical, sensible thing."

"I know, what I did *seems* to bear out your ideas. You're always teasing me about my ideals being mostly pretense. Well, perhaps they are. It does look like it—doesn't it?"

"Everybody's are," said Courtney, squinting at the picture. "Ideals are paste pearls. One can wear much bigger and finer ones than of the real—and nobody knows they're paste—or need ever know if one's careful to avoid their being tested. I'm glad, dear, you weren't so foolish as you always insisted you'd be."

Helen looked as if her soul were freed of a huge weight. "I will say, Courtney, that I'd never think of confiding in any person who believes like me, while I always feel safe in confiding in you."

"Thank you," said Courtney with genuine gratitude. "You don't know what a flattering compliment that is.... So, you're engaged to Will Arbuthnot?"

"Yes—that is, up at Saint X Will asked me to marry him. He's a nice, clean, thoroughly good fellow. And when Basil went away I supposed he'd gone to that bad——"

"I understand," interrupted Courtney. "Never mind about her."

"I felt I could grow to like Will, and I put Basil out of my heart." There she fluttered a guiltily uneasy glance at Courtney.

"And now," teased Courtney, "you give the naughty man the preference over the nice one."

"That's just it!" exclaimed Helen in triumph. "Basil needs me. I did hesitate—at least, I tried to—until he begged me to strengthen him by saying yes. Then I felt it was clearly my duty." Helen took Courtney's amused nod at her landscape as approval. "And while I hated to do a thing that in a way might seem deceitful—still, Basil has such an exalted opinion of me—and it helps him, to feel that way—and if he had found out that I hadn't loved him all along—or if I'd asked him to wait—I might have lost all chance to help him to be the noble, good man— *Don't* smile that way. Courtney."

And Courtney instantly changed her smile to one of tenderness. "I know you're good and sweet, dear—and beautifully sincere," said she, with perfect honesty; for, experience had left in her little of the familiar self-complacence that condemns human beings for human traits. "Much too good for Basil."

"Of course," said Helen, beaming, "a woman who has kept herself pure is superior to a man who has not been clean and nice."

"Always make Basil feel that," advised Courtney. "He's the kind of man that can behave only when he's on his knees—and you're the kind of woman that prefers worship to love.... I suppose you'll live in the East."

"In New York, I think," replied Helen, reflectively. "He talks of the country. But I've had enough of that. I'm sure he'd be better contented in a city."

Courtney laughed gayly. "What a dear you are!" she exclaimed, looking at her friend tenderly. "And so absolutely unconscious of it."

Helen returned her gaze in unaffected surprise. "I don't know what you mean. Why do you laugh?"

"Nothing." Courtney was painting again. "What are you going to do about Will Arbuthnot?"

"Why, be perfectly honest with him," cried Helen, injured and reproachful. "I simply couldn't be deceitful."

"Tell him you've found you can make a better match? Oh, you mustn't do that."

"I should think not!" exclaimed Helen, horrified. "That wouldn't be the truth. No, I'll tell him I find I don't love him as a woman should love the man she's to give herself to. You know I've got the old-fashioned ideals—that is, ideas—of the sacredness of womanhood. He'll understand."

"Yes," said Courtney gravely, though her eyes were dancing, "he'll have a deeper reverence for true womanhood.... Well, the men deserve it. They're responsible for our not daring to be our natural human selves."

"But I *am* natural, dear," remonstrated Helen warmly.

Courtney was busily trying for a shade of brown on her palette. "You're sure Basil won't hear of your other engagement? Remember, he knows several Saint X people."

"I made an agreement with Will that we'd keep it a secret until we got ready to marry." Courtney laughed again; it was so obvious what lingering longing and hope had prompted this precaution. "What *are* you laughing at *now*?" asked Helen.

"I wouldn't spoil your innocence by telling you," replied Courtney. And she rose and, palette in one hand, brush in the other, kissed her affectionately. "I'm glad you're happy—and I'm sure you'll always be happy."

"Indeed I shall. And he'll be happy too. As he said, he's lived in an atmosphere of deceit and falsehood, and he needs to be lifted up into purity and love and—and—all that makes a good home and life on a high plane."

Courtney was smiling strangely into her color box. "You'll be married in Saint X at Mrs. Torrey's, I suppose?"

Helen began her answer in a place so remote that Courtney, used as she was to the complexities of feminine thought, was completely baffled. Said Helen: "Will Cousin Richard think me disloyal, marrying a man he's at outs with?"

Courtney reflected. "I don't know what he'll think." she said. "But you've got to consider yourself first—and Basil."

"Yes, certainly—" Again Helen was only half listening. "About the wedding," she presently said. "I was thinking it out, while Basil and I were talking——"

"Helen—Helen!" And the small head with its auburn crown shook in mock disapproval. "Not while he was making his first love to you?"

Helen reddened. "I had to think about things. You know, a woman can't afford to let herself loose like a man. And I decided it'd be best for us not to announce the engagement, but just to marry. And not at Saint X. I'll go up to Aunt Lida's in Laporte. What is it, dear? Why do you look so queer?"

"Nothing—nothing." Courtney had no desire—indeed, what would have been the use?—to tell her thoughts as she viewed the swamp of deceit and double dealing into which Helen and Basil were dragging each other in pursuit of those will-o'-the-wisp ideals. Ideals! But Courtney's lip did not curl in scorn as it would have curled a few months before. She had learned that supreme lesson of tolerance—even when you are sure you are right, not to fancy that what is right for you is right for anyone else.

"No," Helen was saying, "I'll not tell Richard. It would annoy him and do no good. Oh, I ought to be ashamed of myself, to be so happy when you are unhappy."

"I—unhappy?"

"I know you conceal it, dear. You're brave and self-reliant. But— Isn't there *anything* I could do to bring you and Dick together again? You're a woman, dear. You simply have to be taken care of, and——"

"Don't shadow your romance with worry about me," said Courtney nervously. She was all confusion and restlessness.

"But I can't help it," pleaded Helen. "I know Richard was neglectful. And he's not an attractive man to a woman, as Basil is—isn't livable and lovable like Basil——"

Helen went on and on contrasting the two men, to Richard's disadvantage at every point. In former days she had been too much "afraid Richard'll find out how foolish I am and how little I know" to get in the least acquainted with him; since the divorce they had talked only constrained commonplaces, when she took Winchie to him. Thus, the comparison was grotesque distortion of Richard. But Courtney was not tempted to try to set her right. Helen, of small mentality and in love with Basil, would not appreciate, would not be convinced, would simply be irritated—would probably misunderstand and be encouraged to pursue her absurd scheme for bringing them together. But parallel with Helen's talk there was in Courtney's mind a juster contrasting of the two men—the one strong, the other weak; the one real, the other idealist; the one simple, the other a *poseur*; the one intelligent, the other merely conceited; the one master of his emotions, the other their slave; the one an original, the other a pattern, an identical sample of thousands turned out by the "best families" and the "best colleges" and the "best society." And then it came to her why she had estimated Basil quickly and accurately, once she began it—that it was because in Richard she for the first time had a measure to do her measuring with. The mists of his abstraction had completely hid his personality from her, as from everybody. Those mists had blown away in the cyclone of the disruption of their marriage, and he had stood revealed—and Basil also—Basil, the dwarf beside the giant. She could see how the lesser man had made what was, in the circumstances, irresistible appeal to the imperious craving that must be satisfied before the need of heart for sympathy and of mind for comradeship could gain a hearing, the craving that in gaining its ends will compel the imagination to play any necessary sorry trick upon the intelligence. She could see this; and she could also see how sorry the trick upon intelligence had been—how absurd was her dream of founding a life-long content and happiness upon what Basil could give her and she Basil.

"I'm sure," Helen was saying, "with a little management you could get Richard back."

These words fell upon Courtney's ears just as into her mind again came that scene between her and Richard at the laboratory—the childish, the coarse taunts she had hurled at him, and how he had met them. She was hot with the shame of it when Helen spoke. The suggestion that Richard could be got back overwhelmed her with a crushing, stinging sense of how in contempt he must hold her now. The red of her skin flamed up into scarlet. "Don't speak of those things," she commanded harshly. Then, instantly ashamed of this misdirected outburst of temper, she put on her most careless, frivolous air—put it on well enough to deceive Helen. "Let's talk trousseau," said she. "You haven't much time, you know. June's very near."

But Helen was too curious about the trouble that had so abruptly changed a friendship into hatred. "It must have been exciting—that quarrel between them," she hinted encouragingly. "You were there, weren't you?"

"Yes."

"Tell me, Courtney."

"It cured my cold," said Courtney. "I'd been feeling queer in the nose and eyes——"

"How *can* you be so light!" exclaimed Helen. "Well—let's talk trousseau." She felt that she had done her duty, that it was a waste of time to try to induce Courtney to be serious— "She *never* will have any sense of responsibility—or of the graver side of life." And with a clear conscience she took up trousseau and thought and talked dress steadily the rest of the afternoon, straight through until the supper gong sounded. And she asked so many questions, so much minute advice about every little detail that Courtney's attention could not wander.

At supper Courtney got a real pleasure from Helen's rapt, tenderly smiling countenance—they could not talk before Lizzie as the engagement was to be kept secret. Also, she got pleasure mingled with amusement out of Helen's delightful swift assumption of the ways of a married woman, and out of her immense satisfaction—as shown in a certain sweet and loving condescension to Courtney— over Basil's superiority as a catch. Helen was in fancy already married and installed in grandeur. But after supper, when Helen went up to write her first love letter— (those to Will Arbuthnot didn't count)—Courtney made no attempt to save herself from the attack of the blues that had been threatening ever since she calmed sufficiently to recall what she had said to Dick at the laboratory. She sat at the piano playing softly. Helen's face was haunting her—that expression telling of dreams she understood so well—so well! Would Helen's dream fade too? Probably—yes, certainly—for, the Helen sort of woman soon discouraged love in a man, and the Basil sort of man looked askance at love as tainted of that devil whom no one believed in any more yet everyone feared. Fade—wither—die. And she herself— would she seek on and on, deceived always by hopes and longings—as she had been twice already—the second time worse deceived than the first——

Into her thoughts came an image of Richard. The image grew stronger. Very gradually she realized that he was actually before her, was the tall figure in the doorway of the sitting room——

"I didn't dare interrupt," he said. "It would have been like disturbing a funeral."

"Not quite so bad as that," replied she with an attempt to smile. Though her rose-bronze coloring enabled her to blush deeply without detection, had the corner where she was sitting been less dim he must have seen into what shamefaced confusion his coming threw her.

She went on playing; he seated himself at some distance from her to gaze into the fire and smoke. She was on the grill of humiliating thoughts about herself—what she had said and done that afternoon. She did not lift her eyes until she had made sure by several furtive glances that she could look at him in safety. She watched him—the cigarette gracefully between the long first and second fingers of his hand of the aristocrat and the artist—the poise of his curiously long head so well proportioned—the long, sensitive, mobile features—that indescribable look which proclaims at a glance the man of high intelligence—the man of the finely organized nervous system. Then she observed that he was in evening half dress—one more reason for his looking unusually handsome and distinguished. But all the time she was seeing those two expressions which had transformed him that afternoon—had transformed him and had made her feel mean and poor beside him. A man who could be such a wild hot blast of primeval passion; the man who could be stronger than passion, even such passion—there was indeed a man! And what must he think of her! "But no worse than I deserve."

To break the current of her own thoughts, she interrupted his with a trivial "You are dressed this evening."

"Because I've come to call," he replied, rousing himself from his reverie.

"I'll tell Helen."

"I want to talk to you—if you'll listen." She stopped the soft wandering of her fingers over the keys. "No, go on playing, please."

She resumed. Now her eyes were on the keyboard, and she was having no easy task of it finding the right keys and striking the right chords, all the time conscious of his steady penetrating gaze. "It's nearing the time you fixed for going East," he began.

She nodded slowly in time to the music. He was so seated that the piano prevented his seeing any of her but her bare shoulders and graceful head with its masses of auburn hair, against a background of palms and ferns. "I'm glad the spring is so backward this year," she said; for, she had learned not to fear his misunderstanding, if she spoke out her thoughts. "If it were really spring with the grounds all in bloom and the windows wide— It makes me sad to think of that."

She had thought she might perhaps soften his contempt by reminding him that there was another and a less repellant side to her character. But as soon as the words were out, she wished she had not spoken; it was useless to try to make him think well of her. He was probably regretting that he had let her have Winchie. She looked appealingly toward him, hoping he would speak—say anything—no matter what, so long as it broke that silence of painful suspense. When she could endure it no longer, she suddenly burst out: "You've come to ask me to leave at once. You are right, I'll go as soon as I can pack."

"On the contrary," said he, eyes still intent upon the tall shafts of flame leaping toward the cavernous blackness of the chimney. "I've come to ask you not to go at all."

His tone was calm and self-controlled. It contained no suggestion of ominous meaning; nor did his face.

"I—I don't understand," she ventured, nervously.

"I want to propose," explained he, in the same deliberate way, "that we give each other another trial."

There was no mistaking his meaning. In the sudden reversal from all she had been expecting and fearing, her thoughts became mere chaos. Hands resting upon the keys, she sat silent, rigid—waiting.

He turned his chair, leaned toward her, his elbows on his knees. "Is the idea—is it—distasteful to you?" he asked.

Carefully, with her tapering fingers she measured chords without striking them. "Not *distasteful*," said she.

"You do not dislike me—now?"

"I never have, except for a few minutes now and then—when you said or did tyrannical things." Painfully embarrassed, she was trying to regain control of herself under cover of arranging the chiffon round the edge of the bosom of her dress.

"Courtney, I'm a different man from what I was."

"Yes," she assented, without reserve. "Very different. But——"

"Don't, please," he said, before she could begin to explain. "When you've heard my reasons for asking you to stay, you may think well of them. If not, why you at least can refuse more intelligently. This afternoon, when Gallatin was down at the laboratory making an ass of himself, you whirled upon me with some very vivid reminders of what you had been to him."

"I was insane with rage—not that it wasn't all true—only—I—it was—" She hung her head—"Oh, I'm so ashamed!—so ashamed!" she cried.

"I'm glad you did," interrupted he, heartily. "You thought to infuriate me. And you did, for a moment. Then—I was astonished to find myself quite calm. Do you know why?"

"Yes. Because you care nothing about me."

"Because I care nothing about him. Because I know you've ceased to think you care about him—care, you never did. Since I've come to my senses, I've been getting acquainted with you. And I know you do not and never did and never could love Basil Gallatin. That is, the woman you are now—the only one that interests either of us—never did and never could."

The deep green eyes glanced gratefully toward him. "That's true."

"It was simply what you and I went through with when we first met—and became engaged—and got married."

"Yes," said she. "Much the same. But—" Her eyes met his fully. "It wouldn't be honest if I didn't say too that I do not regret—about him. I suppose there's something wrong with me, but somehow I don't seem able to regret anything I do—even the things I'm ashamed of—like what I said this afternoon. It all seems part of experience. It seems necessary. That experience with him—it helped me toward learning to live."

She expected that he would be offended by her frankness. But he was not. "It helped you toward learning to live," he assented, like one stating an indisputable truth. "And it helped me. No, more than that. It *taught* me.... I wish the lesson could have been got in some—some other way. Perhaps you do, too." She nodded, gazing thoughtfully across the piano into the fire. "But," he went on, "fate doesn't let us choose our way—or, perhaps, there's no nice, refined way of getting one's full growth, any more than there is for a tree. It's simply got to stand outdoors in all weathers, and learn to survive and grow strong, no matter what comes."

"And the things that seem to hinder, often help most—and those that look like helps are enemies."

She saw his understanding, appreciative look, though her eyes were gazing past him; and she liked it. "We've both learned," said he. "And we've both been put in the way of learning more. Now why shouldn't you and I use our experience to the best advantage?"

"I intend to try," said she.

"Then it's simply a question of what is the best advantage. Isn't it for us both to stay on here?"

"I don't think so," was her slow reply. "Not for either of us."

"But you'll listen to my reasons? Really listen, I mean. You know, you caught my bad habit of not listening."

"Yes," she said with a forced, uneasy smile. "I'll listen."

"Well—first, there's this place. You like it, don't you? You must, since you made it. I've found that out, too."

"I love it," she answered. "But—" She shook her head.

"Now, do try to be patient with me. You must consider all three of my reasons together. That was only number one. Number two is Winchie."

She searched his face with swift terrified eyes. He smiled a frank and winning reassurance that instantly convinced her. "Please put that kind of thoughts about me out of your mind forever," he urged. "I've learned my lesson—that the beginning of fear is the end of trust. The boy's yours. You've got the right to him; he's got the right to you. Even if I could do for him, it'd be my duty— But I didn't come here this evening to talk about duty. That's a rotten hypocrisy."

"Is this Richard Vaughan?" she cried laughingly.

"The same—minus his grandfather," replied he, eyes and voice echoing her laugh. "No more duty for me. When anybody talks about doing his duty, he'd better be watched. If he boasts of having done his duty he'd better be locked up while they find out what mischief he's been at. No, I'm out for honest, selfish inclination only. That brings me to my third reason. I want you to stay. But—for very selfish sensible reasons I want you to want to stay. I've gotten acquainted with you. I need you. There's nobody who could take your place."

She smiled at what seemed to her the extravagant kindness of this.

"I mean just that," he went on. It wasn't the words he was saying; it never is a matter of words. It was the way he said it—the force behind the words, like the force behind the projectile. "I need you. Don't you think you could learn to need me? A man needs a woman. A woman needs a man. We've never given each other a fair trial. Why shouldn't we? Now that you've taught me, I don't want you to abandon me. And why should you begin all over again with another man?"

She sat motionless, hardly breathing, it seemed, from the stillness of her bosom. He waited long but no answer came. He went to the big old-fashioned chimneypiece, stood with his back to the logs; a look of somberness came into his face. "Well," he said, "I've said my say." There was silence in the room. He drew a long breath. "What do you think?"

She lifted her head. With flushed face and reproachful, almost resentful eyes she cried: "You've no right to come at me that way. You make it hard for me to do as I wish."

"You wish to go? Then it's settled." He turned his face to the fire, and she could not see it. "We'll not speak of this again." His voice seemed natural; but there must have been some subtle quality in it that set her nerves to vibrating.

"And you," she cried, "are thinking 'How mean and ungrateful she is—after my generosity to refuse to——'"

"Not so!" he protested sharply, wheeling round. "I've not been generous. When I told you the fault was chiefly mine, I meant it."

"When a man treats a woman as if she were a human being, it's generosity, as the world goes," insisted she. And then the words began to pour from her as if they had suddenly found an outlet. "You make me feel small and mean in refusing. Oh, I'm grateful for the way you've treated me—but I hate myself for being grateful—and I'm ashamed that it is hateful. But I can't be different. Your generosity—your forgiveness hurt my pride. They make me feel I'm your inferior—and I am. But I mustn't stay where I'd feel humble. You make me ashamed to go, but I know I've the right to go—and that I ought to go. I must!"

"Then—you are going," was his unhesitating reply. "I don't want you to stay. I see you don't believe me—don't understand me—and no wonder. It'd be useless to try again, unless we were both determined with all our hearts to make a success if success was at all possible."

"And it couldn't be a success," said she, a touching melancholy in her voice, in her deep, mysterious eyes. "For, a man doesn't want an equal woman but a dependent—wants his woman to be like his dog. Oh, what a world it is!—where everybody cants about self-respect, and everybody prefers cringers to friends, fear to love!"

"Not I," said Vaughan, in the quiet forceful manner that fitted so well his air of reserve power, of strength without strenuosity. "And that's why I want you. Courtney, don't you see that you're free and independent here, now? Don't you see it'd be a waste of time, a waste of energy, for you to go away? You may not need me, but I need you—in every way. You can get along without me. But how can I get along without you? Where would I find a woman who could take your place?"

Her bosom was rising and falling stormily. Her eyes wandered, as if she were desperately seeking a way of escape and had scant hope of finding it.

"Can't you give 'us' another trial?" he asked, with proud humility.

"I cannot," she cried, starting up in her agitation. "I cannot! I must go. There's everything here but the one thing I must have—what you never could give me, after all that's happened—and then, there's what I said to you this afternoon. We never could look at each other without my feeling that you— Oh, let's not talk about it. I must go—I must! I cannot live without love—equal love. I must seek until I find it—find some one who needs me—all of me—all I have to give—and must give."

He left the hearth and faced her with the length of the piano between them. "Could you love me?" he asked.

His voice set to vibrating nerves she had thought would never again respond to him. She trembled, and her eyes sank. "Even if I could—you couldn't love me. You could forgive—could be generous and kind. But you couldn't love."

"But I do love you," he said. And she, looking at him in wonder, thought there had never shone eyes so near to being the very soul itself. "I began to love you when you sent Gallatin away and faced me alone and did not lie. I came back because— You were like the air to me, Courtney. One isn't conscious of the air unless he hasn't it, and can't breathe. I've loved you more and more, day by day, ever since. And I shall love you more and more—need you more and more—every day until I die. Courtney—can't you forgive me? I am sorry for what I did—and—I love you."

She sank upon the piano seat, flung her slim white arms along the keyboard, buried her face in them. "I've found it!" she sobbed. "I've found it!"

Several discoveries in chemistry give Richard Vaughan fame, and Courtney shares it. But they value it all at nothing beside the discovery which gives them happiness: That the wise make of their mistakes a ladder, the foolish a grave.

www.ingramcontent.com/pod-product-compliance
Lightning Source LLC
Chambersburg PA
CBHW080842250626
47161CB00010B/3160